THE PEABODY LIBRARY
Columbia City, Indiana

Allende, Isabel
Eva Luna

ALSO BY
ISABEL ALLENDE

The House of the Spirits

Of Love and Shadows

EVA LUNA

Eva Luna

ISABEL ALLENDE

Translated from the Spanish by Margaret Sayers Peden

ALFRED A. KNOPF   NEW YORK

1988

THIS IS A BORZOI BOOK
PUBLISHED BY ALFRED A. KNOPF, INC.

Copyright © 1988 by Alfred A. Knopf, Inc.

All rights reserved under International and Pan-American Copyright
Conventions. Published in the United States by Alfred A. Knopf, Inc.,
New York, and simultaneously in Canada by Random House of
Canada Limited, Toronto. Distributed by Random House, Inc.,
New York.
Originally published in Spain by Plaza y Janés Editores, S.A.,
Barcelona
Copyright © 1987 by Isabel Allende

Library of Congress Cataloging-in-Publication Data

Allende, Isabel.
Eva Luna.

I. Title.
PQ8098.1.L54E813   1988   863   88-45272
ISBN 0-394-57273-4

Manufactured in the United States of America

First Trade Edition

A signed first edition of this book
has been privately printed by The Franklin Library

TO MY MOTHER,
who gave me a love of stories

Then he said to Scheherazade: "Sister, for the sake of Allah, tell us a story that will help pass the night...."

—*A Thousand and One Tales of the Arabian Nights*

EVA LUNA

O N E

My name is Eva, which means "life," according
to a book of names my mother consulted. I was born in the back
room of a shadowy house, and grew up amidst ancient furniture,
books in Latin, and human mummies, but none of those things
made me melancholy, because I came into the world with a breath
of the jungle in my memory. My father, an Indian with yellow
eyes, came from the place where the hundred rivers meet; he smelled
of lush growing things and he never looked directly at the sky,
because he had grown up beneath a canopy of trees, and light
seemed indecent to him. Consuelo, my mother, spent her childhood in an enchanted region where for centuries adventurers have
searched for the city of pure gold the conquistadors saw when they
peered into the abyss of their own ambitions. She was marked
forever by that landscape, and in some way she managed to pass
that sign on to me.

Missionaries took Consuelo in before she learned to walk; she appeared one day, a naked cub caked with mud and excrement, crawling across the footbridge from the dock like a tiny Jonah vomited up by some freshwater whale. When they bathed her, it was clear beyond a shadow of doubt that she was a girl, which must have caused no little consternation among them; but she was already there and it would not do to throw her into the river, so they draped her in a diaper to cover her shame, squeezed a few drops of lemon into her eyes to heal the infection that had prevented her from opening them, and baptized her with the first female name that came to mind. They then proceeded to bring her up, without fuss or effort to find out where she came from; they were sure that if Divine Providence had kept her alive until they found her, it would also watch over her physical and spiritual well-being, or, in the worst of cases, would bear her off to heaven along with the other innocents. Consuelo grew up without any fixed niche in the strict hierarchy of the Mission. She was not exactly a servant, but neither did she have the status of the Indian boys in the school, and when she asked which of the priests was her father, she was cuffed for her insolence. She told me that a Dutch sailor had set her adrift in a rowboat, but that was likely a story that she had invented to protect herself from the onslaught of my questions. I think the truth is that she knew nothing about her origins or how she had come to be where the missionaries found her.

The Mission was a small oasis in the heart of an expanse of voluptuous vegetation writhing and twisting from the banks of the river to the feet of the monumental geologic towers that rose toward the firmament like one of God's mistakes. There time is bent and distances deceive the human eye, persuading the traveler to wander in circles. The humid, heavy air smells of flowers, herbs, man's sweat, and animal breath. The heat is oppressive, unalleviated by any breeze; the stones steam and blood boils in the veins. At dusk the sky is filled with phosphorescent mosquitoes whose bites produce endless nightmares, and the still night air carries the distinct cries of birds, the chattering of monkeys, and the distant roar of the waterfalls born high in the mountains to crash far below like the thunder of warfare. The modest mud-and-wattle Mission building, with its tower of woven stakes and a bell to toll for Mass, balanced, like all the huts, on piles driven into the mud of a river of opalescent waters whose banks evaporated in the reverberating light. The dwellings seemed to drift amid silent canoes, garbage, carcasses of dogs and rats, and inexplicable white blossoms.

Consuelo was easy to distinguish even from a distance, her long red hair like a whip of fire against the eternal green of that landscape. Her playmates were young Indians with swollen bellies, an impudent parrot that recited an "Our Father" salted with curses, and a monkey chained to a table leg; from time to time she would let the monkey loose to look for a sweetheart in the jungle, but he always returned to the same spot to scratch his fleas. Even in those days Protestants were everywhere, distributing their Bibles, preaching against the Vatican, and hauling their pianos through heat and rain so their converts could celebrate salvation in public song. Such competition demanded the total dedication of the Catholic priests, and they paid little attention to Consuelo, who was growing up scorched by the sun, poorly nourished on yucca and fish, infested with parasites, bitten by mosquitoes, free as a bird. Aside from helping with domestic chores, attending religious services and a few classes in reading, arithmetic, and catechism, she had no obligations; she roamed outdoors, sniffing the flora and chasing the fauna, her mind filled with images, smells, colors, and myths borne on the river current.

She was twelve when she met the man with the prospecting chickens, a weathered Portuguese who was dry and hard outside and bubbling with laughter inside. His birds pillaged the countryside, devouring anything that glittered, and after a certain amount of time their owner would slit open their craw and harvest his grains of gold—not enough to make him rich, but enough to nourish his dreams. One morning, El Portugués glimpsed a white-skinned girl with a blaze of hair, knee-deep in the swamp with her skirt tucked up around her legs, and thought he had suffered another of his periodic attacks of fever. His whistle of surprise would have set off a mule train. The sound reached the girl's ears; she looked up, their eyes met, and both smiled the same smile. After that day they met frequently: he, bedazzled, to gaze at her and she to learn to sing Portuguese songs.

"Let's go harvest gold," El Portugués said one day.

They set off into the jungle and soon were out of earshot of the Mission bell, deeper and deeper into the tangled growth along paths visible only to him. All day, crowing like roosters, they looked for the hens, catching them on the wing once they spied them through the dense foliage. She clamped them between her knees, and with one surgical slash he slit open the craw and stuck in his fingers to pull out the seeds of gold. If the hen survived, they stitched it up with needle and thread to continue to serve its owner; the others they put in a sack to sell in the village or use as bait. They burned the feathers because chicken feathers bring bad luck and spread the pip. Tangle-haired, Consuelo returned at dusk, content and spattered with blood. As she climbed the ladder from the rowboat to the terraced riverbank, her nose bumped into four filthy sandals belonging to two friars from Extremadura who were waiting for her with crossed arms and fearsome expressions of repudiation.

"It is time for you to go to the city," they said.

Nothing was gained by begging. Nor was she allowed to take the monkey or the parrot, two companions judged inappropriate for the new life awaiting her. She made the trip along with five native girls, all tied by the ankle to prevent their jumping from the pirogue and disappearing into the river. As he bid her farewell, El Portugués took one long last look at Consuelo; he did not touch her, but as a remembrance he gave her a tooth-shaped gold nugget strung on a cord. She would wear it around her neck most of her life, until she met someone she would give it to as a gift of love. El Portugués saw her for the last time dressed in a stained cotton jumper, a straw hat pulled down to her ears, barefoot and dejected, waving goodbye with one hand.

The journey began by canoe, down tributaries that wound through a landscape to derange the senses, then on muleback over rugged mesas where the cold freezes night thoughts, and finally in a truck, across humid plains through groves of wild bananas and dwarf pineapple and down roads of sand and salt; but none of it surprised the girl, for any person who first opens her eyes in the most hallucinatory land on earth loses the ability to be amazed. On that long journey she wept all the tears stored in her soul, leaving none in reserve for later sorrows. Once her tears were exhausted, she closed her lips, resolving from that moment forward to open them only when it could not be avoided. Several days later, when they reached the capital, the priests took the terrified girls to the Convent of the Little Sisters of Charity, where a nun with a jailer's key opened an iron door and led them to a large shady patio with cloistered corridors on four sides; in the center, doves, thrushes, and hummingbirds were drinking from a fountain of colored tiles. Several young girls in gray uniforms sat in a circle; some were stitching mattresses with curved needles while others wove wicker baskets.

The nun, hands hidden beneath the folds of her habit, recited something that sounded like "Through prayer and toil shall you atone for your sins. I have come not to heal those of you who are whole, but to minister unto those who are suffering and afflicted. The shepherd rejoices more when he finds the lost sheep than in all the ninety and nine. Word of God, praise be His Holy Name, amen."

Consuelo did not understand the meaning of that peroration; she did not even listen to it, she was too exhausted and too assailed by claustrophobia. She had never before been inside a walled enclosure, and when she looked up and saw the sky reduced to a rectangle, she felt that she was suffocating. When they separated her from her traveling companions and took her to the office of the Mother Superior, she had no inkling that it was because of her light skin and eyes. The Little Sisters had not received anyone like her in many years, only girls of mixed blood from the barrios, or Indian girls dragged there bodily by the missionaries.

"Who are your parents?"

"I don't know."

"When were you born?"

"The year of the comet."

Even at that age, Consuelo supplanted with poetic flourishes what she lacked in information. The moment she heard of the comet she decided to adopt it as the year of her birth. During her childhood, someone had told her how everyone had awaited the celestial prodigy with fear and trembling. It was supposed to blaze across the sky like a fiery dragon, and when it entered the earth's atmosphere its tail would envelop the planet in poisonous gases, and heat like molten lava would put an end to any form of life. Some people committed suicide to avoid being scorched to death; others preferred to anesthetize themselves with last-minute gluttony, drunkenness, and fornication. Even El Benefactor was impressed when he saw the sky turn green and he learned that under the comet's influence mulattos' hair had unkinked and the hair of Chinese had curled into ringlets, and he freed some political opponents who had been in prison so long they had forgotten what sunlight looked like—although a few had kept alive the germ of rebellion and were prepared to bequeath it to future generations. Consuelo was seduced by the idea of being born in the midst of all that fear, in spite of the rumor that babies born during that period were abominations and would remain so years after the comet had faded from sight as a ball of ice and stellar dust.

"The first thing we must do is get rid of this Satan's tail," declared the Mother Superior, hefting in both hands the burnished copper coil hanging down the back of the new interne. She gave the order that those long locks be cut and the girl's head washed with a mixture of lye and Aureolina Onirem to kill the lice and tone down the insolent color; therewith, half the hair fell, and what was left was dulled to the color of clay—much more suitable to the climate and goals of a religious institution than the original, naturally incandescent mane.

Consuelo spent three years in that place, chilled in body and soul, sullen and solitary, convinced that the pale sun in the patio was not the same as the one that scalded the jungle in the home she had left behind. No profane babel penetrated these walls, nor any of the national prosperity that had begun when someone dug a well and, instead of water, struck a heavy, fetid black substance that gushed out as if from a dinosaur's entrails. The nation was sitting on a sea of petroleum. The consequence stirred ever so slightly the somnolence of the dictatorship, because it raised the fortunes of the tyrant and his family so high that some trickled down to everyone else. There were signs of progress in the cities, and in the oil fields contact with the hearty foremen from the North rocked the old traditions; a breeze of modernity lifted the women's skirts, but in the Convent of the Little Sisters of Charity none of this mattered. Life began at 4 a.m. with the first prayers; the day progressed with unvarying routine, ending at six o'clock when the bells signaled the hour of the Act of Contrition to cleanse the spirit and prepare for the eventuality of death, since night might be a journey of no return. Long silences, cloisters of waxed paving stones, the odor of incense and lilies, the whisper of prayers, the dark wooden benches, white unadorned walls. God's presence was absolute. In addition to the nuns and a pair of servants, only sixteen girls occupied the vast adobe-and-tile building, most of them orphaned or abandoned. They learned to wear shoes, eat with a fork, and master a few elementary domestic skills, so that later they could be employed in humble serving positions, for it was assumed that they were incapable of anything else. Consuelo's appearance set her apart from the others, and the nuns, sure that this was not accidental but a sign of benevolent divine will, spared no effort in cultivating her faith, in the hope she would decide to take her vows and serve the Church; all their efforts, however, came to naught before the girl's instinctive rejection. She made the attempt in good faith, but never succeeded in accepting the tyrannical god the nuns preached to her about; she preferred a more joyful, maternal, and compassionate god.

"That is the Most Holy Virgin Mary," the nuns explained to her.

"She is God?"

"No, she is the Mother of God."

"Yes, but who has the say in heaven, God or his Mama?"

"Quiet, silly girl. Be quiet and pray. Ask the Lord to give you light," they counseled.

Consuelo would sit in the chapel and stare at the altar dominated by a terrifyingly realistic Christ and try to recite the rosary, but soon she would be lost in endless adventures in which her memories of the jungle alternated with the figures of Sacred History, each with his bundle of passions, vengeance, martyrdom, and miracles. She soaked it in greedily, all of it: the ritual words of the Mass, the Sunday sermons, the pious readings, the night noises, the wind in the colonnades, the witless expressions of the saints and anchorites in the niches of the church. She learned to hold her tongue, and prudently suppressed the treasure of her prodigious flow of fables until I gave her the opportunity to unloose the torrent of words stored within her.

Consuelo spent so much time in the chapel—motionless, hands clasped, placid as a cow chewing her cud—that the rumor spread through the convent that she was blessed with heavenly visions. The Mother Superior, however, a practical Catalan woman less inclined than the other nuns of the congregation to believe in miracles, realized that Consuelo was touched not by saintliness but by an incurable bent for daydreaming. As the girl did not, in addition, show any enthusiasm for stitching mattresses, making the hosts for Mass, or weaving baskets, she judged her training to be complete, and placed her in the house of a foreign doctor named Professor Jones. She herself led Consuelo by the hand to a somewhat run-down but still splendid French-style mansion on the outskirts of the city, sitting at the foot of a hill authorities have now designated as a National Park. Conseulo's first impression of the doctor was so intense that it was months before she lost her fear of him. He came into the large parlor wearing a butcher's apron and carrying a strange metallic instrument. He was so preoccupied in his project that he did not even say hello; he dispatched the nun with four incomprehensible sentences and, with a grunt, packed Consuelo off to the kitchen. She, on the other hand, studied him in detail; she had never seen such a threatening individual. But she also noticed that he was as handsome as a picture of Jesus, all gold, with the same blond beard as the Prince of Peace, and eyes of an impossible color.

The only employer Consuelo was to have in her lifetime had spent years perfecting a system for preserving the dead, a secret he carried finally to the grave—to the relief of all mankind. He was also seeking a cure for cancer; he had observed that this illness is rare in areas where malaria is rife, and had deduced quite logically that he could palliate the malady by exposing its victims to the bite of the swamp mosquito. Following the same logic, he experimented with thumping the head of idiots, whether by birth or by vocation, because he had read in *The Physician's Friend* that a person had been transformed into a genius as the result of cerebral trauma. He was a dedicated anti-Socialist. He calculated that if the world's riches were equally distributed, each of the planet's inhabitants would receive less than thirty-five cents, and that therefore revolutions were ineffectual. Physically, he was healthy and strong; he suffered from unrelenting bad humor, and possessed the knowledge of a sage and the cunning of a sexton. His formula for embalming, like most great inventions, was of admirable simplicity. No nonsense about extracting the viscera, scooping out the cranium, plunging the body into Formol, and then stuffing it with pitch and tow, only to end up with something as wrinkled as a prune whose glass eyes stared at you with stupefaction. He merely drew the blood of the still-fresh cadaver and replaced it with a liquid that conserved the body as it had been in life. The skin, although pale and cold, did not decompose, the hair remained firmly rooted, and in some cases even the fingernails and toenails survived, and continued to grow. The only drawback, perhaps, was a certain penetratingly acrid odor, but after a while the family would grow accustomed to it. At that time, few patients voluntarily submitted to the bite of curative insects, or to blows on the head to increase intelligence, but news of Jones's prestige as an embalmer had crossed the oceans, and he was frequently visited by European scientists or North American businessmen avid to wrest his formula from him. They always left empty-handed. His most famous case—one that spread his fame around the globe—was that of a local lawyer well known in life for his liberal inclinations; El Benefactor had ordered him killed as he left a performance of the musical *La Paloma* in the Municipal Theater. The family carried the still-warm body containing more bullet holes than could be counted, but with the face intact, to Professor Jones. Although he considered the victim his ideological enemy—he himself was a supporter of authoritarian regimes and he distrusted democracy, which he considered vulgar and too much like Socialism—Jones devoted himself to the task of preserving the body. The results were so spectacular that the family seated the dead man, dressed in his best suit and holding a pen in his right hand, in the library, and for several decades protected him from moths and dust as a reminder of the brutality of the dictator, who did not dare intervene; it is one thing to engage in battle with the living, but quite another matter to quarrel with the dead.

Once Consuelo succeeded in overcoming her initial fright, and understood that her employer's slaughterhouse apron and graveyard smell were inconsequential details compared to the fact that he was a person who was easy to get along with, vulnerable, at times even sympathetic, she felt quite at ease in his house; next to the convent, it seemed like paradise. No one in this house rose at dawn to say the rosary in behalf of all humankind, nor did anyone have to kneel on a fistful of peas to atone with her own suffering for the sins of others. The Professor's house did have one thing in common with the crumbling Convent of the Little Sisters of Charity: discreet ghosts also roamed here, perceived by everyone except Professor Jones, who for want of any scientific basis insisted on denying they were there. Although Consuelo was assigned the most onerous chores, she still found time for her daydreams, and here no one bothered her or interpreted her silences as wondrous gifts.

She was strong, she never complained, and she obeyed without asking questions, as the nuns had taught her. Besides carrying out the garbage, washing and ironing the clothes, cleaning the water closets, and being responsible every day for seeing that the iceboxes had ice, which was transported on the backs of burros and packed in heavy salt, she helped Professor Jones prepare the large apothecary jars of his formula; she readied the corpses, removed the dust and nits from all their joints; she dressed them, combed their hair, and tinted their cheeks with rouge. The learned doctor was pleased with his servant. Until she had come, he had worked alone in absolute secrecy, but with time he became accustomed to Consuelo's presence and allowed her to help him in his laboratory, for he sensed the trustworthiness of this silent woman. He was so sure of her always being there when he needed her that he would take off his jacket and hat and, without a backward glance, drop them for her to catch before they fell to the floor, and as she never failed he came to have a blind faith in her. She was a kind of extension of the inventor. Consuelo, therefore, became the only other person in possession of the miraculous formula, but she did not benefit in any way from that knowledge, since the thought of betraying her employer or making money from his secret never entered her mind. She detested handling the cadavers, and could not see the point in embalming them. If there was any reason to do so, she thought, nature would have foreseen it and would not allow the dead to putrefy. Nevertheless, toward the end of her life she found an explanation for the age-old desire of humans to preserve their dead when she discovered that having the bodies nearby makes them easier to remember.

Many years went by without surprises for Consuelo. She did not notice the changes taking place around her, for she had substituted the cloister of Professor Jones's house for that of the convent. They could have listened to news on the radio, but it was rarely turned on; her employer preferred the sound of the opera records he played on the latest Victrola. Nor were there newspapers in that house, only scientific journals, because the Professor was indifferent to events happening in the nation or the world. He was much more interested in abstract knowledge, the annals of history, or predictions concerning a hypothetical future, than the vulgar emergencies of the present. The house was a vast labyrinth of books. Volumes were stacked from floor to ceiling on every wall, dark, crackling, redolent of leather bindings, smooth to the touch, with their gold titles and translucent gilt-edged pages and delicate typography. All the works of universal learning were to be found on those shelves, arranged without apparent order—although the Professor remembered the exact location of each one. The works of Shakespeare rested alongside *Das Kapital*; the maxims of Confucius rubbed elbows with *The Book of Sea Lions*; ancient navigational maps lay beside Gothic novels and the poetry of India. Consuelo spent several hours a day dusting the books. When she finished the last bookcase, it was time to begin again with the first, but this was the best part of her duties. Gently, she picked up each one and wiped the dust from it as if caressing it; she leafed through its pages, sinking for a few minutes into its private world. She learned to recognize each one and to know its place on the shelves. She never dared ask to borrow them, so she smuggled them to her room, read them at night, and replaced them the following day.

Consuelo did not know much about the upheavals, catastrophes, or the progress of her times, but she did learn in detail of the student unrest in the country because of what happened one day when Professor Jones was passing through the center of town and was almost killed by mounted *guardias*. It fell to her to place poultices on his bruises and feed him soup and beer from a baby bottle until his loosened teeth were firm again. The doctor had gone out to buy some supplies essential to his experiments, not remembering for a minute that it was Carnival, a licentious festival that each year left its residue of wounded and dead, although that year drunken quarrels passed unnoticed in the shock of other events that jolted the nation's drowsy complacency. Professor Jones was just crossing the street when the riot broke out. In fact, the problems had begun two days earlier when the university students had elected a beauty queen in the nation's first democratic vote. After the coronation, and the accompanying flowery speeches in which some speakers' tongues had slipped and spoken of liberty and sovereignty, the young people had decided to march. Nothing like it had ever been seen; it was forty-eight hours before the police reacted, and they did so precisely at the moment Professor Jones was emerging from a pharmacy with his vials and powders. He saw the mounted police galloping toward him, machetes drawn, but he changed neither direction nor pace, as he was absorbed in thoughts of his chemical formulas and all that noise seemed in very bad taste. He regained consciousness on a stretcher on the way to the hospital for indigents and, holding his teeth in place to keep them from scattering in the street, managed to mumble some instructions to take him to his house. While he recovered, sunk in his pillows, the police arrested the young leaders of the uprising and threw them into a dungeon; they were not beaten, however, because among them were sons of the most prominent families. Their detention produced a wave of solidarity, and on the following day dozens of young men appeared at the jails and barracks to offer themselves as voluntary prisoners. They were locked up in order of arrival, but after a few days had to be released; there was not space enough in the cells for so many youths, and the clamor of their mothers had begun to disturb El Benefactor's digestion.

Months later, when Professor Jones's teeth were again firm in his gums and he was recuperating from his psychological bruises, the students again rebelled, this time with the complicity of a few young officers. The Ministry of War crushed the insurrection in seven hours, and those who managed to save themselves left the country and remained in exile for seven years, until the death of the Leader of the Nation, who granted himself the luxury of dying peacefully in his bed and not, as his enemies had desired and the North American Ambassador had feared, hanging by his testicles from a lamppost in the plaza.

Faced with the death of the aged caudillo and the end of that long dictatorship, Professor Jones was on the point of returning to Europe, convinced—like so many others—that the country would inexorably sink into chaos. For their part, the Ministers of State, terrified at the possibility of a popular uprising, held a hasty meeting in which someone proposed they call for the Professor, thinking that if the cadaver of El Cid lashed to his steed could lead the charge against the Moors, there was no reason why the embalmed President for Life could not continue to govern from his tyrant's seat. The learned doctor appeared, accompanied by Consuelo, who carried his doctor's black bag and impassively observed the red tile-roofed houses, the streetcars, the men in straw hats and two-toned shoes, the singular mixture of luxury and disorder of the Presidential Palace. During the months of El Benefactor's long agony, security measures had been relaxed and in the hours following his death tremendous confusion reigned. No one stopped the visitor and his servant. They walked down long passageways and through salons, and finally entered the room where that powerful man—father of a hundred bastards, master of the lives and deaths of his subjects, and owner of an incalculable fortune—lay in his nightshirt, wearing kid gloves and soaked in his own urine. Members of his retinue and a few concubines trembled outside the door while the Ministers argued among themselves whether to flee the country or remain to see if the mummy of El Benefactor could continue to direct the destinies of the nation. Professor Jones stopped before the cadaver, examining it with an entomologist's fascination.

"Is it true, Doctor, that you can preserve dead bodies?" asked a fat man with mustaches very like the dictator's.

"Mmm . . ."

"Then I advise you not to do so, because now it is my turn to govern. I am his brother, from the same cradle and the same blood"— a threat underscored by the blunderbuss stuck in the sibling's belt.

At that moment the Minister of War appeared; he took the scientist by the arm and led him aside for a private word.

"You're not thinking of embalming the President—?"

"Mmm . . ."

"You'd be better off not to meddle in this, because now it's my turn to command, and I hold the Army right in this fist."

Disquieted, the Professor, followed by Consuelo, departed. He was never to know why or by whom he had been summoned. As he left the Palace, he was muttering that he would never understand these tropical peoples and the best thing he could do would be to return to the beloved city of his birth, where the laws of logic and urbanity were in full sway—and which he should never have left.

The Minister of War took charge of the government without knowing exactly what he should do; he had always been under the thumb of El Benefactor and did not remember having taken a single initiative in all his career. These were uncertain times. The people refused to believe that the President for Life was actually dead; they thought that the old man displayed on the bier fit for a pharaoh was a hoax, another of that sorcerer's tricks to trap his critics. People locked themselves in their houses, afraid to stick a foot out the door, until the *guardia* broke down the doors, turned the occupants out by brute force, and lined them up to pay their last respects to the Supreme Leader, who was already beginning to stink in state among the virgin wax candles and lilies flown in from Florida. When they saw that various dignitaries of the Church in their finest ceremonial robes were presiding over the pomp of the funeral, the populace were finally assured that the tyrant's immortality was only a myth, and came out to celebrate. The country awakened from its long siesta, and in a matter of hours the cloud of depression and fatigue that had weighed over it dissipated. People began to dream of a timid liberty. They shouted, danced, threw stones, broke windows, and even sacked some of the mansions of the favorites of the regime; and they burned the long black Packard in which El Benefactor always rode, its unmistakable klaxon spreading fear as he passed. Then the Minister of War rose above the confusion, installed himself in the Presidential Seat, gave instructions to deflate high spirits with gunfire, and at once addressed the people over the radio, announcing a new order. Little by little, calm was restored. The jails were emptied of political prisoners to leave space for those still arriving, and a more progressive government was set in motion that promised to bring the nation into the twentieth century—not a far-fetched idea, considering that it was already three decades behind. In that political desert the first parties began to emerge, a Parliament was organized, and there was a renaissance of ideas and projects.

The day they buried the lawyer, his most cherished mummy, Professor Jones was so enraged he suffered a cerebral hemorrhage. At the urging of the authorities, who did not want to be burdened with the visible dead of the previous regime, the family of the celebrated martyr of tyranny provided him with a grandiose funeral, in spite of the widespread impression, created by his still-excellent state of preservation, that they were burying him alive. Jones left no stone unturned in trying to prevent his work of art from ending up in a mausoleum, but to no avail. He stood with outstretched arms at the gates of the cemetery, trying to block the passage of the black hearse transporting the silver-riveted mahogany coffin, but the coachman drove straight ahead, and if the doctor had not stepped aside he would have been flattened without a moment's hesitation. As the niche was sealed, the embalmer was felled by apoplexy, half his body rigid, the other half trembling convulsively. With that burial, the most conclusive evidence that the Professor's formula could thwart the process of decomposition for an indefinite period disappeared forever behind a marble tombstone.

———

Those were the only major events of the years Consuelo served in the house of Professor Jones. For her, the difference between dictatorship and democracy was occasionally being able to attend a Carlos Gardel movie—formerly forbidden to women—and, following her employer's attack of apoplexy, having to care for the invalid as if he were a baby. Their routine was monotonously unvarying, until the July day the gardener was bitten by a viper. He was a tall, strong Indian, smooth-featured but with a secretive, taciturn expression. Consuelo had never exchanged more than ten words with him, in spite of the fact that he helped her with the cadavers, the cancer patients, and the idiots. He would pick up a patient as if he were a feather pillow, sling him over his shoulder, and lope up the stairs to the laboratory without a trace of curiosity.

"A *surucucú* just bit the gardener," Consuelo announced to Professor Jones.

"As soon as he dies, bring him to me," the scientist enunciated through twisted lips, immediately preparing to create an indigenous mummy posed as if pruning the Malabar plums, and then install him as a garden ornament. By this time the Professor was quite elderly and was beginning to have artistic delusions; he dreamed of representing all the trades, thus forming his personal museum of human statues.

For the first time in her entire silent existence, Consuelo disobeyed an order and took the initiative. With the help of the cook, she dragged the Indian to his room in the back patio and laid him on his straw pallet; she was determined to save him, because it seemed shameful to think of him transfigured into an ornament to satisfy her employer's whim— and also because once or twice she had felt an indescribable nervousness as she watched the man's large, dark, strong hands tending the plants with such singular delicacy. She cleaned his wound with soap and water, made two deep cuts with the knife used for cutting up chicken, and slowly and patiently sucked out the poisoned blood, spitting it into a receptacle. Between every mouthful she rinsed her mouth with vinegar, so she herself would not die. Then she wrapped him in turpentine-soaked cloths, purged him with herbal teas, applied spiderwebs to the wound, and allowed the cook to light candles to the saints—although she herself had little faith in that recourse. When the victim began to pass blood in his urine, she spirited the Sándalo Sol from the Professor's cabinet, a heretofore infallible remedy for discharges of the urinary tract; but in spite of her painstaking care, the leg began to turn gangrenous and the man, lucid, silent, not once complaining, began to die. However, Consuelo became aware that notwithstanding pain, fear of death, and shortness of breath, the gardener responded with ardent enthusiasm when she rubbed his body or soothed him with poultices. That unexpected erection so moved her mature virgin's heart that when he held her arm and gazed at her entreatingly, she realized that the moment had come for her to justify the name Consuelo and console this man in his misfortune. Furthermore, she reflected that in all her thirty-some years of existence she had never known pleasure, and had not sought it, believing that it was something reserved for actors in the movies. She resolved to give herself pleasure, for once, and at the same time offer herself to the victim in the hope that he would pass contented to the other world.

I knew my mother so well that I can imagine the ceremony that followed, although she never told me the details. She had no false modesty, and always answered my questions forthrightly, but at any mention of her Indian, she would abruptly fall silent, adrift in pleasant memories.

She removed her cotton outer garment, her linen petticoat and underpants, and pulled the pins from the hair she wore in the large bun required by her employer. The long strands fell loose over her body, and, thus robed in her finest attribute, gently, with infinite care, she straddled the dying man, trying not to exacerbate his agony. She did not know exactly what to do next, because she had absolutely no experience in such tasks, but what she lacked in knowledge she made up for in instinct and good will. The muscles beneath the man's dark skin tensed, and she had the sensation of galloping upon a great, majestic animal. Whispering newly invented words, and drying his sweat with a cloth, she eased herself to the exact position, and then moved cautiously, like a young wife accustomed to making love to an elderly husband. Soon he tumbled her over and embraced her with the urgency dictated by the proximity of death; even the shadows in the corners were transformed by their brief joy. And that is how I was conceived, on my father's deathbed.

But, contrary to the hopes of Professor Jones and the French scientists at the serpentarium, all of whom wanted his body for their experiments, the gardener did not die. Against all logic he began to improve; his temperature went down, his breathing became normal, and he asked for food. Consuelo realized that without intending it she had discovered an antidote for poisonous snakebites, and continued to administer it with tenderness and enthusiasm as often as requested, until the patient was once again on his feet. Soon afterward, the Indian came to tell her goodbye; she made no attempt to detain him. They held hands for a minute or two, kissed each other with a certain sadness, and then she removed her gold nugget, its cord worn thin from wear, and hung it around the neck of her only lover as a remembrance of their shared cantering. He went away grateful, and almost well. My mother says he left smiling.

Consuelo displayed no emotion. She continued to work as she always had, ignoring the nausea, the heaviness in her legs, and the colored spots that clouded her vision, never mentioning the extraordinary medicament she had employed to save the dying man. She did not tell it even when her belly began to swell, nor when Professor Jones called her in to give her a purgative, believing that she was bloated as the result of a digestive disorder; nor did she tell it when, in her appointed time, she gave birth. She bore the pain for thirteen hours, continuing with her chores, and when she could stand it no longer she went to her room, prepared to live that moment, the most important in her life, to the fullest. She brushed her hair, hastily braided it, and tied it with a new ribbon. She removed her clothing, washed herself from head to foot, then placed a clean sheet on the floor and squatted on it in a position she had seen in a book on Eskimo customs. Bathed in sweat, with a rag in her mouth to choke back her moans, she strained to bring into the world the stubborn creature still clinging inside her. She was no longer young, and it was not an easy task, but scrubbing floors on her hands and knees, carrying loads up steep stairs, and washing clothes till midnight had given her firm muscles, and finally the baby began to emerge. First she saw two minuscule feet kicking feebly as if attempting the first steps of an arduous journey. She took a deep breath and, with a last moan, felt something tearing in the center of her body as an alien mass slipped from between her thighs. She was shaken to her soul with relief. There I lay, tangled in a bluish cord, which she carefully removed from around my neck to allow me to breathe. At that moment the door opened; the cook had noticed her absence, guessed what was happening, and had come to help. She found my mother naked, with me on her belly, still joined to her by a pulsing cord.

"Bad luck, it's a girl," said the impromptu midwife after she had tied and cut the umbilical cord and was holding me in her arms.

"But she came feet first, and that's a sign of good luck," my mother smiled as soon as she could speak.

"She seems strong, and she has good lungs. If you want, I can be the godmother."

"I hadn't planned to christen her," Consuelo replied, but when she saw the other woman cross herself, scandalized, she did not want to offend her. "All right, a little holy water never hurt anyone, and—who knows?—it might even do some good. Her name will be Eva, so she will love life."

"And her last name?"

"None. Her father's name isn't important."

"Everybody needs a last name. Only a dog can run around with one name."

"Her father belonged to the Luna tribe, the Children of the Moon. Let it be Luna, then. Eva Luna. Give her to me, please, godmother. I want to see if she's whole."

Sitting in the pool of my birth, her bones as weak as cotton wool, dripping with sweat, Consuelo examined my body for any ominous sign transmitted by the venom and, discovering no abnormality, breathed a deep sigh of relief.

I do not have fangs, or reptilian scales—at least no visible ones. The somewhat unusual circumstances of my conception had, instead, only positive consequences: these were unfailing good health and the rebelliousness that, although somewhat slow to evidence itself, in the end saved me from the life of humiliations to which I was undoubtedly destined. From my father I inherited stamina; he must have been very strong to fight off the serpent's venom for so many days and to give pleasure to a woman when he was so near death. Everything else I owe to my mother. When I was four, I had one of those diseases that leave little pockmarks all over the body, but she healed me, tying my hands to keep me from scratching myself, coating my body with sheep's tallow, and shielding me from natural light for one hundred and eighty days. During that period, she also brewed squash blossoms to rid me of parasites, and fern root to flush out the tapeworm. I have been healthy and sound ever since. I have no marks on my skin, only a few cigarette burns, and I expect to be free of wrinkles in my old age because the effect of sheep's tallow is everlasting.

My mother was a silent person, able to camouflage herself against the furniture or to disappear in the design of a rug. She never made the slightest commotion; it was almost as if she were not there. In the privacy of the room we shared, however, she was transformed. When she talked about the past, or told her stories, the room filled with light; the walls dissolved to reveal incredible landscapes, palaces crowded with unimaginable objects, faraway countries that she invented or borrowed from the Professor's library. She placed at my feet the treasures of the Orient, the moon, and beyond. She reduced me to the size of an ant so I could experience the universe from that smallness; she gave me wings to see it from the heavens; she gave me the tail of a fish so I would know the depths of the sea. When she was telling a story, her characters peopled my world, and some of them became so familiar that still today, so many years later, I can describe the clothing they wore and the tone of their voice. She maintained intact her memories of her childhood in the Mission; she retained all the anecdotes she had heard and those she had learned in her readings. She manufactured the substance of her own dreams, and from those materials constructed a world for me. Words are free, she used to say, and she appropriated them; they were all hers. She sowed in my mind the idea that reality is not only what we see on the surface; it has a magical dimension as well and, if we so desire, it is legitimate to enhance it and color it to make our journey through life less trying. The characters she summoned to the enchanted world of her stories are the only clear memories I have of my first years; the rest existed in a kind of mist where the household servants, the aged Pro-

fessor prostrate in his bicycle-wheeled armchair, and the string of patients and cadavers he attended in spite of his infirmity, all blended
together. Children annoyed Professor Jones, but he was usually lost in
his own thoughts, and when he ran into me in some corner of the house,
he scarcely saw me. I was a little afraid of him because I did not know
whether the old man had fabricated the mummies or whether they had
engendered him; they all seemed to belong to the same parchment-
skinned family. His presence had no effect on me because we lived in
different worlds. I roamed through the kitchen, the patios, the servants'
quarters, the garden, and when I followed my mother to the other parts
of the house, I moved very quietly so the Professor would think I was
a prolongation of her shadow. The house had so many different smells
that I could go around with my eyes closed and guess where I was:
aromas of food, clothing, coal, medicines, books, and dankness fused
with the characters from the stories, enriching those years.

I was brought up on the theory that all vices issue from idleness, an
idea implanted by the Little Sisters of Charity and cultivated by the
learned doctor with his despotic discipline. I had no conventional toys,
although the truth was that everything in the house served me in my
games. During the day, there was no time for rest; idle hands were
considered a source of shame. Beside my mother I scrubbed the wood
floors, hung clothes out to dry, chopped vegetables, and at the time of
siesta tried to knit and embroider—but I do not remember those tasks
as being oppressive. It was like playing house. The Professor's sinister
experiments did not disturb me either; my mother explained that the
head-thumping and the mosquito-bite treatments—fortunately, in-
frequent—were not indications of her employer's cruelty, but the most
rigorous scientific therapy. With her confident manner of handling the
embalmed bodies like relatives down on their luck, my mother nipped
in the bud any blossoming of fear, and never allowed the other servants
to frighten me with their macabre ideas. I think she must have tried to
keep me away from the laboratory. In fact, I almost never saw the
mummies; I simply knew they were there on the other side of the door.
Those poor people are very fragile, Eva, she used to tell me. I don't
want you to go into that room. Just a little push and you might break
one of their bones, and then the Professor would be very angry. For
my peace of mind she gave a name to each body and invented a past

for every one, transforming them into friendly spirits like elves and fairies.

We did not often leave the house. One of the rare occasions we did was to watch a procession during the drought, an occasion when even atheists were prepared to pray, because it was a community event more than an act of faith. I remember hearing people say that not a drop of rain had fallen in the country for three years; the earth had split open in thirsty cracks, all the vegetation had died; animals had perished with their muzzles buried in the dust; and, in exchange for water, people who lived in the plains trudged to the coast to sell themselves into slavery. In view of this national disaster, the Bishop had decided to carry the image of the Nazarene through the streets and implore the Almighty to bring an end to this punishment, and as it was the last hope, all of us came—rich and poor, young and old, believers and agnostics. Professor Jones sputtered with rage when he learned of it—Barbarians! Indians! Black savages!—but he could not prevent his servants from dressing in their best clothes and going off to see the procession. The multitudes, with the Nazarene in the lead, set out from the Cathedral but did not get even as far as the Public Utility Company before they were overtaken by a violent cloudburst. Forty-eight hours later, the city had become a lake; storm sewers were clogged, roads inundated, residences flooded. In the country, houses were carried off by the downpour, and in one town on the coast it rained fish. A miracle, a miracle! the Bishop clamored. And we joined in the chorus, unaware that the procession had been organized after a meteorologist had forecast typhoons and torrential rains throughout the Caribbean—as Jones proclaimed from his wheelchair: Superstitious, ignorant, illiterate fools! the poor man howled. But no one listened. That miracle accomplished what neither the Mission priests nor the Little Sisters of Charity had been able to achieve: my mother accepted God, because now she visualized him seated on his celestial throne gently mocking mankind, and to her this god was very different from the awesome patriarch of religious books. Perhaps one manifestation of his sense of humor was to keep us in a state of confusion, never revealing his plans and proposals to us. But every time we remembered the miracle of the rain, we would die laughing.

The world was bounded by the iron railings of the garden. Within them, time was ruled by caprice; in half an hour I could make six trips around the globe, and a moonbeam in the patio would fill my thoughts for a week. Light and shadow created fundamental changes in the nature of objects: books, quiet during the day, opened by night so their characters could come out and wander through the rooms and live their adventures; the mummies, so humble and discreet when the morning sunlight poured through the windows, at twilight became stones lurking in the shadows, and in the blackness grew to the size of giants. Space expanded and contracted according to my will: the cubby beneath the stairs contained an entire planetary system, but the sky seen through the attic skylight was nothing more than a pale circle of glass. One word from me and *abracadabra!* reality was transformed.

I grew up free and secure in that mansion at the foot of the hill. I had no contact with any other children, nor was I accustomed to strangers, except a man in a black suit and hat, a Protestant with a Bible beneath his arm who reduced Professor Jones's last years to ashes. I feared him much more than I did the Professor.

TWO

Eight years before I was born—on the same day El Bene-factor died in his bed like any innocent grandfather—in a village in the north of Austria, a boy named Rolf came into the world. He was the last son of Lukas Carlé, the most feared of all the upper-school masters. Corporal punishment was a part of schooling; spare the rod and spoil the child was sustained by both popular wisdom and pedagogical theory, and so no parent in his right mind would have protested its application. But when Carlé broke a boy's hands, the school administration forbade him to use the ferule, because it was clear that once he began he lost all self-control in a frenzy of lust. To get even, the students would follow his son Jochen and, if they could catch him, beat him up. The boy grew up fleeing bands of boys, denying his surname, hiding as if he were the hangman's son.

Lukas Carlé had imposed in his home the same rule of fear he maintained at school. His marriage was one of convenience: romantic love had no place in his plans; he considered romance barely tolerable in opera or novels, and totally inappropriate in everyday life. He and his wife had been married without any chance to get to know one another, and from her wedding night on she despised him. To Lukas Carlé, his wife was an inferior being, closer to animal than to man, God's only intelligent creation. Although in theory a woman was a creature deserving of compassion, in practice his wife drove him out of his mind. When he arrived in that village after long weeks of wandering—he had been uprooted from his birthplace by the First World War—he was about twenty-five years old; he had a teaching diploma and money enough to survive for one week. First he looked for work, and then a wife. He had chosen her because he liked the sudden gleam of terror he saw in her eyes, and he approved of her broad hips, which he considered necessary for begetting male offspring and for doing heavy housework. He was also influenced in his decision by two hectares of land, a half-dozen head of cattle, and a small income the girl had inherited from her father; all of which he immediately claimed as legitimate wealth.

Lukas Carlé liked women's shoes with very high heels, and best of all he liked red patent leather. When he traveled to the city, he paid a prostitute to strut around naked, clad only in that uncomfortable footwear, while he, fully dressed, wearing even his overcoat and hat, and ensconced in an armchair like a feted dignitary, tingled with indescribable pleasure at the sight of her buttocks—as ample as possible, white, with dimples—jiggling with every step. He did not touch her, of course. He never touched such women, because he was fanatic about hygiene. Since he did not have the means to indulge in such luxuries as often as he would like, he bought some gay high-heeled French ankle-high boots and hid them in the most inaccessible part of the wardrobe. From time to time he locked his children in their room, turned up the record player to full volume, and summoned his wife. She had learned to gauge her husband's changes of mood and could anticipate—even before he himself knew—when he was feeling the urge to humiliate her. She would begin to tremble with dread, and dishes would fall from her hands and shatter on the floor.

Carlé did not tolerate any noise in his house—I have enough to put up with from my students, he would say. His children learned not to cry or laugh in his presence, to steal about like shadows and talk in whispers, and they developed such skill for passing unnoticed that sometimes their mother thought she could see through them, and was terrified that they might become transparent. The schoolmaster was convinced that he had been dealt a bad hand by the laws of genetics. His children were a total failure. Jochen was slow and clumsy, the worst possible student; he dozed in class, wet his bed, and was not suited for any of the plans his father had made for him. About Katharina, better not even to speak. The girl was an imbecile. Of one thing he was sure: there were no congenital flaws in his bloodline, so it was not he who was responsible for that poor sickly spawn. In fact, how could he be sure she was really his daughter? He would not put his neck on the block for anyone's fidelity, least of all his own wife's. Fortunately Katharina had been born with a heart defect and the doctor had predicted that she would not live very long. Much better that way.

Considering the relative lack of success of his first two children, Lukas Carlé was not overjoyed when he learned of his wife's third pregnancy, but when a large rosy boy was born, with wide-open gray eyes and strong hands, he felt greatly cheered. Maybe this was the son and heir he had always desired: a true Carlé. He would have to keep the child's mother from spoiling him; nothing so dangerous as a woman for corrupting a fine male seedling. Don't dress him in wool; he needs to get used to the cold so he will be strong. Leave him in the dark; that way he will never be afraid of it. Don't pick him up; it doesn't matter if he cries till he turns purple, it's good for his lungs. Those were his orders, but behind his back the mother wrapped her son warmly, gave him double rations of milk, cuddled him, and sang him cradle songs. This regimen of adding and removing clothing, of striking and cosseting him without apparent logic, of closing him in a dark wardrobe and then consoling him with kisses would have driven most children to madness. But Rolf Carlé was fortunate: he was not only born with the mental fortitude to bear what would have broken most others, but the Second World War erupted and his father enlisted in the Army, thus freeing him from his father's presence. The war was the happiest time of his childhood.

While in South America embalmed bodies were accumulating in the house of Professor Jones and a copulation inspired by a serpent's bite engendered a little girl whose mother would call her Eva so she would love life, also in Europe reality took on abnormal dimensions. The war sank the world into confusion and fear. By the time the little girl was walking, clinging to her mother's skirts, peace was being signed on the other side of the Atlantic on a continent in ruins. Meanwhile, on this side of the ocean, few lost any sleep over that distant violence. They were sufficiently occupied with violence of their own.

As he grew up, Rolf Carlé proved to be observant, proud, and tenacious, with a certain inclination toward romanticism that he looked on as a sign of weakness. In that age of glorification of war, he and his friends played at bloodshed in the trenches and shooting planes from the sky; but secretly he was moved by the buds of each spring, the flowers of summer, the gold of autumn, and the melancholy whiteness of winter. In each of the seasons, he walked through the woods collecting leaves and insects to study under his magnifying glass. He tore pages from his notebooks and wrote poems, which he then hid in the hollows of tree trunks or beneath stones with the inadmissible hope that someone might find them. He never spoke of this to anyone.

He was ten years old the afternoon they took him to bury the dead. He was happy that day, because his brother Jochen had trapped a hare and the house was filled with the aroma of the meat, marinated in vinegar and rosemary, stewing over a slow fire. He had not smelled that smell in a very long time, and his mouth was watering with such anticipated pleasure that only his strict upbringing prevented him from lifting the lid and sticking a spoon in the pot. It was also baking day. He loved seeing his mother bent over the enormous kitchen table, elbow-deep in dough, moving to the measured rhythm of making bread. She kneaded the ingredients, formed long rolls of dough, divided them, and from each piece produced a round loaf. Before, in times of plenty, she had put aside a bit of the dough, added milk, eggs, and cinnamon, and made buns that she stored in a tin—one for each child for each day of the week. Now the flour was mixed with bran, and the result was dark and harsh, like bread made of sawdust.

The day had begun with a commotion in the street—movement of the occupation troops, shouted orders—but no one was overly startled; their fear had been exhausted in the rout of defeat, and they had little left to expend in premonitions of bad omens. Following the armistice, the Russians had moved into the village. Rumors of brutality preceded the soldiers of the Red Army, and the terrified populace awaited a bloodbath. They are beasts, people said; they slash open the bellies of pregnant women and throw the fetuses to the dogs; they run their bayonets through old people; they stick dynamite up men's asses and blow them to bits; they rape, burn, destroy. However, none of that happened. Searching for an explanation, the mayor concluded that they were indeed fortunate; the soldiers who occupied their town had not come from the most war-ravaged part of the Soviet Union, and therefore they had less stored-up bitterness and unfulfilled revenge. They had rumbled into town, heavy vehicles pulling all their matériel, under the command of a young officer with Asian features; they had requisitioned all the food, stowed everything they could find of value in their knapsacks, and had shot six prominent members of the community accused of collaborating. The soldiers set up camp on the edge of the village and stayed to themselves. That day, however, they had rounded up all the townspeople, mustering them over loudspeakers and going into houses to roust out the hesitant. Frau Carlé wrapped a jacket around Katharina's shoulders and hurried outside before the soldiers could come in and commandeer the hare and the week's bread. With her three children, Jochen, Katharina, and Rolf, she went to the public square. The village had survived those war years in better shape than most, in spite of the bomb that had fallen on the school one Sunday night, converting it to rubble and scattering splinters of desks and blackboards far and wide. Part of the medieval cobblestones were missing, because various troops had used the stones to construct barricades. The enemy had appropriated the clock in the mayor's office, the church organ, and the last wine harvest, the only local treasures. Buildings were all in need of paint, and here and there some were bullet-pocked, but the village had not lost the charm acquired over centuries of existence.

The people congregated in the square, circled by enemy soldiers; the Soviet commandant, in his tattered uniform, worn-out boots, and several days' growth of beard, walked past the group, closely observing each one. No one looked him in the eye; they stood with heads lowered, shoulders bowed, expectant; only Katharina fixed her meek eyes on the officer, and stuck a finger in her nose.

"Is she retarded?" asked the officer, pointing to the girl.

"She was born that way," Frau Carlé replied.

"Then she doesn't have to go. Leave her here."

"She can't stay here by herself, please. . . . Let me take her with us."

"As you like."

Under a pale spring sun they stood and waited for more than two hours, at gunpoint, the elderly leaning on the strongest, the children asleep on the ground, the youngest in their parents' arms, until finally the order was given, and they set off, following behind the commandant's jeep, under the watchful eye of soldiers who tried to hurry the slow-moving line headed by the mayor and the school principal, the only authorities surviving from the catastrophe of the last years. They walked in silence, uneasy, turning to look back at the roofs of their houses still visible among the hills, asking each other where they were being taken—until it became obvious that they were being led in the direction of the prison camp, and their hearts closed like fists.

Rolf knew the way, because he had often walked there when he went with Jochen to hunt snakes, trap foxes, or gather wood. Sometimes the brothers had sat beneath the trees, looking in the direction of the barbed-wire fence hidden by foliage; they were so far away they could not see clearly, and had to be satisfied with listening to the sirens and sniffing the air. When the wind was blowing, a peculiar odor drifted into their houses, but no one seemed to notice; certainly it was never mentioned. This was the first time that Rolf Carlé, or any of the other villagers, had passed through the metal gates; they were immediately struck by the eroded soil stripped of vegetation, arid as a desert of sterile dust, far different from the soft, green-growing fields of the season. The column filed along a long path, crossed through various barriers of rolled barbed wire, walked beneath guard towers and emplacements that had only recently housed machine guns, and finally reached a large open area. On one side were windowless sheds, on the other a brick building with large chimneys, and, at the rear, latrines and a gallows. Spring had halted at the gates of the prison: here everything was gray, shrouded in the fog of an eternal winter. The villagers came to a stop before the barracks; they huddled together, touching each other for courage, oppressed by that stillness, that immense silence, that sky turned to ash. The commandant gave an order and the soldiers herded them like cattle in the direction of the main building. And then everyone could see. There were dozens of them piled on the ground, one on top of another, a tangled, dismembered mass, a mountain of pale firewood. At first they could not believe they were human bodies, they looked like the marionettes of some macabre theater, but the Russians poked the villagers with their weapons, prodded them with their rifle butts, and they had to move closer, to smell, to look, to allow those bony, eyeless faces to be burned into their memories. Each of them heard the thudding of his own heart, and no one spoke, because there was nothing to say. For long moments they stood motionless, until the commandant picked up a shovel and handed it to the mayor. The soldiers distributed other tools.

"Begin digging," said the officer without raising his voice, almost in a whisper.

They sent Katharina and other small children to sit beneath the gallows while the rest worked. Rolf stayed with Jochen. The ground was hard; his hands and fingernails were grimy from the flinty soil, but he did not stop; stooped over, his hair fallen over his face, he was shaken by a shame he would never forget, a shame that like a relentless nightmare would pursue him throughout his lifetime. He never looked up, not once. All he heard around him was the sound of metal striking rock, harsh breathing, the sobs of some women.

It was night by the time they finished digging the pits. Rolf noticed that the spotlights in the guard towers had been turned on, and night had become as bright as day. The Russian officer gave an order, and people were dispatched two by two to bring the bodies. The boy brushed off his hands, wiping them on his pants legs; he dried the sweat from his face, and with his brother Jochen walked forward to what awaited them. With a hoarse cry their mother tried to stop them, but the boys continued on; they bent down and picked up a cadaver by the ankles and wrists: naked, hairless, bones and skin, weightless, cold and hard as porcelain. They lifted it effortlessly and, tightly gripping the rigid form, started back toward the graves they had dug in the open square. Their load swayed slightly to and fro, and the head lolled backward. Rolf turned and looked at his mother; he saw her doubled over with nausea. He wanted to make a gesture of consolation, but his hands were occupied.

It was past midnight before they completed the task of burying the prisoners. They filled the graves and covered them with earth, but the time had not yet come to leave. The soldiers forced them to go through the barracks, to enter the death chambers, to examine the ovens, to walk beneath the gallows. No one dared pray for the dead. In their hearts they knew that from that moment they would try to forget, to tear that horror from their souls, resolved never to speak of it, with the hope that time would erase it. Finally, slowly, exhausted, feet dragging, they returned home. Last came Rolf Carlé, walking between two rows of skeletons, all equal in the desolation of death.

One week later, Lukas Carlé returned. His son Rolf did not recognize him; when his father had left for the front, the boy was not yet at the age of reason, and the man who burst into the kitchen that night did not in any way resemble the photograph on the mantel. During the years he had lived without a father, Rolf had invented one of heroic dimensions. He had clad him in an aviator's uniform and covered his chest with medals, imagining a proud, brave warrior with boots so shiny a child could see himself in them. He did not associate that image with the person who appeared so suddenly that night and, thinking he was a beggar, did not even bother to say hello. The man in the photograph had a carefully trimmed mustache, and his eyes were as leaden as winter skies—authoritarian and cold. The man who flung open the kitchen door was wearing an oversized pair of pants held up by a cord around the waist, a threadbare jacket, a filthy kerchief around his neck, and, in place of the mirror-shine boots, rags wrapped around his feet. He was a rather small man, badly shaven, his bristling hair cut in clumps. No, that was not anyone Rolf knew. The rest of the family, on the other hand, remembered all too well. When his wife saw him, she clapped both hands to her mouth; Jochen leaped to his feet, overturning his chair in his haste to retreat; and Katharina ran to hide beneath the table, something she had not done in a long time, but which was an instinctive act lodged in her memory.

Lukas Carlé had not returned out of any nostalgia for the hearth.

Being a solitary person without a sense of country, he had never felt he belonged to that village—or to any other. He had returned because he was hungry and desperate; he preferred to risk falling into the hands of the victorious enemy rather than drag himself around the countryside any longer. He had deserted, and had survived by hiding during the day and traveling by night. He had stolen the identification papers of a fallen soldier, planning to change his name and erase his past, but soon realized that he had nowhere on that vast destroyed continent to go. The memory of the village with its pleasant houses and orchards and vineyards, as well as the school where he had taught so many years, held little attraction for him, but he had no other choice. He had won several decorations during the course of the war, not for bravery but for exercising cruelty. He was different; he had explored the murky depths of his soul; he knew exactly to what lengths he would go. After having tested the extremes, having passed the boundaries of evil and pleasure, it seemed a lowly fate to return to his former life and resign himself to teaching groups of runny-nosed, ill-bred children. It was his belief that man is made for war. History demonstrates that progress is never achieved without violence: grit your teeth and bear it; close your eyes and deal it out—that's why we're soldiers. Everything he had suffered had failed to instill in him any desire for peace; instead, it had etched in his mind the conviction that only gunpowder and blood can produce men capable of steering the foundering ship of humanity to port—abandoning the weak and helpless on the high seas, in accordance with the implacable laws of nature.

"What's this? Aren't you happy to see me?" he asked, closing the door behind him.

Absence had not diminished Carlé's capacity for terrorizing his family. Jochen tried to say something, but the words stuck in his throat; only a guttural sound escaped him as he moved in front of his brother to protect him from an undefined danger. Frau Carlé's first act, as soon as she recovered, was to run to the linen chest and take out a large white tablecloth, which she spread over the table so her husband would not see Katharina—would not, perhaps, even remember she existed. With nothing more than a quick glance around, Lukas Carlé took over the house and regained control of his family. His wife seemed no less stupid, but the fear in her eyes and the firmness of her rump were as apparent as ever. Jochen had grown into a tall, husky young man, and Carlé could not understand how he had escaped being conscripted into the youth brigades. He scarcely recognized Rolf, but it took him only an instant to appreciate that the boy was tied to his mother's apron strings, and needed a jolt or two to wipe the spoiled lapdog look off his face. He would make it his business to make a man of him.

"Warm the water for my bath, Jochen. Is there anything to eat in this house? And you must be Rolf.... Come here and shake hands with your father. Did you hear me? Come here!"

After that night Rolf's life was never the same. In spite of the war and all its hardships, he had never known fear. Lukas Carlé taught him. The boy would not have a good night's sleep until years later when his father was found swinging from a tree in the forest.

The Russian soldiers who occupied the village were crude, destitute, and sentimental. In the evening they sat around the campfires beside their weapons and equipment and sang songs of their homeland, and, hearing the sweet sound of their village dialects, some of them wept with nostalgia. Sometimes they got drunk, and quarreled or danced till they dropped from exhaustion. The villagers avoided them, but a few girls, in exchange for a little food, went to their camps to offer themselves, quietly, never raising their eyes. They always returned with something, despite the fact that the victors were as hungry as the vanquished. The children were also drawn to the camp; they were fascinated by the soldiers' language, their war machines, their strange customs, and they were enthralled by a sergeant with a deeply scarred face who entertained them by juggling four knives in the air at a time. Rolf usually went closer than any of his friends, even though his mother had specifically instructed him not to go there, and one day found him sitting beside the sergeant trying to understand what he was saying, and practicing tossing the knives. Within a few days of their arrival, the Russians had located all the remaining collaborators and deserters in hiding and had begun the war trials—extremely brief because there was little time for formalities. Few people attended; they were worn out and did not want to listen to further accusations. Nevertheless, when it was Lukas Carlé's turn, Jochen and Rolf slipped in and sat at the back of the room. The accused did not seem to regret anything he had done: he merely stated in his own defense that he had obeyed his superiors' orders; he was not in the Army to deliberate, but to win a war. The juggler sergeant saw Rolf in the room, felt sorry for him, and tried to take him outside, but the boy sat firmly in his seat, determined to listen to the end. It would have been difficult to explain to the sergeant that his pallor was not caused by any concern for his father, but by his secret hope that there would be enough evidence to sentence him to the firing squad. When, instead, Carlé was consigned to six months of forced labor in the mines of the Ukraine, Jochen and Rolf considered it an unbelievably light punishment, and secretly prayed that Lukas Carlé would die in that faraway land and never come back.

Hunger did not end with the peace; for years foraging for food had been their first priority, and that did not change. Jochen could scarcely read, but he was strong and persistent, and after his father left and after the shelling had destroyed the fields, he had taken charge of providing for his family by cutting wood, selling blackberries and wild mushrooms, and hunting rabbits and partridges and foxes. Soon Rolf was a partner in his brother's efforts and, like him, learned to pilfer odds and ends in the neighboring villages—always without the knowledge of his mother, who even during times of greatest hardship acted as if the war were a remote nightmare that had nothing to do with her; she was not, furthermore, one to compromise when it came to instilling moral values in her children. The boy became so accustomed to the gnawing in his innards that long afterward, when the markets were overflowing with the earth's bounty and fried potatoes and sweets and sausages were being sold on every street corner, he continued to dream of stale bread hidden in a hollow in the floorboards beneath his bed.

Frau Carlé succeeded in maintaining her serenity and her faith in God until the day her husband returned from the Ukraine to claim his rightful place in the household. Then her courage deserted her. She seemed to shrivel up, and she withdrew, engaged in an unending dialogue with herself. The fear that had always been present finally crippled her; she had no outlet for her hatred, and it destroyed her. Unshirking, she continued to carry out all her responsibilities, slaving from dawn to nightfall, tending to Katharina, serving the rest of her family, but she stopped smiling or speaking—and she did not return to church, because she was not willing to get down on her knees to a merciless God who had ignored her just prayers that Lukas Carlé burn in hell. She also gave up trying to protect Jochen and Rolf from their father's excesses. The yellings, the beatings, the quarrels all came to seem normal to her, and evoked no response. She sat and stared out the window with vacant eyes, escaping into a past where there was no Lukas Carlé and she was still a young girl untouched by affliction.

Carlé held the theory that human beings are divided into anvils and hammers: some are born to beat, others to be beaten. Naturally, he wanted his male children to be hammers. He would tolerate no weakness in them, especially in Jochen, on whom he experimented with his theories on teaching. He was infuriated when the boy's stuttering only grew worse and he began to chew his fingernails. Desperate, Jochen would lie awake at night inventing ways to free himself once and for all from that torment, but with the light of day he would bow to reality, hang his head, and obey his father, never daring to stand up to him, even though he was twenty centimeters taller and as strong as a workhorse. His submissiveness lasted until one winter night when Lukas Carlé felt the mood coming over him to use the red boots. The boys were old enough to guess what that oppressive atmosphere meant, those strained looks, the silence heavy with portents. As he always did, Carlé ordered the children to leave them, to take Katharina and go to their room and not come out for any reason. Before they left, Jochen and Rolf glimpsed the terror in their mother's eyes, and saw her shivering. Soon afterward, lying rigid in their beds, they heard the Victrola blaring at full volume.

"I'm going to go see what he's doing to Mama," Rolf announced when he could no longer bear the knowledge that just across the hall a nightmare was being enacted that had existed in this house for as long as he could remember.

"You stay there," Jochen replied. "I'll go. I'm the oldest."

And, instead of huddling deeper under the covers as he had done all his life, he got out of bed, his mind a blank. With precise movements he pulled on his trousers, his jacket, and his wool cap, and laced up his heavy boots. Then he unlocked their door, crossed the hall, and tried to open the door to the living room, but the bolt was shot. With the same slow and deliberate motions he used when setting his traps or splitting wood, he drew back his leg and with one strong kick burst the metal bolt from the door. Rolf, barefoot and still in his pajamas, had followed his brother, and when the door flew open he saw his mother, totally naked, teetering in a pair of ridiculous red high-heeled boots. Enraged, Lukas Carlé roared at them to get out, but Jochen continued forward; he walked past the table, brushed aside the woman attempting to stop him, and approached his father with such purpose that the man took a hesitant step backward. Jochen's fist struck his father's chin with the strength of a hammer blow, slamming him onto the sideboard, which collapsed with a sound of splintering wood and shattering china. Rolf looked at the inert body on the floor, gulped, ran to his room, pulled a blanket from his bed, and brought it back to cover his mother's nakedness.

"Goodbye, Mama," said Jochen from the front door, not daring to look at her.

"Goodbye, Son," she murmured, relieved that at least one of her sons would be safe.

The next morning, Rolf rolled up the legs of his brother's long trousers and wore them to take his father to the hospital, where a doctor reset his jaw. For weeks Carlé could not speak and had to be fed liquid through a straw. With the departure of her elder son, Frau Carlé sank into depression, and Rolf had to face his detested and feared father alone.

Katharina had a face like a little squirrel and a soul innocent of memory. She was able to feed herself, ask when she needed to go to the bathroom, and run and hide under the table when her father arrived—but that was the extent of her capacity. Rolf used to look for little treasures to bring her: a beetle, a polished stone, a nut she opened carefully to extract the meat. She repaid him with absolute devotion. She waited for him all day, and when she heard his footsteps and saw his upside-down face peering between the table legs, she murmured like a sea gull. She spent hours beneath the huge table, protected by the rough wood, until her father left or fell asleep and someone rescued her. She became adjusted to life in her shelter, attuned to approaching or receding footsteps. Sometimes she did not want to come out even though there was no danger, and then her mother would pass her a bowl of food, and Rolf would get a coverlet and slip under the table with her to curl up for the night. Often when Lukas Carlé sat down to eat, his feet nudged his children—mute, motionless, hands tightly clasped—beneath the table, isolated in their refuge where sounds, odors, and alien presences were muffled by the illusion of being underwater. The brother and sister spent so much time there that Rolf Carlé never forgot the milky light beneath the tablecloth, and many years later, on the other side of the world, he awakened one morning weeping under the white mosquito netting where he slept with the woman he loved.

THREE

*O*ne night at Christmas when I was six years old, my mother swallowed a chicken bone. The Professor, eternally absorbed in his insatiable thirst for knowledge, never observed that holiday—or any other—but the household servants always celebrated Christmas Eve. They set up a crèche with crude clay figures in the kitchen; then everyone would sing Christmas carols and give me a present. Several days in advance they prepared a dish that had originally been concocted by slaves. In colonial times, the prosperous families gathered on December 24 around a great table. The remains of the masters' banquet made their way into the bowls of the servants, who chopped all the leftovers, rolled them in cornmeal dough and banana leaves, and boiled them in great kettles, with such delicious results that the recipe was handed down through the centuries and is still repeated every year. Today, however, the dish is not made from the table scraps of the masters; each ingre-

dient must be cooked separately in a tedious and time-consuming process. In the back patio, Professor Jones's servants raised chickens, turkeys,
and a pig they fattened all year for that one occasion of gluttony. A
week before the event, they began forcing nuts and rum down the gul-
lets of the fowls and feeding the pig liters of milk with brown sugar
and spices so the animals would be juicy and tender. While the women
steamed the banana leaves and readied the pots and braziers, the men
slaughtered the fowls and the pig in an orgy of blood, feathers, and
squeals, until everyone was drunk from liquor and death, and sated from
tasting the meat, swigging the thick broth in the kettles, and singing
lively tunes to the Baby Jesus until they were hoarse. Meanwhile, in the
other wing of the house, the Professor lived a day like any other, not
even realizing it was Christmas. The fateful bone passed undetected in
a morsel of dough, and my mother did not feel it until it lodged in her
throat. After a few hours she began to spit blood, and three days later
she slipped away without any fuss, just as she had lived. I was at her
side, and I have never forgotten that moment, because from that day I
have had to sharpen my perception in order not to lose her among the
shadows-of-no-return where disembodied spirits go to rest.

She did not want to frighten me, so she died without fear. Perhaps
the chicken bone severed something vital and she bled internally, I do
not know. When she realized that her life was draining away, she took
me with her to our room off the patio, to be together until the end.
Slowly, not to hasten death, she washed herself with soap and water to
get rid of the odor of musk that was beginning to disturb her. She
combed her long hair, put on a white petticoat she had sewn during the
hours of siesta, and lay down on the same straw mattress where she
and a snakebitten Indian had conceived me. Although I did not understand then the significance of that ritual, I watched with such attention
that I still remember her every move.

"There is no death, daughter. People die only when we forget them,"
my mother explained shortly before she left me. "If you can remember
me, I will be with you always."

"I will remember you," I promised.

"Now go call your godmother."

I went to look for the cook, the enormous mulatto woman who had helped me into the world and who at the proper time had carried me to be christened.

"Take good care of my girl, *madrina*. I'm leaving her in your hands," my mother said, discreetly wiping away the thread of blood trickling down her chin. Then she took my hand and, with her eyes, kept telling me how much she loved me, until a fog clouded her gaze and life faded from her body without a sound. For a few seconds I thought I saw something translucent floating in the motionless air of the room, flooding it with blue radiance and perfuming it with a breath of musk, but then everything was normal again, the air merely air, the light yellow, the smell the simple smell of every day. I took my mother's face in my hands and moved it back and forth, calling "Mama, Mama," stricken by the silence that had settled between us.

"Everyone dies, it's not so important," my *madrina* said, cutting off my mother's long hair with three clicks of the scissors, planning to sell it later in a wig shop. "We need to get her out of here before the *patrón* discovers her and makes me bring her to the laboratory."

I picked up the braid of hair, wrapped it around my neck, and huddled in a corner with my head between my knees; I did not cry, because I still did not realize the magnitude of my loss. I stayed there for hours, perhaps all night, until two men came in, wrapped the body in the bed's only cover, and carried it away without a word. Then the room was pervaded by unremitting emptiness.

After the modest funeral coach had left, my *madrina* came to look for me. She had to strike a match to see me because the room was in shadows; the light bulb had burned out and dawn seemed to have stopped at the threshold. She found me in a little bundle on the floor. She called me twice by name, to bring me back to reality: Eva Luna . . . Eva Luna. In the flickering flame of the match, I saw large feet in house slippers and the hem of a cotton dress. I looked up and met her moist eyes. She smiled in the instant the uncertain spark died out; then I felt her bend over in the darkness. She picked me up in her stout arms, settled me on her lap, and began to rock me, humming some soft African lament to put me to sleep.

———

"If you were a boy, you could go to school and then study to be a lawyer and provide for me in my old age. Those sticky-fingered lawyers are the ones who make the money. They sure know how to keep things in a muddle. Muddy waters," she used to say, "means money in their pockets."

She believed that men had it best; even the lowest good-for-nothing had a wife to boss around. And years later I reached the conclusion that she may have been right, although I still cannot imagine myself in a man's body, with hair on my face, a tendency to order people around, and something unmanageable below my navel that, to be perfectly frank, I would not know exactly where to put. In her way, my *madrina* was fond of me, and if she never showed it, it was because she thought she had to be strict, and because she lost her sanity at an early age. In those days she was not the ruin she is today. She was an arrogant dark-skinned woman with generous breasts, a well-defined waist, and hips that bulged like a tabletop under her skirts. When she went out on the street, men turned to stare; they shouted indecent propositions at her, and tried to pinch her bottom. She did not shy away, but rewarded them with a smack of her pocketbook—What you think you're doin', you black devil, you?—and then she would laugh and show her gold tooth. She bathed every night standing in a tub splashing water over herself from a pitcher and scrubbing with a soapy rag. She changed her blouse twice a day, sprinkled herself with rose water, washed her hair with egg, and brushed her teeth with salt to make them shine. She had a strong sweetish odor that all her rose water and soap could not subdue, an odor I loved because it made me think of warm custard. I used to help her with her bath, splashing water on her back, enraptured at the sight of that dark body with the mulberry teats, the pubis shadowed by kinky fuzz, the buttocks as stout as the overstuffed armchair that cushioned Professor Jones. She would stroke her body with the rag, and smile, proud of her voluminous flesh. She walked with defiant grace, head high, to the rhythm of the secret music she carried inside. Everything else about her was coarse, even her laughter and her tears. She became angry at the drop of a pin, and would shake her fist in the air and swing at anything in reach; if one of those swipes landed on me, it sounded like cannon shot. Once, not meaning to, she burst one of my eardrums.

In spite of the mummies, which she did not like at all, she worked as the Professor's cook for many years, earning a miserable wage and spending most of it on tobacco and rum. She looked after me because she had accepted a responsibility more sacred than blood ties. Anyone who neglects a godchild is damned to hell, she used to say. It's worse than abandoning your own child. It's my obligation to raise you to be good and clean and hardworking, because I will have to answer for you on Judgment Day. My mother had not believed in original sin, and had not thought it necessary to baptize me, but my godmother had insisted with unyielding stubbornness. All right, *comadre*, Consuelo had finally agreed. You do whatever you want. Just don't change the name I chose for her. For three months my *madrina* went without smoking or drinking, saving every coin, and on the designated day she bought me a strawberry-colored organdy dress, tied a ribbon on the four straggly hairs that crowned my head, sprinkled me with her rose water, and bore me off to church. I have a photograph from the day of my baptism; I was done up like a happy little birthday present. She did not have enough money, so she paid for the service with a thorough cleaning of the church—from sweeping the floors and waxing the wooden benches to polishing the altar ornaments with lime. That is how I came to have a little rich girl's baptism, with all the proper pomp and ceremony.

"If it weren't for me, you'd still be a pagan. Children who die without the sacraments go to limbo and stay there forever," my *madrina* always reminded me. "In my place, anyone else would have sold you. It's easy to place girls with light eyes. I've heard the gringos buy them and take them to their country. But I made a promise to your mother, and if I don't fulfill it, I'll stew in hell!"

For her, the boundaries between good and evil were very precise, and she was ready to save me from sin if she had to beat me to do it. That was the only way she knew, because that was how she had learned. The idea that play and tenderness are good for children is a modern discovery: it never entered her mind. She tried to teach me to be quick about my work and not waste time in daydreams. She hated wandering minds and slow feet; she wanted to see me run when she gave an order. Your head's full of smoke and your legs are full of sand, she used to say, and she would rub my legs with Scott's Emulsion, a cheap but famous liniment made from cod-liver oil, which, according to the advertisement, when it came to tonics was equal to the philosopher's stone.

My *madrina*'s brain was slightly addled from rum. She believed in all the Catholic saints, some saints of African origin, and still others of her own invention. Before a small altar in her room she had aligned holy water, voodoo fetishes, a photograph of her dead father, and a bust she thought was St. Christopher but was, I later discovered, Beethoven—although I have never told her because he is the most miraculous figure on her altar. She carried on a continuous conversation with her deities in a colloquial yet proud tone, asking them for insignificant favors; later, when she became a fan of the telephone, she would call them in heaven, interpreting the hum of the receiver as parables from her divine respondents. She believed that was how she received instructions from the heavenly court concerning even the most trivial matters. She was devoted to St. Benedict, a handsome blond high-living man women could not leave alone, who stood in the fire until he crackled like firewood and only then could adore God and work his miracles in peace, without a passel of panting women clinging to his robes. He was the one she prayed to for relief from a hangover. She was an expert on the subject of torture and gruesome deaths; she knew how every martyr and virgin in the book of Catholic saints had died, and was always eager to tell me about them. I listened with morbid terror, begging in each telling for new particulars. The martyrdom of Santa Lucia was my favorite. I wanted to hear it over and over, in minute detail: why Lucia rejected the emperor who loved her; how they tore out her eyes; whether it was true that her eyeballs had shot a beam of light that blinded the emperor, and that she grew two splendid new blue eyes much more beautiful than the ones she had lost.

My poor *madrina*'s faith was unshakable; no misfortune that ever befell her could change it. Only recently, when the Pope came here, I got permission to take her from her nursing home to see him; it would have been a shame for her to miss seeing the Pontiff in his white habit and gold cross, preaching his indemonstrable convictions in perfect Spanish and Indian dialects—as demanded by the occasion. When she saw him advancing down the freshly painted streets in his fishbowl of bulletproof glass, amid flowers, cheers, waving pennants, and bodyguards, my *madrina*, who is now absolutely ancient, fell to her knees, persuaded that the Prophet Elias was on a tourist's trip. I was afraid she would be crushed in the crowd and I tried to get her to leave, but she would not move until I bought a hair from the Pope's head as a relic. Many people seized that opportunity to become righteous; some promised to forgive their debtors and, to avoid saddening the Holy Father, not to mention the class struggle or contraceptives. In my own heart I had no enthusiasm for the illustrious visitor, because I had no happy memories of religion. One Sunday when I was a little girl, my *madrina* took me to our parish church and made me kneel down in a curtained wooden box; my fingers were clumsy and I could not cross them as she had taught me. I became aware of a strong breath on the other side of the grille: Tell me your sins, the voice commanded, and instantly I forgot all the sins I had invented. I did not know what to answer, although I felt obliged to try to think of something, even something venial, but I could not dredge up a single transgression.

"Do you touch yourself with your hands?"

"Yes . . ."

"Often, daughter?"

"Every day."

"Every day! How often?"

"I don't keep count . . . many times . . ."

"That is a most serious offense in the eyes of God!"

"I didn't know, Father. And if I wear gloves, is that a sin, too?"

"Gloves! But what are you saying, you foolish girl? Are you mocking me?"

"No-no," I stammered in terror, at the same time thinking how difficult it would be to wash my face, brush my teeth, or scratch myself while wearing gloves.

"You must promise not to do that again. Purity and innocence are a girl's best virtues. You will pray five hundred Ave Marías in penance, so God will pardon you."

"I can't, Father," I answered, because I could only count to twenty.

"What do you mean, you *can't!*" the priest bellowed, and a rain of saliva sprayed over me through the grille. I burst from the box, but my *madrina* nabbed me and held me by one ear while she consulted with the priest on the advisability of putting me out to work before my character was even more warped and I lost my almighty soul forever.

After my mother's death came the hour of Professor Jones. He died
of old age, disillusioned with the world and his own learning, but I
would swear that he died in peace. Faced with the impossibility of embalming himself, thus assuring a dignified eternity amid his English furniture and his books, he left instructions in his will for his remains to
be sent to the distant city of his birth. He did not want the local cemetery to be his final resting place, to lie covered with foreign dust beneath
a merciless sun, and in promiscuous proximity with who knows what
kind of people, as he used to say. He spent his last days beneath the
ceiling fan in his bedroom, steaming in the sweat of his paralysis, and
with no company but the man with the Bible, and me. I lost my last
fear of him when his thundering voice changed to the unrelieved shal-
low breathing of the dying.

I wandered freely through that house closed to the outside world,
headquarters to death ever since the doctor had begun his experiments.
The servants' discipline collapsed the minute the Professor could no
longer leave his room to threaten them from his wheelchair and harass
them with contradictory orders. I watched them, every time they left
the house, carrying off silverware, rugs, paintings, even the crystal flasks
containing the Professor's formulas. The master's table with its starched
tablecloth and spotless china stood unattended; no one lighted the crystal chandeliers or brought the Professor his pipe. My *madrina* lost interest in the kitchen and served up fried bananas, rice, and fish every meal.
The other servants gave up on the cleaning, and grime and mildew
advanced along the floors and walls. No one had tended the garden since
the incident of the *surucucú* several years before, and the consequence of
this neglect was an aggressive vegetation threatening to devour the house
and overrun the sidewalk. The servants slept through the siesta, went
out at any hour of the day, drank too much rum, and played a radio all
day long, blaring boleros, cumbias, and rancheras. The miserable Professor, who in good health had tolerated nothing but classical records,
suffered inexpressible torment from all the racket, and tugged unceas-
ingly at his bellpull to summon a servant, but none came. When he was
asleep, my *madrina* climbed the stairs to sprinkle him with holy water
she had filched from the church; it seemed a sin to let the man die
without the sacrament, like a common beggar.

The morning the Protestant pastor was shown in by a maid dressed only in underpants and brassière because of the sweltering heat, I suspected that order had sunk to its lowest point and I had nothing left to fear from the Professor. I began to visit him often, at first peering in from the threshold, then going farther and farther into the room, until finally I was playing on the bed. I spent hours with the old man, trying to communicate with him, until I was able to understand the mumbling blurred by both his stroke and his foreign accent. When I was with him, the Professor seemed temporarily to forget the humiliation of his decline and the frustration of his paralysis. I brought books from the sacred bookshelves and held them for him so he could read. Some were written in Latin, but he translated them for me, apparently delighted to have me for a student, loudly lamenting the fact that he had not realized sooner I lived in his house. I may have been the first child he had known, and he discovered too late his vocation as a grandfather.

"Where did this girl come from?" he would ask, his gums chewing air. "Is she my daughter? My granddaughter? A figment of my sick mind? She has dark skin, but her eyes are like mine. Come here, child. Come close so I can see you."

He was unable to connect me with Consuelo, although he remembered very well the woman who had served him loyally for more than twenty years and once had swelled up like a zeppelin following a bad attack of indigestion. He often talked about her, certain that his last days would have been different if she had been there to care for him. She would not have betrayed me, he used to say.

It was I who put wads of cotton in his ears so the songs and dramas on the radio would not drive him mad. I washed him, and slipped folded towels beneath his body to prevent his mattress from being soaked with urine; I aired his room, and spooned pap into his mouth. The old man with the silver beard was my doll. One day I heard him tell the pastor that I was more important to him than all his scientific discoveries. I told the old man a few lies: that he had a large family waiting for him in his country; that he had several grandchildren, and a lovely flower garden. In the library there was a stuffed puma, one of the Professor's earliest experiments with his miraculous embalming fluid. I dragged it to his room, put it on the foot of his bed, and told him it was his pet dog —didn't he remember? The poor animal was pining for him.

"Write in my will, Pastor. I want this little girl to be my sole heir.

Everything is to go to her when I die." I heard him say this in his half-language to the minister who visited him almost every day, ruining the pleasure of his death with threats of eternity.

My *madrina* set up a cot for me beside the dying man's bed. One morning the invalid awoke more pale and tired than usual; he would not accept the *café con leche* I tried to give him, but did allow me to wash him, comb his beard, change his nightshirt, and sprinkle him with cologne. Propped up on his pillows, he lay absolutely silent until midday, his eyes on the window. He refused his strained food for lunch, and when I settled him for his siesta, he asked me to lie down beside him. We were both sleeping peacefully when he stopped living.

The pastor arrived at dusk and took charge of all the arrangements. Sending the body back to Professor Jones's homeland was not at all practical, especially since no one there wanted it, so he ignored those instructions and buried the Professor without fanfare. Only we servants were present at the dismal service; Professor Jones's reputation had been eclipsed by new advances in science, and no one bothered to accompany him to the cemetery, even though the notice had been published in the newspaper. After so many years of seclusion, few remembered who he was, and if some medical student referred to him it was to mock his head-thumping for stimulating intelligence, his insects for combating cancer, and his fluid for preserving cadavers.

After the *patrón* was gone my world crumbled. The pastor inventoried and disposed of the Professor's goods, using the excuse that he had lost his reason in his last years and was not competent to make decisions. Everything went to the pastor's church, except the puma, which I did not want to lose; I had ridden horseback on it since I was a baby and had so many times told the sick man it was a dog that I ended up believing it. When the movers tried to put it on the truck, I kicked up a fearful row, and when the minister saw me foaming at the mouth and screaming, he chose to yield. I suppose, besides, that it was no use to anyone, so I was allowed to keep it. It was impossible to sell the house; no one wanted to buy it. It was marked by the stigma of Professor Jones's experiments, and it sits abandoned to this day. As the years went by, it was said to be haunted, and boys went there to prove their manliness by spending a night among scurrying mice, creaking doors, and moaning ghosts. The mummies in the laboratory were transferred to the

Medical School where they lay piled in a cellar for a long time. Then, one day, there was a sudden resurgence of interest in the doctor's secret formula, and three generations of students industriously hacked off pieces and ran them through different machines, until they were reduced to a kind of unsavory mincemeat.

The pastor dismissed the servants and closed the house. That is how I came to leave the place where I was born—I carrying the puma by its hind legs and my *madrina* carrying the front.

"You're grown up now, and I can't keep you. You'll have to go to work and earn your living and be strong, the way it should be," said my *madrina*. I was seven years old.

My madrina and I waited in the kitchen; she sat ramrod straight in a rush chair, her bead-embroidered plastic handbag in her lap, her breasts swelling majestically above the neckline of her blouse, her thighs over-flowing the seat of the chair. I stood beside her, inspecting out of the corners of my eyes the iron utensils, rusty icebox, cats sprawled beneath the table, the cupboard with its fly-dotted latticed doors. It had been two days since I left Professor Jones's house, but I was still bewildered and confused. Within a few hours I had become very surly. I did not want to talk with anyone. I sat in the corner with my face buried in my arms, and then, as now, my mother would appear before me, faithful to her promise to stay alive as long as I remembered her. A dried-up, brusque black woman, who kept eyeing us with suspicion, was fussing about among the pots of that unfamiliar kitchen.

"Is the girl yours?" she asked.

"How could she be mine—you see her color, don't you?" my *madrina* asked.

"Whose is she, then?"

"She's my goddaughter. I've brought her here to work."

The door opened and the mistress of the house came in, a small woman with an elaborate hairdo of waves and stiff curls. She was dressed in strict mourning and around her neck she wore a large gold locket the size of an ambassador's medal.

"Come here where I can see you," she ordered, but I could not move, my feet seemed nailed to the floor. My *madrina* had to push me

forward so the *patrona* could examine me: the scalp for lice, the fingernails for the horizontal lines typical of epileptics, the teeth, ears, skin,
the firmness of the arms and legs.

"Does she have worms?"

"No, *doña*, she's clean inside and out."

"She's skinny."

"She hasn't had much appetite lately, but don't worry, she's a good
worker. She learns easy, and she's got good sense."

"Does she cry a lot?"

"She didn't even cry when we buried her mother—may God rest
her soul."

"She can stay a month, on trial," the *patrona* declared, and left the
room without a goodbye.

My *madrina* gave me her last advice: don't talk back; be careful not
to break anything; don't drink water in the evening so you won't wet
the bed; behave and do what you're told. She started to lean over and
kiss me, but thought better of it, gave me a clumsy pat on the head, and
turned and marched purposefully out the servants' entrance—but I knew
she was sad. We had always been together; it was the first time we had
ever been separated. I stood where she left me, eyes on the floor, fists
clenched. The cook had just fried some bananas; she put her arm around
my shoulders and led me to a chair, then sat down beside me and
smiled.

"So, you're going to be the new girl. . . . Well, little bird, eat," and
she set a plate before me. "They call me Elvira. I was born on the coast.
The day was Sunday the 29th of May, but I don't remember the year.
All I have ever done in my life is work, and it looks like that will be
your lot, too. I have my habits and my ways, but if you're not sassy,
we'll get along fine. I always wanted grandchildren, but God made me
too poor ever to have a family."

That day was the beginning of a new life for me. I had always
worked, but not, until then, to earn a living, just to imitate my mother,
like a game. The house where I held my first job for pay was filled with
furniture and paintings and statues and ferns on marble columns, but
those adornments could not hide the moss growing on the pipes, the
walls stained with humidity, the dust of years accumulated beneath the
beds and behind the wardrobes. Everything seemed very dirty to me,

very different from Professor Jones's mansion where, before his stroke, he had crawled on all fours to run a finger around corners for dust. This house smelled of rotted melons, and in spite of the shutters closed against the sun, it was suffocatingly hot. The owners were an elderly brother and sister—the *doña* of the locket and a fat sexagenarian with a pitted, fleshy nose tattooed with an arabesque of blue veins. Elvira told me that for a good part of her life her *doña* had worked in a notary's office, writing away in silence and storing up a craving to scream that only now, retired and in her own house, she could satisfy. She spent the day issuing orders in a piercing voice, pointing with a peremptory finger, untiringly haranguing and harassing, angry with the world and with herself. Her brother limited himself to reading his newspaper and racing form, drinking, dozing in a rocking chair in the corridor, and walking around in pajamas, slapping his slippers on the tiled floor and scratching his crotch. In the evenings he roused from his daytime lethargy, dressed, and went out to play dominoes in the cafés—every evening, that is, except Sunday, when he went to the racetrack to lose what he had won during the week. Besides the brother and sister, the inhabitants of the house were a maid—big-boned and birdbrained, who worked from morning to night and at the hour of the siesta disappeared into the bachelor's room—the cook, the cats, and a scruffy, tongue-tied parrot.

The patrona ordered Elvira to bathe me with disinfectant soap and burn all my clothing. She did not shave my head, as they did to servant girls in those days to get rid of lice, because her brother kept her from it. The man with the strawberry nose spoke gently; he smiled often, and was always pleasant to me even when he was drunk. He took pity on my misery at the sight of the scissors and rescued the long hair my mother had kept so well brushed. It is strange that I cannot remember his name. . . . In that house I wore a dress the *doña* had sewed on her sewing machine, and went barefoot. After the month's trial had passed, she explained I had to work harder because now I was earning wages. I never saw them; my *madrina* collected the money every two weeks. At first I anxiously awaited her visits and, the minute she appeared, clung to her skirt and begged her to take me with her, but slowly I got used to the new house. I looked to Elvira for help and made friends with the cats and the parrot. When the *patrona* washed out my mouth with baking soda to cure my habit of muttering to myself, I stopped talking aloud with my mother, but continued doing it in secret. There was a lot to be done; in spite of the broom and the scrub brush, the house looked like a cursed caravel run aground on a reef; there was no end to cleaning that shapeless florescence that crept along all the walls. The food was not varied or abundant, but Elvira hid the masters' leftovers and gave them to me for breakfast because she had heard on the radio that it was good to begin the day with something on your stomach: So it will go to your brain, little bird, she used to say, and you will grow up to be smart. No detail escaped the spinster: today I want you to scrub the patios with Lysol; remember to iron the napkins, and be careful not to scorch them; clean the windows with newspaper and vinegar, and when you get through I will show you how to polish the master's shoes. I never hurried to obey, because I soon discovered that if I was careful I could dawdle and get through the day without doing much of anything. The *doña* of the locket began issuing instructions the minute she arose; she was up at the crack of dawn, dressed in her strict mourning, locket in place and hair intricately combed, but she would get confused about what orders she had given and it was easy to fool her. The *patrón* showed very little interest in domestic affairs; he lived for his horse races, studying bloodlines, calculating the law of probabilities, and drinking to console himself when he lost his bets. There were times his nose turned the color of an eggplant, and then he would call me to help him get into bed and to hide the empty bottles. The maid wanted nothing to do with anyone, least of all me. Only Elvira paid any attention to me, making me eat, teaching me how to do domestic chores, relieving me of the heaviest tasks. We spent hours talking and telling each other stories. It was about that time that some of her eccentricities began to surface, like her irrational hatred of blond foreigners, and her horror of cockroaches, which she battled with every weapon in reach, from quicklime to broom. On the other hand, she said nothing when she discovered that I was feeding the mice and guarding their babies so the cats could not eat them. She feared a pauper's death, that her bones would be tossed into a common grave, and to avoid posthumous humiliation she had bought a coffin on credit, which she kept in her room and used as a catchall for odds and ends. It was a box of ordinary wood, smelling of carpenter's glue, lined in white satin, and trimmed with blue ribbons she had taken from a small pillow. From time to time I was given the privilege of lying inside and closing the lid, while Elvira feigned inconsolable grief and between sobs recited my nonexistent virtues: "Oh, Most Heavenly Father, why have You taken my little bird from me? Such a good girl, so clean, so tidy—I love her more than if she was my own granddaughter. Oh, Lord, work one of Your miracles and return her to me." The game would last until we both burst out laughing, or till the maid lost control and began to howl.

All the days were exactly the same except Thursday, whose approach I calculated on the kitchen calendar. All week I looked forward to the moment we would walk through the garden gate and set off to market. Elvira would help me put on my rubber-soled shoes and my clean dress, and comb my hair into a ponytail; then she would give me a centavo to buy a brilliantly colored round lollipop, almost impervious to the human tooth, that I could lick for hours without noticeably reducing its size. That treat lasted for six or seven nights of intense bliss and many giddy licks between difficult chores. The *patrona* always took the lead, clutching her handbag: keep your eyes peeled, pay attention, stay right beside me, the place is alive with pickpockets. She marched through the market briskly, looking, squeezing, bargaining: these prices are a scandal; jail is the only place for moneygrubbers like these. I walked behind the maid with a bag in each hand and my lollipop in my pocket. I used to watch people, trying to guess their lives and secrets, their virtues and adventures. I always returned home with shining eyes and a joyful heart. I would run to the kitchen, and while I helped Elvira put things away I besieged her with stories of enchanted carrots and peppers that turned into princes and princesses when they fell into the pot and jumped out of it with sprigs of parsley tangled in their crowns and broth streaming from their royal garments.

"Sh-h-h! The *doña* is coming. Grab the broom, little bird."

During the siesta, the hour when quiet reigned in the house, I used to abandon my tasks and go to the dining room. A large painting in a gilded frame hung there, a window open onto a marine horizon: waves, rocks, hazy sky, and sea gulls. I would stand there with my hands behind my back, my eyes fixed on that irresistible seascape, lost in neverending voyages and sirens and dolphins and manta rays that sometimes leapt from my mother's fantasies and other times from Professor Jones's books. Among the countless stories my mother had told me, I always preferred those in which the sea played some part; afterward I would dream of distant islands, vast underwater cities, oceanic highways for fish navigations. We must have a sailor ancestor, my mother said every time I asked for another of those stories, and thus was born the legend of the Dutch grandfather. In the presence of that painting, I recaptured those earlier emotions, either when I stood close enough to hear it speak or when I watched it while I was doing my household chores; each time I could smell a faint odor of sails, lye, and starch.

"What are you doing here!" the *patrona* would scold if she discovered me. "Don't you have anything to do? We don't keep that painting here for your sake."

From what she said, I believed that paintings wear away, that the color seeps into the eyes of the person beholding them, until gradually they fade and vanish.

"No, child. Where did you get such a silly notion? They don't wear away. Come here, give me a kiss on my nose and I'll let you look at the sea. Give me another and I'll give you a centavo. But don't tell my sister, she doesn't understand. Does my nose disgust you?" And the *patrón* and I would hide behind the ferns for that clandestine caress.

I had been told to sleep in a hammock in the kitchen, but after everybody was in bed I would steal in the servants' room and slip into the bed shared by the maid and the cook, one sleeping with her head toward the top and the other with her head toward the foot. I would curl up beside Elvira and offer to tell her a story if she would let me stay.

"All right. Tell me the one about the man who lost his head over love."

"I forgot that one, but I remember one about some animals."

"There must have been a lot of sap in your mother's womb to give you such a mind for telling stories, little bird."

I remember very well, it was a rainy day; there was a strange odor of rotted melons and cat piss on the hot breath blowing from the street; the odor filled the house, so strong you could feel it on your fingertips.

I was in the dining room on one of my sea voyages. I did not hear the *patrona*'s footsteps, and when I felt her claws on my neck, the surprise jerked me back from a great distance, leaving me petrified in the uncertainty of not knowing where I was.

"You here again? Go do your work! What do you think I pay you for?"

"I finished everything, *doña* . . ."

The *patrona* picked up a large vase from the sideboard and turned it upside down, dashing stinking water and wilted flowers to the floor.

"Clean it up!" she ordered.

The sea disappeared, the fogbound rocks, the red tresses woven through my nostalgia, the dining-room furniture—all I saw were those flowers on the tiles, growing, writhing, taking on a life of their own, and that woman with her tower of curls and locketed throat. A monumental *"No!"* swelled inside me, choking me; I heard it burst forth in a scream that came from my toes, and watched it explode against the *patrona*'s powdered face. When she slapped me I felt no pain, because long before she touched me I felt only rage, an urge to leap upon her, drag her to the floor, claw her face, grab her hair, and pull with all my might. But the bun yielded, the curls crumbled, the topknot came loose, and that entire mass of brittle hair lay in my hands like a dying fox. Horrified, I realized that I had snatched the *doña* bald-headed. I bolted from the room, ran through the house and the garden, and rushed into the street without any sense of where I was going. After a few minutes the warm summer rain had soaked me through, and fear and wetness brought me to a halt. The shaggy trophy was still in my hands; I flung it to the edge of the sidewalk where it was carried off with other debris in the drainage ditch. I stood for several minutes observing the shipwrecked curls swirling sadly away, and once they were out of sight I began to walk aimlessly, convinced I had come to the end of my road, sure there was no place I could hide after the crime I had just committed. I left familiar streets, passed the site of the Thursday market, continued through the residential zone of houses shuttered for the siesta, and walked on and on like a sleepwalker. The rain had stopped and the late afternoon sun was evaporating moisture from the wet asphalt, swathing the world in a sticky veil. People, traffic, noise—a lot of noise: construction sites with gigantic, roaring yellow machines, ringing steel, screeching brakes, horns, the cries of street vendors. A vague odor of swamp and fried food drifted from the cafés, and I remembered that I usually had something to eat at this hour. I was hungry, but I had no money, and in my flight I had left behind the remnants of my weekly lollipop. I reckoned that I had been walking in circles for several hours. I was awestruck. In those days the city was not the hopeless disaster it is now, but it was already growing—shapelessly, like a malignant tumor, assailed by lunatic architecture in an unholy mixture of styles: Italian marble palaces, Texas ranch houses, Tudor mansions, steel skyscrapers, residences in the form of ships, mausoleums, Japanese teahouses, Swiss chalets, and wedding cakes with plaster icing. I was in shock.

Toward evening, I came to a plaza bordered with ceibas, solemn trees that had stood guard over that place since the War of Independence; in the center was a bronze equestrian statue of the Father of the Nation, a flag in one hand and reins in the other, humiliated by the irreverence of pigeon shit and the disillusion of history. In one corner of the square, surrounded by curious onlookers, I saw a white-clad *campesino* in a straw sombrero and sandals. I walked closer to watch. He was reciting in a singsong voice, and for a few coins, in response to the individual client, he would change his theme but continue to improvise verses without pause or hesitation. Under my breath I tried imitating him, and discovered how much easier it is to remember stories when you rhyme—the story dances to its own music. I stood listening until the man picked up his coins and went away. For a while I amused myself by searching for words that sounded the same: what a good way to remember; now I would be able to tell Elvira the same story twice. The minute I thought of Elvira, I could almost smell the odor of fried onion; I felt a cold chill down my back as I realized the truth of my predicament. Again I saw my *patrona*'s curls rippling down the drainage ditch like a dead cat, and the prophecies my *madrina* had so often repeated rang in my ears: Bad, bad girl. You'll end up in jail, that's how it begins. You don't mind, and then you act smart—and you end up behind bars. Listen to what I'm telling you, that's how it's going to be. I sat down on the edge of a fountain to look at the goldfish and at the water lilies drooping from the heat.

"What's the matter?" It was a dark-eyed boy wearing khaki pants and a shirt much too large for him.

"I'm going to be arrested."

"How old are you?"

"Nine, more or less."

"Then you have no right to be in jail. You're a minor."

"But I scalped my *patrona*."

"How?"

"With one jerk."

He sat down beside me, watching me out of the corner of his eye and digging the dirt from beneath his fingernails with a penknife.

"My name is Huberto Naranjo. What's yours?"

"Eva Luna. Would you be my friend?"

"I don't hang around with women." But he stayed, and until it got late we were showing each other our scars, sharing secrets, getting to know each other, and beginning a long relationship that would lead us along the paths of friendship and love.

From the moment he could look after himself, Huberto Naranjo had lived in the street, first shining shoes and selling newspapers and then scratching a living through hustling and petty thievery. He had a natural gift for conning the gullible, and I was given immediate proof of his talent there at the plaza fountain. He began a spiel to catch the attention of passersby, and soon had gathered a small crowd of clerks, old men, poets, and a few *guardias* stationed there to be sure that everyone walking past the equestrian statue showed the proper respect. His challenge was to see who could grab a fish from the fountain; it meant plunging your upper body into the water, rooting around among the aquatic plants, and blindly feeling along the slimy bottom. Huberto had cut the tail of one fish, and the poor creature could only swim in a circle like a top or lie motionless beneath a lily pad, where Huberto knew to fish him out with one swoop. As he triumphantly hoisted his catch, the losers paid up—with both shirt-sleeves and dignity considerably dampened. Another way of earning a few coins consisted of betting on finding the pea beneath one shell of the three he moved rapidly across a piece of cloth unfolded on the ground. He could slip off a stroller's watch in less than two seconds, and in the same amount of time make it vanish in thin air. Some years later, dressed like a cross between a cowboy and a Mexican charro, he would sell everything from stolen screwdrivers to shirts bought in factory closeouts. At sixteen he would be the leader of a street gang,

feared and respected; he would own several carts selling roasted pea-
nuts, sausages, and sugarcane juice; he would be the hero of the whores
in the red-light district, and the nightmare of the *guardia*, until other
concerns took him off to the mountains. But that came much later. When
I first met him, he was still a boy, but if I had observed him more
carefully I might have seen a sign of the man he would become; even
then he had ready fists and fire in his heart. If you want to get ahead,
you have to be macho, Huberto Naranjo used to say. It was his crutch,
based on male attributes that were no different from those of other boys,
but that he put to the test, measuring his penis with a ruler or demonstrating how far he could urinate. I learned that much later, when he
himself scoffed at such standards—after someone told him that size is
not irrefutable proof of virility. Nevertheless, his ideas about manhood
were deeply rooted from childhood, and the things that happened to
him later, all the battles and passions, all the encounters and arguments,
all the rebellions and defeats, were not enough to change his mind.

After dark we made the round of nearby restaurants, looking for something to eat. Sitting in an alley across from the back door of a cheap
café, we shared a steaming pizza that Huberto had traded for a postcard
of a smiling blonde with stupendous breasts. Then, climbing fences and
violating private property, we twisted our way through a labyrinth of
courtyards until we reached a parking garage. We slipped through a
ventilation duct to avoid the fat guard at the entrance, and scrambled
down to the lowest level. There, in a dark corner between two columns,
Huberto had improvised a nest of newspapers where he could go when
nothing better presented itself. We settled in for the night, lying side by
side in the darkness, drowning in fumes of motor oil and carbon mon-
oxide as thick as an ocean liner's exhaust. I made myself comfortable
and offered him a story in payment for being so nice to me.

"All right," he conceded, slightly baffled, because I believe that in all
his life he had never heard anything remotely resembling a story.

"What shall it be about?"

"About bandits," he said, to say something.

I took inspiration from several episodes I'd heard on the radio, some ballads I knew, and a few ingredients of my own invention, and began spinning a story of a damsel in love with an outlaw, a real jackal who resolved even minor disagreements with bullets, strewing the landscape with widows and orphans. The girl never lost hope of redeeming him through the strength of her love and the sweetness of her character, and while he went around perpetrating his evil deeds, she gathered in the very orphans created by the insatiable pistols of the evildoer. When he showed up at the house, it was like a gale from hell; he stomped in, kicking doors and emptying his pistols into the air. On her knees she would plead with him to repent of his cruel ways, but he mocked her with guffaws that shook the walls and curdled the blood. "How've you been, honey!" he would shout at the top of his lungs, while terrified youngsters ran to hide in the wardrobe. How are all the kids? and he would open the door and pull them out by the ear to see how tall they were. Aha! I see they're getting big, but don't you worry. Before you can say *boo!* I'll be off to town and I'll make some new orphans for your collection. And so the years went by and the number of mouths to be fed kept growing, until one day the sweetheart, weary of such abuse, realized the futility of continuing to hope for the bandit's salvation and decided to stop being so good. She got a permanent, bought a red dress, and turned her house into a place for parties and good times where you could buy the most delicious ice cream and the best malted milks, play all kinds of games, and dance and sing. The children had a wonderful time waiting on the customers; poverty and misery were ended and the woman was so happy that she forgot all the unhappiness of the past. Things were going very well, but gossip reached the ears of the jackal and one night he appeared as usual, beating down doors and shooting holes in the ceiling and asking for the children. But he got a surprise. No one began to tremble in his presence, no one ran to hide in the wardrobe, and the girl did not throw herself at his feet to beg for mercy. They all just went about their business, some serving ice cream, one playing the drums, while the former sweetheart, in a fabulous turban decorated with tropical fruit, danced the mambo on a tabletop. So the bandit, furious and ashamed, slunk away with his pistols to look for a new sweetheart who *would* be afraid of him. And that was the end of the story.

Huberto Naranjo listened to the end.

"That's a stupid story. . . . But, all right, I would like to be your friend," he said.

We roamed the city for a couple of days. Huberto taught me the advantages of street life and tricks of survival: always steer clear of a uniform because you're screwed for good if they get their hands on you; to rob somebody on a bus, stand in the back and when the doors open make your pinch and jump off; the best food is to be had mid-morning on the garbage heap at the Central Market and midafternoon in the garbage pails of hotels and restaurants. Following him in his adventures, I knew for the first time the headiness of freedom, the com-bination of nervous excitement and deathly vertigo that since that time has haunted my dreams as clearly as if I were living it again. But by the third night of sleeping outdoors, tired and filthy, I suffered an attack of homesickness. First, grieving that I could not return to the scene of the crime, I thought of Elvira, and then of my mother; I missed the switch of red hair and I wanted to see my stuffed puma again. So I asked Huberto Naranjo to help me find my *madrina*.

"Why? Aren't we doing all right? You're a stupid girl."

I did not dare explain the reasons, but I begged so much that finally he agreed to help me, after warning that I would regret it all the days of my life. He knew every corner of the city, and went anywhere he wanted by hitching rides on the steps and bumpers of buses. With my sketchy description and his knack for locating places, we found a hillside where shacks made out of scrap—cardboard boxes, bricks, old tires, sheets of zinc—rose one after the other. It looked like every other bar-rio, but I recognized it immediately by the garbage dumped in the bar-rancas. This was where the city garbage trucks disgorged their filth, and as we looked on the dumps from above they shimmered with the blue-green iridescence of flies.

"There's my *madrina*'s house!" I shrieked when I spied the blue-stained boards. I had been there only once or twice, but since it was the closest thing I ever had to a home, I remembered it well.

The shack was closed but a neighbor woman shouted from across the street to wait; my *madrina* had gone down to market and would be right back. The time had come for us to say goodbye, and Huberto Naranjo, cheeks blazing, stuck out his hand to shake mine. Instead, I threw my arms around his neck, but he pushed me away so hard I almost fell backward. I held on to his shirt, though, and gave him a kiss. I meant it for his mouth but it landed right in the center of his nose. Huberto trotted down the hill without looking back, and I sat down on the doorstep to sing a song.

It was not long before my *madrina* returned. I saw her climbing the hill along the crooked street, big and fat and decked out in a lemon-yellow dress; she had a package in her arms, and was sweating from the effort of the climb. I called to her and ran to meet her, but she did not even wait for me to explain what had happened; she had had a report from the *patrona*, who had told her of my disappearance and the unpardonable treatment she had received at my hands. My *madrina* lifted me off my feet and shoved me inside the shack. The contrast between the noonday light and the darkness inside left me blinded, and before my eyes could adjust, she walloped me so hard I flew across the room and landed on the ground. She beat me until the neighbors came. Then they used salt to cure me.

Four days later, I was marched back to my place of employment. The man with the strawberry nose patted me affectionately on the cheek, and took advantage of the others' inattention to tell me he was happy to see me; he had missed me, he said. The *doña* of the locket received me in the living room; seated in a chair, stern as a judge, she seemed to have shrunk to half her size. She looked like a little old rag doll dressed in mourning. Her bald head was not, as I expected, wrapped in bloodstained bandages; she sat there in the same towering curls and iron-hard waves, of a different color but intact. Dumbfounded, I searched my mind for a possible explanation of this incredible miracle, ignoring both the *patrona*'s harangue and my *madrina*'s pinches. The only comprehensible part of the reprimand was that from that day on I was to work twice as hard: thus I would have no time to waste in the contemplation of art—and the garden gate would be kept locked to prevent a second escape.

"I will tame her," the *patrona* assured my *madrina*.

"It will take some good smacks, God knows," my *madrina* replied.

"Keep your eyes lowered when I'm speaking to you, you naughty girl. The devil is in your eyes, but I'll not tolerate any insolence," the *patrona* threatened. "Do you understand me?"

I stared at her, unblinking, then turned and, with my head very high, went to the kitchen where Elvira was waiting, eavesdropping behind the door.

"Ah, little bird . . . Come here and let me put something on those bruises. Are you sure nothing's broken?"

The *patrona* never mistreated me again, and as she never mentioned the vanished hair, I came to believe the whole thing was a nightmare that had filtered into the house through some crack or other. Neither did she stop me from gazing at the painting; she must have guessed that if I had to, I would sink my teeth in her to see it. That painting of the sea with its foaming waves and motionless gulls was essential to me; it was the reward for the day's labors, the door to freedom. At the time of the siesta, when the others lay down to rest, I repeated the same ritual, never asking permission or offering an explanation, ready to do whatever was necessary to defend that privilege. I would wash my face and hands, run a comb through my hair, straighten my dress, put on the shoes I wore to market, and go to the dining room. I placed a chair in front of this window on storyland, sat down—back straight, knees together, hands in my lap, as I sat at Mass—and set out on my voyage. Sometimes I saw the *patrona* watching me from the open doorway, but she never said anything. She was afraid of me now.

"That's good, little bird," Elvira would say approvingly. "You have to fight back. No one tries anything with mad dogs, but tame dogs they kick. Life's a dogfight."

It was the best advice I ever received. Elvira used to roast lemons in the coals, then quarter and boil them, and give me a drink of the mixture to make me more courageous.

For several years I worked in the house of that elderly bachelor and spinster, and during that time many things happened to change the country. Elvira used to tell me about them. After a brief interval of republican freedom, we once again had a dictator. He was a military man so harmless in appearance that no one imagined the extent of his greed. The most powerful man in the government was not the General, however, but the Chief of Political Police, the Man of the Gardenia. He had many affectations, among them slicked-down hair and manicured fingernails,

impeccable white linen suits—always with a flower in the buttonhole—
and French cologne. No one could ever accuse him of being common
—and he was not the homosexual his many enemies accused him of
being. He personally directed the torture of prisoners, elegant and courteous as ever. It was during his time that the penal colony of Santa
María was reopened, a hellhole on an island in the middle of a crocodile-
and piranha-infested river at the edge of the jungle, where political prisoners and criminals, equals in misfortune, perished from hunger, beatings, and tropical diseases. Not a breath of any of this was reported on
the radio or published in the newspapers, but Elvira found out through
rumors on her days off, and often talked about them. I loved Elvira very
much; I called her grandmother; *abuela*, I would say. They'll never part
us, little bird, she promised, but I was not so sure; I already sensed that
my life would be one long series of farewells. Like me, Elvira had started
working when she was a little girl, and through the long years weari-
ness had seeped into her bones and chilled her soul. The burden of work
and grinding poverty had killed her desire to go on, and she had begun
her dialogue with death. At night she slept in her coffin, partly to become accustomed to it, to lose her fear of it, and partly to irritate the
patrona, who never got used to the idea of a coffin in her house. The
maid could not bear the sight of my *abuela* lying in her mortuary bed
in the room they shared, and one day simply went away, without ad-
vising even the *patrón*, who was left waiting for her at the hour of the
siesta. Before she left, she chalked crosses on all the doors in the house,
the meaning of which no one ever deciphered, but for the same reason
never dared erase. Elvira treated me as if she were my true *abuela*. It
was with her that I learned to barter words for goods, and I have been
blessed with good fortune, for I have always been able to find someone
willing to accept such a transaction.

I did not change much during those years; I remained rather small
and thin, but with defiant eyes that nettled the *patrona*. My body developed slowly, but inside something was raging out of control, like an
unseen river. While I felt I was a woman, the windowpane reflected the
blurred image of a little girl. Even though I did not grow much, it was
still enough that the *patrón* began to pay more attention to me. I must
teach you to read, child, he used to say, but he never found time to do
it. Now he not only asked for kisses on his nose; he began giving me a

few centavos to help him bathe and sponge his body. Afterward he would lie on the bed while I dried him, powdered him, and put his underwear on him as if he were a baby. Sometimes he sat for hours soaking in the bathtub and playing naval battles with me; other times he went for days without even looking in my direction, occupied with his bets, or in a stupor, his nose the color of eggplant. Elvira warned me with explicit clarity that men have a monster as ugly as a yucca root between their legs, and tiny babies come out of it and get into women's bellies and grow there. I was never to touch those parts for any reason, because the sleeping beast would raise its horrible head and leap at me —with catastrophic results. But I did not believe her; it sounded like just another of her outlandish tales. All the *patrón* had was a fat, sad little worm that never so much as stirred, and nothing like a baby ever came from it, at least when I was around. It looked a little like his fleshy nose, and that was when I discovered—and later in life proved—the close relationship between a man's nose and his penis. One look at a man's face and I know how he will look naked. Long noses and short, narrow and broad, haughty and humble, greedy noses, snooping noses, bold and indifferent noses good for nothing but blowing—noses of all kinds. With age, almost all of them thicken, grow limp and bulbous, and lose the arrogance of upstanding penises.

Every time I looked outside from the balcony, I realized that I would have been better off had I not come back. The street was more appealing than that house where life droned by so tediously—daily routines repeated at the same slow pace, days stuck to one another, all the same color, like time in a hospital bed. At night I gazed at the sky and imagined that I could make myself as wispy as smoke and slip between the bars of the locked gate. I pretended that when a moonbeam touched my back I sprouted wings like a bird's, two huge feathered wings for flight. Sometimes I concentrated so hard on that idea that I flew above the rooftops. Don't imagine such foolish things, little bird, only witches and airplanes fly at night. I did not learn anything more of Huberto Naranjo until much later, but I often thought of him, placing his dark face on all my fairy-tale princes. Although I was young, I knew about love intuitively, and wove it into my stories. I dreamed about love, it haunted me. I studied the photographs in the crime reports, trying to guess the dramas of passion and death in those newspaper pages. I was always hanging on to adults' words, listening behind the door when the *patrona* talked on the telephone, pestering Elvira with questions. Run along, little bird, she would say. The radio was my source of inspiration. The one in the kitchen was on from morning till night, our only contact with the outside world, proclaiming the virtues of this land blessed by God with all manner of treasures, from its central position on the globe and the wisdom of its leaders to the swamp of petroleum on which it floated. It was the radio that taught me to sing boleros and other popular songs, to repeat the commercials, and to follow a beginning English class half an hour a day: *This pencil is red, is this pencil blue? No, that pencil is not blue, that pencil is red.* I knew the time for each program; I imitated the announcers' voices. I followed all the dramas; I suffered indescribable torment with each of those creatures battered by fate, and was always surprised that in the end things worked out so well for the heroine, who for sixty installments had acted like a moron.

"I say that Montedónico is going to recognize her as his daughter. If he gives her his name, she can marry Rogelio de Salvatierra," Elvira would sigh, one ear glued to the radio.

"She has her mother's locket. That's proof. Why doesn't she tell everyone she's Montedónico's daughter and get it over with?"

"She couldn't do that to the man who gave her life, little bird."

"Why not? He left her locked up in an orphanage for eighteen years."

"He's just mean, little bird. They call people like him sadists."

"Look, *abuela*, if she doesn't change her ways, she's going to have a hard time all her life."

"Well, you needn't worry, everything will work out fine. Can't you see she's a good girl?"

Elvira was right. The long-suffering always triumphed and the evil received their due. Montedónico was struck down by a fatal illness, pleading from his deathbed for forgiveness; his daughter cared for him until he died, and then, after inheriting his fortune, married Rogelio de Salvatierra, giving me in passing an abundance of material for my own stories—although only rarely did I respect the standard happy ending. Little bird, my *abuela* used to say, why don't people in *your* stories ever get married? Often only a word or two would string together a rosary of images in my mind. Once I heard a delicious new word and flew to ask Elvira, *Abuela*, what is snow? From her explanation I gathered it was like frozen meringue. At that moment I became the heroine of stories about the North Pole; I was the abominable snow woman, hairy and ferocious, battling the scientists who were on my trail hoping to catch me and experiment on me in their laboratory. I did not find out what snow really was until the day a niece of the General celebrated her début; the event was so widely heralded on the radio that Elvira had no choice but to take me to see the spectacle—from a distance, of course. A thousand guests gathered that night at the city's best hotel, transformed for the occasion into a wintertime replica of Cinderella's castle. Workmen trimmed back philodendron and tropical ferns, decapitated palm trees, and in their place set Christmas trees from Alaska trimmed with angel hair and artificial icicles. For ice-skating they installed a rink of white plastic imitating polar ice. They painted frost on the windows and sprinkled so much synthetic snow everywhere that a week later snowflakes were still drifting into the operating room of the Military Hospital five hundred meters away. The machines imported from the North failed to freeze the water in the swimming pool; instead of ice, all they obtained was a kind of gelatinous vomit. They decided to settle for two swans, dyed pink, awkwardly trailing a banner between them bearing the name of the débutante in gilt letters. To give more panache to the party, they flew in two scions of European nobility and a film star. At midnight the honoree, swathed in sable, was lowered from the ceiling in a swing built in the shape of a sleigh, swaying four meters above the heads of the guests, half-swooning from heat and vertigo. Those of us on the fringes outside did not see this, but it was featured in all the magazines; no one seemed surprised by the miracle of a tropical capital hotel shivering in Arctic cold—much more unbelievable events had happened there. In all that spectacle, I had eyes for only one thing: some enormous tubs filled with natural snow that had been placed at the entrance to the festivities so the elegant guests could throw snowballs and build snowmen, as they had heard is done in lands of ice and snow. I pulled free from Elvira, slipped between the waiters and guards, and ran to take that treasure in my hands. At first I thought I had been burned, and screamed with fright, but I was so fascinated by the color of light trapped in the frozen, airy matter that I could not let go. A guard nearly caught me, but I stooped down and scooted between his legs, clutching the precious snow to my chest. When it melted away, trickling through my fingers like water, I felt deceived. Some time later, Elvira gave me a transparent hemisphere containing a miniature cabin and a pine tree; when you shook it, it set loose a blizzard of snowflakes. So you will have a winter of your own, little bird, she told me.

At that age I was not interested in politics, but Elvira filled my head with subversive ideas to offset the beliefs of our employers.

"Everything in this country is crooked, little bird. Too many yellow-haired gringos, I say. One of these days they'll carry the whole country off with them, and we'll find ourselves plunk in the middle of the ocean—that's what I say."

The *doña* of the locket was of exactly the opposite opinion.

"How unfortunate that we were discovered by Christopher Columbus and not an Englishman. It takes determined people of sturdy stock to build roads through the forests, sow crops on the plains, and industrialize the nation. Wasn't that what they did in the United States? And look where that country is today!"

She agreed with the General when he opened the border to anyone wanting to flee the misery of postwar Europe. Immigrants arrived by the hundreds, bringing wives, children, grandparents, and distant cousins; with their many tongues, national dishes, legends, holidays; and nostalgias. Our exuberant geography swallowed them up in one gulp. A few Asians were also allowed to enter and, once in the country, multiplied with astounding rapidity. Twenty years later, someone pointed out that on every street corner there was a restaurant decorated with wrathful demons, paper lanterns, and a pagoda roof. Once the newspaper reported the story of a Chinese waiter who left the customers unattended in the dining room, climbed the stairs to the office, and with a kitchen cleaver cut off the head and hands of his employer because he had not shown the proper respect for a religious tradition when he placed the image of a dragon beside that of a tiger. During the investigation of the case, it was discovered that both protagonists of the tragedy were illegal immigrants. Asian passports were used a hundred times over; since the immigration officers could barely determine the sex of an Oriental, they certainly were not able from a passport photograph to tell them apart. Foreigners came with the intention of making their fortune and returning home but, instead, they stayed. Their descendants forgot their mother tongue, conquered by the aroma of coffee and the happy nature, the spell, of a people who still did not know envy. Very few set out to cultivate the homesteads granted by the government, because there were too few roads, schools, and hospitals, and too many diseases, mosquitoes, and poisonous snakes. The interior was the territory of outlaws, smugglers, and soldiers. Immigrants stayed in the cities, working diligently and saving every centavo, ridiculed by the native-born, who thought extravagance and generosity were the greatest virtues any decent person could have.

"I don't believe in machines. This business of copying the gringos' ways is bad for the soul," Elvira maintained, scandalized by the excesses of the newly rich, who were trying to live life as they had seen it in the movies.

Since they lived on their respective retirement pensions, the elderly brother and sister had no access to easy money; as a result, there was no money squandered in that house, although they were aware of how the practice was spreading around them. Every citizen thought he had to own an executive-model automobile, until soon it became almost impossible to drive through the choked streets. Petroleum was traded for telephones in the shapes of cannons, seashells, and odalisques; so much plastic was imported that highways inevitably became bordered by indestructible garbage; eggs for the nation's breakfasts arrived daily by plane, producing enormous omelets on the burning asphalt of the landing strip when a crate was cracked open.

"The General is right. Nobody dies of hunger here—you reach out your hand and pluck a mango. That's why there's no progress. Cold countries have more advanced civilizations because the climate forces people to work." The *patrón* made these assertions lying in the shade, fanning himself with a newspaper and scratching his belly. He even wrote a letter to the Ministry of Trade, suggesting the possibility of towing an iceberg from the polar zone, crushing it, and scattering it from airplanes to see whether it might change the climate and combat the laziness of his countrymen.

While those in power stole without scruple, thieves by trade or necessity scarcely dared practice their profession: the eyes of the police were everywhere. That was the basis for the story that only a dictator could maintain order. The common people, who never saw the telephones, disposable panties, and imported eggs, lived as they always had.

The politicians of the opposition were in exile, but Elvira told me that in silence and shadow enough anger was brewing to cause the people to rebel against the regime. The *patrones* were unconditionally loyal to the General, and when members of the *guardia* came by the house selling his photograph, they showed them with pride the one already hanging in a place of honor in the living room. Elvira developed a relentless hatred of that chubby, remote, military man with whom she had never had the slightest contact, cursing him and casting the evil eye on him every time she dusted his portrait.

FOUR

he day the postman found Lukas Carlé's body, the forest was freshly washed, dripping and shining, and from its floor rose a strong breath of rotted leaves and a pale mist of another planet. For some forty years, every morning, the man had ridden his bicycle down the same path. Peddling that trail, he had earned his daily bread and had survived unharmed two wars, the occupation, hunger, and many other misfortunes. Because of his work, he knew all the inhabitants of the area by name and surname, just as he could identify every tree in the forest by its species and age. At first sight, that morning seemed no different from any other, the same oaks, beeches, chestnuts, birches, the same feathery moss and mushrooms at the base of the tallest trees, the same cool, fragrant breeze, the same shadows and patches of light. It was a day like all the rest, and perhaps a person with less knowledge of nature would not have noted the warnings, but the mailman was on edge, his skin prickling, because he perceived signs no other human eye would have registered. He always imagined the forest as a huge green beast with gentle blood flowing through its veins, a calm-spirited animal; but today it was restless. He got off his bicycle and sniffed the early morning air, seeking the reason for his uneasiness. The silence was so absolute he feared he had gone deaf. He laid his bicycle on the ground and took a couple of steps off the path to look around. He did not have to go far; there it was, waiting for him, hanging from a branch above his head, a thick cord around its neck. He did not need to see the hanged man's face to know who it was. He had known Lukas Carlé ever since he arrived in the village years before—come from God knows where, somewhere in France, maybe, with his trunkloads of books, his map of the world, and his diploma—and immediately married the prettiest of the village girls, and within a few months destroyed her beauty. The mailman recognized Carlé by his high-top shoes and schoolmaster's smock, and he had the impression of having seen this scene before, as if for years he had been expecting a similar dénouement. At first he felt no panic, only a sense of irony, the urge to say to him: I warned you, you scoundrel. It was several seconds before he grasped the enormity of what had happened, and at that instant the tree groaned, the body slowly turned, and the hopeless eyes of the hanged man met his. He could not move. There they were, staring at each other, the postman and the father of Rolf Carlé, until they had nothing more to say to each other. Only then did the old man react, hurrying back to his bicycle. As he bent over to pick it up, he felt a dagger thrust in his chest, as deep and burning as the stab of love. He straddled his bicycle and started off as quickly as he was able, doubled over the handlebars, a moan trapped in his throat.

He reached the village, peddling with such desperation that his aged courier's heart nearly burst. He managed to give the alarm before collapsing in front of the bakery, with a buzzing like a wasps' nest in his brain and the glitter of fear in his eyes. The bakers picked him up and laid him on the table where they made their pastries, and there he lay, gasping for breath, dusted with flour, and repeating that at last Lukas Carlé was strung up on a gallows as he should have been long ago, the scoundrel, the damned scoundrel. And that was how the town learned the news. The word flashed through the village, startling the inhabitants, who had not heard such an uproar since the end of the war. Everyone rushed into the street to comment on the death, except five students from the top form, who hid their heads beneath their pillows, pretending to be fast asleep.

Within a brief time the police had pulled the doctor and the judge from their beds and had set off, followed by various neighbors, in the direction indicated by the trembling finger of the postal employee. They found Lukas Carlé very near the road, swinging like a scarecrow, and then they realized that no one had seen him since Friday. Because the forest was cold and the dead man's weight had become monolithic, it took four men to cut him down. The doctor needed only a glance to know that before dying of asphyxia Carlé had received a severe blow to the back of the head, and the policeman needed only another to deduce that the sole witnesses who might offer an explanation were the students themselves, whom Carlé had accompanied on the school's annual outing.

"Bring the boys in," ordered the Chief of Police.

"Why? This is no sight for children," replied the judge, whose grandson was one of the victim's students.

But they could not overlook them. During the brief investigation, which the local authorities carried out more from a sense of duty than from any authentic desire to know the truth, the students were called to testify. They said they knew nothing. They had gone to the forest, as they did every year at that time; they had played soccer, conducted the usual wrestling matches, eaten their lunches, and, baskets in hand, scattered to collect mushrooms. In accord with their instructions, when it had begun to grow dark they met at the roadside, even though the schoolmaster had not blown his whistle to summon them. They looked for him, without success, then sat down to wait, but as night fell decided to return to the village. It had not occurred to them to inform the police because they supposed that Lukas Carlé had either returned home or gone back to the school. That was all. They did not have the least idea how he had come to meet his fate hanging from the branch of that tree.

Rolf Carlé, in his school uniform, his shoes recently polished and his beret pulled down to his ears, walked beside his mother along the corridor of the Prefecture. The youth had the ungainly and urgent air of many adolescents; he was thin, freckled, with alert eyes and delicate hands. They were led to a bare, cold room with tiled walls; in the center, on a stretcher beneath a bright white light, lay the body. The mother took a handkerchief from her sleeve and carefully cleaned her glasses. When the coroner lifted the sheet, she leaned over and for an interminable minute observed the distorted face. She made a sign to her son and he, too, stepped forward to look; then she lowered her eyes and covered her face with her hands to hide her joy.

"That is my husband," she said finally.

"That is my father," Rolf Carlé added, trying to keep his voice steady.

"I-I am very sorry. This is very distressing for the two of you," the doctor stammered, not understanding the source of his embarrassment. He covered the body, and the three stood in silence, staring uncomfortably at the silhouette beneath the sheet. "I haven't as yet performed the autopsy, but it looks like a suicide. I am truly sorry."

"Well, I suppose that's that," said the mother.

Rolf took her arm and, unhurriedly, they left the room. The echo of footsteps on a cement floor would be forever linked in their memories to a feeling of peace and relief.

"It was not a suicide. Your schoolmates killed your father," Frau Carlé declared once they were home.

"How do you know that, Mama?"

"I just know, and I am grateful they did it, because if they hadn't, we would have had to do it ourselves one day."

"Don't talk that way, please," whispered Rolf, frightened. He had always thought that his mother was resigned to her fate, had never imagined that her heart harbored such rancor against her husband. He thought he was the only one who hated his father. "It's all behind us now, we must forget about it."

"No, on the contrary, we must always remember it." She smiled with an expression he had never seen before.

The inhabitants of the village tried so stubbornly to erase the death of Professor Carlé from their collective memory that had it not been for the murderers themselves, they would have succeeded. But for years the five boys had been working up courage to perform that crime and they were not inclined to keep silent; they sensed that it would be the most important act of their lives, and they did not want it to vanish in the smoke of forgotten deeds. At the schoolmaster's funeral they were there in their Sunday suits to sing hymns and to lay a funeral wreath in the name of the school; they kept their eyes lowered so no one would surprise them exchanging guilty glances. For two weeks they were as quiet as the tomb, expecting each morning that the town would awake with enough evidence to send them to jail. Fear possessed their being, and it persisted until they decided to give it words. Following a soccer game, the opportunity presented itself in the dressing room where the sweat-drenched, high-spirited players were changing their clothes, joking and roughhousing. Without any prior agreement, the five lingered in the showers until all the others had left, and then, still naked, they stood before the mirror and studied one another, verifying that none of them bore visible signs of what had happened. One smiled, dissolving the shadow that had divided them, and they were themselves again, punching and backslapping and playing around like the overgrown boys they were. Carlé deserved it; he was a beast, a psychopath, they agreed. They reviewed all the facts and realized with amazement that they had left such a trail of clues it was incredible they had not been arrested. It was then they understood that they would not be punished, that no one was going to raise a voice to accuse them. One of their fathers was the Chief of Police, and would be in charge of any investigation; another's grandfather would be the judge at the trial; and the jury would be composed of relatives and neighbors. Everybody knew everybody else; they were all interrelated and no one had any desire to stir the mud of that murder, not even the family of Lukas Carlé. In fact, everyone suspected that the wife and son had been hoping for Carlé's demise for years, and that the general wind of relief caused by his death had blown first through their house, sweeping it from top to bottom and leaving it cleaner and fresher than it had ever been.

The boys vowed to keep the memory of their deed alive, and they succeeded so well that the story passed from mouth to mouth, enhanced at every telling, until it was transformed into a heroic feat. They formed a club and sealed their brotherhood with a secret oath. Occasionally they met by night at the edge of the forest to commemorate that unprecedented Friday in their lives, preserving the memory of the stone that had stunned him, the previously prepared noose, the way they had climbed the tree and then slipped the lasso around the neck of the still-unconscious schoolmaster, how at the instant they were hauling him up his eyes had opened, and how his body had jerked in its death spasms. They sewed an identifying circle of white cloth on the left sleeve of their jackets, and in no time at all the villagers guessed the meaning of that symbol. Rolf Carlé also knew, torn between gratitude for having been liberated from his tormentor, humiliation at bearing the hated man's name, and shame for not having either the spirit or the strength to avenge his father.

Rolf Carlé began to grow thin. Every time he lifted his food from his plate, his spoon was transformed into his father's tongue; at the bottom of the bowl, through the soup, he could see the dead man's terrified eyes; the bread was the color of a hanged man's skin. At night he trembled with fever and in the daytime he invented excuses not to leave the house. He had excruciating headaches but his mother made him eat and go to school. He bore it for twenty-six days, but on the morning of the twenty-seventh, the day that his five schoolmates appeared at recess with white circles on their jacket sleeves, he suffered an attack of vomiting so severe that the principal became alarmed and called an ambulance to take him to the hospital in the neighboring town, where he stayed for the remainder of the week, vomiting up his soul. When Frau Carlé saw her son's condition, she knew instinctively that his symptoms were not caused by ordinary indigestion. The village doctor, the same who had attended his birth and issued his father's death certificate, examined him carefully; he prescribed a series of medications and advised his mother not to worry: Rolf was a strong, healthy boy, his anxiety would soon pass, and before she knew it he would be back on the playing field and flirting with the girls. Frau Carlé administered the remedies faithfully, and when she saw no improvement doubled the dosage on her own. Nothing seemed to work; the boy, numbed by his misery, did not regain his appetite. The image of his hanged father blended with the memory of the day they had been taken to bury the dead in the prison camp. Katharina's mild eyes never left her brother; she followed him all over the house, and finally she took his hand and tried to pull him under the kitchen table to hide, but by now they were both too big. So she huddled beside him and began to whisper one of the long litanies of their childhood.

Early one Thursday morning, Frau Carlé went in to wake her son for school and found him lying facing the wall, pale, exhausted, and clearly determined to die; he could not any longer withstand the assault of so many ghosts. She realized that he was being consumed in flames of guilt for having wished to commit the murder himself. Without a word, Frau Carlé went straight to the wardrobe and began rummaging through it. She found belongings that had been lost for years: outgrown clothing, children's toys, the X-rays of Katharina's brain, Jochen's shotgun. There she also found the stiletto-heeled red patent-leather boots, and she was surprised that they evoked so little bitterness. She did not even have the impulse to throw them out; instead, she carried them to the mantel and placed them beside the portrait of her deceased husband, one on each side, as if on an altar. Finally she found the green bag with heavy leather trim that Lukas Carlé had carried during the war; and in the same meticulous way that she performed her household and garden chores, she placed in the bag her younger son's clothing, a photograph taken on her wedding day, a silk-lined cardboard box containing one of Katharina's curls, and a packet of oatmeal cookies she had baked the day before.

"Get dressed, son, you are going to South America," she announced with unshakable determination.

That was how Rolf Carlé found himself on the Norwegian ship that carried him to the other side of the world, far away from his nightmares. His mother traveled with him by train to the nearest port; she bought him a third-class ticket, wrapped the remaining money and his Uncle Rupert's address in a handkerchief, and sewed the handkerchief inside his trousers, instructing him not to remove them for any reason. She did all this without any sign of emotion and, when she said goodbye, gave him a quick kiss on the forehead, just as she did every morning when he left for school.

"How long shall I be far away, Mama?"

"I do not know, Rolf."

"I shouldn't go. I'm the only man in the family now and I have to take care of you."

"I will be fine. I will write you."

"Katharina is sick, I can't leave her like this."

"Your sister will not live much longer—we always knew it would be that way, there's no use in worrying about her. What is this? Are you crying? You're no son of mine, Rolf—you're too big to act like a little boy. Wipe your nose and get on board before people begin staring at us."

"I don't feel good, Mama. I want to throw up."

"I forbid you! Don't shame me. Go on now, up the gangway. Walk forward to the bow and stay there. Don't look back. Goodbye, Rolf."

But the boy hid at the stern where he could see the dock, and so learned that his mother did not move until the ship was out of sight. He never forgot that vision of her, dressed in black, with her felt hat and imitation-crocodile pocketbook, standing, like a solitary statue, facing the sea.

Rolf Carlé spent almost a month deep in the bowels of the ship among refugees, émigrés, and other impecunious passengers without— both from shyness and pride—exchanging so much as a word with any of them. He scanned the sea, however, with such determination that he plumbed the depths of his sadness and finally depleted it. He never again suffered the affliction that brought him to the brink of jumping overboard. Twelve days in the salt air restored his appetite and ended his bad dreams; his nausea passed and he was enchanted by the smiling dolphins that accompanied the ship for long stretches. By the time they reached the coast of South America, the color had returned to his cheeks. He examined himself in the tiny mirror of the bathroom he shared with the other passengers in steerage, and saw that his face was that of a man, not a tortured adolescent. He liked what he saw; he took a deep breath and, for the first time in a long while, he smiled.

When the ship docked, the passengers debarked down an open gangway. Feeling like a freebooter from an old adventure novel, his hair ruffled by a warm breeze and his eyes filled with wonderment, Rolf Carlé was one of the first to step ashore. An incredible sight was revealed in the morning light. He saw dwellings of all colors hanging from the hillsides around the port, twisting streets, lines of drying clothes, and an exuberant vegetation in every possible shade of green. The air was vibrant with sound—hawkers' cries, women singing, children's laughter, parrots' squawking—and steamy with sensuality and odors warm from the food stalls. Amid the hubbub of stevedores, sailors, and passengers, the bundles, suitcases, onlookers, and peddlers, waited his

Uncle Rupert, his Aunt Burgel, and their daughters, two sturdy, red-cheeked girls Rolf immediately fell in love with. Rupert was a distant cousin of his mother, a carpenter by trade, a great beer drinker and dog lover. With his family he had come to these far reaches of the world fleeing the war. He had no taste for soldiering; it seemed stupid to him to be killed for a flag that in his estimation was nothing more than a piece of cloth tied to a pole. He had not the slightest patriotic inclination, and when he became certain that war was inevitable, he remembered some remote ancestors who had long ago embarked for America to found a colony, and he decided to follow in their footsteps. From the ship Rupert drove Rolf Carlé directly to a fairy-tale village preserved in a bubble where time had stopped and geography was illusory. Life went on there as it had in the nineteenth century in the Alps. For Rolf, it was like walking into a movie. He knew nothing of the rest of the country, and for months he believed there was little difference between the Caribbean and the shores of the Danube.

In the mid-nineteenth century, an illustrious South American who owned these fertile lands nestled in the mountains a short distance from the sea and not too far from civilization had dreamed of populating them with colonists of good stock. He went to Europe, chartered a ship, and spread the word among farmers impoverished by wars and plagues that a utopia was awaiting them on the other side of the Atlantic. There they would construct a perfect society in which peace and prosperity reigned, a society regulated by sound Christian principles, far from the vices, ambitions, and mysteries that had assailed humanity since the beginnings of civilization. Eighty families were selected on the basis of merit and good intentions, among whom were representatives of various trades, a schoolmaster, a doctor, and a priest, along with their tools and instruments and a background of several centuries of tradition and learning. When they stepped onto that tropical soil, some were frightened, convinced that they would never get used to such a place, but their ideas changed as they ascended a path toward mountain peaks and found themselves in the promised paradise, a cool, mild region where they could cultivate the fruits and vegetables of both Europe and America. There they erected a replica of the villages of their homeland: wood-trimmed houses, Gothic-lettered signs, window boxes filled with flowers, and a small church where they hung the bronze bell they had carried with them on the ship. They closed the entrance to La Colonia and blocked the road, making it impossible to enter or leave, and for a hundred years they fulfilled the dream of the man who had brought them to that land, living in accord with the precepts of God. But the secret of such a utopia could not be hidden indefinitely, and when the press published the story it created a sensation. The government, little inclined to allow within its sovereign territory a foreign colony with its own laws and customs, forced them to open their doors and welcome national authorities, tourism, and commerce. Visitors found a village where no one spoke Spanish, where everyone was blond and blue-eyed, and where a significant proportion of the children had some defect resulting from inbreeding. A highway was constructed to link the village with the capital, making La Colonia a favorite site for outings; families with cars drove there to buy seasonal fruit, honey, sausage, home-baked bread, and embroidered linens. The colonists turned their homes into restaurants and inns for the visitors, and a few hostels accepted lovers, which may not have precisely corresponded to the ideas of the community's founder, but times change and it was necessary to modernize. Rupert had arrived when the village was still closed but, after establishing his European blood and demonstrating his good will, had managed to be accepted. When communications were opened with the outside world, he was one of the first to understand the advantages of the new arrangement. He stopped building furniture, now that it was possible to buy better and more varied furnishings in the capital, and began producing cuckoo clocks and reproducing hand-painted antique toys to sell to the tourists. He also began breeding dogs, and set up a school for training them, an idea that had never occurred to anyone in the country; until then, animals had been born and bred haphazardly, without papers, clubs, shows, grooming, or special handling. But Rupert had quickly learned that German shepherds were the fashion in some quarters, and wealthy owners wanted dogs with the proper papers. Those who could afford them bought their animals, then left them for a while in Rupert's school. When the dogs graduated, they had been trained to walk on their hind feet, salute with a front paw, carry the master's newspaper or slippers in their mouth, and play dead when given a command in a foreign tongue.

Uncle Rupert was the owner of a sizable piece of land and a large, many-roomed house that he had converted into an inn; he had built and furnished it with his own hands in the light wood of the Heidelberg style, in spite of the fact that he had never set eyes on that city but had copied everything from a magazine. His wife raised strawberries and flowers and kept chickens that supplied eggs for the whole village. They made a good living from dog-breeding, cuckoo clocks, and tourists.

Rolf Carlé's life underwent a great change. He had finished school, and there was no place for further study in La Colonia; besides, his uncle had plans to teach him his own trades, hoping Rolf would help him and perhaps take over his business. He had high hopes of seeing one of his daughters married to Rolf, whom he had liked from the moment he saw him. He had always wanted a male heir, and Rolf was exactly the son he had dreamed of: strong, of high character, good with his hands, and red-haired like the men in his family. Rolf learned quickly to master the tools of the carpentry shop, to assemble the clocks, to harvest the strawberries, and to wait on the guests in the inn. His aunt and uncle, in turn, learned that he would do anything they wanted as long as he believed it was his own idea, and if they appealed to his emotions.

"What do you think we should do about that henhouse roof, Rolf?" Burgel would ask, with a sigh of helplessness.

"It needs some tar."

"I'm afraid I'll lose all my hens when the rains begin."

"Leave it to me, Aunt, it won't take any time at all to fix it." And for the next three days the youth would be stirring a kettle of hot tar, doing a balancing act on the roof, and explaining his theories on waterproofing to anyone passing by, before the admiring gaze of his cousins and the veiled smile of his aunt.

Rolf was determined to learn the language of the country and was not satisfied until he found someone to teach him in a methodical way. He was gifted with a good ear for music, and that talent was evident when he played the church organ, entertained visitors with his accordion, and absorbed Spanish—with a good supply of forbidden words that he used only rarely, but treasured as part of his culture. In his free moments, he read, and in less than a year had consumed all the books in the village, which he borrowed, then returned with obsessive punctuality. He had a good memory and he stored information—almost always useless and impossible to dispute—to impress his family and neighbors. Without a moment's hesitation he could state the population of Mauritania, or the width of the English Channel in nautical miles, usually because he remembered, but occasionally invented by him on the spot, and spoken with such arrogance that no one dared question him. He learned several Latin phrases to spice his conversation and, even though he did not always use them correctly, earned a solid reputation in that small community. He had inherited his mother's courteous and somewhat old-fashioned manners, which helped him capture everyone's heart, particularly the ladies', who had little exposure to finesse in that rather rough society. He was particularly attentive to his Aunt Burgel, not out of affectation but because he was truly fond of her. She had a way of dispelling his despair with such simplicity that afterward he would ask himself why he had not thought of the solution. Whenever he fell into the vice of nostalgia or tortured himself thinking about the evils of mankind, she restored him with her magnificent desserts and steady stream of little jokes. She was the first person, apart from Katharina, to hug him without needing a reason or permission. Each morning she greeted him with resounding kisses, and before he fell asleep she came in to tuck him in—affection his mother had been too shy to bestow. At first, Rolf himself seemed timid; he blushed easily and spoke in a low voice. In fact, he was vain and even at an age to see himself as the center of the universe. He was much quicker than most of the people around him and he knew it, but he was intelligent enough to affect a certain modesty.

Every Sunday morning, people from the city drove out for the show in his Uncle Rupert's school for dogs. Rolf would lead them to a large courtyard with tracks and jumps where the dogs performed their feats amid enthusiastic applause. Sunday was the day the dogs were sold, and the youth always watched them go with a heavy heart, because nothing was more dear to him than those animals he had cared for since birth. He would throw himself down on the bitches' matting and let the pups nuzzle him and chew his ears and fall asleep in his arms. He knew each one by name and spoke with them as if they were equals. Rolf had a hunger for love, but as he had never been coddled or babied he felt free to demonstrate affection only with the pups; it took much longer to learn to accept human contact—first Burgel's and then that of others. His memories of Katharina formed a secret source of tenderness, and sometimes, thinking of her in the darkness of his room, he hid his head beneath the sheet and wept.

He never spoke of his past, for fear of evoking sympathy and also because he had not yet come to grips with it in his mind. The unhappy years with his father were a broken mirror in his memory. He prided himself on his coldness and pragmatism, two qualities he considered particularly manly, but in truth he was an incorrigible dreamer. He was disarmed by the slightest gesture of sympathy and outraged by injustice, and he suffered the ingenuous idealism of youth that never withstands confrontation with reality. His childhood of privation and terror had given him the ability to sense intuitively the dark side of situations and people, with a clairvoyance that flared before him like a powder flash, but his pretense of rationalism kept him from giving credence to those mysterious warnings or following his impulses. He denied his emotions, but at any unguarded moment was demolished by them. He also refused to respond to the demands of his senses, and tried to control the part of his nature inclined toward voluptuousness and pleasure. He understood from the beginning that La Colonia was a naïve dreamworld he had stumbled into by accident, and believed that life was filled with harshness that would require strong armor if he was to survive. Nevertheless, those who knew him could see that his shell was nothing but smoke and that it would dissipate in the slightest breeze. Rolf went through life with his emotions bared, tripping over his pride, falling, and struggling to his feet again.

Rupert, Burgel, and their daughters were simple, lively folk with large appetites. Food was central: their lives turned around the labors of the kitchen and the ceremony of the table. They were all plump, and could not get used to seeing Rolf so thin in spite of their constant efforts to nourish him. Aunt Burgel had created an aphrodisiac dish that attracted the tourists and kept her husband inflamed. Look at him, she would say with the contagious laughter of a contented matron; he's steaming like a tractor. The recipe was simple: in a huge pot she browned onion, bacon, and tomato seasoned with salt, peppercorns, garlic, and coriander. To this she added, in layers, chunks of pork and beef, boned chicken, broad beans, corn, cabbage, pimiento, fish, clams, and lobster;

then she sprinkled in a little raw sugar and added four steins of beer. Before putting on the lid and simmering the stew over a slow fire, she threw in a handful of herbs grown in her kitchen flowerpots. That was the crucial moment, because no one else knew the combination of spices, and she meant to carry her secret to the grave. The result was a dark rich stew that was spooned from the pot and served in reverse order to its preparation. The grand finale was the broth, served in cups, and the effect was a formidable heat in the bones and a lustful passion in the soul. Rolf's aunt and uncle slaughtered several hogs a year and turned out the best pork products in the village: smoked hams, pork sausage, salami, and enormous tins of lard. They bought fresh milk by the can in order to have cream and churn butter and make cheese. From dawn to dusk delicious odors drifted from that kitchen. In the patio, copper kettles simmered over open wood fires, filled with conserves of plum, apricot, and strawberry for the guests' breakfasts. From spending so much time around the aromatic pots, Rolf's two cousins smelled of cinnamon, clove, vanilla, and lemon. At night Rolf slipped like a shadow into their room to bury his nose in their clothes and breathe in a sweet fragrance that filled his head with sin.

On the weekends the routine changed. Thursday they aired the rooms, decorated them with fresh flowers, and brought wood for the fireplaces —at night there was a cool breeze and the guests liked to sit before the fire and imagine they were in the Alps. From Friday to Sunday the house was filled with guests, and from early dawn the family worked to make them happy. Burgel never left the kitchen, while the girls, with the embroidered felt vests and skirts, white stockings, starched aprons, and ribbon-braided hair of village girls in German folktales, served the tables and cleaned the rooms.

It took four months for Frau Carlé's letters to arrive. They were all very brief, and almost identical: Dear son, I am fine. Katharina is in the hospital. Take good care of yourself and remember everything I taught you so you will grow up to be a good man. Your Mama sends kisses. Rolf, in contrast, wrote his mother frequently, filling both sides of page after page, telling her about what he had read, because after describing the village and his uncle's family there was little more to say; he felt that nothing ever happened to him that was worth reporting in a letter, and he preferred to astound his mother with long philosophical ideas based on his reading. He also sent her photographs he took with his uncle's ancient camera, immortalizing the moods of nature, people's expressions, and minor events, the kinds of details that ordinarily pass unnoticed. That correspondence meant a great deal to him, not only because it kept his mother alive for him, but also because he discovered how much he enjoyed observing the world and preserving it in images.

Rolf Carlé's cousins were being wooed by a pair of suitors who were direct descendants of La Colonia's founders, the owners of a unique industry, elegant candles sold throughout the country and beyond. The factory still exists, and its fame is so widespread that on the occasion of the Pope's visit, the government ordered a candle seven meters tall and two meters in diameter, to be kept burning in the Cathedral; not only was it molded to perfection, decorated with scenes of the Passion, and perfumed with the scent of pine, but beneath a burning sun it was transported by truck from the mountain to the capital without loss of its obelisk shape, scent of Christmas, or antique ivory tone. The young men's conversation tended to center on candle molds, colors, and perfumes. At times they were rather boring, but both were handsome, quite prosperous, and permeated inside and out with the aroma of beeswax and scents. They were the best catch in La Colonia, and all the girls looked for excuses to go and buy candles wearing their filmiest dresses. Rupert, however, had sowed the seed of doubt in his daughters' minds that those youths, bred through generations of interrelated families, had watered-down blood and might produce defective offspring. In candid opposition to theories of purity of race, he believed that crossbreeding gave the best progeny, and to prove it he liked to breed his registered dogs with mongrels. He obtained regrettable-looking mutts with unpredictable coats and configuration that no one wanted to buy, but also were much more intelligent than their pedigreed kindred, as was apparent when they learned to walk a tightrope and waltz on their hind legs. Better to look for sweethearts outside, Rupert used to say, defying his beloved Burgel, who wanted to hear nothing of such a possibility. The idea of seeing her girls married to dark men with the rhythm of the rumba in their hips seemed disgraceful to her. Don't be dense, Burgel. *You're* the one who's dense—do you want mulatto grandchildren? The people of this country may not be blond, wife, but not all of them are black, either. To avoid further argument, both would sigh, with the name of Rolf Carlé on their lips, lamenting they did not have two nephews like him, one for each daughter, because despite the blood relationship and the precedent of Katharina's mental retardation, they would swear that Rolf was not the bearer of deficient genes. In their minds he was the perfect son-in-law: hardworking, educated, cultivated, good-mannered—what more could they ask? For the moment, his youth was the only stumbling block, but everyone is cured of that.

The girls were slow to sympathize with their parents' aspirations; they were true innocents, but once awakened to the idea, they left far behind the norms of modesty and discretion they had been raised by. They saw the fire in Rolf Carlé's eyes; they watched him steal into their room like a wraith to paw furtively through their clothes, and they interpreted those actions as signs of love. They talked the matter over, contemplating the possibility of a platonic relationship between the youth and the two sisters, but when they saw Rolf naked to the waist, his coppery hair tousled by the wind, sweating over the farm machinery or the carpentry tools, they began to change their minds, coming to the blissful conclusion that God had something obvious in mind when He created two sexes. The girls were cheerful by nature, and accustomed to sharing a bedroom, bathroom, clothes, and almost everything else, so they saw nothing wicked in sharing a lover. Besides, it was easy to see the excellent physical condition of the youth, who had, they were sure, sufficient strength and good will to carry out the heavy chores their father demanded of him and still have energy left over for a good romp with them. The matter was not that simple, however. The villagers were not sufficiently sophisticated to understand a triangular relationship, and even their father, though he might boast of modernity, would never tolerate such an arrangement. Not to speak of their mother: she would be quite capable of picking up a kitchen knife and sinking it into her nephew's most vulnerable parts.

Soon Rolf Carlé began to notice a change in the girls' behavior. They insisted he take the largest slice of the roast, piled mountains of whipped cream on his dessert, whispered behind his back, fluttered when he caught them watching him, touched him as he passed by—always in some casual way, but with such an erotic charge that not even an anchorite would have remained unmoved. Until then he had kept a prudent distance and watched them covertly, in order not to offend the norms of courtesy—or face the possibility of a rejection that would have been fatal to his self-esteem. Little by little, because he did not want to make any hasty decisions, he began to look at them more boldly. Which should he choose? They were both enchanting, with robust legs, straining breasts, aquamarine eyes, and baby-fine skin. The older sister was more amusing, but he was also attracted by the gentle flirtatiousness of the younger. Poor Rolf argued the matter with himself, undecided, until the girls tired of waiting for his initiative and launched a frontal attack. They cornered him in the strawberry patch, tripped him up, then piled on top of him and tickled him unmercifully, shattering his mania for taking himself seriously and arousing his lust. They burst the buttons of his trousers, pulled off his shoes, ripped open his shirt, and put their mischievous nymphet hands where he never imagined anyone would explore. From that day on, Rolf Carlé abandoned his reading, neglected the pups, forgot the cuckoo clocks, the letters to his mother, even his own name. He wandered around in a trance, his instincts aflame and his mind in a daze. From Monday to Thursday, when there were no guests in the house, the rhythm of the domestic chores slowed and the three young people had a few hours of liberty, which they seized to disappear into the unoccupied guest rooms. They did not want for excuses: airing the eiderdowns, cleaning the windows, spraying for cockroaches, waxing the wood furniture, changing the beds. The girls had inherited their parents' sense of fairness and orderliness, and while one closed herself in a room with Rolf the other stood guard in the corridor to give the alarm if anyone approached. They were scrupulous in taking turns, but fortunately the youth was not aware of that humiliating detail. What did they do when they were alone? Nothing new; they played the same games cousins have played for six thousand years. Things became interesting when they decided to spend nights three in a bed, calmed by Rupert's and Burgel's snoring in the adjacent room. To keep an eye on the girls, the parents slept with their door open, and that also allowed the girls to keep an eye on them. Rolf Carlé was as inexperienced as his two companions, but from the first encounter he took precautions not to get them pregnant, and poured into the erotic games all the enthusiasm and inventiveness needed to make up for his amatory ignorance. His energies were endlessly fed by the formidable gifts of his cousins—open, warm, smelling of fruit, breathless with laughter, and exceedingly receptive. Furthermore, having to maintain absolute silence—terrified at the creaking bedsprings, huddled beneath the sheets, enveloped in one another's warmth and aromas—was a spur that set their hearts aflame. They were at the perfect age for inexhaustible love-making. The girls were flowering with a summery vitality, the blue of their eyes deepening, their skin becoming more luminous, and their smiles happier; as for Rolf, he forgot his Latin and went around bumping into furniture and falling asleep on his feet; he was only half awake as he waited on the tourists, his legs trembling and his eyes unfocused. The boy is working too hard, Burgel. He looks pale, we must give him some vitamins, Rupert would say, never suspecting that behind his back his nephew was devouring great portions of his aunt's famous aphrodisiac stew so that his strength would not desert him in his hour of need. Together the three cousins discovered the basic requirements of levitation, and on occasion defied gravity for brief periods. The youth resigned himself to the idea that his companions had the greater capacity for pleasure and could repeat their feats several times in the same session, so in order to keep his reputation intact and not cheat the girls, he improvised techniques to ration his energy and pleasure. Years later, he learned that the same methods had been employed in China since the time of Confucius, and concluded that there is nothing new under the sun, as his Uncle Rupert said each time he read the newspaper. Some nights the three lovers were so contented that they forgot to say good night and fell asleep in a tangle of arms and legs, the young man buried in a soft and fragrant mountain of flesh, lulled by his cousins' dreams. They would awake at the first rooster's crow, just in time for them to leap into their own beds, before their elders surprised them in such delicious misbehavior. For a while the sisters were planning to flip a coin for the indefatigable Rolf Carlé, but during the process of those memorable tourneys they discovered they were joined to him by playful and festive emotions totally inappropriate as a basis for a respectable marriage. They, practical young women that they were, decided it would be more convenient to marry the aromatic candlemakers, keeping their cousin in reserve as a lover and, when feasible, as father of their children, thus avoiding the risk of boredom—though not, perhaps, of bringing half-witted children into the world. Such an arrangement never entered Rolf Carlé's mind, nurtured as he had been by romantic literature, chivalric novels, and strict and honorable teachings learned in childhood. While the girls were planning audacious combinations, he was striving to ease his guilt at loving them both by pretending that this was a temporary arrangement, the ultimate aim of which was to know one another better before selecting a partner; in his mind, a long-term contract would be an abominable perversion. He struggled with the insoluble conflict between desire—always spiritedly revived by those two opulent and generous bodies—and the severity that caused him to view monogamous marriage as the only possible course for a decent man. Don't be foolish, Rolf. Don't you see it doesn't matter to us? I don't love you for myself alone, and neither does my sister. We can go on like this until we marry—even after. Their proposal was a brutal blow to the young man's vanity. For thirty hours he was sunk in indignation, but finally his concupiscence won out. He scraped his dignity off the floor and came back to sleep with the girls. And they, his precious cousins, one on each side, laughing in their glorious nakedness, again enveloped him in a delicious mist of cinnamon, clove, vanilla, and lemon, driving him mad and obliterating the last of his stodgy Christian virtues.

Three years passed in this manner, more than enough to replace Rolf Carlé's macabre nightmares with lovely dreams. It is possible that the girls would have triumphed over his scruples and he would have remained by their side for the rest of his days, humbly fulfilling the dual role of lover and surrogate father, had fate not led him down a different path. And the person charged with showing him the way was a *señor* Aravena, a newspaperman by profession and filmmaker by vocation.

Aravena wrote for the country's most important newspaper. He was Rupert and Burgel's best client and he spent almost every weekend at their inn, where a room was always kept for him. His pen was so highly respected that not even the dictatorship had been able to still it completely, and during his years in the profession he had acquired an aureole of honesty that allowed him to publish what his colleagues would never have dared. Even the General and the Man of the Gardenia treated him with respect, abiding by a mutually beneficial formula that allowed him, within specific limitations, unmolested freedom, while the government projected an image of liberalism by exhibiting his moderately daring articles. A man with an obvious taste for the good life, he smoked enormous cigars, ate like a lion, and was a prodigious drinker, the only man able to defeat Uncle Rupert in the Sunday beer fests. He alone was allowed the luxury of pinching Rolf's cousins' magnificent buttocks, because he did it with grace, in no spirit of offense, merely of rendering due tribute. Come here, my adorable Valkyries, let this humble news-paperman feel your heavenly ass; and even Burgel would laugh as her daughters turned a backside and he ceremoniously lifted the embroi-dered felt skirts and fell into rhapsodies at the sight of those orbs en-cased in girlish underdrawers.

Señor Aravena owned a movie camera and a noisy portable type-writer, its keys discolored with use, and he sat before it all day Saturday and half of Sunday on the terrace of the inn, pecking out his columns with two fingers and eating sausages and drinking beer. Ah, it does me good to breathe this pure mountain air, he would say from behind a cloud of black smoke. Sometimes he arrived with a girl—never the same one—whom he introduced as his niece, and Burgel always went along with the pretense. We don't run one of those shady hotels. Do you think I'd put up with such a thing? I allow Aravena to bring a friend because he's such a well-known gentleman. Haven't you seen his name in the newspaper? Aravena's enthusiasm for the lady in question would last only one night; after that he would have had his fill of her and would pack her off with the first truckload of vegetables bound for the capital. In contrast, he would spend days talking with Rolf Carlé as they strolled around the village. He maintained a running commentary on international news, initiated Rolf into national politics, supervised his readings, taught him the basics of the camera and some rudiments of typing. You can't stay in La Colonia forever, he said. It's fine for a neurotic like myself to come here to fortify my body and get the poisons out of my system, but no normal young man should live in this stage set. Rolf Carlé was familiar with the works of Shakespeare, Molière, and Calderón de la Barca, but he had never been in a theater and could not see its relationship with the village; he was disinclined, however, to argue with the maestro for whom he felt such unbounded admiration.

"I'm very pleased with you, Rolf," his Uncle Rupert told him the day he turned twenty. "In a couple of years' time, you can take complete charge of the clocks—it's a profitable business."

"The truth is, Uncle, that I don't want to be a clockmaker. I think that cinematography would be a better profession for me."

"Cinematography? And what good is that?"

"To make films. I'm interested in documentaries. I want to know what's going on in the world, Uncle."

"The less you know, the better, but if that's what you like, then do it."

Burgel was almost ill when she learned that Rolf was going off to live alone in the capital, that den of peril, drugs, politics, and sickness, where all the women are bitches—pardon my French—like those women who come sailing into La Colonia with their stern wagging and their bow breasting the waves. Desperate, the cousins tried to dissuade Rolf by refusing him their favors, but in view of the fact that the punishment was as painful for them as it was for him, they changed their tactics and made love to him with such ardor that Rolf lost weight at an alarming rate. Those most affected, nonetheless, were the dogs, who when they sniffed the preparations in the air lost all appetite and slunk around with their tail between their legs, ears drooping, and an unbearable gaze of supplication in their eyes.

Rolf Carlé withstood all emotional appeals, and two months later set off for the university, after promising his Uncle Rupert that he would spend the weekends with them, his Aunt Burgel that he would eat the biscuits, hams, and marmalades she packed in his suitcases, and the cousins that he would remain absolutely chaste in order to return with renewed energies for their frolics beneath the eiderdown.

FIVE

While these things were happening in Rolf Carlé's life, I was growing up only a short distance away. It was during that time that my *madrina*'s misfortune began. I heard about it on the radio, and saw her picture in the scandal sheet Elvira used to buy behind the *patrona*'s back. That's how I learned my *madrina* had given birth to a monster. Specialists informed the public that the creature belonged to Tribe III—that is, it was characterized by a fused body with two heads: genus *Xiphoid*, meaning it had a single vertebral column; and class Omphalosian, one umbilicus for two bodies. The great curiosity was that one head was white by race, and the other black.

"The poor thing had two fathers, that's for sure," said Elvira, with a grimace of disgust. "A horror like that happens only if you sleep with two men on the same day. In all my fifty years, I've never done a thing like that. You won't catch me letting the juices of two men mix in my belly. The fruit of that sin is circus freaks."

My *madrina* had been earning her living nights as a scrubwoman. She was on a tenth floor scrubbing the stains from a carpet when she felt her first pangs; she continued working, however, because she was not sure how to time the delivery, and because she was furious with herself for having succumbed to temptation, paying with a shameful pregnancy. A little past midnight she felt warm liquid trickling between her thighs, and knew she should get to a hospital, but it was too late; she did not have the strength to get to the elevator. She yelled at the top of her lungs, but there was no one in all the lonely building to come to her aid. Resigned to staining what she had just cleaned, she lay down on the floor and pushed with desperation until she expelled the fetus. She was so befuddled when she saw the strange two-headed creature she had given birth to that her first reaction was to get rid of it as quickly as possible. As soon as she could struggle to her feet, she carried the baby into the corridor and threw it down the incinerator chute, and then, still gasping for breath, went back to clean the rug all over again. The next day when the janitor went into the basement, he found the tiny body in the trash that had been discarded from the offices; there were few signs of injury, because it had fallen on shredded paper. Waitresses from the cafeteria came running in response to his cries, and in a few minutes the news had reached the street and spread like wildfire. By noon the scandal was news throughout the nation; even foreign newspapermen came to photograph the infant's corpse, because in all the annals of medicine that combining of races was unique. For a week, no one talked of anything else; the event overshadowed even the deaths of two students who had been shot by the *guardia* at the gates of the university for waving red flags and singing the "Internationale." My *madrina* was called an unnatural mother, a murderess, and a foe of science because she would not give the body to the Anatomical Institute for examination, but insisted on burying it in the cemetery, according to Catholic teaching.

"First she kills it and throws it in the trash like a rotten fish, and then she wants to give it a Christian burial. God will never forgive a crime like that, little bird."

"But, *abuela*, no one has proved that my *madrina* killed it."

"And who did, then?"

The police kept the mother in isolation for several weeks, until the coroner finally succeeded in making himself heard. He had insisted from the first, although no one paid any attention, that being thrown down the incinerator chute was not the cause of death; the infant had been stillborn. Finally the authorities freed the poor woman, who was marked for life, in any case; for months she was followed by newspaper headlines, and no one ever believed the official version. The sympathies of an unforgiving public were all for the baby, and they called my *madrina* "The Little Monster Murderess." All this trauma was the final blow to her nerves. She could not get over the guilt of having given birth to a sideshow freak, and was never the same person after getting out of jail. She was obsessed with the idea that the birth was a divine punishment for some abominable sin that not even she could remember. She was ashamed to show herself in public, and sank into misery and despair. As a last resort, she went to see witch doctors; they wrapped her in a shroud, laid her on the ground inside a circle of lighted candles, and blanketed her beneath a suffocating cloud of smoke, talcum, and camphor, until there issued from the depths of her being a visceral scream that they interpreted as the expulsion of the evil spirits. Then they hung sacred necklaces around her neck to prevent the evil from re-entering her body. When I went with Elvira to visit her, I found her living in the same blue-painted shack. She had fallen away, and had lost the unabashed sauciness that had once put pepper in her walk; she had surrounded herself with pictures of Catholic saints and African gods, her only company the stuffed puma.

When she saw that the prayers and the witchcraft and the herbalists' brews did not bring an end to her adversity, my *madrina* swore before the altar of the Virgin Mary never again to have carnal contact with a man, and to ensure that vow she had a midwife stitch up her vagina. The infection nearly killed her. She never knew whether she was saved by the hospital's antibiotics, the candles lighted to Santa Rita, or the medicinal teas she so faithfully imbibed. From that moment she could not do without rum and the witch doctors' *santería*. Life lost its meaning; often she did not recognize people she knew, and she roamed the city streets mumbling unintelligibly about a devil's spawn, a creature of two bloods born from her belly. She was totally mad, and could not earn a living because, in her disturbed state and with her photograph in the police files, no one would give her work. She disappeared for long stretches at a time, and I would fear she was dead, but when I least expected her, she would reappear haggard and wretched, her eyes bloodshot. She always brought a cord with seven knots in it to measure my skull, a surefire way, someone had told her, to verify whether I was still a virgin. That's your only treasure. As long as you're untouched, you're worth something, she would say; but when you lose it, you're nobody. I did not understand why the part of my body that was so sinful and forbidden could at the same time be so valuable.

She might let months go by without collecting my salary, then, pleading or threatening, suddenly show up to ask to borrow money. You are mistreating my little girl—she's stunted and skinny, and everyone tells me that the *patrón* can't keep his hands off her. That's not what I like to hear, they call that corruption of minors. Whenever she came to the house, I ran and hid in the coffin. Adamant, the spinster would refuse to raise my wages and would tell my *madrina* that the next time she bothered her she would call the police. They know you, they know all about you. You should be grateful that I've taken the girl off your hands. If it weren't for me, she would be as dead as your two-headed baboon. The situation became intolerable, and finally one day the *patrona* lost her patience and fired me.

Leaving Elvira was very difficult. We had been together for more than three years; she had given me affection and I had filled her head with romantic stories. We had helped each other and shared our laughter. Sleeping in the same bed and playing funeral in the same coffin, we had formed an enduring friendship that protected us from loneliness and the harshness of a servant's life. Elvira swore never to forget me, and visited me when she could, somehow managing to find out where I was. She would show up like a kindly *abuela*, always with a bottle of guayaba syrup, or lollipops she had bought in the market. Our affection needed no words, and we would just sit and look at each other the way we used to before I was taken away. Elvira would ask me for a long story to last till the next visit. And so we saw each other for a time, until a twist of fate caused us to lose track of each other.

———

That was when I began moving from one house to another. My *madrina* was constantly seeking new employers, each time demanding more money—but no one was disposed to pay decent wages, considering that many girls my age asked for no salary at all, only their keep. I lost count of, and now cannot remember, all the places I worked, except a few that are impossible to forget, like the house of the lady of the stone-hard *porcelana*, whose art served me well in later years in an unusual adventure.

This lady was a widow who had been born in Yugoslavia. She spoke a halting Spanish, but her cooking skills were inspired. She had discovered a recipe for a Universal Matter, as she modestly called her mixture of wet newspapers, unmilled flour, and dental cement, which she kneaded into a grayish dough that was malleable while moist but rock-hard when it dried. She could imitate any substance except the transparency of glass or the vitreous humor of the eye. She would mix up a batch, wrap it in a wet cloth, and keep it in her refrigerator until she needed it. It could be molded like clay or rolled as thin as silk, cut, given different textures, or folded in any way desired. Once it was dry and hard, she sealed it with varnish and then painted it to resemble wood, metal, cloth, fruit, marble, human skin—any substance she wanted. Her home was a showroom for the possibilities of this miraculous material: a Coromandel screen in the entry; four musketeers dressed in velvet and lace, swords unsheathed, presiding over the living room; an elephant decorated in the Indian manner serving as a telephone table; a Roman frieze at the head of her bed. One of the rooms had been transformed into a pharaoh's tomb: the doors were trimmed with mortuary bas-reliefs; the lamps were black panthers with light bulbs for eyes; the table imitated a burnished sarcophagus with incrustations of false lapis lazuli; and the ashtrays reproduced the serene and eternal form of the Sphinx, with a depression in the back for crushing out cigarettes. I would tiptoe through that museum terrified that I would break something with the feather duster, or that one of the figures would come to life and I would be wounded by a musketeer's sword, the elephant's tusk, or the panther's claws. That was where my fascination with the culture of ancient Egypt was born, and my horror of bread dough. The Yugoslavian *patrona* sowed in my heart a lasting suspicion of inanimate objects, and ever since I must touch things to know whether they are what they seem, or Universal Matter. In the months I worked there, I became her apprentice, but I had the good fortune not to become addicted to her art. *Porcelana* is a dangerous temptation, because once its secrets are known, nothing stands in the way of the artist's copying everything imaginable, constructing a world of lies, and getting lost in it.

This *patrona*'s nerves had been destroyed by the war. She was convinced that invisible enemies were spying on her and planned to harm her, and she built a high wall topped with glass shards all around her property, and kept two loaded pistols in her night table: This city is overrun with thieves and a poor widow must be ready to defend herself—the first intruder who dares enter my house will get a bullet right between the eyes. But the bullets were not to be reserved for robbers alone. The day this country falls into the hands of the Communists, Evita, I will kill you so you won't suffer at their hands, and then blow my own head off, she said. She treated me with kindness, even a certain tenderness. She worried that I did not eat enough; she bought me a good bed; and every afternoon she invited me into the living room to listen to the serials on the radio: "Let the sonorous pages of the airwaves open before you as we bring to life the emotion and romance of a new chapter of . . ." Sitting side by side, munching crackers between the musketeers and the elephant, we listened to three programs in a row—two love stories and one mystery. I was happy with this *patrona*, and had a sense of belonging somewhere. Perhaps the only drawback was that the house was located in an isolated neighborhood and it was difficult for Elvira to come and visit. Even so, she tried to come every time she had an afternoon off: I get weary of coming so far, little bird, but I'm more weary when I don't see you. Every day, I ask God to make you strong and to grant me good health to keep loving you, she told me.

I would have stayed there much longer; my *madrina* had no reason to complain—she was paid punctually and generously—but a strange incident ended my employment. One windy night about ten o'clock, we heard a prolonged rumbling, something like a drumroll. The widow forgot her pistols; trembling, she locked the shutters, refusing to look out to try to see the source of the racket. The next morning we found four dead cats in the garden, strangled, beheaded, or gutted, and curses scrawled in blood on the wall. I remembered having heard on the radio about similar incidents, attributed to gangs of boys who made a sport of such cruel antics, and I tried to convince the *señora* that there was no cause for alarm—but in vain. My Yugoslavian *patrona*, crazed with fear, was determined to escape the country before the Bolsheviks did to her what they had done to the cats.

"You're in luck," my *madrina* announced. "I've got you a job in the house of a Cabinet Minister."

The *patrón* turned out to be an insipid type, like most public figures in that time when political life was congealed and any hint of originality could lead to a cellar room where a man awaited with a flower in his buttonhole, reeking of French cologne. By name and fortune my new *patrón* was a member of the old aristocracy, which guaranteed a certain impunity for his vulgarity, but he had exceeded the bounds of acceptable behavior and even his family had repudiated him. He was fired from his post in the Chancery when he was caught urinating behind the green brocade drapes of the Hall of Heraldry, and dismissed from an embassy for the same reason. That unpleasant habit, however unacceptable in diplomatic protocol, was no impediment to heading a Ministry. His greatest virtues were his capacity for fawning over the General and his talent for passing unnoticed—although years later his name became famous when he fled the country in a private plane and, in the tumult and haste of departure, left behind on the tarmac a suitcase filled with gold, which he did not miss in exile anyway. This paragon lived in a colonial mansion in the center of a shadowy park where ferns grew as large as octopuses and wild orchids clung to the trees. At night red dots glowed in the rank foliage, eyes of gnomes and other garden sprites, or bats swooping low from the rooftops. Divorced, without children or friends, the Minister lived alone in that enchanted place. The house he had inherited from his grandparents was much too large for him and his servants; many rooms were empty and under lock and key. My imagination took wing when I saw that corridor of locked doors; behind every one I thought I heard whispers, moans, laughter. At first I put my ear to the doors and peeked through the keyholes, but soon I found I did not have to do that to divine the universes hidden there, each with its own laws, time, and inhabitants, safe from the decay and contamination of the everyday world. I gave each room a name that recalled my mother's tales—Katmandu, Palace of the Bears, Merlin's Cave—and it took only the slightest effort of imagination to pass through the door and enter the extraordinary stories unfolding on the other side of the walls.

Besides the chauffeurs and bodyguards, who dirtied the parquet floors and stole the liquor, the Minister employed a cook, an aged gardener, a butler, and me. I never learned exactly what I was hired to do or what the financial arrangement was between the *patrón* and my *madrina*. I spent most of my time in idleness, exploring the garden, listening to the radio, daydreaming about the sealed rooms, or telling ghost stories to the other servants in exchange for sweets. Only two chores were exclusively mine: shining the Minister's shoes, and emptying his chamberpot.

The same day I arrived, there was a banquet for ambassadors and politicians. I had never witnessed such preparations. A truck unloaded round tables and gilded chairs; from large chests in the pantry came embroidered tablecloths and from the dining-room sideboards the best china and silverware with the family monogram engraved in gold. The butler handed me a cloth to shine the crystal, and I marveled at the perfect sound when one goblet grazed another and how each shimmered like a rainbow in the light. Masses of roses were delivered and arranged in tall vases in all the rooms. From the armoires flowed gleaming silver trays and carafes; from the kitchen an unending procession of fish and roasts, wines, cheeses from Switzerland, candied fruits, and tortes baked by nuns. Ten white-gloved waiters attended the guests, while I watched from behind the draperies of the grand salon, fascinated with the refinements that furnished a wealth of new material for embellishing my stories. Now I would be able to describe royal feasts, reveling in details I could never have invented, such as musicians in tails playing dance music on the terrace, chestnut-stuffed pheasants crowned with tufts of feathers, roast meat soaked in liqueur and served in a wreath of blue flames. I did not go to bed until the last guest had left. We spent the next day cleaning up, counting the silver, throwing away wilted flowers, and putting everything back in place. I was absorbed into the normal rhythm of the household.

The Minister's bedchamber was on the second floor, a large room with a huge bed carved with chubby-cheeked angels. The coffered ceiling was a century old, the carpets had been brought from the Orient, the walls were crowded with colonial *santos* from Quito and Lima and a collection of photographs of the Minister himself in the company of various dignitaries. Before the jacaranda-wood desk stood an antique plush bishop's armchair with gilt arms and legs and a hole in the seat. There the *patrón* ensconced himself to satisfy the demands of nature, the end results of which fell into a basin strategically placed beneath the hole. He would sit for hours on that anachronism, writing letters and speeches, reading the newspaper, drinking whisky. When he was through, he rang a bell that resounded through the house like a clap of doom, and I, outraged, climbed the stairs to fetch the vessel, unable to understand why the man could not use the toilet like any normal human being. Don't ask so many questions, girl—the *señor* has always been like that, was the butler's only explanation. After a couple of days I began to feel as if I were drowning; I could not get my breath. I had a perpetual choking sensation, a tickling in my hands and feet, a sheen of cold sweat. Neither the anticipation of witnessing a second banquet nor the fabulous adventures of the locked rooms could rid my mind of that plush chair, the *patrón*'s expression as he pointed out my duty, or the trip to empty that vessel. On the fifth day when I heard the summons of the bell, I pretended for a while to be deaf, busying myself in the kitchen, but within a few minutes the sound was thundering in my brain. Finally, I started slowly up the stairs, getting more worked up with every step. I entered the luxurious room that stank like a stable, knelt down behind the chair, and removed the basin. With absolute aplomb, as if it were something I did every day, I lifted the receptacle high and emptied it over the head of the Minister of State—with a single motion of the wrist liberating myself from humiliation. For an eternal second the Minister sat motionless, eyes bulging.

"Adios, *señor*." I turned on my heel, hurried from the room—in passing bidding farewell to the figures sleeping behind the locked doors—dashed down the stairs, darted past the chauffeurs and bodyguards, ran through the park, and made my escape before the victim could recover from his shock.

I did not dare look for my *madrina*; I had been afraid of her ever since, in the haze of her madness, she had threatened to have me sewed up, too. In a café I asked if I could use the telephone, and I called the house of the bachelor and the spinster to talk with Elvira. I was told she had gone away one morning, carting her coffin in a hired van, and was not coming back. They did not know where she had gone; she had vanished without a word, leaving behind the rest of her belongings. I had the sensation of having lived through this desertion before. I invoked the spirit of my mother to give me courage and, with the manner of someone on her way to an appointment, I started off instinctively toward the center of the city. When I reached the plaza of the Father of the Nation, I almost did not recognize the equestrian statue; it had been cleaned up, and now, instead of being spattered by pigeons and dulled by the verdigris of time, it sparkled with glory. Huberto Naranjo, the nearest thing to a friend I had ever had, was on my mind; I never considered the possibility that he might have forgotten me, or that he might be difficult to find—I had not lived enough to become a pessimist. I sat down on the edge of the fountain where he used to win bets with the tailless fish, and watched the birds and black squirrels and sloths in the trees. By dusk I decided I had waited long enough. I left the fountain and plunged into side streets that had conserved their colonial charm, still untouched by the jackhammers of Italian construction workers. I asked for Naranjo in the shops in the barrio, in the kiosks and cafés where many people knew him—this had been his theater of operations, after all, since he was a young boy. Everyone was pleasant to me, but no one wanted to hazard an answer to my question. I suppose the dictatorship had taught people to keep their mouths shut; you never knew, even a girl in a servant's apron with a dustrag tucked in her belt could be suspect. Finally one person took pity on me and whispered, Go to the Calle República, he hangs around there at night. At that time the red-light district was only a couple of poorly lighted blocks, innocent in comparison with the small city it was to become, but there were already signs displaying girls wearing the black patch of censorship across naked breasts, streetlamps lighting by-the-hour hotels, discreet brothels, and gambling houses. I remembered I had not eaten, but did not dare ask anyone for help: Better dead than beg, little bird, Elvira had drummed into my head. I found a spot in a dark alley, made a nest behind some cardboard cartons, and immediately fell asleep. I was wakened several hours later by strong fingers digging into my shoulder.

"I hear you've been looking for me. What the hell do you want?"

At first I did not recognize him, nor he me. The boy I had known had been left behind long ago. In my eyes Huberto Naranjo was elegant: dark sideburns, oily pompadour, tight pants, cowboy boots, and metal-studded belt. His expression was vaguely arrogant, but in his eyes danced the spark of mischief that nothing in his stormy life could erase. He was barely fifteen, but he looked older because of the way he stood: legs apart, knees slightly bent, head thrown back, a cigarette dangling from his lower lip. I recognized him by his desperado-like bearing; he had walked exactly the same way as a kid in short pants.

"I'm Eva."

"Who?"

"Eva Luna."

Huberto Naranjo ran his hand over his hair, stuck his thumbs in his belt, spit his cigarette to the ground, and peered at me from on high. It was dark where I was and he could not see me very well, but my voice was the same and he caught a glimpse of my eyes in the shadows.

"The one who told stories?"

"Yes."

He immediately dropped his pose as a tough, and was again the boy who as he told me goodbye one day long ago had been mortified by a kiss on the nose. He knelt on one knee, leaned forward, and grinned as happily as if he had found his lost dog. I smiled, too, still groggy with sleep. We shook hands shyly, two sweating palms; flushed, we looked each other over with growing excitement—Hey, how've you been!—until I jumped up, threw my arms around Huberto, and buried my face in his chest, rubbing my cheek against the rock-star shirt and brillian-tined collar, while he gulped and clumsily patted my back in consola-tion.

"I'm a little hungry" was the only thing I could think of to say to keep from bursting into tears.

"Wipe your nose and we'll get something to eat," he said, taking out his pocket comb and reshaping his pompadour from memory.

He led me through empty and silent streets to the one run-down bar still open. He pushed open the doors, playing the cowboy, and we found ourselves in the semi-darkness of a room obscured in cigarette smoke. A jukebox was playing sentimental songs while bored customers were killing time at the pool tables or getting drunk at the bar. Naranjo took me by the hand—behind a counter, down a hallway, and into the kitchen. A young mulatto with a large mustache was slicing meat, wielding his knife like a saber.

"Cut this girl a beefsteak, Negro, and make it a big one, you hear? With two eggs, rice, and fried potatoes. I'm paying."

"Whatever you say, Naranjo. Isn't this the kid who was going around asking for you? She came by here this afternoon. She your girlfriend?" He grinned, with a wink.

"Don't be a shit, Negro. She's my sister."

El Negro served me more food than I could eat in two days. While I ate, Huberto Naranjo watched in silence, measuring with an expert eye the visible changes in my body—little enough, because I was slow to develop. Nevertheless, budding breasts like two lemons were poking out beneath my cotton dress, and already Naranjo was the connoisseur of women he is today; he could envision the future shape of hips and other protuberances, and draw his conclusions.

"Once you asked me to stay with you," I said.

"That was a long time ago."

"I've come to stay now."

"We'll talk about that later. Now eat El Negro's dessert, it's tasty stuff," he replied, and a shadow clouded his face.

You can't stay with me. A woman can't live on the street," Huberto Naranjo announced about six, when not a soul was left in the bar and even the love songs on the jukebox had died. Outside, day was breaking as always: traffic was beginning to move and a few people were hurrying by.

"But it was your idea!"

"Yes, but then you were a kid."

The logic of this reasoning escaped me completely. I felt much better prepared to face my fate now that I was a little older and thought I knew the world. Naranjo explained that it was just the opposite: because I was older, I needed even more to be protected by a man, at least while I was young; later it wouldn't matter, because no one would be interested in me, anyway. I'm not asking you to protect me, no one is after me. I just want to go with you, I argued. He was inflexible, and he put an end to the discussion by banging his fist on the table. O.K., kid, that's all well and good, but I don't give a shit what you say; so shut up. As soon as the city was awake, Huberto grabbed my arm and half-dragged me to the apartment of La Señora; she lived on the sixth floor of a building on Calle República that was in better shape than others of the barrio. The door was opened by a middle-aged woman wearing a dressing gown and slippers with pompons, still muzzy with sleep and grumbling from the taste of a late night in her mouth.

"What do you want, Naranjo?"

"I've brought a friend to you."

"You have a nerve getting me out of bed at this hour!"

But she invited us to come in, offered us a chair, and said she would be right back. After a long wait she returned, switching on lights as she came, and stirring the air with the flutter of her nylon negligee and the scent of overpowering perfume. I had to look twice to realize it was the same person: her eyelashes had grown, her skin looked like china, her pale, lackluster curls lay in petrified rows, her eyelids were two blue petals, her mouth a crushed cherry. But those astounding changes had not spoiled her sympathetic expression or the charm of her smile. La Señora, as everyone called her, laughed at the least excuse, wrinkling her face and rolling back her eyes, a friendly and contagious habit that won me immediately.

"Her name is Eva Luna and she's come to live with you," Naranjo announced.

"You're mad, Naranjo."

"I'll pay."

"Let's see, girl. Turn around and let me look at you. I'm not in that part of the business, but—"

"She's not come to work!" he interrupted.

"I'm not thinking of starting her now—no one would have her, not even gratis—but I can begin to teach her a few things."

"None of that. I want you to think of her as my sister."

"And what do I want with your sister?"

"She can keep you company, she knows how to tell stories."

"What?"

"Tell stories."

"What kind of stories?"

"Oh, love, war, horror—whatever you ask her."

"Is that right!" exclaimed La Señora, observing me with kindness. "Well, whatever we do, we'll have to fix her up a little, Huberto. Look at those elbows and knees, she has skin like an armadillo. You'll have to learn some graces, my girl, and not sit in a chair as if you were riding a bicycle."

"Forget all that junk, just teach her to read."

"Read? Why? Do you want an intellectual?"

Huberto was a man of quick decisions and even at his age already believed his word was law, so he slapped a few bills in the woman's hand, promised to come back often, and left, reeling off instructions to the accompaniment of the loud tapping of his boot heels: "Don't even think of dyeing her hair, because you'll have me to answer to. I don't want her going out at night, things have gone to hell ever since they killed those students—they're finding dead bodies every morning. Don't get her tangled up in your affairs. Remember, she's like my own family. Buy her some classy clothes. I'll pay for everything. Make her drink milk, they say it's fattening. And if you need me, leave a message at El Negro's bar and I'll come flying! Oh . . . and thanks, you know I'm at your service."

He was scarcely out the door when La Señora turned toward me with her wonderful smile, circled around me, examining me, while I stood crestfallen, with downcast eyes and blazing cheeks, for until that moment I had never had reason to take inventory of my own insignificance.

"How old are you?"

"Thirteen, more or less."

"Don't worry, no one is born pretty, it takes patience and hard work to get that way. But it's worth it, because if you're pretty, all your troubles are over. To begin with, lift your head, and smile."

"I'd rather learn to read."

"That's Naranjo's foolishness. Pay no attention to him. Men are arrogant, always telling you what to do. It's better to say yes to everything and then do whatever you please."

La Señora had nocturnal habits: heavy drapes shielded her apartment from daylight; it was illuminated by so many colored lights that at first you thought you had walked into a circus. She showed me the leafy ferns—all plastic—decorating the corners, the bar with its assortment of bottles and glasses, the pristine kitchen without a hint of a pot, her bedroom where a Spanish doll dressed like a flamenco dancer lay on a round bed. In the bathroom, crammed with pots and jars of cosmetics, there were large rose-colored towels.

"All right, strip."

"Uh . . ."

"Take off your clothes. Don't worry," La Señora laughed, "I'm just going to give you a bath."

She ran the water in the bathtub, poured in a handful of bath salts that filled the water with fragrant foam, and I lowered myself into it, timidly at first, then with a sigh of pleasure. When I was almost asleep amid jasmine vapors and a meringue of soapsuds, La Señora reappeared to scrub me with a horsehair mitt. Then she helped me dry myself, sprinkled talcum powder under my arms, and dabbed a few drops of perfume at my neck.

"Get dressed. We'll get something to eat and then go to the hairdresser's," she announced.

Along the way, people turned to stare at La Señora, fascinated by her provocative walk, her air of challenge daring even in this atmosphere of brilliant color and women who moved like toreadors. Her dress was skintight, outlining valleys and hills; jewels glittered at her neck and wrist; her skin was chalk-white—still appreciated in this sector of the city, even though among the wealthy suntans had become the fashion. After breakfast we went to the beauty shop; La Señora's presence—boisterous greetings, perfect smile, courtesan voluptuousness —filled the room. The hairdressers hovered over us with the deference reserved for only the very best clients. Afterward, we set off happily for the arcades in the heart of the city—I with a troubadour's mane, and she with a tortoiseshell butterfly trapped in her curls—leaving behind us a wake of patchouli and hair spray. When it was time to make our purchases, La Señora made me try on everything in the shop except trousers; in her mind, a woman in man's clothing was as grotesque as a man in a skirt. Finally she picked out outfits like those in the movies: ballet slippers, full skirts, elastic belts. My most precious acquisition was a diminutive brassière in which my ridiculous breasts bobbed like two lost plums. When she was finished with me, it was five o'clock in the afternoon, and I was transformed. I stared in the mirror but could not find myself; the glass reflected the image of a disoriented mouse.

Melesio, La Señora's best friend, arrived at dusk.

"Who's this?" he asked, surprised to find someone there.

"To make a long story short, let's say she's the sister of Huberto Naranjo."

"You're not planning to . . ."

"No. He left her here to keep me company."

"*Just* what you need!"

But after a few minutes he had adopted me, and both of us were playing with the doll and listening to rock 'n' roll records—an extraordinary discovery for someone accustomed to the salsas, boleros, and rancheras of the kitchen radio. That night for the first time I tasted cream-filled pastries and rum with pineapple juice, the basic diet in that house. Later, La Señora and Melesio went off to their respective jobs, leaving me on the round bed hugging the Spanish doll, lulled to sleep by the frenetic rock rhythm, and with the absolute certainty that it had been one of the happiest days of my life.

Melesio tweezed his facial hairs, then ran ether-soaked cotton over his face, so his skin was the texture of silk; he took pains with his long-fingered, slender hands, and every night brushed his hair one hundred times. He was tall, with strong bones, but he moved with such delicacy that he gave the impression of being fragile. He never talked about his family and it would be years later, during his time in the penal colony on Santa María, that La Señora learned anything about his past. His father had been a bear of a man who had emigrated from Sicily and who every time he found his son playing with his sister's toys gave him a beating accompanied by cries of *Ricchione! Pederasta! Mascalzone!* His mother dutifully cooked the ritual pasta but stood her ground like a tigress when the father tried to force his son to kick a ball, box, drink, or, later, go to whorehouses. When she was alone with her son, she tried to find out what his true feelings were, but Melesio's only explanation was that there was a woman inside him and she could not get used to the male body in which she was trapped as surely as if she were in a straitjacket.

That was all he ever said, and later when psychiatrists addled his brain with their questions, his answer was always the same: I am not homosexual, I am a woman. This body is a mistake. Nothing more, nothing less. He left home as soon as he could convince his *mamma* that it would be worse to stay and die at the hands of his own father. After working at several jobs, he ended up teaching Italian in a language institute where they paid very little but the schedule was convenient. Once a month he met his mother in the park, handed her an envelope with twenty percent of his earnings, whatever they were, and soothed her with lies about fictitious courses in architecture. His father's name never crossed their lips, and after a year his mother began wearing widow's weeds; although the bear remained in perfect health, she had killed him in her heart. Melesio got by for a while, but only rarely did he have enough money, and there were days when he kept on his feet with coffee alone. It was at that point that he met La Señora, and from the moment of their meeting his life took a turn for the better. He had grown up in a climate of tragic opera, and the musical-comedy tone of his new friend was balm for the wounds he had suffered at home and continued to suffer every day in the street because of his effeminate behavior. They were not lovers. For her, sex was nothing but the mainstay of her business, and at her age she had no energy to waste on that kind of nonsense; for Melesio, intimacy with a woman was out of the question. With uncommon wisdom they established from the beginning a relationship devoid of jealousy, possessiveness, rudeness, and other disadvantages of carnal love. She was twenty years older than he, but in spite of that difference—perhaps even because of it—they had a splendid friendship.

"I heard about a job that would be just right for you. Would you like to sing in a bar?" La Señora asked one day.

"I don't know . . . I've never done it."

"No one would recognize you, you'd be masquerading as a woman. It's a cabaret for transvestites, but don't worry about that—they're decent people and they pay well. The work's easy, you'll see . . ."

"Even *you* think I'm one of those!"

"Don't take offense. Singing there doesn't mean anything. It's just like any other job," replied La Señora, whose good sense reduced everything to a practical level.

With some difficulty she succeeded in overcoming Melesio's prejudices, and convinced him of the advantages of the offer. At first he was
shocked by the atmosphere of the place, but with his first performance
he discovered he not only had a woman inside him, but an actress as
well. He had a talent for music and theater unrevealed until then, and
his act, which began as an opening number in the program, ended with
star billing. He began to live a double life, by day the sober schoolteacher and by night a fantastic creation smothered in feathers and
rhinestones. His finances prospered; he was able to buy his mother presents, move to a decent room, eat and dress respectably. He would have
been happy had he not been invaded by uncontrollable distress every
time he thought of his genitals. He suffered when he looked at himself
naked in the mirror, or demonstrated—quite against his will—that he
functioned like a normal man. He was tormented by a recurrent obsession: he imagined a self-mutilation with a pair of pruning shears; a
single contraction of his biceps and *zap!* the hated appendage fell to the
floor like a bloody snake.

He moved into a rented room in the Jewish district on the far side
of the city, but every evening before work he took time to visit La
Señora. He arrived about dusk, when the red and green and blue lights
were coming on and the ladies of the night positioning themselves in
windows and working the streets in full battle dress. Even before I heard
the doorbell, I would know Melesio was there and run to meet him.
After he held me up in his arms, he always said, You haven't gained an
ounce since yesterday, don't they give you anything to eat? and, like a
magician, he would pluck some sweet out of the air. He liked contem-
porary music, but his public demanded romantic ballads in French or
English. He spent hours learning new songs for his repertoire, and as
he learned them, taught me. I memorized them without understanding
a single word; there was no *"This pencil is red, is this pencil blue?"* or any
other phrase from the beginning English course I had listened to on the
radio. We used to play children's games that neither of us had had a
chance to play when we were young; we made houses for the Spanish
doll, sang rounds in Italian, and danced and chased each other around.
I loved to watch him as he put on his makeup, and I helped him sew
the beads on the costumes for the cabaret.

In her youth La Señora had analyzed her possibilities and concluded that she lacked the patience to earn a living through respectable means. So she began working as a specialist in erudite massage, and enjoyed a certain success at first, because such novelties were unknown in these latitudes; with the population growth and uncontrolled immigration, however, she encountered unfair competition. Asian women brought with them centuries-old techniques impossible to improve upon, and Portuguese girls offered unthinkably low prices. That removed La Señora from this ceremonial art, since she was not inclined to perform acrobatics, or to give anything away—not even to her husband, if she'd had one. Another woman would have resigned herself to exercising her trade in the conventional way, but La Señora was a woman of imagination. She invented some bizarre devices with which she planned to invade the marketplace, but she could not find anyone willing to finance her. For lack of commercial vision in this country, her ideas—like so many others—were grabbed up by North Americans, who now hold the patents and sell her models around the globe. The automatic telescoping penis, the battery-operated finger, and the never-fail breast with candy nipple were her creations, and if she were paid the just royalty she would be a millionaire. But she was ahead of her time; no one dreamed then that such contrivances would have mass-market appeal, and it did not seem profitable to manufacture them to specification for the use of a few specialists. Nor could she obtain loans to open her own factory. Blinded by the petroleum boom, the government ignored non-traditional industries. She was not discouraged by that setback. She prepared a mauve velvet-bound catalogue of her girls and discreetly sent it to the nation's highest officials. A few days later she received the first inquiry; it was for a party on La Sirena, a coral-reef- and shark-protected private island that does not appear on any navigation charts and can only be reached by small plane. Once her original enthusiasm had passed and she became aware of the magnitude of her responsibility, she began to ponder the best way to satisfy such a distinguished clientele. At that moment, as Melesio told me years later, her eyes fell on us. We had set the Spanish doll in one corner and from the opposite side of the room were tossing coins into her ruffled skirt. As she watched us, La Señora's creative mind began shuffling possibilities, and she came up with the idea of substituting one of her girls for the doll. She remembered other childhood games, and to each she added some obscene touch, transforming it into a novel diversion for the party guests. After that, she was in constant demand with bankers, magnates, and leading government figures, who paid for her services from public funds. The best thing about this country, she used to sigh with delight, is that there is enough corruption for everyone. She was very strict with her girls. She did not recruit them with the deceitful tricks of the barrio pimps, but told them exactly what she had in mind, to avoid any misunderstandings and dispose of scruples right from the beginning. If one of the girls failed to show up—whether because of illness, grief, or unforeseen catastrophe—she was immediately dismissed. Do your job with enthusiasm, girls, we're working for high-class gentlemen. In this business, she told them, you have to have a mystique. She charged more than the local competition, because she had proved that inexpensive peccadilloes are neither enjoyed nor remembered. On one occasion, when it came time to settle the bill, a colonel of the *guardia* who had spent the night with one of her girls pulled out his service revolver and refused to pay, threatening to arrest her if she insisted. La Señora never batted an eyelash. Within a month the officer called and asked for three well-disposed ladies to entertain some foreign delegates, and quite amiably she suggested that he invite his wife, his mother, and his grandmother if he wanted to fuck for free. Two hours later an orderly appeared with a check and a crystal box containing three royal purple orchids, which, as Melesio explained, in the language of flowers represented three supremely potent feminine charms, although possibly the customer did not know it and chose them only for the elegant packaging.

Eavesdropping on the girls' conversations, I learned in a few weeks more than many persons discover in a lifetime. Intent on improving the quality of her services, La Señora bought numbers of French books that were furtively supplied by the blind man of the local kiosk. I doubt, really, that they were of much use, for the girls complained that when the pants were down, the high-class gentlemen bolted a few drinks and repeated the same old routines, so all their study was for nothing. When I was alone in the apartment, I used to take the forbidden books from their hiding place and settle into a comfortable chair. They were eye-opening. Even though I could not read them, the illustrations alone put ideas in my head that went, I am sure, beyond anatomical possibilities.

That was a good time in my life, in spite of having the sensation of floating on a cloud, surrounded by both lies and things left unspoken. Occasionally I thought I glimpsed the truth, but soon found myself once again lost in a forest of ambiguities. In that house day and night were reversed, you lived at night and slept during the day; the girls became entirely different creatures once they put on their makeup; my *patrona* was a tangle of contradictions; Melesio was without sex or age; even the food we ate seemed like birthday treats, not ordinary everyday food. Money itself became unreal. La Señora kept fat bundles of bills in shoe boxes from which she took enough for daily expenses, apparently never keeping accounts. I found money everywhere, and at first thought she left it where I would find it to test my honesty; later I realized it was not a trap, but mere profusion and total disorder.

More than once I heard La Señora say she had a horror of senti-mental ties, but I think she was betrayed by her true nature and, as had happened with Melesio, she ended up being fond of me. Let's open the windows and let in the noise and light, I urged her, and she agreed. Let's buy a bird to sing to us and a flowerpot with real ferns we can watch grow, I suggested, and she did that as well. I want to learn to read, I insisted, and she was willing to teach me but other affairs inter-fered. Now that so many years have passed and I can remember her from the perspective of experience, I think she did not have a happy life; she survived in a brutal milieu, debased by a vulgar profession. She must have imagined that somewhere there were a chosen few who could allow themselves the luxury of goodness, and decided to protect me from the sordidness of Calle República, to see if she could play a trick on fate and rescue me from a life like hers. In the beginning she meant to lie to me about her business activities, but when she found me ready to devour the world, errors and all, she changed her mind. I learned later through Melesio that La Señora made a compact with the other women to keep me innocent, and clung to it so stubbornly that I ended up embodying the best of each of them. They tried to keep me isolated from what was gross and shoddy, and in doing so won new dignity for their own lives. They would beg me to tell them what was happening in the current radio serial, and I would invent a dramatic ending that never coincided with the real one, but that did not matter to them. They invited me to go with them to Mexican movies, and afterward we would go to the Espiga de Oro tearoom to talk about the performance. They liked me to improve on the plot, changing the restrained love story of a simple Mexican cowboy to a blood-and-guts tragedy. Your stories are better than the movies, there's more suffering, they would sob, mouths filled with chocolate cake.

Huberto Naranjo was the only one who never asked me for stories; he thought they were a stupid diversion. When he came to visit, he arrived with his pockets filled with money that he bestowed with open hands, never explaining where he had got it. He brought me presents of frilly dresses with ruffles and lace, baby-doll shoes, little-girl pocketbooks, which all the girls praised because they wanted to keep me in the limbo of childish purity, but which I rejected, offended. "I wouldn't put this on the Spanish doll. Can't you see I'm not a baby anymore?"

"You can't go around looking like a streetwalker. Are they teaching you how to read?" he would ask, and be furious when he learned my illiteracy had not been reduced by so much as one letter.

I was very careful not to tell him that in other ways my education was advancing by leaps and bounds. I loved him with one of those adolescent passions that leave their mark for life, but I could never get Naranjo to notice my fervent adoration; each time I hinted at it, he would push me away, his ears red as fire.

"Leave me alone. What you need to do is study to be a teacher or a nurse—those are decent jobs for a woman."

"Don't you love me?"

"I take care of you, that's enough."

Alone in my bed I would hug my pillow, praying that my legs would fill out and my breasts hurry up and grow. I never, however, connected Huberto Naranjo with the illustrations in La Señora's books of instruction, or the chatter I overheard from the girls. I could not imagine that such capers had any relation to love: they were simply a trade you practiced for a living, like sewing or typing. Love was what was in songs and the serials on the radio—sighs, kisses, ardent words.

I wanted to lie in the same bed with Huberto, my head on his shoulder, sleeping by his side, but my fantasies were still chaste.

Melesio was the only real artist in the cabaret where he worked nights. The rest were a sorry lot: a group of queens billed as the Blue Ballet strung together by the tail to form a regrettable chorus line; a dwarf who performed indecent feats with a milk bottle; and a gentleman of advanced years whose act consisted of lowering his trousers, turning his rear to the spectators, and expelling three billiard balls. The audience laughed uproariously at these vaudeville tricks, but when Melesio, swathed in feathers, his wig worthy of a royal courtesan, made his entrance singing in French, absolute silence reigned in the room. The audience did not whistle or shout insulting jokes the way they did at the chorus line, because even the least sensitive of the customers could appreciate his talent. During those hours in the cabaret, he was a star, desired and admired, sparkling beneath the spotlights, the center of all eyes; there he fulfilled his dream of being a woman. After his act, he retired to the unsanitary hole he had been assigned as a dressing room and removed his diva's costume. From a hook, his feathers resembled a dying ostrich; on the table his wig was a trophy from the guillotine, and the rhinestones scattered across a tin tray were the booty of a cheated pirate. As he removed his makeup with cold cream, his masculine face appeared. He put on trousers and jacket, closed the door, and, once outside, was assaulted by profound sadness, knowing he had left the best of himself behind. He would go to El Negro's bar and get something to eat, sitting alone at a corner table and reliving his hour of happiness on the stage. Then, in the night air, he walked home through empty streets, climbed the stairs to his room, bathed, and fell into bed to stare into the darkness until he fell asleep.

When homosexuality ceased to be taboo and showed itself in the light of day, it became fashionable, as people said, to "visit the queers on their own turf." The wealthy arrived in chauffeur-driven cars, elegant, noisy, brightly colored birds who shouldered their way through the regular customers and sat down to drink watered champagne, sniff a line of cocaine, and applaud the artists. The women were the most enthusiastic: refined descendants of prosperous immigrants, dressed in

Paris gowns, exhibiting paste replicas of jewels kept in safe-deposit boxes; it was they who invited the performers to the table to drink a toast. They repaired the damage the next day: Turkish baths and beauty treatments to counter the effects of cheap liquor, smoke, and late hours. But it was worth it: those excursions were the *de rigueur* subject of conversation at the Country Club. The prestige of the extraordinary Mimí, Melesio's stage name, spread from mouth to mouth that season; the echo of her fame, however, did not ripple beyond the living rooms of the very rich. In the Jewish quarter where Melesio lived, or in Calle República, no one knew and no one cared that the quiet professor of Italian and Mimí were one and the same.

The residents of the red-light district had organized as a matter of survival. Even the police respected their tacit code of honor, restricting themselves to intervening in public fights, patrolling the streets from time to time, collecting their commissions, and keeping an ear to the ground through informers, more interested in political vigilance than anything else. Every Friday a sergeant appeared at La Señora's apartment; he parked his car on the sidewalk where everyone could see it and know he was collecting his share of the earnings—no one should think for a minute that the authorities were ignorant of that madam's business. His visit lasted no more than ten or fifteen minutes, enough time to smoke a cigarette, tell a couple of jokes, and leave happy, with a bottle of whisky under his arm and his percentage in his pocket. The arrangements were the same for everyone and were basically fair, allowing the officers to fatten their incomes and their victims to work in peace. I had been living at La Señora's house for only a few months when a new sergeant was assigned, and overnight the good relations went down the drain. Business was threatened by the demands of the new officer, who had no respect for tradition. His ill-timed raids, threats, and blackmail put an end to the peace of mind so necessary for prosperity. The community tried to reach an agreement with him, but the man was so greedy it affected his judgment. His presence broke the delicate equilibrium of the Calle República and spread confusion everywhere. People gathered in bars to discuss the issue: It's not possible anymore to live the way God intended us to. We must do something before this bastard wrecks everything. Moved by the chorus of laments, Melesio decided to intervene even though he was not directly affected;

he offered to draft a letter to be signed by all concerned and to take it
to the Chief of Police, with a copy for the Minister of the Interior, since
both had been benefiting for years and therefore had a moral obligation
to listen. All too soon it would be proved that not only was the plan
ill-conceived, but putting it into practice was even worse. Nevertheless,
within a few days they had gathered an impressive list of signatures—
not an easy task since the details had to be explained to each
individual—and La Señora went in person to deliver the petition. Twenty-
four hours later, at dawn, an hour when everyone was sleeping, El
Negro awakened La Señora with the news that they were searching the
area house by house. The damned sergeant had brought a vanload of
officers from the vice squad, which was notorious for slipping weapons
and drugs into pockets to implicate the innocent. Breathless, El Negro
recounted how they had burst into the cabaret like commandos and
arrested all the artists and part of the audience—discreetly excluding
elegant clientele. Among those arrested had been Melesio, surprised in
his carnival costume of glitter and plumed tail and charged with peder-
asty and trafficking, two words unknown to me at that time. El Negro
rushed off to spread the bad news to the rest of his friends, leaving La
Señora in an acute state of nerves.

"Get dressed, Eva! Get going! Put everything in a suitcase. No!
There isn't time for that! We have to get out of here . . . Poor Melesio!"

She raced around the apartment half-naked, bumping into chrome
chairs and mirrored tables as she threw on her clothes. Last, she picked
up the shoe box filled with money and rushed to the service stairs,
followed by me, still half-asleep and totally unaware of what was
happening—although it was obvious it was something very serious. We
ran down the stairs just as the police were pouring into the elevator
downstairs. On the ground floor we were met by the concierge in her
nightgown, a Galician woman with a motherly heart who in normal
times used to trade us delicious potato-and-sausage omelets for bottles
of cologne. When she saw our disarray and heard the shouting of the
uniformed men and the sirens of patrol cars in the street, she understood
that it was no moment to ask questions. She motioned us to follow and
led us to the basement of the building; there an emergency door communicated with a nearby parking garage and we were able to escape
without crossing Calle República, which was swarming with police. Af-

ter that undignified flight, La Señora stopped, gasping for breath, and leaned against the wall of a hotel, nearly fainting. Then for the first time she seemed to see me.

"What are *you* doing here?"

"I'm escaping, too."

"Go away! If they find you with me, they'll accuse me of corrupting minors!"

"Where do you want me to go? I don't have any place."

"I don't know, child. Look for Huberto Naranjo. I have to hide and then get help for Melesio. I can't worry about you now."

She disappeared down the street, and the last I saw of her were her hips in the flowered skirt, bobbling not with the old daring but, rather, with frank uncertainty. I hunched against a building as police cars howled and pimps, perverts, and prostitutes streamed past me. Someone told me to get away quick; the letter Melesio had written and everyone signed had fallen into the hands of the newspapers, and the scandal, which was costing the job of more than one Minister and several high-level police officers, would soon be taking its toll on us. They were searching every building, house, hotel, and bar in the district; they were arresting everyone in sight—even the blind man of the kiosk—and they had set off so many tear-gas bombs that several people had been poisoned and one baby had died because his mother was with a client and could not rescue him. For three days and nights, the only topic of conversation was the "War on the Underworld," as the press labeled it. It was immediately branded the "Revolt of the Whores" by popular wit, however, and immortalized in the verses of poets.

I found myself without a centavo, as had so often happened in the past, and would happen again in the future. And Huberto Naranjo was no help; he was on the far side of the city when all the ruckus began. Shaken, I sank down between two columns of a building and gathered strength to combat the sense of abandonment I had felt on other occasions, and was beginning to experience now. I buried my face between my knees and summoned my mother; almost immediately I was aware of the scent of clean starched cotton. Then she was before me, long hair rolled in a bun at her neck, smoke-colored eyes shining in her freckled face, telling me that I was not to blame for all this pandemonium and there was no reason to be afraid: I should forget my fear and we would walk along together. I stood up and took her hand.

I could not find anyone I knew, and did not dare return to the Calle República; every time I went near it I saw parked patrol cars I supposed must be waiting for me. No one had heard anything of Elvira for a long time; and I rejected the idea of looking for my *madrina*, who by then was completely mad, interested only in playing the lottery, counting on the saints to give her the winning number on the telephone, but the celestial court was as mistaken in their predictions as any mortal.

The famous Revolt of the Whores threw everything into turmoil. At first the public applauded the energetic action of the government, and the Bishop issued a declaration supporting the hard line against vice. Public opinion was reversed, however, when in an issue entitled *Sodom and Gomorrah* a humor magazine edited by a group of artists and intellectuals published caricatures of important officials implicated in the corruption. Two of the drawings were perilously like the General and the Man of the Gardenia, whose participation in trafficking of all kinds was well known, although until that moment no one had dared suggest it in print. Security forces leveled the editorial offices, smashed the presses, burned paper stock, arrested any employees they could locate, and declared the publisher a fugitive from justice. The next day his body—with throat slit and bearing clear signs of torture—was found in a parked car in the center of the city. No one had a moment's doubt about who was responsible for the death: the same persons responsible for the deaths of university students and the disappearance of countless others tossed into bottomless wells in the hope that by the time their bodies were found they would be mistaken for fossils. The affair of the magazine, however, was the last straw for a public that for years had endured the abuses of dictatorship, and within a few hours a massive demonstration was organized that was very different from the flash-in-the-pan rallies the opposition had mounted in vain protests against the government. The streets near the plaza of the Father of the Nation were flooded with thousands of students and workers waving flags, pasting up posters, and burning tires. It seemed that at last fear had given way to rebellion. In the midst of the tumult a small, bizarre column came marching down one of the side streets: the citizens of the Calle República, who had failed to recognize the extent of the public indignation and believed the protest to be in their defense. Greatly moved, several nymphs clambered onto an improvised platform to offer appreciation for the massive gesture of solidarity with the "forgotten of society," as they called themselves. And it is only right that this is so, my fellow citizens, for how would mothers, sweethearts, and wives get a peaceful night's sleep if we weren't here to carry out our job? Where would their sons, sweethearts, and husbands let off steam if we did not fulfill our duty? The crowd roared its approval so enthusiastically that it almost seemed like Carnival. That mood did not last long because the General had ordered the Army into the streets. Tanks rumbled forward with the solemnity of pachyderms, but not very far: the colonial paving in the heart of the city caved in, and the people used those same cobblestones to resist authority. There were so many wounded and battered that a state of siege was declared and a curfew imposed. These measures merely increased the violence, which exploded across the city like summer fires. Students placed homemade bombs even in the pulpits of the churches; mobs tore down the metal shutters of Portuguese shopkeepers and looted their merchandise; a group of students captured a policeman and marched him naked down the Avenida Independencia. There was widespread destruction, as well as victims to mourn, but this stupendous brawl offered the public an occasion to shout until they were hoarse, to be unruly, and to feel free once again. There were scores of impromptu bands playing on empty gasoline drums, and conga lines snaking to the rhythms of Cuba and Jamaica. The riot lasted four days, but finally spirits were subdued, primarily because everyone was exhausted and no one could remember the exact cause for the uprising. The Minister responsible tendered his resignation and was replaced by someone I once knew. As I passed a kiosk, I saw his picture on the front page of a newspaper; I barely recognized him, because the image of that stern and frowning man with upraised hand did not correspond to the one of the man I had left sitting humiliated in a bishop's plush chair.

By the end of the week the government had regained control of the city and the General had left for a rest on his private island, basking in the Caribbean sun, confident that he held even his compatriots' dreams in his fist. He expected to govern for the rest of his life; why else did he have the Man of the Gardenia on the alert for conspiracies in barracks and streets? Besides, he was satisfied that the spark of democracy had not lasted long enough to leave a permanent mark in people's memories. The final outcome of that unparalleled free-for-all was a few dead and an undetermined number of prisoners and exiles. Once again the casinos and seraglios of Calle República opened for business, and the occupants returned to their habitual labors as if nothing had happened. The authorities continued to receive their cut and the new Minister held his post without mishap, after ordering the police not to bother anyone engaged in criminal activities but to devote themselves, as usual, to persecuting political enemies and hunting down madmen and beggars: shave their heads, douse them with disinfectant, and release them on the highways to disappear through *natural* means. The General was immutable before the storm of gossip, certain that accusations of abuse and corruption would merely solidify his prestige. He had taken as his own El Benefactor's lesson, and believed that history hallows audacious leaders, and that the people consider honesty to be an undesirable trait in a real man, something befitting priests and women. He was convinced that learned men exist for the purpose of being honored with statues, and that it is nice to have two or three to exhibit in textbooks, but when it is a question of power, only the high-handed, feared caudillo comes out on top.

I wandered around for days after the Revolt of the Whores. I had no part in it because I was trying to keep my distance from any disturbances. In spite of the visible presence of my mother, at first I felt a vague burning in the pit of my stomach, and my mouth felt dry—sour and gritty—but I got used to it. I abandoned the habits of cleanliness my *madrina* and Elvira had drilled into me, and stopped going to the fountains and public water taps to bathe. I turned into a filthy urchin who rambled aimlessly by day, scavenging food, and by night took refuge in dark corners to wait out the curfew when the cars of the Security Force were all that were moving through the streets.

Then one evening about six I met Riad Halabí. He was walking down the street, and when he reached the corner where I was standing, he stopped and stared at me. I looked up and saw a heavy, middle-aged man with thick-lidded, sleepy eyes. I think he was wearing a light-colored suit and a necktie, but I always think of him in the impeccable batiste guayabera shirts that I would soon be ironing with such painstaking care.

"Psst, little girl," he called in a hoarse voice.

It was then I noticed the disfiguration of his mouth, a deep cleft between upper lip and nose, and separated teeth that revealed the tip of his tongue. He produced a handkerchief and placed it over his mouth to hide the deformity, smiling at me with his olive eyes. I started to back away but suddenly was overcome by extreme fatigue, an irresistible longing to give up and go to sleep. My knees doubled under me and I sank to the sidewalk, gazing up at this stranger through a thick mist. He bent over, took my arms, lifted me to my feet, forced me to take one step, two, three, until I found myself sitting in a café before an enormous sandwich and a glass of milk. I took them in trembling hands, breathing the aroma of warm bread. As I chewed and swallowed, I felt the dull pain, the sharp pleasure, the fierce anxiety that I had known since only infrequently in the embrace of love. I gulped my food, but was unable to finish; again I felt dizzy, and this time the nausea was uncontrollable and I vomited. All around me people turned away in revulsion and the waiter began to shout insults, but the man silenced him with a banknote, and with his arm around my waist led me outside.

"Where do you live, hija? Do you have a family?"

I shook my head, ashamed. We walked to a nearby street where a broken-down pickup truck was waiting, loaded with boxes and sacks. He helped me in, covered me with his jacket, started the motor, and headed off toward the east.

We drove all night through a dark landscape where the only lights were the checkpoints of the guardia, the trucks rolling toward the oil fields, and the Palace of the Poor, which for thirty seconds materialized like a hallucination at one side of the road. Once it had been the summer home of El Benefactor. The most beautiful mulatto women in the Caribbean had danced there, but the very day the tyrant died, indigents began to take it over, timidly at first, and then in droves. They walked into the gardens and, since no one stopped them, continued to advance; they climbed broad stairways rimmed with bronze-studded carved columns; they wandered through sumptuous marble salons—white from Almería, rose from Valencia, and gray from Carrara—and arborescent, arabesque, and cipolin marble corridors; they invaded bathrooms of onyx, jade, and malachite; and finally they settled in with children, grandparents, chattel, and livestock. Invisible lines divided the commodious rooms, and each family staked out its place: hammocks were hung, rococo furniture was splintered to fuel cookstoves, children dismantled the chromium plumbing, adolescents made love among the garden statuary, and the elderly sowed tobacco in gilded bathtubs. Someone ordered the *guardia* to remove the interlopers, with firearms if necessary, but the officials became lost along the way. They could not evict the occupants because the palace and everything inside had become invisible to the human eye; it had entered another dimension where life continued without aggravation.

The sun had risen by the time we reached our destination: Agua Santa, one of those towns drowsing in the doldrums of the provinces, washed by rain, radiant in the incredible tropical light. The truck bumped down a main street lined with colonial houses, each with a small garden and chicken coop, and came to a stop before a whitewashed dwelling that was more solid and sturdy than the others. At that hour the main door was still closed and I did not realize it was a shop.

"We're home," the man said.

SIX

R iad Halabí was one of those persons who are un-
done by their own compassion. He loved others so much that he
tried to spare them the unpleasantness of his cleft lip: he always
carried a handkerchief in his hand to conceal it; he never ate or
drank in public; he rarely smiled; and he tried always to stand
either with his back to the light or in the shadow, to hide his
defect. He lived his whole life without realizing the sympathy he
evoked, or the love he sowed in my heart. He had come to this
country when he was fifteen, alone, without money or friends,
carrying a tourist visa stamped on a false Turkish passport his
father had bought from a dishonest consul in the Near East. His
mission was to make his fortune and send money to his family,
and although he did not accomplish the former, he never failed in
the latter. He educated his brothers, provided a dowry for each of
his sisters, and bought an olive grove for his parents, a mark of

prestige in the land of refugees where he had grown up. He spoke Spanish with all the native idioms but with the undeniable accent of the desert; from the desert, too, came his sense of hospitality and passion for water. During his first years as an immigrant, he lived on bread, bananas, and coffee. He slept on the floor of a textile factory owned by a compatriot; in exchange for a roof over his head, he was expected to clean the building, carry the bundles and bales of thread and cotton, and tend to the mousetraps; the part of the day not devoted to these responsibilities was spent in various other chores. Soon he realized that more substantial earnings were to be had, and chose to dedicate himself to commerce. He peddled underclothes and watches in offices; in the homes of the middle class he tempted maids with cosmetics and cheap necklaces; he dispensed maps and pencils in schools; in the barracks he sold photos of naked film stars and religious prints of Saint Gabriel, patron saint of soldiers and recruits. The competition was fierce and the possibilities for advancement almost nil; for him, the only virtue in being a salesman was his pleasure in bargaining, which he did not use to drive a hard bargain but as an excuse for exchanging ideas with his customers and making friends. He was honest and unambitious; he lacked all the attributes for success in that trade, at least in the capital. For these reasons, his countrymen advised him to take his merchandise to the small towns of the interior where people were more ingenuous. Riad Halabí set off with the same trepidation his ancestors had felt as they began a long trek across the desert. At first he traveled by bus, until he was able to buy a motorcycle on credit and strap on a large box behind the seat. Astride that machine he traveled burro paths and sheer mountainsides with the endurance of the tribesmen from whom he was descended. Later he acquired an ancient but rugged automobile, and finally a truck. There was no place he could not go in that vehicle. He climbed the peaks of the Andes over indescribable roads, offering his wares in hamlets where the air was so clear that you could see angels at dusk; he knocked on every door up and down the coast, sweltering in the hot breath of the siesta, feverish in the humidity, stopping from time to time to give assistance to iguanas whose feet were stuck in the melted asphalt; he crossed dunes, navigating without a compass across a sea of sands shifting in the wind, never looking back, so that the seduction of oblivion would not turn his blood to chocolate. At last he came to a region that had been prosperous in bygone years; dugouts laden with aromatic cacao beans had floated down its rivers, but now it was a place ruined by oil fever, left to be devoured by the jungle and man's indolence. Enamored of that geography, he traveled the countryside with wondering eyes and grateful heart, recalling his own dry and harsh land where an antlike tenacity was required to cultivate an orange, in contrast to this place prodigal in fruit and flowers, a paradise protected from all evil. There, even for someone as disinclined toward profit as he, he found it easy to sell any trinket, but he had a soft heart and could not make himself rich at the expense of the ignorance of others. He was taken with the people, lords in their poverty and abandonment. Wherever he went he was received as a friend, just as his grandfather had welcomed strangers to his tent in the belief that a guest is sacred. In each country hovel, he was offered a glass of lemonade, a black and aromatic coffee, a chair where he could rest in the shade. These were happy, generous, and plain-speaking people whose word had the force of a contract. He would open his suitcase and display his merchandise on the hard dirt floor. His hosts would examine those goods of dubious utility with a courteous smile, and buy something not to offend him; but many had no way to pay because only rarely did they have money in hand. They were, in fact, suspicious of the paper money that today was worth something and tomorrow might be withdrawn from circulation, according to the whim of the current leader, printed paper that could vanish if you turned your back—as had happened with the collection for Aid to Lepers, devoured by a goat that ambled into the treasurer's office. They preferred coins, which at least weighed in the pocket, rang on the counter, and shone as real money should. The oldest among them still hid their savings in clay jugs and kerosene tins buried in the patio, for they had never heard of a bank. Very few lost any sleep over financial matters and most bartered for goods. Riad Halabí adjusted to these conditions and renounced the paternal edict to amass a fortune.

One of his trips took him to Agua Santa. When he drove into the town there was not a soul in the streets and at first he thought it was abandoned; but then he came upon a crowd gathered in front of the post office. That was the memorable morning when the son of the schoolteacher Inés had died of a gunshot wound to the head. The murderer was the owner of a house surrounded by steep hillsides where mangoes thrived without the hand of man. The children used to pick up the fallen fruit, in spite of the threats of the owner, an outsider who had inherited the small hacienda and still had not shed the avarice of some city men. The trees were so heavy with fruit that the branches broke beneath the weight, but it was pointless to try to sell the mangoes. Who would buy them? There was no reason to pay for something that the good earth gave away. That day the son of the schoolteacher Inés, like all his schoolmates, took the long way to school to pick a mango. The bullet entered his forehead and exited through the back of his neck before he had time to realize what the spark and thunder that exploded in his face might be.

Riad Halabí stopped his truck in Agua Santa moments after the children had carried in the body on a makeshift stretcher and set it down before the post-office door. The whole town came to look. The mother stared at her son, still not comprehending what had happened, while four uniformed men held back the townspeople from taking justice into their own hands; they fulfilled that duty with little enthusiasm, however, because they knew the law and were aware that the homicide would go unpunished. Riad Halabí joined the crowd with the presentiment that this place would play a role in his destiny; he had come to the end of his pilgrimage. As soon as he heard the details of what had happened, he took charge without a moment's hesitation. No one seemed surprised by his behavior; it was as if they had been waiting for him. He opened a path through the crowd, picked up the child's body in his arms, and carried it to the schoolteacher's house where he improvised a bier on the dining-room table. Then he brewed and served coffee, producing no little surprise among the mourners, who had never seen a man busying himself in the kitchen. He sat through the wake with the mother, and his firm and discreet presence led many to believe he was a distant relative. The next morning, he organized the burial and helped lower the coffin into the grave with such sincere anguish that *señorita* Inés wished that the stranger were the father of her son. When they had tamped down the earth over the grave, Riad Halabí turned toward the people assembled there and, covering his mouth with his handkerchief, proposed a plan for channeling their collective anger. Straight from the cemetery, each of them went to pick mangoes; they filled sacks, baskets, bags, and wheelbarrows, and then converged upon the property of the murderer, who when he saw them approaching had the impulse to fire and frighten them off, but thought better of it and ran and hid among the reeds by the riverbank. The crowd advanced in silence, surrounded the house, broke windows and doors, and emptied their load inside. Then they went back for more. All day they hauled mangoes, until there were none left on the trees and the house was filled to the rooftop. The juicy fruit burst open, soaking the walls and running across the floor like sweet blood. At nightfall, when the harvesters had returned home, the criminal crept from the water and jumped into his car and escaped, never to return. In the days that followed, the sun beat down on the house, converting it into an enormous saucepan in which the mangoes slowly simmered; the building took on an ocher color; it grew soggy and weak, and burst open and rotted, impregnating the town for years with the odor of marmalade.

From that day, Riad Halabí considered himself a native of Agua Santa; he was accepted as such, and there he built his home and his shop. Like many rural dwellings, his was square, with rooms arranged around a patio filled with tall, leafy vegetation to provide shade—palms, ferns, and a few fruit trees. This patio was the heart of the house; it afforded passage from one room to another, and there life unfolded. In its center Riad Halabí constructed a large and serene Arabian fountain that soothed the spirit with the incomparable music of water over stones. Around the edge of this interior garden he installed a tile trough with clear flowing water, and in every room he placed a pottery bowl filled with moist flower petals whose perfume made the suffocating heat more bearable. The dwelling had many doors, like the houses of the wealthy, and with time it grew in order to make space for new storerooms. The shop occupied the three large front rooms; the living quarters, kitchen, and bathroom were in the rear. Little by little, Riad Halabí's business became the most prosperous in the region. Anything could be bought there: food, fertilizer, disinfectants, cloth, medicines; if something was not in stock, the Turk was charged with fetching it on his next trip. He called the shop The Pearl of the Orient, in honor of Zulema, his wife.

Agua Santa was a modest village, with adobe, wood, and reed houses lining the roadway; machetes defended it against a wild vegetation that would engulf it in an instant's inattention. The country's waves of immigrants had not washed as far as this backwater, nor had the uproar of modern life; people were affable, their pleasures simple, and if it had not been for the proximity of the penal colony on Santa María, Agua Santa would have been a hamlet like any other in that region. The presence of the *guardia* and the whorehouse, however, gave it a touch of cosmopolitanism. For six days of the week, life went along without incident, but on Saturday they changed the guard at the prison and the off-duty sentries came to town to amuse themselves, altering the routine of the villagers, who tried to ignore them, pretending that the racket they raised came from a sabbat of monkeys in the treetops, but nonetheless taking the precaution of bolting their doors and locking up their daughters. The Indians also came to town on Saturday, to beg a banana, a swig of alcohol, or bread. They came in single file, ragged, followed by a pack of dwarf dogs, the children naked, the old worn by time, the women pregnant—all with a faint expression of mockery in their eyes. The priest kept a coin from the tithe box for each of them, and Riad Halabí gave each a cigarette or a piece of candy.

Before the arrival of the Turk, as he became known, commerce had been limited to an occasional sale of produce to the truck drivers who passed on the highway. In the early morning, children would set up canvas tents to protect themselves from the sun, and on a box display vegetables, fruits, and cheese they fanned constantly to keep away the flies. If they were lucky, they would sell something and return home with a few coins. It was Riad Halabí's idea to make a formal agreement with the drivers, who hauled cargo to the oil camps and returned empty to the capital, to carry the produce of Agua Santa to the city. He himself arranged for it to be sold at the stand of one of his countrymen in the Central Market, thus bringing a modicum of prosperity to the town. Shortly afterward, when he realized that in the city there was interest in pottery and wood and wicker handicrafts, he organized some of the townspeople to produce such objects for a sale in the tourist shops, and in less than six months that had become the principal source of income for several families. No one doubted his good intentions or questioned his prices, because in the years the Turk had lived in the town, he had given numerous examples of his honesty. Without intending it, his store had become the center of the commercial life of Agua Santa; almost all the business of the area passed through his hands. He enlarged his storeroom, built additional rooms on his house, bought beautiful iron and copper utensils for his kitchen, gave a satisfied look around, and came to the conclusion that he had everything necessary to make a woman happy. Then he wrote his mother and asked her to find him a wife in his native land.

Zulema agreed to marry Halabí because in spite of her beauty she still did not have a husband, and was already twenty-five years old when the marriage broker spoke to her of Riad Halabí. She was told that he had a harelip, but she did not know what that meant, and in the photo they showed her she saw only a shadow between mouth and nose, which looked more like a twisted mustache than an obstacle to marriage. Her mother convinced her that physical appearance is not important at the hour of forming a family, and that any alternative would be preferable to ending up an old maid and becoming a servant in the house of one of her married sisters. Furthermore, her mother said, you always learn to love your husband, if you really try. It is the will of Allah that two people who sleep together and bring children into the world end up feeling affection for each other. Also, Zulema believed that her suitor was a wealthy businessman in South America, and though she did not have the least idea where that place with the exotic name might be, she had no doubt that it would be more agreeable than the fly- and rat-infested quarter where she lived.

When he received his mother's affirmative reply, Riad Halabí said goodbye to his friends in Agua Santa, closed the store and house, and traveled to the country where he had not set foot for fifteen years. He wondered whether his family would recognize him; he felt like a different person, as if the American landscape and the hard life he had lived had formed him anew, but in fact he had changed very little. Although he was a heavyset man with an incipient paunch and double chin, and no longer a thin young boy with enormous eyes and a hook nose, he was still timid, insecure, and sentimental.

Because the bridegroom could afford to pay, the marriage between Zulema and Riad Halabí was celebrated with full rituals. It was a memorable event in that poor village where real festivities had been almost forgotten. Perhaps the only bad omen was that at the beginning of the week the *khamsin* blew from the desert and sand invaded everything: it

filtered into houses, abraded clothing, cracked skin, and by the day of
the actual marriage, the bride and groom had sand in their eyelashes.
But that detail did not hinder the celebration. The first day of the ceremony, women friends and family members gathered to inspect the bride's
trousseau, all orange blossoms and pink ribbons, while enjoying eggfruit,
"gazelle horns," almonds, and pistachios, and ululating with happiness,
a sustained *yuyuyu* that spread through the street to the café where the
men had congregated. The following day, Zulema was led to the public
bath in a procession headed by an elder beating a bottle-shaped tam-
bourine to warn the men to look away during the passing of the bride,
who was clothed in seven gauzy robes. When her clothing was removed
in the bath, so that the parents of Riad Halabí could see that she was
well nourished and had no flaws, her mother broke into tears, following
tradition. Zulema's hands were stained with henna; all her body hair
was removed with wax and sulfur; she was massaged with cream; her
hair was braided with imitation pearls; and everyone sang and danced
and ate sweets and drank mint tea—with the louis d'or the bride gave
to each of her friends never far from their minds. The third day was the
ceremony of the *neftah*. Zulema's grandmother touched her forehead with
a key to open her mind to frankness and affection, and then her mother
and Riad Halabí's father placed her feet in slippers anointed with honey,
so that she enter married life along a path of sweetness. The fourth day,
dressed in a simple tunic, she welcomed her in-laws, honoring them
with dishes prepared by her own hands; she lowered her eyes demurely
when they said that the meat was tough and the couscous lacked salt,
but that the bride was pretty. The fifth day, they tested Zulema's de-
pendability by bringing to her three troubadours who sang suggestive
songs; she maintained a stony indifference behind her veil, and each
obscenity that bounced against her virginal face was rewarded with a
coin. Meanwhile the men's feast was being celebrated in another room,
where Riad Halabí was the brunt of all jokes. The sixth day, they were
married in the office of the *alcadia*, the town hall, and the seventh, they
received the *cadi*, the local magistrate. The guests placed their presents
at the feet of the newly married couple, shouting the price they had
paid; the father and mother drank the last cup of chicken broth with
Zulema, and then delivered her to her husband, unwillingly, as they
were supposed to do. The women of the family led her to a chamber

prepared for the occasion and changed her bridal gown for a shift, then joined the men in the street, waiting for the bloodstained sheet of purity to be displayed at the window.

At last Riad Halabí was alone with his wife. They had never seen each other except from a distance, or exchanged words or smiles. Custom demanded that she be frightened and trembling, but it was he who felt that way. As long as he had kept a prudent distance and not opened his mouth, his defect was not terribly noticeable, but he did not know how it would affect his wife at a more intimate moment. Apprehensive, he walked toward her and reached out to touch her, attracted by the nacreous glow of her skin, the abundance of her flesh, the shadows of her hair, but when he saw the expression of revulsion in her eyes, the gesture was frozen in midair. He took out his handkerchief and put it to his face, holding it there with one hand while with the other he undressed and caressed her, but his patience and tenderness were not enough to overcome Zulema's rejection. The encounter was wretched for both of them. Later, as his mother-in-law flourished the sheet from the balcony—painted blue to fend off evil spirits—and, below, neighbors shot off rifles and the women ululated deliriously, Riad Halabí hid in a corner. His humiliation was like a fist in his belly. He was never rid of the silent moan of that sorrow, and he never spoke of it until the day he told it to the first person who kissed him on the lips. He had been educated in the rule of silence: it is forbidden for a man to demonstrate his feelings or secret desires. His position as husband had made him Zulema's master; it was not proper that she should know his weaknesses, because she might use them to wound or dominate him.

They returned to America and Zulema quickly understood that her husband was not wealthy, and never would be. From the first moment, she despised that new land, that town, that climate, that people, that house. She refused to learn Spanish or help in the shop, using the excuse of unbearable headaches. She closed herself in the house and lay on her bed, stuffing herself with food and growing increasingly fat and bored. She depended on her husband for everything, even as interpreter for communication with the neighbors. Riad Halabí thought that all she needed was time to adjust. He was sure that when there were children everything would be different; but children did not come in spite of the nights and impassioned siestas he shared with her—never forgetting to cover his face with his handkerchief. And so a year had gone by, two, three, ten, until I walked into The Pearl of the Orient and into their lives.

It was very early and the town was still asleep when Riad Halabí parked the truck. He led me inside the house through the back entrance, across the patio where frogs were croaking and water was trickling from the fountain, and left me in a bathroom with soap and towel in my hands. For a long time I let the water run over my body, washing away the drowsiness of the trip and the grime of the last weeks, until my skin, forgotten beneath layers of neglect, was once again its normal color. Then I dried myself, combed my hair and fastened it at my neck, and put on a man's shirt, which I tied at the waist with a cord, and canvas espadrilles Riad Halabí brought from the shop.

"Now, eat slowly so you don't get a bellyache," said the master of the house, seating me in the kitchen before a feast of rice, meat pies, and unleavened bread. "They call me the Turk. And you?"

"Eva Luna."

"When I go on a trip, my wife is left alone. She needs a companion. She never goes out. She has no women friends, she doesn't speak Spanish."

"You want me to be her servant?"

"No. You will be something like a daughter."

"It's a long time since I have been anyone's daughter, and I don't remember how to do it. Do I have to do everything she says?"

"Yes."

"What will she do to me if I don't?"

"I don't know, we'll have to see."

"I'm telling you, I won't let anyone beat me . . ."

"No one will beat you, child."

"I'll try it for a month, and if I don't like it, I'll run away."

"Agreed."

Zulema chose that moment to appear in the kitchen, still half-asleep. She looked me up and down, seemingly not surprised to see me; she had long ago resigned herself to accepting the incurable hospitality of a husband who was apt to take in anyone with a look of need. Ten days earlier, he had brought home a vagabond and his burro, and while the guest regained strength to resume his travels, the beast devoured the laundry that had been spread in the sun to dry and a good part of the merchandise in the shop. Zulema—tall, white-skinned, black-haired, with two beauty spots near her mouth and large, melancholy, protuberant eyes—was wearing a cotton tunic that covered her to the ankles. She was adorned with gold earrings and bracelets that jingled like little bells. She observed me with a marked absence of enthusiasm, obviously believing I was a beggar girl her husband had dragged home. I greeted her with an Arabic phrase Riad Halabí had taught me only moments before. A broad smile sent a tremor through her body; she took my face in her hands and kissed my forehead, replying with a stream of words in her language. The Turk laughed happily, covering his mouth with his handkerchief.

That greeting was all it took to soften the heart of my new *patrona*, and from then on I felt as if I had grown up in the house of Riad Halabí. My habit of getting up early served me well. I awakened at dawn, hopped out of bed, and for the rest of the day was constantly on the go, singing as I worked. First I prepared coffee, following careful instructions. I brought it to a boil three times in a copper jug and spiced it with cardamom seeds; then I poured it into a small cup and carried it to Zulema, who drank it without opening her eyes and fell back to sleep until late afternoon. Riad Halabí, on the other hand, ate breakfast in the kitchen. He liked to prepare this first meal himself, and gradually he lost his shyness about his lip and allowed me to eat with him. Later we would raise the metal shutter on the storefront, wipe the counter, tidy the merchandise, and sit down to wait for customers—who were not long in appearing.

For the first time in my life, I was free to come and go; until then I had always been confined behind walls or forced to wander lost in a hostile city. I looked for excuses to talk with the neighbors or to go out in the afternoons and stroll around the plaza. The church was there, the post office, the school, the police headquarters; there was where drums rolled every year on St. John's day; where a rag effigy was burned to commemorate the betrayal of Judas; where the Queen of Agua Santa was crowned; and where every Christmas the schoolteacher Inés organized the Tableaux Vivants, with students dressed in crêpe paper and sprinkled with silvery frost to represent the Annunciation, the Nativity, and the slaughter of the innocents ordered by King Herod. I would walk among the crowd, talking in a loud voice, happy, defiant, mingling with the others, rejoicing in being a part of that community. In Agua Santa there was no glass in the windows and doors were always open; it was the custom to visit, to stand in front of houses chatting, to step inside and have a cup of coffee or a glass of fruit juice; everyone knew everyone else, and no one could complain of loneliness or neglect. Not even the dead were alone there.

Riad Halabí taught me to sell, weigh, measure, do figures, make change, and bargain—the basic activities of commerce. He did not bargain in order to get the better of his customers, he used to say, but to prolong the pleasure of conversation. I also learned a few words of Arabic to be able to communicate with Zulema. Soon Riad Halabí decided that I could not pull my weight in the store or go through life without knowing how to read and write, and he asked the schoolteacher Inés to give me private lessons, because I was much too big to attend the first grade. Every day, proud of being a student, I walked the four blocks with my book in full view, so everyone would see it. For two hours, I sat before the schoolteacher's desk, beside the photograph of her murdered son: *hand, boot, eye, cow, the dog digs deep, Pepe puffs a pipe*. Writing was the best thing that had happened to me in all my life; I was euphoric. I read aloud, and walked around with my notebook tucked under my arm so I could use it at any moment; I jotted down thoughts, the names of flowers, birdcalls; I made up words. Being able to write allowed me to remember without rhyme, and I could make my stories more complex, with multiple characters and adventures. If I noted a couple of brief sentences, I could remember the rest and repeat them to my *patrona*—but that was later, when she began to speak Spanish.

To give me practice in reading, Riad Halabí bought an almanac and some movie magazines with pictures of stars, which enchanted Zulema. When I could read without difficulty, he brought me romantic novels, all in the same vein: a secretary with fleshy lips, silken breasts, and trusting eyes meets an executive with muscles of bronze, temples of silver, and eyes of steel; she is always a virgin, even in the unusual instance of being a widow; he is authoritarian and superior to her in every way; there is a misunderstanding over jealousy or an inheritance, but everything works out and he takes her in his steely arms and she sighs trochaically, and both are transported with passion—but nothing gross or carnal. The culmination was always a single kiss that led to the ecstasy of the paradise of no return: matrimony. Nothing followed the kiss, only the words "The End," embellished with flowers or doves. Soon I could predict the plot line by the third page, and amuse myself by revising it, directing it toward a tragic ending very different from the one imagined by the author and more in keeping with my incurable tendency toward morbidity and violence, so that the girl would become an arms dealer and the impresario would go off to cure lepers in India. I peppered the plot with spicy ingredients I had heard on the radio or read in newspaper crime reports, along with information I had surreptitiously absorbed from the illustrations in La Señora's books of instruction. One day, the schoolteacher Inés mentioned *A Thousand and One Nights* to Riad Halabí, and on his next trip he brought it to me as a present: four enormous volumes bound in red leather, in which I submersed myself so deeply I completely lost sight of reality. Eroticism and fantasy blew into my life with the force of a typhoon, erasing all limitations and turning the known order of things upside down. I do not remember how many times I read each story. When I knew them by heart, I began to transfer characters from one story to another, to change the anecdotes, to add and remove details—a game of infinite possibilities. Zulema spent hours listening to me, her senses alert to every gesture and sound, until one day she awoke speaking fluent Spanish, as if for ten years the language had been in her throat waiting only for her to open her mouth and let it escape.

I loved Riad Halabí like a father. We were united by laughter and play. The man who at times seemed grave and sad was in fact a merry man, but only in the privacy of his house and far from the stares of strangers did he dare laugh and not cover his mouth. Whenever he did it, Zulema turned away, but I thought of his imperfection as a gift of birth, something that made him different from others—unique in this world. We used to play dominoes, betting all the merchandise of The Pearl of the Orient, nonexistent gold nuggets, vast plantations and oil Wells. I became a multimillionaire, because he always let me win. We shared a taste for proverbs, popular songs, and naïve jokes; we discussed the news in the papers, and once a week we went to see a movie shown from a truck that went from town to town setting up its spectacle on playing fields or in plazas. The real proof of our friendship was eating together. Riad Halabí would bend over his plate and push food in with bread or his fingers, sipping, licking, and using a paper napkin to wipe away food that escaped his mouth. When I saw him hunched over that way, in the darkest corner of the kitchen, he reminded me of a huge and kindly animal, and I always wanted to stroke his curly hair or pet him on the back. I never dared. I tried to show my affection and gratitude with small attentions, but he would not allow it; he was not used to receiving affection, although it was his nature to squander it on others. I washed his business shirts and guayaberas, bleached them in the sun, and starched them lightly; I ironed them meticulously, folded them, and stored them in the armoire with sweet basil and mint leaves. I learned to cook hummus and tahini; grape leaves stuffed with meat and piñon nuts; falafel; chicken with couscous, dill, and saffron; baklava with honey and nuts. When there were no customers in the store and we were alone, Riad Halabí tried to translate the poems of Harun al-Rashid for me. He sang songs of the East, long and beautiful laments. Sometimes he covered the lower half of his face with a dishcloth, in the manner of an odalisque's veil, and danced for me, clumsily, arms uplifted, belly gyrating wildly. So it was, amid shouts of laughter, that I learned the belly dance.

"It is a sacred dance—you will dance it only for the man you love most in your life," Riad Halabí told me.

Zulema was perfectly amoral, like a babe at the breast; all her energy had been diverted or suppressed. She did not involve herself in life, but was preoccupied only with personal satisfactions. She was afraid of everything: of being abandoned by her husband, of having children with a harelip, of losing her beauty, of her headaches muddling her brain, of growing old. I am sure that in her heart she loathed Riad Halabí, but neither could she leave him; she chose to put up with him rather than work to support herself. Intimacy with him repelled her, but at the same time she was consciously seductive as a means to hold him, terrified that he might find pleasure with another woman. As for Riad, he loved her with the same humble and mournful ardor of their first meeting, and went to her often. I learned to read his expressions, and when I glimpsed that certain smoldering spark, I would go out for a stroll or go tend the store, while they closed themselves in their room. Afterward Zulema would soap herself furiously, rub her body with alcohol, and give herself vinegar douches. It took me a while to connect that rubber apparatus and nozzle with my *patrona*'s sterility. Zulema had been educated to serve and please a man, but her husband asked nothing of her and, probably for that very reason, she fell into the habit of doing nothing at all, and eventually became a kind of enormous toy. My stories did not make her happy; they merely filled her head with romantic ideas, and led her to dream of impossible escapades and borrowed heroes, distancing her totally from reality. Her only enthusiasms were gold and jewels. When her husband traveled to the capital, he spent a good part of his earnings to buy her jewelry, which she kept buried in a box in the patio. Obsessed with the fear that someone would steal it, she changed the place almost every week; often she could not remember where she had buried it, and would spend hours searching, until I learned all the possible hiding places and observed that she used them always in the same sequence. It was a local belief that jewels should not be kept buried too long: mushrooms would destroy even precious metals and after a while phosphorescent vapors would rise from the earth and attract thieves to the treasure trove. That was why Zulema occasionally sunned her ornaments during the siesta. She would leave me there to guard them, puzzled by her passion for a concealed treasure she never had an opportunity to show off: she did not receive visitors, she did not travel with Riad Halabí or parade through the streets of Agua Santa, but limited herself to fantasizing a return to her country when everyone would be crazed with envy of her opulence, thus justifying the years lost in such a remote region of the world.

In her own way Zulema was good to me; she treated me like a lapdog. We were not friends, but Riad Halabí would get nervous if we were alone for very long; and if he surprised us talking in low voices, he looked for reasons to interrupt us, as if he feared our complicity. When her husband was away on a trip, Zulema forgot her headaches and seemed almost happy. She would call me to her room and ask me to rub her body with milk and cucumber slices to lighten her skin. She would lie on her back on the bed, naked except for earrings and bracelets, eyes closed, her blue hair spread across the sheet. Seeing her like that, I was always reminded of a great pale fish abandoned to its fate on the beach. The heat could be overpowering, and some days her skin burned beneath my hands like a stone in the sun.

"Oil my body, and later, when it gets cooler, I will color my hair," Zulema ordered in her newly acquired Spanish.

She could not bear body hair; to her it was a sign of bestiality tolerable only in men, who were half animal anyway. She screamed as I pulled hers, using a mixture of hot sugar and lemon, leaving only a small dark triangle on her pubis. She was offended by her own odor and washed and perfumed herself obsessively. She demanded that I tell her love stories, to describe the protagonist, the length of his legs, the strength of his hands, the muscles of his chest. She would question me on the amorous details: whether he did this or that, how many times, what he whispered in bed. Her sensuality was like a disease. I tried to weave into my stories an occasional hero who was less handsome, one with a physical defect, maybe a scar on his face near the mouth, but that put her in a bad mood; she would threaten to throw me out in the street, and immediately sink into sullen melancholy.

As the months went by, I felt more secure; I got over my homesickness and did not mention my trial period, hoping that Riad Halabí had forgotten it. In a way my *patrones* were my family. I grew accustomed to the heat, to iguanas sunning themselves like prehistoric monsters, to Arabic food, to the long hours of the afternoon, to the sameness of the days. I liked that forgotten village joined to the world by a single telephone line and a curving road, surrounded by vegetation so thick that once when a truck ran off the road before the eyes of several witnesses, they could not find it in the barranca because it had been swallowed up by ferns and philodendron. Everyone knew each other by name, and no one had any secrets. The Pearl of the Orient was a meeting place where people came to chat, to conduct business, to meet lovers. No one asked about Zulema; she was merely a foreign ghost hidden in the back rooms, whose scorn for the town was returned in equal measure. On the other hand, Riad Halabí was greatly esteemed, and he had been forgiven for never eating or drinking with his neighbors, as demanded by the rituals of friendship. Despite the doubts of the priest, who objected to his Muslim faith, he was godfather to a number of children named after him, a judge in disputes, an arbiter and counselor in moments of crisis. I moved in the shadow of his prestige, happy to belong to his house, and I planned to stay on in that large white dwelling with the cooling perfume of flower petals in every room and shady trees in the patio. Gradually I stopped missing Huberto Naranjo and Elvira; I developed a tolerable image of my *madrina*, and suppressed bad memories so I could remember my past as happy. My mother also found her place in the shadows of the rooms and often appeared at night like a breath beside my bed. I was content, at peace. I grew a little; my face began to change, and when I looked in the mirror I no longer saw an insecure waif. I was beginning to look the way I look now.

"You can't go through life like a bedouin. We'll have to get your name in the Bureau of Records," my *patrón* said one day.

Riad Halabí provided me with some essential baggage for my travels through life. Two gifts were of special importance: writing, and proof of existence. I had no papers to prove my presence in this world: no one had registered my birth; I had never been inside a school—it was as if I had never been born. But he spoke with a friend in the city, paid the necessary bribe, and obtained a certificate on which, through an official error, I am recorded as three years younger than I really am.

Kamal, the second son of one of Riad Halabí's uncles, came to live in the house a year and a half after I arrived. His entrance into The Pearl of the Orient was so discreet that no one saw the fatal omens or suspected he would have the effect of a hurricane in our lives. He was twenty-five years old, small and thin, with fine fingers and long eyelashes; he seemed unsure of himself, and greeted people ceremoniously by placing one hand over his heart and bowing his head, a gesture that Riad immediately adopted and then was impishly imitated by all the children of Agua Santa. Kamal was a man accustomed to misery. Escaping from the Israelis, his family had fled their village after the war, leaving behind all their earthly possessions: the small orchard they had inherited from their ancestors, their burro, and a handful of domestic animals. Kamal had grown up in a camp for Palestine refugees, and his destiny may have been to become a guerrilla fighter against the Jews, but he was not cut out for the hazards of battle, and neither did he share his father's and brothers' indignation at having lost a past to which he felt no ties. He was drawn more to Western customs; he longed to go to a Western country and begin a new life where no one knew him and where he owed no one respect. He spent his childhood peddling items on the black market, and his adolescence seducing the widows in the camp, until one day his father, weary of beating him and hiding him from enemies, remembered Riad Halabí, the nephew located in a remote South American country whose name he could not recall. He did not ask Kamal's opinion; he simply took him by the arm and dragged him to the port; there he was hired as a cabin boy on a merchant vessel, with the injunction that he not return until he had made his fortune. So it was that this youth, like so many immigrants, came to the same steamy coast where five years earlier Rolf Carlé had disembarked from a Norwegian ship. From there he traveled by bus to Agua Santa and into the arms of his kinsman, who welcomed him with effusive hospitality.

The Pearl of the Orient was closed for three days and the house of Riad Halabí thrown open for an unforgettable fiesta attended by all the townspeople. While Zulema stayed in her room, suffering one or more of her countless afflictions, the *patrón* and I, assisted by the schoolteacher Inés and other neighbor women, cooked so much food that it looked like a wedding feast in the courts of Baghdad. On large tables covered with snowy cloths we placed huge platters of saffron rice, piñon nuts, raisins and pistachios, peppers and curry, and around them some fifty trays of Arabic and American dishes, some salty, some hot, some sweet and sour, along with meats, fish brought on ice from the coast, and every imaginable grain with its sauces and condiments. There was one table only for desserts, evenly divided between Oriental sweets and native Latin recipes. I served enormous pitchers of rum with fruit, which, like good Muslims, the two cousins did not taste, but which the others drank until they rolled happily beneath the tables, and those still standing danced in honor of the new arrival. Kamal was introduced to each guest, and to each he had to tell the story of his life in Arabic. No one understood a word of his account, but everyone commented that he seemed a pleasant young man—which, in fact, he was. He may have had a kind of feminine fragility, but there was something hirsute, dark, and ambiguous in his nature that disturbed all the women. When he walked into a room, his aura was felt in the farthest corner; when he sat in the doorway of the shop to enjoy the cool evening air, the whole street felt his magnetism; he enveloped everyone in a kind of spell. He could barely make himself understood by gestures and exclamations, but all of us listened with fascination, following the rhythm of his voice and the harsh melody of his words.

"Now I can travel in peace, knowing that a man of my own family is here to look after the women and the house and the store," said Riad Halabí, clapping his cousin on the back.

Many things changed with the advent of that visitor. I was not as close to the *patrón;* he did not call me to tell him my stories or comment on the news; he put aside the jokes and reading aloud; the domino games became a man's affair. From the first week, he began going alone with Kamal to the traveling movie theater, because his cousin was not used to female company. Except for a few women doctors from the Red Cross and the evangelical missionaries who visited the refugee camps —almost all dry as sticks—the only time the youth had seen a woman over fifteen with her face uncovered in the street was when he first left the camp where he had grown up. On that occasion he had made a difficult trip one Saturday by truck to the capital; there he and his companions had driven to the North American colony where gringas were washing their cars in the street, dressed only in shorts and scoop-neck T-shirts, a spectacle that attracted hordes of males from remote towns of the region. The men rented chairs and umbrellas and settled down to watch. The area was alive with street vendors but the women were not even aware of the commotion, totally oblivious to the heavy breathing, sweating, trembling, and erections they provoked. For those young women transplanted from a different civilization, the men swathed in tunics, with dark skin and beards of prophets, were simply an optical illusion, an existential error, a delirium brought on by the heat. When Kamal was around, Riad Halabí was curt and authoritarian with Zulema and me, but when we were alone he made amends with little gifts, and was once again the affectionate friend of old. He assigned to me the task of teaching Spanish to the new cousin, a none too simple task since Kamal was humiliated if I told him the meaning of a word or pointed out an error of pronunciation; nevertheless, he quickly learned a kind of slang, and soon could help in the shop.

"Keep your knees together when you're sitting down," Zulema commanded me, I think with Kamal in mind, "and button up all your buttons."

The cousin's sorcery spread through the house and The Pearl of the Orient, spilled through the town, and was carried even farther on the wind. Girls came to the shop from morning to night on the most transparent errands. They ripened before Kamal like wild fruit, swelling beneath their short skirts and tight blouses, so perfumed that after they left, their scent permeated the room. They came in groups of two or three, laughing and whispering; they leaned on the counter so that their breasts were exposed and their bottoms, atop dark legs, invitingly elevated. They waited for him in the street; they invited him to their homes for the afternoon; they initiated him into the dances of the Caribbean.

I felt an unrelenting restlessness. It was the first time I had ever experienced jealousy, and that emotion clung to my skin day and night like a dark stain, a contamination I could not shed; it became so unbearable that when finally I rid myself of it, I was freed forever of the desire to possess another person or the temptation ever to belong to anyone. From the instant I saw Kamal I was deranged; my nerves were raw, chafed by the supreme pleasure of loving him and the unendurable ache of loving him in vain. I followed him everywhere, like a shadow; I waited on him; I made him the hero of my solitary fantasies. But he ignored me completely. I became conscious of myself; I studied myself in the mirror; I touched my body; I tried different hairstyles during the silence of the siesta; I applied a touch of rouge to my cheeks and lips, careful that no one should notice. Kamal walked by without seeing me. He was the protagonist of all my love stories. Now I was not content with the final kiss of the novels I had read to Zulema, and I began to live tempestuous nights with him in my imagination. I was fifteen years old and a virgin, but if the cord with seven knots my *madrina* invented had measured intentions as well, I would not have passed the test.

All our lives changed when Riad Halabí went away for the first time and left Zulema, Kamal, and me alone. The *patrona*'s indisposition vanished as if by a miracle, and she awakened from a lethargy of almost forty years. She got up early and prepared breakfast; she put on her best clothes; she adorned herself in all her jewels; she fastened half her hair at her neck and let the rest fall loose about her shoulders. She had never looked so beautiful. At first Kamal eluded her; when he was with her, he kept his eyes lowered and scarcely spoke; he spent the entire day in the shop, and at night went out to roam through the town. Soon, however, it was impossible to escape the power of the woman, the sultry scent, the heat of her tread as she passed by, the bewitchment of her voice. The atmosphere was heavy with secret urgencies, with omens, with summonses. I sensed that something of great magnitude was happening from which I was excluded, a private war between those two, a titanic battle of wills. Kamal beat a constant retreat, digging his trenches, defended by centuries of taboos, by respect for the laws of hospitality and the bonds of blood that joined him to Riad Halabí. Zulema, avid as a carnivorous flower, fluttered her fragrant petals to lure him to her trap. That lazy and docile woman, who had lived her life lying on a bed with cold cloths pressed to her forehead, was transformed into a stupendous female, a pale spider tirelessly spinning her web. I wanted to be invisible.

Zulema, sitting in the shade of the patio painting her toenails, her massive legs exposed to mid-thigh. Zulema smoking, the tip of her tongue playing with the mouthpiece of the cigarette holder, lips shimmering. Zulema, bending forward, her dress slipping to reveal a plump shoulder that captured the sunlight in its impossible whiteness. Zulema, eating a piece of ripe fruit, the yellow juice splashing one breast. Zulema, toying with her blue hair, covering part of her face, and gazing at Kamal with the eyes of a houri.

The cousin resisted heroically for seventy-two hours. The tension was building to an excruciating level, and I feared the air would explode like lightning, reducing us all to cinders. On the third day, Kamal worked from early morning, not showing his face in the house, performing meaningless tasks in The Pearl of the Orient to pass the time. Zulema called him to eat, but he said he was not hungry, and spent another hour counting the till. He waited to close the shop until the town had gone to bed and the sky was black, and when he calculated that the evening drama had begun on the radio, he stole into the kitchen to look for leftovers from our meal. But for the first time in many months Zulema was prepared to miss an episode. To throw him off the track, she left the radio turned on in her room, and the door ajar; then she stationed herself in the semi-darkness of the corridor. She had put on an embroidered tunic; beneath it she was naked, and when she raised her arm, milky flesh glowed to her waist. She had spent the afternoon removing body hair, brushing her hair, rubbing herself with creams, perfecting her makeup; her body was perfumed with patchouli and her breath freshened with licorice; she was barefoot and jewelless, ready for love. I saw everything, because she had not sent me to my room; she had forgotten I existed. For Zulema, all that mattered was Kamal and the battle she was about to win.

She cornered her prey in the patio. The cousin had half a banana in his hand and was chewing the other half; a two-day growth of beard shadowed his face, and he was sweating, because it was hot and because it was the night of his defeat.

"I am waiting for you," Zulema said in Spanish, to avoid the shame of saying it in her own language.

The youth froze, his mouth full and his eyes alarmed. She walked toward him slowly, as inexorable as a ghost, until she was only centimeters away. Suddenly the crickets began chirping, a shrill, sustained chorus that grated on my nerves like the drone of an Oriental instrument. I noticed that my *patrona* was half a head taller and twice as heavy as her husband's cousin, who, in addition, seemed to have shrunk to the size of a boy.

"Kamal . . . Kamal . . ." A murmur of words in their tongue followed as her finger touched his lips and traced their outline with a feathery touch.

Kamal groaned, vanquished; he swallowed what was left of the banana in his mouth and dropped the other half. Zulema pulled his head to her bosom where it disappeared in her enormous breasts as if sucked under by bubbling lava. She held him there, rocking him the way a mother rocks her child, until he pulled away and they stared at each other, panting, minds racing, measuring the risks. Desire won out and, clinging to each other, they hurried to Riad Halabí's bed. I followed them, but they were not perturbed. I believe I truly had become invisible.

I crouched down in the doorway, my mind a blank. I felt no emotion. I forgot my jealousy; it was as if I were watching a movie being projected from the mobile truck. Standing beside the bed, Zulema wrapped

Kamal in her arms and kissed him until his arms seemed to rise of their own accord and encircle her waist as he responded to her caresses with a sob of anguish. She covered his eyelids, his neck, his forehead with rapid kisses, insistent flicks of her tongue, love bites; she unbuttoned his shirt and yanked it off him. He tried to remove her caftan but became entangled in its folds and, instead, tore at the low neck to reach her breasts. Without interrupting her fondling for an instant, Zulema turned him so his back was to her, and continued to cover his neck and shoulders with her kisses while her fingers unzipped his trousers and tugged them down over his hips. Only a few steps from me, I saw his masculinity pointed directly at me, unobscured. Kamal was even more compelling naked; without his clothes he lost that feminine delicacy. His slight build suggested synthesis, not fragility, and just as his prominent nose dominated his face without making it ugly, he was not made bestial by his great, dark sex. Stunned, for almost a minute I forgot to breathe, and when I did, I choked on a sob. He was right before me and for an instant our eyes met, but his passed on, unseeing. Outside, a torrential summer rain began to fall, and the clash of the cloudburst and thunder was joined to the dying song of the crickets. Finally, Zulema disrobed and stood revealed in all her splendid abundance, like a clay Venus—although the contrast between the woman's prodigal flesh and the thin body of the youth to me seemed obscene. Kamal pushed her onto the bed; she screamed, imprisoning him between her heavy legs and clawing his back. He shuddered several times and fell limp with a visceral moan. She had not, however, spent all that time in preparation only to have everything over in one moment, so she rolled him from atop her, propped him among the pillows, and devoted herself to resuscitating him, whispering inducements in Arabic, with such good results that in a brief time he was ready. Then he surrendered himself, eyes closed, while she caressed him until he seemed near death: finally she swung astride him, smothering him with her voluptuousness and the wealth of her hair, completely obliterating him, absorbing him in her quicksands, devouring him, draining him, and leading him to the gardens of Allah where he was celebrated by all the odalisques of the Prophet. Then they rested, calm, entwined like two children in the crescendo of the rain and the crickets of that sweltering night that had become as hot as midday.

I waited until the horses stampeding in my chest had slowed, then stumbled away. I stood in the middle of the patio, water streaming from my hair, soaking my clothes and my soul, afire, with a strong presentiment of catastrophe. My first thought was that if we kept silent, it would be as if nothing had happened—what is not voiced scarcely exists; silence would gradually erase everything, and the memory would fade. But the smell of desire had drifted through the house, impregnating the walls, the clothing, and the furniture, filling rooms, sifting into cracks, affecting flowers and living creatures, warming subterranean rivers, saturating the very sky of Agua Santa; it was as visible as a beacon and would be impossible to hide. I sat down beside the fountain, in the rain.

Finally it stopped raining and the moisture in the patio began to evaporate, enveloping the house in a light fog. I had spent those long hours in darkness, gazing inward. I felt hot and cold; it must have been due to the persistent odor that for some days had floated in the air and clung to everything. It's time to sweep out the shop, I thought when I heard the tinkling of the milk seller's bells in the distance, but my body was so heavy I had to examine my hands to be sure I hadn't turned to stone. I dragged myself to the fountain and plunged my head into the water; as I stood up, the cold water trickling down my back awakened me from the paralysis of that sleepless night and washed away the image of the lovers in the bed of Riad Halabí. I went to the shop without looking toward Zulema's door. Let it be a dream, Mama, make it just be a dream. I spent the morning behind the refuge of the counter, without a glance toward the corridor but with one ear cocked to the silence of my *patrona* and Kamal. At noon I closed the shop, but still I was reluctant to leave those three rooms filled with merchandise, and I lay down among some grain sacks to get through the heat of the siesta. I was afraid. The house had been transformed into a lewd beast breathing at my back.

Kamal spent that morning dallying with Zulema; during the siesta, they made a lunch on sweets and fruit, and then, while she was sleeping from exhaustion, he gathered his things, packed his cardboard suitcase, and crept out the back door like a thief. As I watched him leave, I was sure he would never return.

Zulema awoke in the late afternoon with the shrill of the crickets.

She walked into The Pearl of the Orient in her bathrobe, hair un-combed, lips swollen, dark circles beneath her eyes, but she looked beautiful, complete, satisfied.

"Close the shop and come help me," she ordered.

As we cleaned and aired the room, putting fresh sheets on the bed and changing the flower petals in the pottery bowls, Zulema was singing in Arabic, and she continued to sing in the kitchen while she prepared yogurt soup, kibbeh, and tabbouleh. Then I filled the bathtub, perfumed it with lemon essence, and Zulema sank into the water with a happy sigh, her eyelids half-closed, smiling, lost in who knows what memories. When the water cooled, she asked for her cosmetics; she regarded her-self in the mirror, gratified, and began to powder her face; she put rouge on her cheeks, lipstick on her lips, pearly shadow around her eyes. She emerged from the bathroom wrapped in towels and lay down on the bed for her massage; then she brushed her hair, pinned it in a knot, and put on a low-necked dress.

"Am I pretty?" she wanted to know.

"Yes."

"Do I look young?"

"Yes."

"How young?"

"As young as the photograph of your wedding day."

"Why did you mention that? I don't want to remember my wedding! Get out, you stupid girl. Leave me alone . . ."

She took a seat in a wicker rocking chair beneath the eaves of the patio to enjoy the evening and await her lover's return. I waited with her, lacking the courage to tell her that Kamal had gone. Zulema sat for hours, rocking and summoning him with all her senses, while I nodded in my chair. The food in the kitchen turned rancid and the faint perfume of flower petals faded in the bedroom. At eleven I awoke, frightened by the silence; the crickets had stopped chirping and the air was still; not a leaf was stirring in the patio. The odor of desire had dissipated. My *patrona* still sat motionless in the chair, her dress wrinkled, her hands clenched; tears wet her face and her makeup was streaked. She looked like a mask left out in the rain.

"Go to bed, *señora*, don't wait any longer. Maybe he isn't coming until tomorrow," I begged, but she did not move.

We sat there the whole night. Although my teeth were chattering, a strange sweat was running down my back. I attributed those signs to the malign fate that had fallen over the house. I realized that something had shattered in Zulema's heart and that this was not the moment to worry about my own discomfort. I was horrified when I looked at her. She was not the person I had known; she seemed to be turning into a kind of enormous vegetable. I prepared coffee for the two of us and brought it to her with the hope of restoring her old self, but she did not want to taste it. She sat rigid, a caryatid with eyes fixed on the patio door. I drank a sip or two, but it tasted strong and bitter. Finally I managed to raise my *patrona* from her chair and lead her by the hand to her room. I removed her dress, washed her face with a damp cloth, and put her to bed. She was breathing easily, but desolation clouded her eyes and she continued to weep, quietly and persistently. Then, like a sleepwalker, I opened the shop. It had been hours since I had eaten; I was reminded of my time of great misfortune, before Riad Halabí had taken me in, when my stomach was tied in knots and I could not swallow. I sucked on a medlar fruit and tried not to think. Three girls came into The Pearl of the Orient and asked for Kamal; I told them he was not in, that there was no point even in remembering him, because in fact he was not human, he had never been a flesh-and-blood creature; he was an evil genie, an *efrit* come from the other side of the world to stir their blood and trouble their hearts, but they would never see him again; he was gone, carried off by the same fateful wind that had blown him from the desert to Agua Santa. The girls went straight to the plaza to tell the news, and soon the curious began to drop by to find out what had happened.

"I don't know anything. Wait till the *patrón* returns," was the only answer I could think to give.

At noon I carried a bowl of soup to Zulema and tried to spoon it into her mouth, but I kept seeing shadows, and my hands trembled so that the liquid spilled onto the floor. Suddenly she began to rock back and forth with her eyes closed, mourning, first a moaning monotone and then a sharp and uninterrupted *ayayay* like the wail of a siren.

"Be quiet! Kamal will not be back. If you can't live without him, get up and go look for him. There's nothing else you can do. Do you hear me, *señora?*" I shook her, frightened at the magnitude of that suffering.

But Zulema did not respond; her Spanish was forgotten, and no one would ever hear her speak a word in that language again. Then I put her to bed, and lay down beside her, listening to her sighs until we both fell into an exhausted sleep. That was where Riad Halabí found us when he returned in the middle of the night. His truck was loaded with new merchandise, and he had not forgotten gifts for his family: a topaz ring for his wife, an organdy dress for me, and two shirts for his cousin.

"What's going on here?" he asked, amazed at the wind of tragedy that swept his house.

"K-Kamal's gone," I stammered.

"What do you mean, gone? Gone where?"

"I don't know."

"But he is my guest—he can't leave like this, without telling me, without saying goodbye."

"Zulema isn't well."

"I think you're even sicker, child. You have a high fever."

In the days that followed, I sweated out my terror; my fever went away, and I regained my appetite. In contrast, it was evident that Zulema was not suffering from a passing illness. She was stricken with lovesickness, and everyone realized it except her husband, who did not want to see it and refused to connect Kamal's absence with his wife's despair. He did not ask what had happened, because he guessed the answer, and had he been certain of the truth, he would have had to take revenge. He was too softhearted to slice off his unfaithful wife's breasts or to hunt down his cousin, cut off his genitals, and stuff them in his mouth, in keeping with the traditions of his ancestors.

Zulema continued silent and sullen, weeping at times, with no trace of interest in food, the radio, or her husband's gifts. She began to lose weight, and at the end of three weeks' time her skin had turned a light sepia, like a photograph from another century. She reacted only when Riad Halabí attempted to caress her; then she crossed her arms tightly, hunched her shoulders, and glared at him with implacable hatred. For a while my classes with the schoolteacher Inés and my work in the store were interrupted, and the weekly visits to the mobile movie theater were not resumed, because now I could not leave my *patrona*'s side. I spent all day and a large part of the night caring for her. Riad Halabí hired two girls to do the cleaning and help in The Pearl of the Orient. The only good thing about that period was that he began to pay attention to me as he had before Kamal had come: he asked me to read aloud to him or to tell him tales of my own invention; he invited me to play dominoes and again let me win. In spite of the oppressive atmosphere in the house, we found reasons to laugh.

Several months went by without noticeable improvement in Zulema's health. The inhabitants of Agua Santa and neighboring towns came to inquire about her, each bringing a different remedy: some sprigs of rue for a healing tea; a syrup to cure trauma; vitamins in pill form; chicken broth. They did not do it out of consideration for that haughty and friendless foreigner, but from affection for the Turk. What she needed, they said, was to see an expert healer, and one day they brought a Goajira woman of few words, who smoked tobacco leaves, blew the smoke on the patient, and concluded that she had no illness known to science, only a prolonged attack of love sadness.

"She misses her family, poor woman," her husband explained, and dismissed the Indian woman before she went further and divined his shame.

We had no news of Kamal. Riad Halabí never again mentioned his name, wounded by the ingratitude with which Kamal had repaid his hospitality.

SEVEN

Rolf Carlé began working with *señor* Aravena the same month the Russians launched a space capsule containing a dog.

Rolf's Uncle Rupert was infuriated when he heard the news: "That's the Soviets for you, they don't even respect animals!"

"What's all the fuss, husband? She was only a mutt, not even pedigreed," Aunt Burgel replied without looking up from the pastry she was rolling out.

That unfortunate comment unleashed one of the worst fights the couple ever had. They spent all of Friday shouting at each other and hurling insults stored up during thirty years of married life. Among many other deplorable remarks, Rupert heard his wife confess for the first time that she had always detested the dogs; she was sick of raising and selling them, and she prayed every single one of the damned German shepherds would get distemper and die and get the hell out of her life. In turn, Burgel learned that her husband knew of an infidelity she had committed in her youth, but had not mentioned so they could live in peace. They said unthinkable things, and both ended in a state of collapse. When Rolf arrived Saturday at La Colonia, he found all the doors closed, and thought the family was down with the Asian flu that was taking its toll that season. Burgel was prostrate, lying on the bed with sweet-basil compresses on her forehead, and Rupert, purple with rage, had locked himself in the carpentry shop with his bitches and fourteen whelps, and was methodically destroying all the cuckoo clocks he had built for the tourist trade. The cousins' eyes were swollen from crying. The girls had married their candlemakers, adding the delicious aroma of beeswax to their natural bouquet of cinnamon, clove, vanilla, and lemon. They lived on the street where they had lived as children, dividing the day between their own housekeeping and helping their parents with the hotel, chickens, and dogs. No one reacted to Rolf Carlé's excitement over his new movie camera or, as they usually did, begged to hear detailed accounts of his activities and the political unrest at the university. The argument had so radically disturbed the spirit of that tranquil home that for once he could not even pinch and nuzzle his cousins: they went around with long faces and failed to show any enthusiasm whatever for airing the eiderdowns in the unoccupied rooms. Sunday night Rolf returned to the capital, inflamed but celibate, wearing last week's dirty clothes, without the usual biscuits and sausages his aunt always packed in his suitcase, but with the uncomfortable sensation that a Muscovite bitch was more important in his family's eyes than he was. Monday morning he met *señor* Aravena for breakfast in a corner coffee shop near the newspaper office.

"Forget the damned dog and your aunt and uncle's tiff," his mentor said, attacking the toothsome dishes that helped him begin a new day. "Something important's in the air."

"What are you talking about?"

"There's going to be a popular election in a couple of months. It's all cut and dried, the General intends to govern another five years."

"That's not news."

"But this time he's going to get his ass reamed, Rolf."

Just as predicted, a referendum was held shortly before Christmas, spearheaded by a publicity campaign that swamped the nation in noise, posters, military parades, and dedications of patriotic monuments. Rolf

Carlé decided to do his work carefully and, within limits, with a degree of humility, beginning at the beginning and the bottom. Well in advance of the event, he began to gauge the situation, making the rounds of campaign offices and talking with officers of the armed forces, with workers and students. On election day, the streets were filled with the Army and the *guardia*, but very few citizens were seen at the polls; it looked like a country Sunday. It was announced that the General had won a crushing majority of eighty percent of the registered voters. The fraud was so brazen that instead of giving the desired effect it made the General look ridiculous. In the several weeks Carlé had spent snooping around, he had gathered a lot of useful information, which he delivered to Aravena with the brashness of a novice, hazarding in passing complex analyses of the political situation. Aravena listened with a sardonic air.

"It isn't that complicated, Rolf. The simple truth is, as long as the General was feared and hated, he had a firm grip on the reins of government, but as soon as he became an object of scorn, his power began to slip through his fingers. He'll be out of office before a month passes."

All the years of tyranny had not abolished opposition to the dictatorship: a few unions still operated in the shadows; political parties, although they were illegal, had survived; and students never let a day go by without showing their discontent. Aravena contended that the masses had never determined the country's course, but only a handful of bold and powerful men. The fall of the dictatorship, he believed, would come through a consensus of the élite, and the people, accustomed to a system of political bosses, would follow wherever they were led. He considered the role of the Catholic Church to be fundamental, because even though no one respected the Ten Commandments, and men bragged of being atheists as another expression of machismo, the Church continued to exercise enormous power.

"You should talk with the priests," Aravena suggested.

"I already have. There is one group inciting the workers and middle class; according to them, the Bishops are going to accuse the government of corruption and repressive measures. When my Aunt Burgel went to confession after the argument with her husband, the priest reached under his cassock and passed her a handful of pamphlets to distribute in La Colonia."

"What else have you heard?"

"That the opposition parties have signed a pact—they've finally banded together."

"Then this is the moment to drive the wedge into the armed forces —divide them and stir up a revolt. The time is ripe, I can smell it," said Aravena, lighting one of his strong Havanas.

From that day forward, Rolf Carlé was not content simply to register events; he used his contacts to advance the cause of the rebellion and at the same time to measure the moral strength of the opposition, which was spreading discontent among the soldiers. Students occupied schools and colleges, seized hostages, took over a radio station, and urged the people to come out into the streets. The Army was called out with specific orders to leave a harvest of corpses, but within a few days discontent had spread among many officers and contradictory orders were being issued to the troops. The winds of conspiracy had begun to blow among them, too. The Man of the Gardenia reacted by flooding his cellars with new prisoners, whom he dealt with personally without disturbing a hair on his Beau Brummel head; but his brutality failed to slow the erosion of power. The country became ungovernable. Everywhere people were talking openly, liberated finally from the fear that had sealed their lips for so many years. Women smuggled weapons beneath their skirts; schoolboys slipped out at night to paint slogans on walls; and Rolf found himself one morning on the way to the university, carrying a load of dynamite sticks for a beautiful girl. He had fallen for her at first sight, but it was a passion that was never to be: she took the bag without so much as a thank-you, hurried away with the explosives over her shoulder, and he never heard from her again. A general strike was called: stores and schools closed; doctors refused to treat patients; priests bolted the church doors; the dead were left unburied. The streets were empty, and at night no one turned on a light; it was as if civilization had suddenly come to an end. Everyone was holding his breath, waiting, waiting.

The Man of the Gardenia left in his private plane to live in luxury in Europe, where he is today, very old but elegant still, writing his memoirs to set the record straight. The same day, the Minister of the bishop's plush chair escaped, carrying with him a large quantity of gold. They were not alone. Within a few hours, many whose consciences were less than clear fled by air, land, and sea. The strike did not last three days, however. Four captains reached an agreement with the political parties of the opposition; they enlisted their junior officers, and soon other regiments joined in, drawn to the conspiracy. The government fell, and the General, his coffers overflowing, fled with his family and his closest collaborators in a military airplane put at his disposal by the Embassy of the United States. A throng of men, women, and children covered with the dust of victory rushed into the dictator's mansion and, while a black man played jazz on a white grand piano adjoining the terrace, they jumped into the swimming pool, turning the water to a human soup. The barracks of the Security Force was attacked. Guards defended it with machine-gun fire, but the mob broke down the doors and stormed the building, killing everyone in their path. The torturers were nowhere to be found; they must have hidden months before to avoid being lynched. The shops and homes of foreigners accused of having grown rich through the General's immigration policy were sacked. Liquor-store windows were shattered and bottles flowed into the street, passed from mouth to mouth to celebrate the end of the dictatorship.

Rolf Carlé did not go to bed for three days, filming events in the midst of frenzied mobs, automobile horns, street dances, and widespread drunkenness. He worked as if in a dream, with so little thought of himself that he forgot fear; he was the only person who dared carry his camera into the Security Force building to record firsthand the piles of dead and wounded, the dismembered agents, the prisoners set free from the infamous cellars of the Man of the Gardenia. He was also at the General's mansion to film the mobs destroying furnishings, slitting paintings, and dragging the First Lady's chinchilla coats and beaded ball gowns into the streets, and he was also present at the Palace when the new Junta composed of rebel officers and prominent citizens was formed. Aravena congratulated him for his work and gave him one last push by praising him at the television station, where his daring reporting made him the most celebrated figure on the news broadcasts.

All the political parties joined in a conclave to outline the basis of an agreement; experience had taught them that if they cannibalized each other the only ones to benefit would again be the military. Exiled leaders tarried a few days before returning to establish themselves and begin to untangle the skein of power. In the interim, the economic right and the oligarchy, who had joined the rebellion at the very last moment, quickly moved in on the Palace and in a few hours had taken over the vital posts, apportioning them so astutely among themselves that when the new President took office, he realized that the only way he could govern was through compromise with them.

Those were confused days, but finally the dust settled, the noise diminished, and the first day of democracy dawned.

In many places people did not learn of the overthrow of the dictatorship because, among other things, they had not known that the General was in power all those years. They lived on the periphery of current events. All ages of history co-exist in this immoderate geography. While in the capital entrepreneurs conduct business affairs by telephone with associates in other cities on the globe, there are regions in the Andes where standards of human behavior are those introduced five centuries earlier by the Spanish conquistadors, and in some jungle villages men roam naked through the jungle, like their ancestors in the Stone Age. It was a decade that had witnessed great upheavals and marvelous discoveries, but for many it was no different from previous times. People are generous and forgive easily; there is no death penalty in the nation, or life imprisonment, so that those who benefited from tyranny—collaborators, informers, secret agents of the Security Force—were soon forgotten.

The details of the news did not reach Agua Santa, so I did not learn what had happened until many years later when, out of curiosity, I was scanning the newspapers of the period. On that fateful day a fiesta was in progress, organized by Riad Halabí to raise funds to repair the school. It began early in the day with the blessing by the priest, who originally had been opposed to such festivities on the grounds they served as an excuse for betting, drinking, and knife fights, but who had taken a broader view when the school had been damaged in a recent storm. After the blessing came the election of the Queen, who was crowned by the mayor with a diadem of flowers and imitation pearls fashioned by the schoolteacher Inés; then later in the afternoon came the cockfights. Visitors came from nearby towns, and when someone with a portable radio interrupted, shouting that the General had fled and mobs were breaking into the prisons and butchering secret agents, people yelled at him to shut up, he was upsetting the gamecocks. The only person to give up his place was the chief of police, who left reluctantly to go to his office to communicate with his superiors in the capital and receive instructions. He returned a couple of hours later, saying that the whole damn thing was a tempest in a teapot; the government had fallen, but nothing had changed. So start up the music and dancing, and give me another beer, let's drink to democracy. At midnight Riad Halabí counted the money, handed it over to the schoolteacher Inés, and returned home, tired but happy, pleased that his project had not been in vain and a roof on the schoolhouse was assured.

"The dictatorship has collapsed," I said the minute he came in. I had spent the day looking after Zulema, who was suffering one of her crises, and I was waiting up for him in the kitchen.

"I know, child."

"That's what they said on the radio. What does it mean?"

"Nothing that involves us. It happened a long way from here."

Two years passed and democratic power was consolidated. With time only the taxi-drivers' union and a few military men felt any nostalgia for the dictatorship. Oil continued to flow with undiminished abundance from the depths of the earth, and no one was overly concerned about investing the profits, because at heart they believed the bonanza would last forever. At the universities, the same students who had risked their lives to topple the General felt betrayed by the new government, and accused the President of bowing to the interests of the United States. The triumph of the Cuban Revolution had sparked a fire storm of hopes across the continent. There men were changing the order of life, and their noble words were borne on the breeze. There was Che, born with a star on his forehead and prepared to fight in any remote area of America. Young men let their beards grow and memorized concepts of Karl Marx and phrases of Fidel Castro. If the conditions for revolution are not ripe, the true revolutionary must create them, is written in indelible letters on the walls of the university. Some, convinced that the people would never obtain power without violence, decided the moment had come to take up arms. That was the beginning of the guerrilla movement.

"I want to film them," Rolf Carlé announced to Aravena.

And that was how he went off to the mountains, following on the heels of a dark, silent, and cautious young man, who led him by night along mountain-goat trails to the place his *compañeros* were hiding. And that is how he became the only journalist in direct contact with the guerrillas, the only one allowed to film their camps, the only one in whom the *comandantes* placed their trust. And that was also how he came to meet Huberto Naranjo.

Naranjo had spent his adolescent years raiding the neighborhoods of the middle class, leading a gang of outcasts in a war against the bands of wealthy youths who, dressed in leather jackets and armed with knives and chains in imitation of movie street gangs, cruised the city on chrome-plated motorcycles. As long as the upper-class youths stayed in their own part of town, strangling cats, slashing movie-theater seats, harassing nursemaids in the park, sweeping through the Convento de las Adoratrices terrorizing the nuns, and crashing débutante birthday parties to urinate on the cake, it was practically a family affair. From time to time the police arrested them, took them to the station, called their fathers to talk things over in a friendly way, and immediately released them without booking them. Innocent pranks, everyone said indulgently; they'll grow up; they'll change their leather jackets for suits and ties and direct their fathers' businesses and the nation's destiny. But when they invaded the downtown streets and smeared beggars' genitals with mustard and hot chili, marked prostitutes' faces with their knives, and trapped and raped homosexuals on Calle República, Huberto Naranjo thought things had gone far enough. He rounded up his cohorts and organized a defense. That was the origin of La Peste, the most feared gang in the city, which confronted the motorcyclists in pitched battles, leaving behind a trail of battered, knifed, and unconscious bodies. If the police showed up in armored vans with attack dogs and anti-riot gear and managed to take them by surprise, the youths with white skins and black jackets returned unmolested to their homes. The rest were taken to jail and beaten until blood trickled between the cobblestones of the courtyard. It was not the beatings that finished La Peste, however, but something much more compelling, something that took Naranjo far from the capital.

One night El Negro, Naranjo's friend from the bar, invited him to a clandestine meeting. After giving the password at the door, they were led to a locked room where they found a number of students who introduced themselves using obvious aliases. Huberto sat on the floor with the others, feeling out of place; both he and El Negro seemed alien to the group—they had not only not gone to the university, they had not even attended high school. Nonetheless, it became apparent that they were respected: El Negro because of prestige from having been trained in explosives during his military service; Naranjo because of deference due the leader, the notoriously courageous leader, of La Peste. That night Naranjo heard a young man put into words the confusion he had carried in his heart for years. It was a revelation. At first he felt incapable of understanding much of that impassioned rhetoric—even less repeating it—but he knew instinctively that his private war against the Country Club *señoritos* and his defiance of police authority were child's play in the light of these ideas he was hearing for the first time. Contact with the guerrillas changed his life. He discovered with amazement that in the minds of those young men injustice was not part of the natural order of things, as he had supposed, but an aberration. They made him see clearly the schisms that determine men's lives from birth, and he vowed to put all his rage, ineffectual until then, to the service of their cause.

Entering the guerrilla force was a test of Huberto's manhood: it had been one thing to battle the black-jackets with chains; it was very different to fight with guns against the Army. He had lived all his life in the street, and believed he was immune to fear. He had not retreated in battles with other gangs or begged for mercy in the courtyard of the jail. Violence was routine for him, but he had never imagined the reserves he would be called upon to test in the years ahead.

In the beginning he was assigned missions in the city: painting walls, printing flyers, pasting up posters, procuring blankets, obtaining arms, stealing medicine, recruiting sympathizers, looking for safe hiding, subjecting himself to military training. With his *compañeros* he learned the many uses of plastic explosives, how to make bombs, to sabotage high-voltage cables, to blow up railways and roads, in order to give the impression that they were many and well organized; that attracted the indecisive, built the morale of the men fighting, and unnerved the enemy. The newspapers at first publicized these criminal acts, as they were called, but later a ban was enforced prohibiting mention of the guerrilla strikes and the country learned of them only by rumor, through broadsides printed on home printing presses, or in clandestine radio broadcasts. The young revolutionaries used every means possible to mobilize the masses, but their zeal was met with impassivity and ridicule. The illusion of petroleum wealth cloaked everything in a mantle of indifference. Huberto Naranjo grew impatient. At the meetings, he heard what was happening in the mountains: the best men were there, the weapons, the seed of revolution. Long live the people, death to imperialism, they shouted, said, whispered: words, words, thousands of words, good and bad words; the guerrillas had more words than bullets. Naranjo was not an orator; he did not know how to use those passionate words, but he soon developed political insight, and although he did not have the rhetoric of an ideologue, he moved people by the force of his courage. He had tough fists and a reputation for bravery; for those reasons he was finally sent to the mountains.

He left one evening without explanations or goodbyes to his friends in La Peste, with whom he had had little contact since the beginning of his new restlessness. The one person who knew his whereabouts was El Negro, and he would not have told it under threat of death. After only a few days in the mountains, Huberto Naranjo learned that everything he had experienced until then was a foolish game; the hour had come for a serious test of his character. The guerrillas were not a shadow army, as was believed, but groups of fifteen or twenty youths scattered throughout the mountains, few in number, barely enough to keep hope alive. What have I got myself into, these are crazy men, was Naranjo's first thought, which he immediately discarded, because the goal was very clear: they had to win. The fact that they were so few forced them to greater sacrifices. The first was pain. Forced marches with thirty kilos of supplies on your back and your weapon in your hand—the sacred weapon that could not get wet or be struck, that could not be set down for an instant; walking, crouching, up, down, single file, not speaking, no food, no water, until all the muscles in your body were one long-drawn-out wail, until the skin of your hands puffed up like a balloon distended with dark liquid, until insect bites sealed your eyes and your feet bled raw inside your boots. Climbing and more climbing, pain and more pain. And the silence. In the impenetrable green of that landscape, he learned the meaning of silence: he learned to move like a breath of air; there a sigh, a scrape of backpack or rifle resounded like a bell, and could cost you your life. The enemy was very near. Patience; waiting motionless for hours. Hide your fear, Naranjo, don't infect the others; bear your hunger, we're all hungry; bear your thirst, we're all thirsty. Always soaking wet, miserable, filthy, in pain, tortured by the cold of night and steaming heat of midday, by mud, rain, mosquitoes and chiggers, by infected wounds, coughs, and chills. At first he felt lost; he could not see where he was going or what he was hacking at with the machete: high grass, weeds, branches, rocks, underbrush beneath treetops so thick they blocked out the sunlight. But gradually his eyes grew as sharp as a mountain lion's, and he learned to orient himself wherever he was. He stopped smillng; his face became hard, his skin the color of dirt, his expression cold. The loneliness was worse than the hunger. He was plagued by a pressing need for contact with another human being, to feel someone's touch, to be with a woman; but they were all men in that place. They never touched; each was sealed in his own body, in his past, in his fears and hopes. Occasionally they saw a *compañera*, and each of them longed to put his head in her lap, but that also was impossible.

Huberto Naranjo was becoming one more animal in the jungle, nothing but instinct, reflex, impulse, nerves, bones, muscles, skin, frown, clenched jaw, tight belly. The machete and rifle fused to his hands, natural extensions of his arms. His hearing and sight were refined; he was constantly alert, even when he slept. He developed a limitless tenacity: fight to the death, to victory, there's no alternative: dream, and fulfill our dream; dream or die; forward. He lost all self-awareness. Externally he was stone, but as the months went by something elemental inside him softened, opened, and something budded. The first symptom was compassion, an emotion unknown to him, something he had never received or had occasion to practice. Something was growing beneath the hardness and silence, something akin to a boundless affection for others, something that surprised him more than any of the changes he had undergone. He began to love his comrades; he wanted to give his life for them; he felt a strong desire to put his arms around each of them and say, I love you, brother. Soon that sentiment expanded until it embraced the anonymous masses of the people, and he understood then that his rage had been transformed.

In that period he met Rolf Carlé, and Carlé had only to exchange three words with him to understand that this was an exceptional man. He had a presentiment that their fates would be intertwined, but immediately rejected it; he always tried to avoid falling into the traps of intuition.

EIGHT

Two years had gone by since Kamal's departure. Zulema's condition had stabilized into melancholy; she had recovered her appetite and was sleeping as well as she used to, but nothing interested her. She whiled away the hours, motionless in her wicker chair, staring toward the patio—off in another world. My stories and the radio serials were the only things that brought a spark to her eyes, although I am not sure she understood them; she seemed to have completely forgotten her Spanish. Riad Halabí bought her a television set, but since she ignored it, and since there was so much interference the picture might as well have been a message from another planet, he brought it into the shop so that at least the neighbors and customers could see it. My *patrona* did not dwell on Kamal, or lament the loss of love; she simply settled into the indolence for which she had always been so well suited. Illness was her way of avoiding boring household duties, her marriage, herself. Sadness and boredom were more bearable than the effort of living a normal life. Perhaps the idea of death began to hover over her during that period, as a kind of higher order of lassitude in which she would not have to move the blood in her veins or the air in her lungs; her repose would be absolute—not to think, not to feel, not to *be*. Her husband put her in the truck and drove her to the regional hospital three hours from Agua Santa; there they administered a number of tests, gave her pills for her melancholy, and told her that in the capital she could be cured by electric shock, a treatment unacceptable to her husband.

"The day she looks in a mirror again, she'll be cured," I said, and I set my *patrona* before a large mirror to rekindle her narcissism. "Do you remember how white your skin used to be, Zulema? Do you want me to make up your eyes?" But all that was reflected in the glass was the vague outline of a jellyfish.

We grew accustomed to thinking of Zulema as a kind of enormous and delicate plant. We had settled back into the routines of the house and The Pearl of the Orient, and I had resumed classes with the schoolteacher Inés. When I began, I had scarcely been able to read two syllables in a row and my handwriting was the illegible scrawl of a three-year-old. My ignorance, however, was not the exception: most of the people in the town were illiterate. You must study so you can look after yourself, child. It isn't good to have to depend on a husband. Remember, Riad Halabí used to say, he who pays has the say. I studied obsessively; I was fascinated with history and literature and geography. The schoolteacher Inés had never been out of Agua Santa, but she had maps on all the walls of her house, and in the evening she would explain the news on the radio, pointing out the unknown places where each event was unfolding. With the help of an encyclopedia and my teacher's knowledge, I traveled the world. On the other hand, I had no head at all for numbers. If you don't learn how to multiply, how can I trust you with the store? the Turk complained. I paid little attention, preoccupied only with mastering words. Reading the dictionary was a passion, and I could spend hours looking for rhymes, checking antonyms, solving crossword puzzles. As I approached my seventeenth year, I grew to my full height and my face became the face I have today. I stopped examining myself in the mirror to compare myself to the perfect beauties of movies and magazines; I decided I was beautiful—for the simple reason

that I wanted to be. And then never gave the matter a second thought.
I wore cotton dresses I made myself, canvas espadrilles, and I combed
my hair in a long ponytail. Some of the boys in Agua Santa, and truck
drivers stopping by to drink a beer, used to say things to me, but Riad
ran them off like a jealous father.

"None of these peasants are right for you, my girl. We're going to
get you a husband who's well placed, who will respect you and love
you."

"Zulema needs me, and I'm happy here. Why would I want to get
married?"

"Women need to get married, because if they don't they're not complete. They dry up inside, their blood sours in their veins. But there's
no hurry, you're still young. You need to be thinking about your future.
Why don't you study to be a secretary? As long as I'm alive, you'll be
taken care of, but you never know—you should have some skill. When
it's time to look for a husband for you, I'm going to buy you pretty
dresses and send you to the beauty shop to get one of those permanents
they wear now."

I kept devouring all the books I could get my hands on, tending the
house and the sick woman, and helping my *patrón* in the shop. I was
too busy to think about myself, but a yearning and restlessness began
to appear in my stories that I had not known were in my heart. The
schoolteacher Inés suggested I write them down in a notebook. So I
began spending part of the night writing, and I enjoyed it so much that
the hours sped by and I often got up in the morning with red eyes. But
those were my best hours. I began to wonder whether anything truly
existed, whether reality wasn't an unformed and gelatinous substance
only half-captured by my senses. There was no proof that everyone
perceived it in the same way; maybe Zulema, Riad Halabí, and others
had a different impression of things; maybe they did not see the same
colors or hear the same sounds I did. If that were true, each of us was
living in absolute isolation. The thought terrified me. I was consoled by
the idea that I could take that gelatin and mold it to create anything I
wanted; not a parody of reality, like the musketeers and sphinxes of my
Yugoslavian *patrona*, but a world of my own populated with living people, a world where I imposed the rules and could change them at will.
In the motionless sands where my stories germinated, every birth, death,

and happening depended on me. I could plant anything I wanted in those sands; I had only to speak the right word to give it life. At times I felt that the universe fabricated from the power of the imagination had stronger and more lasting contours than the blurred realm of the flesh-and-blood creatures around me.

Riad Halabí lived the life he always had, worrying over his neighbors' problems, standing by, counseling, organizing—always at the service of others. He was president of the sports club, and in charge of almost all the projects in that small community. Two nights a week he left the house without explanation, and returned very late. When I heard him trying to tiptoe in the patio door, I turned out the light and pretended to be asleep, to save him embarrassment. Apart from those escapades, we shared everything like father and daughter. Together we attended Mass; we went because the town did not approve of my scant devotion—as the schoolteacher Inés had often told me—and because he had decided that in the absence of a mosque it would do no harm to worship Allah in a Christian temple, especially considering he need not follow the service too closely. Like all the men, he stood in the back of the church, slightly aloof, because genuflections were not considered manly. There he could recite his Muslim prayers without attracting attention. We never missed a performance at the new movie theater in Agua Santa. If something romantic or musical was playing, we took Zulema with us, supporting her on both sides, like an invalid.

When the rainy season was over and they had repaired the road washed out by the river in the last flood, Riad Halabí announced a new trip to the capital; The Pearl of the Orient was low on stock. I never liked staying alone with Zulema, but my *patrón* always used to tell me before he left, It's my job, child. I must go because if I don't I'll lose business, but I'll be back soon and bring you lots of presents. I never mentioned it, but I was still afraid of the house; I felt that the walls held the spell of Kamal. Sometimes I dreamed of him, and in the shadows I sensed him, his scent, his fire, his naked erect sex pointed directly toward me. Then I would call on my mother to make him go away, but she did not always hear my call. In fact, the absence of Kamal was so powerful that I could not imagine how we had ever borne his presence. At night the emptiness left by the cousin filled the silent rooms, possessed objects, permeated the hours.

Riad Halabí left on Thursday morning, but only on Friday at breakfast did Zulema notice her husband was gone, and murmur his name. It was her first show of interest in a long time, and I was afraid it might signal the beginning of a new crisis, but she seemed relieved to know he was away on a trip. That afternoon, to distract her, I put her in a chair in the patio, and went to dig up her jewels. It had been several months since we had sunned them and I could not remember exactly where we had last hidden them; I had to look for more than an hour before I found the box. After I dug it up, I brushed off the dirt and set it before Zulema, removing the jewels one by one, polishing them with a rag to make the gold shine and the stones glow with color. I put earrings in her ears and rings on all her fingers, hung chains and necklaces around her neck, covered her arms with bracelets, and, when she was decked in all her treasures, brought her a mirror.

"See how pretty you look—you look like an idol . . ."

"Find a new place to hide them," Zulema commanded in Arabic, removing the jewelry and sinking back into apathy.

It seemed a good idea to change the hiding place. I put everything back into the box, wrapped it in a plastic bag to protect it from the damp, and carried it behind the house to a hilly piece of ground covered with thick undergrowth. I dug a hole near a tree and buried the package, stamped down the dirt, and with a sharp knife carved a mark on the tree trunk to identify the place. I had heard that was how country people hid their money. This method of saving was so common that years later when the main highway was being built, tractors unearthed more than one cache of jugs stuffed with coins and bills made worthless by inflation.

That night I prepared Zulema's dinner, put her to bed, and then sat sewing in the corridor until very late. I missed Riad Halabí; inside the dark house I could hear only faint sounds of nature; the crickets were silent, no breeze was stirring. At midnight I decided to go to bed. I turned on all the lights, closed the shutters to keep out the frogs, and left the back door open so I could flee if the ghost of Kamal or any other denizen of my nightmares appeared. Before I went to bed, I checked Zulema one last time: she was sleeping peacefully, covered only by a sheet.

As always, I awakened with the first light of dawn and went to the kitchen to prepare the coffee; I poured it into a cup and crossed the

patio to wake the invalid. As I went, I turned out the lights that had
been burning all night and noted that I needed to wash the incinerated
fireflies off the light bulbs. I opened my *patrona*'s door quietly, and went
in.

Zulema was lying half off the bed, arms and legs outflung, her head
toward the wall, her blue-black hair spilling over the pillows; a pool of
red was spreading over her nightgown and sheets. I smelled an odor
stronger than the flower petals in the pottery bowls. I walked forward
slowly, set the coffee cup on the table, and bent over Zulema and turned
her over. She had placed the barrel of a pistol in her mouth; the shot
destroyed her palate.

I picked up the weapon, wiped it off, and put it back in the dresser
drawer among Riad Halabí's underclothes, where it was always kept.
Then I eased the body to the floor and changed the sheets. I brought a
pan of water, a sponge, and a towel; I removed my *patrona*'s nightgown
and bathed her, because I did not want anyone to see her in that state.
I closed her eyes, carefully painted her eyelids with kohl, combed her
hair, and dressed her in her best nightgown. I had great difficulty pulling
her back onto the bed, because in death she was as heavy as stone.
When order was restored, I sat beside Zulema to tell her one last love
story, while outside the morning quiet was being shattered by the sound
of the Indians arriving with their children, elders, and dogs to beg—
like any ordinary Saturday.

The chief of the tribe—an ageless man wearing white cotton pants and a
straw sombrero—was the first to reach Riad Halabí's house. He had
come for the cigarettes the Turk gave out every week, and when he
found the shop closed he had gone around to the back door I had left
open the night before. He walked into the patio, still cool at that hour,
past the fountain and down the hallway to the door of Zulema's room.
He saw me from the threshold and recognized me instantly because he
had seen me so often behind the counter in The Pearl of the Orient.
His eyes took in the clean sheets, the dark shining wood, the mirrored
dressing table with its ornate silver hairbrushes, the body of my *patrona*
laid out like a chapel saint in her lace-trimmed nightgown. He also
noticed the heap of bloody clothing beside the window. He came to me

and without a word put his hands on my shoulders. I felt as if I were returning from a great distance, with an undying scream trapped deep inside.

When the police rushed in later as if they were making a raid, battering doors and pounding out orders, I had not moved; the chief was still there beside me, arms crossed, and the rest of his ragged tribe huddled in the patio. Behind them were arrayed the townspeople of Agua Santa, whispering, pushing, peering, invading the home of the Turk, where they had not set foot since the fiesta of welcome for his cousin Kamal. One look at the scene in Zulema's room and the lieutenant immediately took charge. He began by shooing away the curious and quieting the hubbub with one shot in the air; then he emptied the room, in order, he explained, not to spoil the fingerprints; and last he put me in handcuffs, to the amazement of everyone, including his subordinates. Since the time several years ago that convicts from the penal colony on Santa María had been brought to build the road, no one in Agua Santa had seen a person in handcuffs.

"Don't move," the lieutenant told me, while his men searched the room for the weapon. They discovered the basin and towels, confiscated the silver hairbrushes and the money from the store, and manhandled the Indian, who was still in the room and kept stepping in front of them whenever they came near me. At that moment the schoolteacher Inés came running in, still in her bathrobe because it was her day to clean house. She tried to talk to me, but the lieutenant would not permit it.

"We must notify the Turk!" the teacher exclaimed, but no one knew where he was.

The spirit of the house was transformed by the bedlam of noise, by the running back and forth and the shouting. I reckoned it would take me two days to scrub the floors and clean up the mess. I wondered, completely forgetting that he was away on a trip, why Riad Halabí was allowing such disrespect, and when they picked up Zulema's sheet-wrapped body, I still could not find a reasonable explanation. The protracted scream was still in my chest, cold as winter wind, but it would not come out. The last thing I saw before being dragged to the police jeep was the face of the Indian, who leaned over and whispered something in my ear I did not understand.

They locked me in a cell at headquarters, a small, hot cave. I was thirsty, and I tried to call out to ask for water. The words were born within me, grew, ascended, resonated in my head, and reached my lips, but I could not expel them; they clung to the roof of my mouth. I tried to concentrate on happy images: my mother braiding my hair as she hummed a song; a young girl riding the patient back of a stuffed puma; waves breaking in the dining room of the spinster and the bachelor; the comical sham funerals with Elvira, my beloved *abuela*. I closed my eyes and prepared to wait. Many hours later, a sergeant to whom I had served rum only the day before in The Pearl of the Orient came to get me. He left me standing before the officer on duty, and he sat down at a school desk at one side to record my statement in his slow and laborious handwriting. The room was painted a drab green; there was a row of metal benches along the walls, and a dais to lend the proper authority to the chief's desk. The blades of a ceiling fan stirred the air, repelling mosquitoes without relieving the unrelenting, humid heat. I thought of the Arabic fountain in Riad Halabí's house, the crystalline water running over stones in the patio, the large pitcher of pineapple juice the schoolteacher Inés prepared when I came for my classes. The lieutenant entered and planted himself squarely before me.

"Name," he barked. I tried to say it, but again the words stuck somewhere and I could not dislodge them.

"She's Eva Luna, the girl the Turk brought back from one of his trips. She was just a kid then—don't you remember I told you about it, Lieutenant?" said the sergeant.

"Shut up, numskull. I didn't ask you."

He walked toward me with menacing calm and circled around me, looking me up and down, smiling. He was a cheerful, handsome, dark-haired man who cut a wide swath among the girls of Agua Santa. He had been in town two years, blown in with new winds from the most recent elections when several officials, including some in the police, had been replaced by others from the party in power. I knew him; he often came to Riad Halabí's and sometimes stayed to play dominoes.

"Why did you kill her? To rob her? They say the Turk's woman is rich, and has a treasure buried in the patio. Answer me, whore! Where did you hide the jewels you stole from her?"

It took me an eternity to recall the pistol, Zulema's rigid body, everything I had done before the arrival of the Indian. I finally understood the extent of my predicament, and that tied my tongue irrevocably; I did not even attempt to answer. The officer balled his fist, drew back his arm, and punched me. That is the last thing I remember. I awakened in the same room, tied to a chair and alone. They had stripped my dress from me. Worst of all was the thirst: oh, the pineapple juice, the water in the fountain... It was dark outside, and the room was lighted by a lamp hanging near the ceiling fan. I tried to move, but my body hurt all over, especially my legs, which were pocked with cigarette burns. Shortly afterward, the sergeant came back; he was not wearing his uniform blouse; his undershirt was sweaty, and he had a dark stubble of beard. He wiped the blood from my mouth and brushed my hair back from my face.

"It'll go easier for you if you confess. Don't think the lieutenant has finished with you, he's just begun.... Do you know what he does sometimes to women?"

I tried to tell him with my eyes what had happened in Zulema's room, but again reality vanished and I saw myself sitting on the floor with my head between my knees and a braid of red hair wrapped around my neck. Mama, I called silently.

"You're more stubborn than a mule," the sergeant said, with a sincere expression of pity.

He went to get water and held my head so I could drink; then he wet a handkerchief and carefully wiped the welts on my face and neck. His eyes met mine, and he smiled at me like a father.

"I want to help you, Eva. I don't want you to be hurt anymore, but I'm not in command here. Tell me how you killed the Turk's woman and where you hid what you stole, and I'll fix it with the lieutenant to have you turned over immediately to a juvenile judge. Come on, tell me.... What's the matter? Have you lost your voice? I'm going to give you more water, to see if you can come to your senses and we can understand each other."

I gulped down three glasses, and the pleasure of the cool liquid flowing down my throat was so great that I smiled, too. Then the sergeant untied the ropes around my wrists, gave me back my dress, and patted my cheek.

"Poor kid... The lieutenant'll be back in a couple of hours. He went to see the movie and drink a few beers. But he'll be back, that's sure.

When he comes, I'm going to hit you so hard you'll black out again, and maybe he'll leave you alone till tomorrow.... You want some coffee?"

Word of what had happened reached Riad Halabí long before it was published in the newspapers. The message traveled to the capital from mouth to mouth along secret paths; it spread through streets, sleazy hotels, Arab shops, until it reached the only Arab restaurant in the country; there, in addition to typical dishes, Middle Eastern music, and a Turkish bath on the second floor, a local girl costumed as an odalisque improvised a peculiar dance of the seven veils. A waiter went to the table where Riad Halabí was enjoying an assortment of his country's dishes, and gave him a message from one of the kitchen help, a man born of the same tribe as the Indian who had found me. That was how Riad Halabí learned the news on Saturday night. He drove like lightning to Agua Santa and managed to arrive the following morning, just in time to prevent the lieutenant from resuming his interrogation.

"I want the girl," he demanded.

In the murky green room, again naked and bound to a chair, I heard my *patrón*'s voice but barely recognized it; for the first time it had the ring of authority.

"I can't release a suspect, Turk—you understand my position," said the lieutenant.

"How much?"

"All right. Let's go to my office and discuss this in private."

But everything had gone too far for me to avoid scandal. My photographs—full-face and profile, with a black patch across the eyes because I was still a minor—had already been dispatched to newspapers in the capital, and appeared in the police reports in the next editions beneath the bizarre caption "Dead at the Hands of Her Own Blood." I stood accused of having murdered the woman who had rescued me from the gutter. I still have a newspaper clipping, yellowed and brittle as a dried petal, that recounts the story of this horrendous crime invented by the press; I have read it so many times that at various moments of my life I have been ready to believe it was true.

"Fix her up a little, we're going to hand her over to the Turk," the lieutenant ordered following his conversation with Riad Halabí.

The sergeant cleaned me up as well as he could, but did not want to put my dress back on me because it was stained with Zulema's blood and my own. I was sweating so hard that he threw a water-soaked blanket around me to cover my nakedness and cool me at the same time. I straightened my hair a little but, even so, I looked terrible.

When he saw me, Riad Halabí bellowed: "What have you done to my girl!"

"Don't make such a fuss, Turk, or it will be the worse for her," the lieutenant warned. "Remember, I'm doing you a favor. My duty is to keep her here until this thing is cleared up. What makes you so sure she didn't kill your wife?"

"You know Zulema was crazy—she killed herself!"

"I don't know anything. It hasn't been proved. Take the girl, but don't push me—I can still change my mind."

Riad Halabí encircled me with his arms and we walked slowly to the door. When we stepped across the threshold and looked into the street, we saw all the neighbors and some Indians who had stayed behind in Agua Santa standing quietly and watching from across the plaza. As we emerged from the building and walked toward the truck, the chief of the tribe began to stamp the ground with his feet in a strange dance that produced a sound like a muted drum.

"Get the hell out of here before I shoot the lot of you!" ordered the enraged lieutenant.

The schoolteacher Inés could contain herself no longer and, calling upon the authority conferred by so many years of being obeyed in the classroom, she marched forward, looked him straight in the eye, and spit at his feet. Heaven will punish you, cur, she said loud enough for everyone to hear. The sergeant took one step backward, fearing the worst, but the lieutenant merely smiled scornfully, and did not reply. No one else moved until Riad Halabí had helped me into the cab of the truck and started the motor; then the Indians faded toward the road of the jungle and the townspeople of Agua Santa began to disperse, mouthing curses against the police. That's what happens when you bring in outsiders, my *patrón* muttered furiously in the truck. None of those brutes were born here. If they had been, they wouldn't think they were such big shots.

We were home. The doors and windows were open, but the smell of fear still lingered in the air. The house had been sacked—it was the guards, said the neighbors; it was the Indians, said the guards. It looked like a battlefield: the radio and television were gone; half the dishes were broken; the storerooms were turned upside down—merchandise scattered, all the sacks of grain, flour, coffee, and sugar slit open. Riad Halabí, his arm still around my waist, hurried by the debris of that typhoon without pausing to measure the damage, and led me to the bed where the day before his wife had lain.

"Just look what those dogs did to you," he said, pulling up the covers.

And then the words came; they spilled from my lips, an uncontainable outpouring, one after the other: A huge nose pointing at me, unseeing, and she whiter than ever before, licking and sucking, the crickets in the garden and the heat of the night, all of us sweating, they sweating, I sweating, I didn't tell you so we could forget, he went away, anyway, he evaporated like a mirage, she climbed on him and swallowed him up, weep, Zulema, for a love that is lost, slim and strong, that dark nose poking into her, not me, no, only her, I thought she would start eating again and ask me for stories and sun her gold, that's why I didn't tell you, *señor* Riad, one bullet and her mouth was split like yours, Zulema, all blood, her hair blood, her nightgown blood, the house soaked in blood and the crickets with that deafening shrill, she climbed on him and swallowed him up, he ran away, all of us sweating, the Indians know what happened and the lieutenant knows, too, tell him not to touch me, not to beat me, I swear, I didn't hear the pistol shot, it went off in her mouth and blasted away her palate, I didn't kill her, I dressed her so you wouldn't see her like that, I washed her, the coffee is still in the cup, I didn't kill her, she did it herself, tell them to let me go, tell them I didn't do it, didn't do it, didn't do it . . .

"I know that, child—be quiet now, please," and Riad Halabí cradled me in his arms and wept with sorrow and compassion.

The schoolteacher Inés and my *patrón* put ice packs on my bruises and then dyed my best dress black for the cemetery. The next day I was still feverish and my face was swollen, but my teacher insisted that I dress in mourning from head to foot, with dark stockings, and a veil over my head, as was the custom, to attend Zulema's funeral, which had already been delayed beyond the legal twenty-four hours because no one had been found to perform the autopsy. You must meet the gossip head on, said my teacher. The priest did not attend, so it would be crystal clear it was a suicide, and not a crime as the guards were gossiping. Out of respect to the Turk, and to annoy the lieutenant, all of Agua Santa filed by the grave, and each person embraced me and gave me condolences as if in fact I were actually Zulema's daughter and not the one suspected of having murdered her.

After two days I felt better and was able to help Riad Halabí clean the house and shop. Life began again; we never spoke of what had happened, and never mentioned Zulema's or Kamal's name, but both were visible in the shadows of the garden, the corners of the room, the semi-darkness of the kitchen: he naked, with burning eyes, and she unblemished, plump and white, free of stains of blood or semen, as if alive of natural death.

In spite of all the schoolteacher's precautions, the gossip rose and spread like yeast, and the same people who three months before were ready to swear that I was innocent began to whisper because Riad Halabí and I were living beneath the same roof without being joined by any discernible family tie. By the time the gossip drifted through the windows into the house, it had reached alarming proportions: the Turk and that little bitch are lovers; they killed the cousin Kamal, threw his remains into the river for the current and piranhas to dispose of, and that's why the poor wife lost her reason—and then they killed her too, so they could be alone in the house; and now they spend day and night in an orgy of sex and Muslim heresies; poor man, it isn't his fault, that she-devil has cast her spell on him.

"I don't believe any of that horseshit people are saying, Turk, but when the river roars, stones must be rolling. I'll have to reopen the investigation—we can't leave it like this," the lieutenant threatened.

"How much do you want now?"

"Come by my office and we'll talk about it."

Then Riad Halabí realized that there would be no end to the black-

mail, and that the situation had reached a point of no return. Nothing
could ever be the same again; people would make our lives impossible.
The time had come to go our separate ways. That night, sitting beside
the Arab fountain in his impeccable white batiste guayabera shirt, he
told me just that, choosing his words with care. It was a bright night
and I could see his large sad eyes, two moist black olives, and I thought
of the good things I had shared with that man: the card games and
dominoes, the evenings reading my primers, the movies, the hours in
the kitchen cooking. I realized that I loved him deeply, that I owed him
everything. A gentle warmth stole through my legs, constricted my chest,
made my eyes sting. I got up and walked behind the chair where he
was sitting; for the first time in all the time we had lived in the same
house, I dared touch him. I laid my hands on his shoulders and rested
my chin on his head. For a moment impossible to calculate, he did not
move; perhaps he sensed what was going to happen, and wanted it,
because he took out the handkerchief he used in moments of intimacy
and covered his mouth. No, not with the handkerchief, I said. I grabbed
it and threw it to the ground; then I walked around the chair and sat
on his lap, putting my arms around his neck, very close, and stared at
him unblinking. He smelled of clean maleness, of freshly ironed shirts,
of lavender. I kissed his smooth-shaven cheek, his forehead, his dark,
strong hands. *Ayayay*, my child, sighed Riad Halabí, and I felt his warm
breath on my neck, beneath my blouse. My skin prickled with pleasure,
and my nipples hardened. I was aware that I had never been so close
to anyone before, and that it had been centuries since anyone had caressed me. I took Riad Halabí's face in my hands and slowly drew him
toward me until I was kissing his lips, a long kiss, learning the strange
form of his mouth as fire rippled through my bones and sent shivers
through my belly and thighs. Perhaps for an instant he struggled against
his own desires, but immediately surrendered, to follow my lead and
explore me in turn, until the tension was unbearable, and we drew apart
to breathe.

"No one has ever kissed me on the mouth," he whispered.

"Or me." And I took his hand to lead him to the bedroom.

"Wait, child. I don't want to get you in trouble . . ."

"I haven't had a period since Zulema died. It was the shock, the
schoolteacher says." I blushed. "She thinks I will never have children."

We stayed together that whole night. Riad Halabí had spent a life-time inventing ways to approach a woman while that handkerchief covered his mouth. He was a loving and delicate man, eager to please and to be accepted, and he had devised innumerable ways to make love without using his lips. His hands, and all the rest of his solid body, had been refined into a single sensitive instrument tuned to giving pleasure to a woman who wanted to be fulfilled. That encounter was so momentous for each of us that it might have become a solemn ceremony; instead, it was smiling and joyful. Together we entered a private place where time did not exist; we spent delectable hours in absolute intimacy with no thought for anything but ourselves, freely giving and taking, two uninhibited and playful friends. Riad Halabí was wise and tender, and that night he gave me such pleasure that many years and more than one man would pass through my life before I again felt so complete. He taught me the multiple possibilities of my womanhood, so I would never compromise for less. I gratefully received the splendid gift of my own sensuality; I came to know my body; I learned that I had been born for that enjoyment—and I could not imagine life without Riad Halabí.

"Let me stay with you," I begged at dawn.

"My child, I am much too old for you. When you are thirty, I will be a helpless old man."

"That doesn't matter. Let's use the time we have to be together."

"We could never live down the scandal. I've lived my life, but yours is still ahead of you. You must leave this town, change your name, get an education, forget everything that's happened to us. I will always help you—you're dearer than a daughter to me."

"I don't want to go, I want to stay with you. Don't pay any attention to what people say."

"You must obey me, I know what I'm doing. Can't you see that I know the world better than you? They would hound us until we were both mad. We can't live locked up here—that wouldn't be fair to you, you're just a child." And after a long pause, Riad Halabí added: "There is one thing I've wanted to ask you for days. Do you know where Zulema hid her jewels?"

"Yes."

"Good. Don't tell me. They're yours now, but leave them where they are because you don't need them yet. I'll give you money to live in the capital, enough to go to school and learn to make your living. That way you won't have to be dependent on anyone, not even me. You won't want for anything, my child. Zulema's jewels will be waiting for you, they will be your dowry when you marry."

"I won't marry anyone, only you—please don't make me go."

"I'm doing it because I love you very much. One day you will understand, Eva."

"I'll never understand! Never!"

"Sh-h-h . . . let's not talk about that now. Come here, we still have a few hours."

That morning we walked together to the plaza. Riad Halabí was carrying the suitcase of new clothes he had packed for me; I walked in silence, my head high and my gaze defiant, so that no one would know how near I was to tears. It was a day like any other, and at that hour children were playing in the street and the old women of Agua Santa had brought their chairs out on the sidewalk and were sitting shucking corn into pans in their lap. The implacable eyes of the town followed us to the bus stop. No one waved goodbye to me, not even the lieutenant, who happened to pass by in his jeep but turned his head as if he had seen nothing, carrying out his part of the bargain.

"I don't want to go," I begged for the last time.

"Don't make this harder for me, Eva."

"Will you come see me in the city? Promise me you'll come soon, and we can make love again."

"Life is long, child, and filled with surprises—anything can happen."

"Kiss me."

"I can't, everyone is looking. Get on the bus and don't get off for any reason until you reach the capital. Once you're there, get a taxi and go to the address I wrote down for you—it's a boardinghouse for young ladies. The schoolteacher Inés called the woman in charge. You'll be safe there."

From the bus window, I saw him standing with his handkerchief over his mouth.

———

I traveled, in reverse, the same route I had taken years before asleep in Riad Halabí's truck. Amazing scenery passed before my eyes, but I saw nothing; my gaze was turned inward where I was still blinded by the discovery of love. I knew intuitively that for the rest of my life every time I thought of Riad Halabí, my gratitude would be renewed—and, in fact, it has been so. Nevertheless, I spent those hours trying to shake off the languour of thoughts of love and achieve the clarity of mind needed to review the past and take stock of the possibilities that lay before me. Until that day I had followed other people's orders, starved for affection, with no future beyond the next day and no fortune but my stories. It took a constant effort of imagination to fill in the parts of my past that were missing. Even my mother was an ephemeral shadow I had to sketch clearly in my mind each day if I was not to lose her in the labyrinths of memory. I recalled every word of the previous night, and realized that the man I had loved for five years as a father, and now desired as a lover, was lost to me. I looked at my hands roughened by domestic chores; I ran them over my face, feeling the shape of the bones; I buried my fingers in my hair and sighed, Enough! I repeated the word aloud: Enough, enough, *enough!* I took the paper with the name of the boardinghouse for young ladies from my pocketbook, wadded it up in my fist, and threw it out the window.

I arrived in the capital at a moment of turmoil. As I got off the bus with my suitcase, it was apparent that something alarming was happening: police were running down the street hugging the walls or zigzagging between the parked cars, and I could hear shots. When the bus driver asked what was going on, a policeman shouted for us to get away from there, someone was firing a rifle from the building on the corner. Passengers grabbed their bundles and ran in every direction. I started off in a daze, not knowing which way to go: I had recognized nothing about the city.

Outside the terminal, the atmosphere was heavy with tension; people were closing their doors and windows; shopkeepers were lowering the shutters of their storefronts; the streets were emptying. I looked for a taxi, wanting to get out of there as quickly as possible, but none stopped, and as no other transportation was available, I had to keep walking in the new shoes that were torturing my feet. I heard a roar like thunder and when I looked up saw a helicopter circling in the sky like a disoriented fly. People were rushing by on every side. I tried to find out what was happening, but no one knew for sure: a *coup d'état*, I heard someone say. Though I did not know what the words meant, I kept moving by instinct, aimlessly, the suitcase growing heavier by the minute. Half an hour later, I passed a modest-looking hotel and went in, calculating I had enough money to stay a short while. The next day I began to look for work.

Each morning I set out filled with hope, and in the evening returned exhausted. I read the notices in the newspaper and went to all the places advertising for help, but soon learned that unless I was prepared to be a topless dancer or to work as a bar girl, the only available jobs were for servants, and I had had enough of that. More than once I was on the verge of calling Riad Halabí in desperation, but I refrained. Finally the owner of the hotel, who always sat at the door and had watched my comings and goings, guessed what my problem was and offered to help. He explained that it was very difficult to find work without a letter of recommendation, especially in these days of political upheaval, and he gave me the card of a woman friend of his. As I neared the address, I recognized the neighborhood of the Calle República and my first impulse was to turn around and go back, but then I thought better of it, concluding I had nothing to lose by asking. I never found the building I was looking for, however, because before I got there I was caught up in a street disturbance. A crowd of young people ran by, sweeping me along with them to a small plaza in front of the Church of the Seminarians. Students were brandishing their fists and yelling and shouting slogans, and I was in the middle of it all, without any notion of what was going on. One boy was screaming that the government had sold out to imperialism and betrayed the people; two others were climbing the façade of the church to hang a flag there, while the crowd chanted, *No pasarán, no pasarán!* Then soldiers came and fought their way through with clubs and gunfire. I started to run, looking for a place where I could wait until both the tumult in the plaza and the rhythm of my breathing died down. I saw that the side door of the church was half-open, and I ran straight to it and slipped inside. I could still hear the noise outside, but it was muted, as if happening in some distant time. I sat down in the nearest pew, suddenly weak from the accumulated exhaustion of the last days. I put my feet on the kneeler and rested my head on the back of the pew. Little by little I began to feel calm; it was peaceful in that dark refuge, surrounded by columns and immutable saints, cloaked in silence and coolness. I thought of Riad Halabí and wished I were beside him as I had been evenings in the last few years, the two of us together in the patio at sunset. I shivered at the memory of love, but immediately shut the thought away. After a while I noticed that the echoes from the street had faded and the light filtering through the stained-glass windows had dimmed. It must be getting late, I thought, and looked around. In a nearby pew I saw a woman so beautiful that for a moment I thought she was a divine apparition. She looked toward me and gave a friendly wave of her hand.

"Did you get caught in that mob, too?" the magnificent stranger asked in a subterranean voice as she came and sat beside me. "The whole city's in an uproar. They say the students have dug in at the university and troops have been called out. This country's in a real mess, and our democracy won't last much longer at this rate."

I stared at her, struck by her beauty, studying the sleek, whippet-like bone structure, the long slim hands, the dramatic eyes, the classic line of nose and chin. I had the impression that I had known her before—or, at least, dreamed of her. She stared at me, too, with a quizzical smile on her red lips.

"I've seen you somewhere . . ."

"I was thinking the same thing."

"Aren't you the girl who used to tell the stories? . . . Eva Luna?"

"Yes."

"Don't you recognize me? It's me, Melesio."

"It can't be. . . . What have you done?"

"Do you know what reincarnation is? It's like being born again. Just say I'm reincarnated."

I touched her bare arms, her ivory bracelets, a lock of her hair, still with the feeling I was looking at someone from my own imagination. Melesio, Melesio! And all the good memories of the person I had known from the time I lived with La Señora came rushing back. I saw mascara-stained tears rolling slowly down her perfect face. I threw my arms around her and hugged her, timidly at first, and then with unrestrained joy. Melesio. Eva. Oh, Melesio!

"Don't call me Melesio—my name's Mimí now."

"I like it, it suits you."

"How we've changed! No, don't look at me like that. I'm not gay, I'm a transsexual."

"A what?"

"I was born a man, but by mistake, and now I'm a woman."

"How did you do that?"

"The hard way. I always knew that I wasn't like everyone else, but it was while I was in prison that I decided to undo what nature had done to me. It seems a miracle we met . . . and in a church! I haven't been in a church for twenty years." Mimí laughed, drying the last of her tears.

Melesio had been arrested during the Revolt of the Whores, that memorable riot he himself had incited with his unfortunate letter to the Minister of the Interior complaining about police extortion. When they raided the cabaret where he worked, they hadn't given him time to put on his street clothes but had hauled him down to headquarters still in his fake pearl-and-diamond bikini, pink ostrich tail, blond wig, and platform sandals. His appearance produced a storm of jeers and insults. He was brutally beaten and put into a cell for forty hours with the most hardened prisoners. Then he was referred to a psychiatrist who was trying out an experimental cure for homosexuality based on what he called "emetic persuasion." For six days and nights Melesio had been subjected to a series of drugs that left him only half alive, all the while being shown pictures of male athletes, dancers, and models; the doctor claimed his treatment would ensure a conditioned reflex of revulsion toward the male sex. On the sixth day, Melesio, normally a peaceful person, exploded; he leaped on the doctor, began to tear and bite at him like a hyena, and had they not stopped him would have strangled the doctor with his bare hands. The diagnosis was that he had developed a revulsion for the psychiatrist himself, and he was pronounced incurable and sentenced to Santa María, a prison for criminals without hope of probation and for political prisoners who had survived their interrogations. Santa María, built during the dictatorship of El Benefactor and modernized with new fences and cells in the time of the General, had a capacity of three hundred occupants, but more than fifteen hundred men were crammed together there. Melesio was transported in a military airplane to a ghost town that had prospered in times of gold fever but had declined with the oil boom. From there, bound like an animal, he was taken first by truck and then by motor launch to the hell where he was sentenced to spend the rest of his life. One look and he grasped the hopelessness of his situation. The meter-and-a-half-high wall was topped by iron bars; from behind the bars prisoners stared toward the unchanging green of the jungle and the yellow water of the river. *Libertad, libertad,* the prisoners chanted at the sight of Lieutenant Rodríguez, who had accompanied the new batch of prisoners to carry out his quarterly inspection. The heavy metal gate swung open and they drove to the innermost circle where they were greeted by howls and jeers. Melesio was taken directly to the building for homosexuals; there guards auctioned him off to inmates with the greatest seniority. All things considered, he was fortunate, because he was assigned to The Harem, where fifty privileged inmates had a building to themselves and were organized for self-protection.

"I had never heard of the Maharishi then, and had no spiritual guidance," said Mimí, trembling from those memories; she took a card from her purse and showed me a picture of a bearded man in a prophet's robes, surrounded with symbols of the zodiac. "The only thing that saved me from going mad was knowing that La Señora would not abandon me. You remember her, of course. She's a loyal friend, and she never rested until she rescued me. She spent months greasing the palms of judges and using her contacts in the government. She even went to the General in person to get me out of there."

When he left Santa María a year later, Melesio was less than a shadow of the person he once was. Because of hunger, and bouts with malaria, he had lost twenty kilos; a rectal infection forced him to walk stooped over like an old man; and exposure to violence had burst the dam of his emotions: he shifted from tears to hysterical laughter without transition. The day he was freed he did not believe what was happening; he thought it was a trick, that he would be shot in the back "while attempting to escape," but he resigned himself to his fate, too weak to protest. He was taken back across the river in a launch and then by automobile to the ghost town. He was pushed out of the car—End of the road, faggot—and fell on his knees in the amber dust; he crouched there awaiting the shot that would kill him, but nothing happened. He heard the car driving away, looked up, and saw La Señora, who at first had not recognized him. A chartered plane was waiting, and he was flown directly to a clinic in the capital. For a year, by illegally shipping prostitutes overseas, La Señora had been gathering funds to put at Melesio's disposal.

"It's thanks to her that I'm alive," Mimí told me. "She had to leave the country. If it weren't for my own *mamma*, I'd get a passport under my new name and go live with her."

La Señora had not left by choice, but had fled following the scandal that erupted with the discovery of twenty-five dead girls on a ship bound for Curaçao. I remembered having heard about it on Riad Halabí's radio a couple of years before, but never dreamed that there was any connection with the large-hipped woman whose home Huberto Naranjo had taken me to. The dead were Dominican and Trinidadian women being smuggled in a sealed compartment that contained air for only twelve hours. Because of a bureaucratic foul-up, the women were locked in the hold of the cargo vessel for two days. The women La Señora enlisted were paid in dollars as they embarked, and promised a good job. That part of the transaction was her responsibility, and she carried it out in good faith. When they reached their destination, however, their documents were confiscated and they were placed in squalid brothels where they found themselves trapped in a web of threats and debts. La Señora was accused of having masterminded this modern Caribbean slave traffic, and barely escaped imprisonment; again powerful friends helped her and, provided with false documents, she slipped away just in time. For a year or two, she had lived on her income, trying not to attract attention, but such a creative mind needed an outlet, and she had ended up establishing a business in sadomasochistic paraphernalia—with such success that orders poured in from all corners of the globe for her male chastity belts, seven-tailed whips, dog collars for humans, and other instruments of degradation.

"It's getting dark, we'd better go," said Mimí. "Where do you live?"

"For now, in a hotel. I've only been here a few days. I've lived all these years in Agua Santa, a town you never heard of."

"Come and stay with me, I'm by myself."

"I think I should try to make my own way."

"Loneliness isn't good for anyone. Let's go to my house, and once things calm down you can decide what's best for you," said Mimí as with the help of a mirror from her purse she touched up her makeup, which had suffered from the ordeals of the day.

Mimí's apartment was near Calle República, within sight of the yellow and red lights. What had once been two hundred meters dedicated to modest vices had become a labyrinth of plastic and neon, a center of hotels, bars, cafés, and brothels of every kind. This was also the neighborhood of the Opera House, the best French restaurant in the city, the Seminary, and a number of residences, for in the capital, as in the rest of the nation, everything was jumbled together willy-nilly. Imposing manors sat next to shanties, and every time the nouveau riche tried to build an exclusive development, by the end of the year they found themselves ringed by the hovels of the nouveau poor. This topographic democracy extended to other aspects of national life, to the degree that it was sometimes difficult to determine the difference between a Cabinet Minister and his chauffeur: both seemed of the same social background, wore similar suits, and they treated each other with a familiarity that could be taken as bad manners but actually was based on a strong sense of individual dignity.

"I like this country," Riad Halabí had once said, sitting in the kitchen of the schoolteacher Inés. "Rich and poor, black and white, a single class, a single people. Everyone thinks he's king of the mountain, free of social ranks and rules—no one better than anyone else either by birth or money. That's not how it is where I come from. In my country there are many castes and many codes. A man dies right where he is born."

"Don't be deceived by appearances, Riad," the schoolteacher replied. "This country has as many layers as phyllo dough."

"Yes, but a man can climb or fall, be a millionaire, President, or beggar. It depends on his effort, his luck . . . or the will of Allah."

"Have you ever seen a rich Indian? Or a black general or banker?"

The schoolteacher was right, but no one would admit that race had any bearing on the matter; in fact, they boasted of being a uniformly brown people. Immigrants from all parts of the planet were accepted as equals, without prejudice, and after a few generations not even the Chinese could swear they were pure Asian. Only the oligarchy, entrenched from long before the Independence, could be identified by type and skin color; even among them, however, the subject was never mentioned—it would have been an unpardonable breach of manners in a society supposedly proud of its mixed blood. But even allowing for a history of colonization, political bosses, and tyrants, it was the promised land, as Riad Halabí said it was.

"Money, beauty, and talent open doors in this country," Mimí explained.

"I don't have either of the first two, but I think I have a God-given talent for telling stories . . ." Actually, I doubted whether there was any practical application for my talent; until then it had served only to add a little color to life, and to allow me to escape to other worlds when reality became too difficult to bear. Storytelling seemed an art that had been passed by in the advances of radio, television, and movies: everything transmitted by airwaves or projected onto a screen was true, I thought, while my tales were almost always a string of lies, and not even I knew where they came from.

"If that's what you like, then that's what you should do."

"No one pays to hear stories, Mimí, and I have to earn a living."

"Maybe you'll find someone who will pay you for them. There's no hurry—as long as you stay with me, you won't need anything."

"I don't want to be a burden to you. Riad Halabí always said that freedom begins with financial independence."

"You'll soon learn that I'm the one who's a burden. I need you much more than you need me. I'm a very lonely woman."

I stayed with Mimí that night, then another, and another, and so on for several years, and during that time I gradually worked my impossible love for Riad Halabí out of my heart. I became a woman, and for the first time steered my own course—not always with grace, to tell the truth, but it should be remembered it has always been my fortune to sail on stormy seas.

I had told myself so often it is a curse to be born a woman that I had some difficulty understanding Melesio's struggle to become one. I could not see a single advantage, but he wanted it so much he was willing to go through hell to achieve it. Under the guidance of a physician who specialized in such metamorphoses, he swallowed enough hormones to turn an elephant into a migratory bird; he had hair removed by electric tweezer, silicone breast and buttock implants, and paraffin injections wherever it was considered necessary. The result is unsettling, to say the least. Naked, Mimí is an Amazon with splendid breasts and skin like a baby, whose torso culminates in masculine attributes that are atrophied but quite visible.

"I need one more operation, she told me. La Señora found out that they work miracles in Los Angeles. They can make me into a true woman, but it's still experimental, and it costs a fortune!"

For Mimí, sex is the least vital part of her femininity. Other things attract her: clothes, perfumes, fabrics, jewelry, cosmetics. She loves the feel of her stockings when she crosses her legs, the barely perceptible whisper of lingerie, the swish of hair on her shoulders. At that time, she longed for a male companion to care for and serve—someone who would protect her and offer her lasting affection—but she had not found him. She lived suspended in an androgynous limbo. Some men had approached her thinking she was a transvestite, but she was not interested in ambiguous relationships; she thought of herself as a woman, and she was looking for virile men. They, however, did not dare be seen with her, even though they were fascinated by her beauty; they did not want to be tagged as homosexuals. There were those who seduced her to find out how she looked naked, and how she made love; they found it exciting to hold such a remarkable freak in their arms. When a lover entered her life, the whole house revolved around him; she became his slave, ready to indulge him in his most daring fantasies to atone for the unpardonable sin of not being a complete woman. On those occasions when she bent to a man's will and became fanatically submissive, I tried to defend her from her own madness, to reason with her, to thwart that dangerous passion. But that only irritated her: You're jealous, leave me alone. The men she chose were almost always the same: a tough, macho type, who for several weeks would exploit her, upset the equilibrium of the house, leave his mark on everything he touched, and cause such upheaval that I would fall into a foul mood and threaten to move out. Finally the sane part of Mimí would rebel; she would regain her self-control and throw the bastard out. Sometimes the breakup was violent; sometimes the man, his curiosity satisfied, simply tired of her and left; when that happened, she would take to her bed in a fit of depression. For a while, until she fell in love again, we would return to our normal routine. I would keep track of her hormones, sleeping pills, and vitamins, and she would oversee my education—English classes, driving lessons, books—and bring home stories from the street to offer them to me as a gift. Suffering, humiliation, fear, and illness had scarred her deeply, and shattered her dream of living in a fairy-tale world. She was not naïve—though she might play the ingénue—but there was a part of her that no sorrow, no violence had touched.

As for me, although I never lacked for men in my life, I was no luckier in love than Mimí. From time to time I succumbed to some passion that rocked me to my bones. When that happened, I did not wait for the man to make the overtures; I took the initiative, hoping each time to recapture the happiness I had known with Riad Halabí— but without success. Once or twice I was rebuffed by men who may have been disconcerted by my assertiveness, and who made a point of ridiculing me to their friends. But I felt free, and I never worried about getting pregnant.

"You should see a doctor," Mimí insisted.

"Don't worry about it, I'm perfectly healthy. Everything will be all right once I stop dreaming about Zulema."

Mimí collected porcelain boxes, stuffed animals, dolls, and pillows she embroidered in her spare time. Her kitchen looked like a showcase for kitchen gadgets, and she used them all; although she was a vegetarian and ate like a rabbit, she enjoyed cooking. She considered red meat a deadly poison, another of the many teachings of the Maharishi, whose portrait presided over the living room and whose philosophy guided her life. He was a smiling grandfather with watery eyes, a sage who received divine illumination through mathematics. His calculations had demonstrated that the universe—and, even more, its creatures—were ruled by the power of numbers, principles of cosmogonic knowledge known from Pythagoras to our day. He was the first, however, to apply the science of numbers to futurology. Once he had been invited by the government to consult on matters of state, and Mimí was among the throng waiting at the airport. Before she watched him disappear into an official limousine, she had been able to touch the hem of his robe.

"Man and woman, there's no difference between them in this theory. They are models, on a reduced scale, of the universe, and therefore every occurrence on the astral plane is accompanied by manifestations at the human level, and each person experiences a relationship with a determined planetary order in accordance with the basic configuration associated with him or her from the day breath is drawn," Mimí recited in a rush, without taking breath herself. "Do you understand?"

"Perfectly," I assured her, and from that moment we have never had a problem, because when everything else fails, we communicate in the language of the stars.

NINE

The daughters of Burgel and Rupert became pregnant at the same time, suffered together the ills of gestation, grew as roly-poly as a pair of Renaissance nymphs, and, within a few days of each other, gave birth to their firstborn sons. The grandparents breathed a deep sigh of relief when they saw the babies had been born without visible defects, and they celebrated the event with a lavish double christening on which they spent a good part of their savings. The mothers could not, as they secretly may have wished, attribute their sons' paternity to Rolf Carlé. The babies smelled of beeswax; and for more than a year the girls had been deprived of their frolics with Rolf—not for any lack of willingness on their part, but because the husbands had turned out to be much more vigilant than the girls had anticipated and gave them few opportunities to be alone. On each of Rolf's sporadic visits to La Colonia, his aunt and uncle and the two young matrons had pampered him like a baby, while the two candlemakers had danced attendance but had never taken their eyes off him; amorous acrobatics, therefore, were shunted into the background owing to circumstances beyond the control of anyone. From time to time, even so, the three cousins managed to slip into the pine forest or some empty room in the inn and laugh together for a while, remembering the old days.

As the years went by, the two sisters had other children and settled into the role of wife, but they never lost the freshness that had captivated Rolf Carlé the first time he saw them. The elder was still merry and playful; she had the vocabulary of a sailor and could drink five steins of beer and still walk a straight line. The younger was as delicate and coy as ever, even though she had lost some of the apple-cheeked beauty of adolescence. Both still smelled of cinnamon, clove, vanilla, and lemon, and just remembering that scent could set Rolf's soul on fire—as had happened thousands of kilometers away, when he awakened in the night with the intuition that the girls were also dreaming of him.

Burgel and Rupert were growing old breeding their dogs and challenging the digestion of the tourists with their extraordinary culinary treats; they continued to fight over trifles and love each other wholeheartedly, and generally grew more charming with each new day. Living together through the years had obscured their differences, and they had grown so alike in body and soul that they looked like twins. To entertain the grandchildren, Burgel sometimes pasted on a wooly mustache and put on her husband's clothes, while he donned a rag-stuffed brassière and a woman's skirt—to the children's happy confusion. They had relaxed the rules of the inn, and furtive couples now drove to La Colonia to spend a night at their hotel: Rolf's aunt and uncle knew that love is good for keeping a fine polish on wood, and at their age they themselves did not have the old ardor—in spite of the huge portions of aphrodisiac stew they consumed. They welcomed the lovers with sympathy and without questions about their legal status; they gave them the best rooms and served them succulent breakfasts, grateful that those forbidden larks helped preserve the coffered ceilings and fine furniture.

The political situation had stabilized after the government suppressed an attempted coup and controlled the military's chronic tendency toward subversion. Oil flowed from the earth in an endless torrent, and prosperity lulled consciences and postponed all difficulties to a hypothetical tomorrow.

Rolf Carlé, meanwhile, had become a roving celebrity. He had filmed several documentaries that won him renown outside the country. He had crossed all the continents, and by now spoke four languages. *Señor* Aravena, who after the fall of the dictatorship had been promoted to the directorship of the national television network, and who was an advocate of dynamic and bold programming, always sent Rolf to the source for the news. He considered Rolf the best cameraman on his team— and secretly Rolf agreed with him. The news services slant the news, Aravena used to say. It's best to witness events with our own eyes. So Carlé filmed catastrophes, wars, kidnappings, trials, coronations, summit meetings, and other events that kept him far from his own country. At times—when he found himself knee-deep in a Vietnam quagmire, or trapped for days in a desert trench, half-dead of thirst, his camera over his shoulder and death at his back—he would remember La Colonia and smile. For him, that storybook village nestled in an obscure mountain range in South America was a safe haven; he was always at peace there. He returned when he felt weighed down by the world's atrocities, to lie beneath the trees and stare at the sky, roll on the ground with his nieces and nephews and the dogs, sit at night in the kitchen while his aunt fussed among the pots and his uncle adjusted the mechanism of a clock. There he gave free rein to his ego, dazzling the family with his adventures. Only with them did he indulge his inclination toward pedantry, because he knew in his heart that he was forgiven beforehand.

The nature of his job had kept him from marrying, and his Aunt Burgel scolded him more insistently with each visit. Now he did not fall in love as easily as he had at twenty, and he had begun to resign himself to the idea of loneliness; he knew it would be difficult for him to find the ideal woman—although he never asked himself whether, in the unlikely event this perfect creature appeared in his life, he would meet her requirements. He had one or two affairs that ended in frustration, a few loyal women friends in different cities who welcomed him with affection when he happened to pass through, and enough conquests to nourish his self-esteem. But he had grown tired of transitory relationships, and now with the first kiss began saying goodbye. He had developed into a sinewy man with taut skin and muscles; his eyes were alert, surrounded by fine lines, and he was tanned and freckled. His experiences at the scene of so many violent events had not hardened him: he was still vulnerable to the emotions of his adolescence. He was moved by tenderness and pursued from time to time by the old nightmares, intermixed, it is true, with happy dreams of rosy thighs and rollicking puppies. He was tenacious, restless, untiring. He smiled often, and his smile was so sincere that he won friends everywhere he went. When he was behind his camera, he forgot about himself, interested only in capturing the image, whatever the risk.

One September afternoon I ran into Huberto Naranjo on a street corner. He was watching, at a distance, a factory for military uniforms located farther down the block. He had come to the capital for weapons and boots—how can a man exist without boots in the mountains?—and, while in town, to persuade his superiors to change their strategy, because the Army was decimating the guerrilla forces. His beard had been trimmed and his hair cut, and he was wearing city clothes and carrying a small briefcase. He bore no resemblance to the posters offering a reward for the capture of a heavily bearded man in a black beret who stared defiantly at passersby from every wall. The most elemental precaution demanded that even if he came face to face with his own mother, he would walk straight ahead as if he had not seen her. But I took him by surprise, perhaps at a moment his defenses were down. He told me later that when he saw me crossing the street he recognized me immediately by my eyes, although there was little else to identify the girl he had left with La Señora, years ago, to care for as if she were his sister. He grabbed my arm as I passed him. I turned, startled, and he whispered my name. I tried to remember where I had seen him before, but made no connection between that man who looked like a public official—despite his weather-beaten skin—and the teenager with the brilliantined pompadour, the cowboy boots, and the metal-studded belt who had been my girlhood hero and the protagonist of my first amorous fantasies.

Then he committed his second mistake. "I'm Huberto Naranjo . . ."

I held out my hand, the only thing that occurred to me at the moment, and we both grinned. We stood on that corner, amazed, staring at one another; we had more than seven years to tell each other about, but did not know where to begin. I felt a languid warmth in my knees, and my heart was pounding; a long-forgotten passion suddenly swept over me. I had thought I would love him forever, and in thirty seconds I was in love again. Huberto Naranjo had not been with a woman for a long time. Later I learned that for him the most difficult part of being in the mountains was lack of affection and sex. When he came to the city, he headed for the nearest whorehouse and for a few moments, always too brief, sank into the annihilation of an urgent, raging, and ultimately melancholy sensuality that barely relieved his stored-up hunger without providing any happiness. When he could allow himself the luxury of thinking about himself, he was overwhelmed with a desire to hold a girl in his arms who belonged to him, someone he could possess totally, someone who would wait for him, want only him, be faithful to him. Ignoring all the rules he himself imposed on his guerrillas, he invited me to have a cup of coffee.

I arrived home very late that day, walking on air.

"What happened to you?" asked Mimí, who knew me as well as she knew herself and could guess my moods even from a distance. "Your eyes are brighter than I've ever seen them."

"I'm in love."

"Again?"

"This time it's serious. I've been waiting for this man for years."

"I see. A meeting of twin souls. Who is he?"

"I can't tell you, it's a secret."

"What do you mean, you can't tell me!" She took my shoulders and shook me, visibly upset. "You've just met this man and he's already coming between us?"

"All right, don't be angry. It's Huberto Naranjo, but you must never mention his name."

"Naranjo? The one from Calle República? What's all the mystery?"

"I don't know. He told me that even a word could cost him his life."

"I always knew he would end up in trouble. I knew Huberto Naranjo when he was just a kid. I read his palm and saw his fate in the cards. He's not for you. Listen to what I'm telling you. That one was born to be a bandit or a tycoon—he must be mixed up in smuggling or drugs, or some other dirty business."

"I forbid you to talk about him like that!"

By the time I ran into Huberto Naranjo, we were living near the Country Club in the best neighborhood in the city, where we had found a small, older house within our means. Mimí's fame was greater than she had ever dreamed of and she had become so beautiful she was almost unreal. The determination that had driven her to change her sex was now dedicated to mastering good manners and acting. She shed all excesses that might be considered vulgar and began to set fashion with her couturier clothes and light-and-shadow maquillage; she improved her vocabulary—saving a few expletives for emergencies—and spent two years studying acting in an actors' workshop and grace in a charm school for beauty queens, where she learned to cross her legs as she got into an automobile, eat an artichoke without smearing her lipstick, and descend a stairway trailing an invisible mink stole. She did not try to hide her sex change, but neither did she speak of it. The sensationalist press exploited that air of mystery, fanning the flames of scandal and slander. Her life had changed dramatically. Now when she walked down the street, people turned to stare at her; schoolgirls crowded around her for her autograph; she had contracts for telenovelas and stage perfor-mances in which she demonstrated a talent that had not been seen since 1917 when El Benefactor had brought Sarah Bernhardt from Paris, an-cient, an amputee, but still magnificent. Mimí's appearance on the stage ensured a full house; people poured in from the provinces to see this mythological creature who was said to have a woman's breasts and man's phallus. She was invited to fashion shows, to serve as juror in beauty pageants, to attend charity events. She made her triumphal entry into high society at the Carnival Ball, when the first families added to her cachet by inviting her to the Country Club. On that night Mimí stunned the guests by appearing dressed as a man, wearing an elaborate, fake-emerald-encrusted costume as the king of Thailand, with me on her arm as queen. There were some who remembered having applauded her years before in a sordid cabaret for homosexuals but, rather than damaging her prestige, that merely heightened interest. Mimí knew she would never be accepted among the families of the oligarchy who were, for the moment, seeking her out; she was nothing more than an exotic curiosity to ornament their parties, but entrée to that atmosphere fasci-nated her, and to justify herself she claimed it was useful to her career

as an actress. In this country, she told me whenever I made fun of her
fancies, good contacts are all that matter.

Mimí's success had made us financially secure. Now we lived across
from a park where nursemaids wheeled their employers' children and
chauffeurs walked pedigreed dogs. Before we moved, we had given all
the Calle República girls Mimí's collections of stuffed animals and embroidered pillows, and had stored the figurines she had made from *porcelana*. I had made the mistake of teaching her that craft, and for months
she spent her free time mixing dough and modeling knickknacks. But
when the professional she had hired to decorate her new home saw the
creations made from Universal Matter, he nearly suffered a heart attack.
He begged Mimí to put them away somewhere, and not spoil the plan
of his décor; Mimí agreed, because she was attracted to that pleasant,
mature man with gray hair and dark eyes. They developed such a sincere friendship that she was convinced she had at last found the mate
promised by her horoscope. Astrology never fails, Eva. It's written in
my chart that I'm going to find a great love in the second part of my
life.

For a long time the decorator played a major role in our lives, changing
them in significant ways. Through him we became acquainted with a
culture we never knew existed. We learned to choose the right wines—
until then we had thought you drank red wine at night and white during
the day—to appreciate art, and take an interest in what was happening
in the world. We devoted our Sundays to art galleries, museums, theater, film. It was with him I attended my first concert, and the impression
was so overpowering I did not sleep for three nights; the music kept
resounding inside me, and when finally I could sleep, I dreamed I was
a blond wood stringed instrument with mother-of-pearl inlay and ivory
pegs. For a long time I never missed a performance of the orchestra. I
would sit in a box in the balcony, and when the director lifted his baton
and the hall flooded with music, tears of happiness rolled down my cheeks.
The decorator had done everything in white—modern furniture with an
occasional antique accessory—so different from anything we had seen
that for weeks we wandered around the rooms as if we were lost, terrified to move anything because we might forget its exact place, or to
sit on an Oriental divan because we might flatten the feather cushions.
But, as he had assured us from the beginning, good taste is an addiction,

and we grew to like it and to scorn the trash we had once lived with. One day that delightful man announced he had been hired by a magazine in New York. He packed his suitcases and said goodbye to us with genuine regret, leaving Mimí in a stupor of dejection.

"Come out of it, Mimí," I pleaded. "If he went away, that proves he wasn't your predestined mate. The real one will come along soon." The irrefutable logic of this argument afforded her some consolation.

As time passed, the perfect harmony of the décor suffered a few changes, but they merely made the house more livable. First it was the seascape. I had told Mimí how much the spinster and bachelor's painting had meant to me, and she believed that my fascination must have its source in genetics; surely it had come from some oceangoing ancestor who had transferred to my blood his irrepressible longing for the sea. Since that corresponded to the legend of my Dutch grandfather, we explored the antique and secondhand shops until we found an oil painting of rocks, waves, gulls, and clouds, which we bought without a second's hesitation and hung in a place of honor—with one stroke destroying the effect of the Japanese prints our friend had chosen with such care. Then, little by little, I acquired a family to display on the wall, antique daguerreotypes faded by time: an ambassador covered with medals; an explorer with great mustaches and a double-barreled gun; a grandfatherly type with wooden shoes and a meerschaum pipe, gazing toward the future with hauteur. Once I had my imposing family tree, we looked everywhere for a picture of Consuelo. I rejected everything I saw until at the end of one long day we came upon the picture of a delicate and smiling young girl in a garden of climbing roses, dressed in lace and protected by a parasol. She was beautiful enough to embody my image of my mother. In my childhood I had never seen Consuelo in anything but an apron and canvas shoes, performing everyday household chores, but I always knew in my heart that she was like the exquisite lady of the parasol, because that was what she became when we were alone in the maids' quarters, and that is how I wanted to preserve her in my memory.

I spent those years attempting to make up for lost time. I took evening courses to get a bachelor's degree that was never good for anything, but at the time I thought indispensable. During the day, I worked as a secretary in a factory that manufactured military uniforms, and at night I filled my notebooks with stories. Mimí had begged me to leave that unproductive job and dedicate myself to writing. Ever since she had seen a line of people outside a bookstore waiting to have their books signed by a thickly mustached Colombian writer on a triumphal tour, she had showered me with notebooks, pencils, and dictionaries. That's a good career, Eva. You don't have to get up too early and there's no one to order you around. . . . She dreamed of seeing me devote my life to literature, but I needed to earn a living, and in that regard writing does not offer a very firm footing.

Soon after I left Agua Santa and lived in the capital, I began looking for my *madrina*, because the last time I had heard anything about her she was not well. I found her living in an old section of the city in a room furnished by compassionate souls who had taken pity on her. She had few possessions, apart from her saints and the stuffed puma—miraculously intact in spite of time and the havoc of poverty. A person should always have an altar at home, she used to say. That way you only spend money for candles, not on priests. She had lost a few teeth —among them the gold one, sold out of necessity—and all that remained of her once-voluminous flesh was a memory; but she had not lost her habits of cleanliness, and still filled her water jug each night to bathe. Her mind was so cloudy that I understood it would be impossible to rescue her from the private mazes in which she was lost, and had to limit myself to frequent visits and to bringing her vitamins, cleaning her room, and providing her with treats and with rose water that kept her smelling as sweet as in former times. I tried to have her admitted for treatment, but no one would pay attention to her; she was not seriously ill, they said, and there were so many other priorities that medical services could not be wasted on cases like hers. Then one morning the family she was living with called me in alarm: my *madrina* had fallen into a deep depression and had not stopped crying for twelve days.

"Let's go see her. I'll go with you," Mimí said.

We arrived just as she had reached the limits of her endurance and cut her throat with a razor. From the street we heard the scream that attracted the whole neighborhood. We ran inside and found her lying in a pool of blood spreading like a lake under the feet of the stuffed puma. She had slashed her throat from ear to ear, but she was still alive and paralyzed with fright. She had sliced the muscles of her jaws; her cheeks had contracted and she was grinning a horrifying, toothless smile. All the strength drained from my body and I had to lean against the wall to keep from falling, but Mimí knelt beside her and, using her mandarin fingernails, pressed the edges of the wound together and staunched the outpouring of my *madrina*'s lifeblood until an ambulance arrived. Those fingernails maintained their grip all the way to the hospital, as I trembled uncontrollably. Mimí is a surprising woman. The doctors rushed my *madrina* into the operating room and stitched her up like a sock, miraculously saving her life.

When I went to collect her belongings from the room where she had been living, I found an old pouch containing the long braid of my mother's hair, as red and brilliant as the skin of a *surucucú*. It had lain forgotten all those years, having escaped being made into a wig. I took it and the puma with me. The attempted suicide at least had the effect of focusing attention on the sick woman, but as soon as she was discharged from emergency care, she was transferred to the Hospital for the Insane. After a month we were allowed to visit her.

"This is worse than Santa María," Mimí declared. "We have to get her out of here."

Tied to a cement post in the center of a patio, surrounded by deranged women, my *madrina* no longer wept; she sat silent, motionless, her stitches stretching like a seam across her neck. She wanted her saints; she felt lost without them. Devils were chasing her, threatening to take away her baby, the monster with two heads. Mimí tried to cure her using positive energy waves, following the Maharishi's manual, but my *madrina* was impervious to esoteric therapies. That was the beginning of her obsession with the Pope; she wanted to see him and ask for absolution of her sins, and to calm her I promised to take her to Rome, never dreaming that one day we would see the Holy Father in person dispensing his blessings in the tropics.

We took my *madrina* from the asylum, bathed her, combed her few remaining tufts of hair, dressed her in new clothes, and moved her with all her saints to a private clinic situated on the coast, amid palm trees, cool waterfalls, and huge cages of macaws. It was a nursing home for the rich, but they accepted her in spite of her appearance because Mimí was a friend of the director, an Argentine psychiatrist. She was given a pink room with a view of the ocean and piped-in music; it was very expensive, but it was more than worth the money because for the first time I could remember, my *madrina* seemed content. Mimí paid for the first month, but I knew it was my responsibility. That was when I found the job in the factory office.

"That's not for you. You should study to be a writer," Mimí insisted.

"You can't study to be a writer."

Just as Huberto Naranjo had abruptly re-entered my life, he vanished without explanation only hours later, leaving behind a trail of jungle, mud, and dust. I began to live on expectation, and during that long forbearance I relived many times the afternoon of our first lovemaking when, after drinking our coffee almost without speaking, and staring at each other with passionate resolution, we had walked hand in hand to a hotel and tumbled into bed; he confessed that he had never loved me like a sister and that in all those years he had never stopped thinking of me.

"Kiss me. I shouldn't love anyone, but I can't let you go now. . . . Kiss me again," he whispered as he put his arms around me; afterward, trembling, covered with sweat, he lay with eyes like stone.

"Where do you live? How can I find you?"

"Don't look for me. I'll come back whenever I can." And again, urgent and clumsy, he pulled me to him.

Days went by and I heard nothing from him; Mimí believed it was the consequence of my having surrendered on our first meeting. How many times have I told you? You have to make them beg. Men do everything they can to get you in bed, and then when they get their way they scorn you. Now he thinks you're easy. You can just sit and wait—he won't be back. But Huberto Naranjo did return; again he came up to me on the street, and again we went to the hotel and made love with the same urgency. After that meeting I had the premonition that he would always come back, although on each occasion he hinted it might be the last time. He had come into my life in a mist of secrecy, bringing with him something heroic, something terrible. That something challenged my imagination, and it may be why I resigned myself to loving him under such precarious circumstances.

"You don't know anything about him. I'll bet he's married and has half a dozen kids," Mimí fumed.

"Your mind has been poisoned by those programs of yours. Not everyone is like the villains in your television series."

"I know what I'm saying. I was raised to be a man. I went to a boys' school, I played with boys and tried to keep up with them at the soccer stadium and in bars. I know much more on this subject than you do. I don't know about other places in the world, but here there's no such thing as a man you can trust."

Huberto's visits did not follow any predictable pattern; he might be absent for a week or two, or several months. He did not call or write; he never sent messages, but suddenly, when I least expected, he would intercept me somewhere on a street—as if, hidden in the shadow, he knew all my comings and goings. He always looked different: sometimes it was a mustache, sometimes a beard, or his hair might be combed differently, as if he were in disguise. That worried me, but it also attracted me; I felt as if I had several lovers at the same time. I dreamed of a place where we could be together; I wanted to cook his meals, wash his clothes, sleep with him every night, and stroll through the streets hand in hand, like man and wife. I knew that he was starved for love, for tenderness, for justice, for happiness—for everything. He would crush me in his arms as if trying to satisfy the appetites of centuries, murmuring my name, and suddenly his eyes would fill with tears. We talked about the past, about being children together, but we never referred to the present or the future. Sometimes we were together less than an hour; he seemed to be on the run. He would embrace me with anguish and rush away. If there was more time, I would fondle him, explore his body, count his small scars, his identifying marks, observe that he was thinner, that his hands were more calloused, his skin rougher. What is this?—it looks like a wound. No, it's nothing, come. At each parting I was left with a bitter taste in my mouth, a mixture of passion, depression, and something akin to pity. In order not to upset him, I sometimes feigned a satisfaction I was far from experiencing. My need to make him love me and stay with me was so great that I had decided to follow Mimí's advice and not practice any of the tricks I had learned from La Señora's books, or teach him Riad Halabí's knowing caresses.

I never spoke of my fantasies, or indicated the precise cords Riad had struck, because I sensed he would hound me with questions—Where? Who with? When did you do it? Despite all the boasting about women I had heard when he was a teenager—or maybe because of that very reputation—he was almost prudish with me. I respect you, he told me. You're not like the others. What others? I asked, and he would smile, ironic and remote. I consciously did not tell him of my adolescent passion for Kamal, my futile love for Riad, or my brief affairs with other lovers. When he asked how I had lost my virginity, I answered, Why should you care about my virginity when you can't offer me yours? Huberto's reaction was so violent that I passed over the incomparable night with Riad Halabí and invented the story that I had been raped by the police in Agua Santa when they arrested me for Zulema's death. We had an absurd argument, and finally he apologized: I'm a brute, forgive me, it's not your fault, Eva. Those bastards will have me to pay, I swear. They'll pay for what they did to you.

"When things calm down, it will go much better," I argued in conversations with Mimí.

"If you're not happy now, you never will be. I don't understand why you go on seeing someone that strange."

For a long while, my relationship with Huberto Naranjo affected my everyday life. I was desperate, wild, possessed by a compulsion to enslave him, never to let him leave my side. I slept badly; I had horrible nightmares; I was almost out of my mind. I was unable to concentrate on my work or my stories, and to find some relief I sneaked tranquilizers from the medicine cabinet and took them on the sly. But as time passed the phantom of Huberto Naranjo began to recede, to be less consuming; it dwindled to a more comfortable size and I began to live for other things, not just desiring him. My life still revolved around his visits, because I loved him. I felt like the protagonist of a tragedy or the heroine of a novel, but I was able to live a normal life and do my writing at night. I recalled the vow I had made after loving Kamal: never again to suffer the unbearable hell of jealousy, and I clung to it with sullen and obstinate determination. I would not allow myself even to speculate that he looked for other women when we were apart, or to worry that he was a gangster, as Mimí insisted. I wanted to think there was some higher reason for his behavior, a world of adventure that I could not enter, a world of men governed by unalterable laws. Huberto Naranjo was loyal to a cause that to him was more important than our love. I would have to understand and accept that. I cultivated a romantic love for that man who was becoming increasingly leaner, stronger, more silent; but I stopped making plans for the future.

The day two policemen were killed near the factory where I worked, my suspicions were confirmed that Huberto's secret had something to do with the guerrilla movement. The policemen had been gunned down by machine-gun fire from a moving car. The street immediately filled with people, patrol cars, and ambulances; the whole area was taken over. Inside the factory they shut down the machines, lined up the operators in the courtyards, searched the building from top to bottom, and finally released us on orders to go directly home because the entire city was in a state of emergency. I walked to the bus stop, where Huberto Naranjo was waiting for me. It had been almost two months since I had seen him, and I had difficulty recognizing him; he seemed to have aged overnight. This time I felt no pleasure at all in his arms. I did not even try to pretend; my thoughts were elsewhere. Later when we were sitting on the bed, naked on the rough sheets, I had the feeling that each day we were drifting farther apart, and I grieved for the two of us.

"I'm sorry. I'm not myself. It's been a horrible day. Two policemen were killed. I knew them—they were guards near the factory and always said hello to me. One was named Socrates, can you imagine? What a name for a policeman! He was a good man. They murdered him."

"They executed him," Huberto Naranjo contradicted. "The people executed him. That isn't murder. You ought to choose your words more carefully. The murderers are the police."

"What are you saying? Don't tell me you're in favor of terrorism?"

He pushed me away firmly and, looking me straight in the eye, explained that the violence originated with the government. Weren't unemployment, poverty, corruption, and social injustice forms of violence? The state practiced many forms of abuse and repression. Those policemen were hirelings of the regime; they were defending the interests of enemies of the people, and their execution was a legitimate act.

The people were fighting for their liberation. I did not answer for a long time. Now I understood his absences, his scars, his silences, his haste, his fatalism, and the tremendous magnetism that emanated from him, electrifying the air around him and attracting me like an insect to a bright light.

"Why didn't you tell me this before?"

"It was best for you not to know."

"You don't trust me?"

"Try to understand, this is a war."

"If I had known, these years would have been easier for me."

"Just seeing you at all is madness. Think what would happen if they suspected and interrogated you."

"I wouldn't say anything."

"They can make a mute talk. I need you, I can't get along without you, but every time I come to you I feel guilty because I'm putting the movement and the lives of all my *compañeros* in danger."

"Take me with you."

"I can't, Eva."

"Aren't there women in the mountains?"

"No. This is a man's war, but better times will come, and then we can love each other under different circumstances."

"But how can you sacrifice both our lives?"

"It isn't a sacrifice. We're building a new society; one day we'll all be free and equal. . . ."

I thought of the long-ago afternoon when we first met, a boy and a girl in a crowded plaza. Even then he was an ingrained macho, able to direct his destiny; in contrast, he believed that because I had been born a girl I was at a disadvantage, I should accept my limitations and entrust myself to others' care. In his eyes, I would never be independent. Huberto had thought that way since he could think at all; it was not likely that the Revolution was going to change those attitudes. I realized that our problems were not related in any way to the fortunes of the guerrillas; even if he achieved his dream, there would be no equality for me. For Naranjo, and others like him, "the people" seemed to be composed exclusively of men; we women should contribute to the struggle but were excluded from decision-making and power. His revolution would not change my fate in any fundamental way; under any circumstances, as long as I lived I would still have to make my own way. Perhaps it was at that moment I realized that mine is a war with no end in view; I might as well fight it cheerfully or I would spend my life waiting for some distant victory in order to be happy. Yes, Elvira had been right: you have to be tough, life is a dogfight.

We parted that day in anger, but Huberto Naranjo returned two weeks later and, as always, I was waiting.

TEN

The escalation of guerrilla activities brought Rolf Carlé back to the country.

"For the moment, my boy, your world travels are over," said Aravena from behind his director's desk. He had grown very fat; his heart was not good and the only pleasures that stirred his senses were a good meal, the savor of his cigars, and during his outings at La Colonia, an occasional veiled glance toward the majestic but now forbidden bottoms of the daughters of Uncle Rupert. Physical limitations, however, had not diminished his professional curiosity. "The guerrillas are becoming a nuisance to everyone, and it's time to find out what's going on. All the information we get is censored, the government lies and so does the guerrilla radio. I want to know how many men there are in the mountains, what kind of weapons they have, who's backing them, what their plans are—in short, everything."

"You can't put that on television."

"We need to know what's going on, Rolf. I think those men are a bunch of locos, but it may be that we have another Sierra Maestra right under our noses and just can't see it."

"And if that's so, what then?"

"Nothing. It isn't our role to change the course of history, merely to record the facts."

"That isn't how you thought when the General was in power."

"I've learned with age. Go on, take a look around, get something on film if you can, and tell me everything you find out."

"It won't be easy. They're not going to let me go snooping around their camps."

"That's why I'm asking you and not some other reporter. You were with them a few years back. What was the name of the guy who impressed you so much?"

"Huberto Naranjo."

"Can you get in touch with him again?"

"I don't know. He may not be there—they say that a lot of them have been killed by the Army, and others have deserted. But in any case, I'm interested, and I'll see what I can do."

Huberto Naranjo was not dead, and had not deserted, but no one called him by that name any longer. Now he was known as Comandante Rogelio. He had been at war for years, with his boots on, his gun in hand, his eyes wide open to see beyond the shadows. Violence was the order of his life, but he also had moments of euphoria. Every time he welcomed a group of new recruits, his heart pounded in his chest the way it once had on meeting a new girl. He would walk out to the edge of camp to greet them. There they stood, still untouched, optimistic, forming a line as their patrol leader had taught them, still with an air of the city, with new blisters on their hands, not the calluses of the veterans; but their eyes were gentle and, although weary, they would be smiling. These were his younger brothers, his sons; they had come to fight, and from that moment on he would be responsible for their lives —for keeping their morale high, for teaching them to survive in the mountains, for making them as hard as granite, braver than a lioness, clever, quick . . . hardy, so that each of them would be worth a hundred soldiers. It was good to have them there, he would think, and feel a lump in his throat. Then he would jam his hands into his pockets and greet them with a few brusque phrases, to avoid betraying his emotion.

Naranjo also liked to sit with his *compañeros* around the campfire when it was possible. They were never very long in one place; they had to know the mountains, to move over that terrain like a fish through water, as it said in the manual. But there were idle days; sometimes they sang and played cards and listened to music on the radio like normal human beings. Fairly regularly he had to go down to the city to check with his liaison; then he would walk through the streets pretending he was just like everybody else, breathing forgotten odors of food, traffic, and garbage, looking with new eyes at children, women shopping, stray dogs, as if he were just another person in the crowd, and not a wanted man. Soon on some building or fence he would come on the name "COMANDANTE ROGELIO" in large black letters, and, seeing himself crucified on that wall, would remember with a mixture of pride and fear that he should not be there: he was not like everyone else, he was a guerrilla fighter.

Though Rolf Carlé had heard that most of the guerrillas were recruited from the university, he made no attempt to find the men in the mountains by mixing with students; he had often appeared on television news programs and was too well known. He remembered the contact he had made some years before when he had first interviewed Huberto at the dawn of the armed struggle, and so he made his way back to El Negro's bar. He found El Negro in his kitchen, a little older but as good-natured as before. They shook hands warily. Times had changed, and now no one could be trusted, since repression had become the work of specialists. The guerrilla movement was no longer the ideal of a group of beardless boys with a dream of changing the world, but a conflict without mercy or restraint. Rolf Carlé did not waste words, he went straight to the point.

"I don't know anything about them," El Negro replied.

"I'm not an informer, I never have been. I haven't betrayed you in all these years—why would I do it now? Get in touch with whoever's in charge. Tell him to give me a chance, at least let me explain what I want to do."

El Negro stared at him, studying every detail of his face, and seemed to approve of what he saw, because Rolf Carlé sensed a change in his attitude.

"I'll be back tomorrow, my friend," Carlé said.

He returned the next day and every day for almost a month, until finally he was granted the meeting he wanted, and could explain his plans. The Party realized that Rolf Carlé could be useful to them. He was a first-rate reporter; he seemed like an honest man; he had access to the television network; and he was Aravena's friend. It would be helpful to be able to count on someone like him, and if they took the proper precautions the risks would not be too great.

The guerrilla leaders wanted the people to be informed: "With every victory we win allies."

"Don't alarm the public," the President of the Republic ordered in turn. "I don't want to hear a word about guerrillas—we'll crush them with silence. They're enemies of the government, and that's how we'll deal with them."

Carlé's second trip to the camp was very different from the earlier one: no backpacking into the mountains like a schoolboy on vacation. Part of the time he was blindfolded and transported in the trunk of a car, half-asphyxiated and nearly fainting from the heat. Then he was driven by night through fields that gave no indication of where he might be. His guides took turns, and neither was disposed to talk with him. For two days he was locked in a variety of sheds and barns, moved from place to place with no chance to ask questions. Army troops trained in schools of counterinsurgency had moved in to contain the guerrillas, installing mobile control points on the highways, stopping all vehicles, searching everything that moved. It was not easy to pass their checkpoints. Special troops were concentrated in Operations Centers spread across the country. There was a rumor that such centers also served as prison and torture camps. The Army shelled the mountains until everything was reduced to rubble. Remember the revolutionary code of ethics, Comandante Rogelio pounded into his men. You are not to abuse anyone. Respect property, and pay for everything you consume. That way people will see the difference between us and the Army. They will learn how it will be in zones liberated by the Revolution. Rolf Carlé found that within a short distance of the cities, where life seemed superficially peaceful, there was a nation at war—although officially it was forbidden to speak of it. The only mention of the struggle came from underground broadcasts reporting guerrilla strikes: a dynamited oil pipeline, a guard station blown up, an ambush of Army troops.

After five days, during which he was hauled about like a piece of freight, Carlé found himself on a mountainside chopping his way through undergrowth with a machete—hungry, muddy, and eaten alive by mosquitoes. His guides left him in a clearing with instructions not to move from that spot for any reason, and not to light a fire or make a sound. There he waited, with no company but chattering monkeys. At dawn, just as his patience was nearly exhausted, two ragged, bearded young men armed with rifles appeared.

"Welcome, *compañero*," they said with broad smiles.

"It's about time," he replied, completely spent.

Rolf Carlé shot the only existing 16-millimeter film on the guerrilla movement of the period before defeat ended the revolutionary dream and pacification returned the survivors to everyday life—some to become bureaucrats, others deputies or businessmen. He lived with Comandante Rogelio's troops, moving by night from site to site across savage terrain, occasionally resting during the day. Hunger, fatigue, fear. Life in the mountains was not easy. He had filmed hostilities around the world, but this warfare of ambushes, surprise attacks, loneliness, silence, this constant feeling of being watched, was worse. The total number of guerrillas varied; they were organized into small units for greater mobility. Comandante Rogelio moved from group to group, responsible for the entire front. Rolf observed the training of new combatants; he helped set up radios and emergency posts; he learned to drag himself forward on his elbows, and tolerate pain; living with these young men and listening to them, he came to understand the reasons for their sacrifice. The camps were run with as much discipline as the military, but, unlike Army camps, they lacked clothing, medicine, food, shelter, transport, communications. It rained for weeks, but they were not allowed a fire to dry out; it was like living in an undersea jungle. Rolf had the sensation of walking on a tightrope across a canyon; death was there, hiding behind the next tree.

"We all feel the same. Don't worry, you get used to it," the Comandante joked.

Provisions were considered sacred, but occasionally the need would be too great and someone would steal a tin of sardines. Punishment was harsh not only because food had to be rationed, but even more because the value of solidarity must be respected. From time to time, someone would crack, curl up on the ground and cry for his mother. The Comandante would go to him, help him up, walk with him where no one could see them, and talk with him quietly. But if he identified a traitor, this same man was capable of executing one of his own troops.

"It's normal here to die or be wounded, you have to be ready for anything. Getting out with your life is rare, and victory will be a miracle," Comandante Rogelio told Rolf.

Rolf lost weight in those few months, and felt that he had aged. Toward the end he did not know what he was doing, or why. He lost all sense of time: an hour seemed a week, and suddenly a week would go by as if he had dreamed it. It was difficult to collect accurate information, to get at the essence of things. He was surrounded by a strange silence filled with words and at the same time heavy with portents, a silence throbbing with jungle sounds, screeching and murmurs, distant voices, sleepwalkers' wails and moans. He learned to sleep in spurts, standing, sitting, day, night, half-unconscious from exhaustion, but always alert—a whisper would make him leap. He was disgusted by the filth, his own stench; he dreamed of sinking into a clean tub, of soaping himself to the bone; he would have given anything he owned for a cup of hot coffee. In the skirmishes with the Army, he watched men die whom he had shared a cigarette with the night before. He would lean over them with his camera and film them from somewhere outside himself, as if he were a long way away looking at their bodies through a telescope. I must hang on to my sanity, he kept repeating, as he had often done in similar situations. Childhood images—such as the day he went to bury the dead in the concentration camp—returned along with images from recent wars. He knew by experience that he absorbed everything, that every event was imprinted in his memory, but that sometimes months or years passed before he realized how deeply an episode had marked him. It was as if memory congealed somewhere, then suddenly, through some mechanism of association, appeared before his eyes with blinding intensity. He asked himself why he stayed; why didn't he get the hell out of there, back to the city? That made infinitely more sense than remaining in this labyrinth of nightmares. Leave, go rest for a while at La Colonia, be soothed by the exhalation of his cousins' cinnamon, clove, vanilla, and lemon. But he stayed on. He followed the guerrillas everywhere, lugging his film equipment as others packed their weapons. He was present one afternoon when Comandante Rogelio was carried into camp on an improvised stretcher, wrapped in a blanket, shivering, writhing, poisoned by the sting of a scorpion.

"What's all the fuss, *compañeros?* Nobody dies of a scorpion sting," the Comandante murmured. "Go on, I'll get through this myself."

Rolf Carlé had contradictory feelings about the Comandante; he was never comfortable in his presence. He felt he did not have his full confidence, and for that reason could not understand why he was letting him film. He was troubled by the man's sternness, but he also admired what he accomplished with his men. The Comandante received a contingent of city boys and after a few months he had made them into fighters hardened to fatigue and pain, tough, but somehow still clinging to their youthful ideals.

The first-aid kit was nearly empty; there was no antidote for the sting. Rolf stayed at the victim's side, seeing that he was kept covered, giving him water, keeping him clean. After two days the fever passed, and the Comandante smiled with his eyes; Rolf knew then that in spite of everything they were friends.

For Rolf Carlé, the information he had received while he was with the guerrillas was not enough; he needed the other half of the story. He said very little as he took leave of Comandante Rogelio; they both knew the rules and it would have been inappropriate to speak of them. Without telling anyone what he had seen in the mountains, Rolf Carlé visited Army Operations Centers, accompanied soldiers on sorties, talked with officers, interviewed the President, and even obtained permission to observe military training. When he was finished, he had thousands of meters of film, hundreds of photographs, hours of tapes; he had more information on the subject than anyone in the nation.

"Do you think the guerrillas will win, Rolf?"

"Frankly, *señor* Aravena, no."

"They succeeded in Cuba. They demonstrated there that an army can be overthrown."

"But that was years ago, the gringos will never allow a revolution now. The conditions were different in Cuba. There they were rebelling against a dictatorship and had the support of the people. Here we have a democracy that has its defects, it's true, but people are proud of it. The guerrillas can't count on the sympathy of the people, and with few exceptions their only recruits have come from the universities."

"What do you think of them?"

"They're idealistic, and they're courageous."

"I want to see everything you got, Rolf," Aravena demanded.

"I have to edit the film, and cut the parts that can't be aired. You once told me that we're not here to change the course of history, but to give the news."

"I never get used to your pedantic fits, Rolf. So you think your film could change the country's destiny?"

"Yes, I do."

"That's a documentary I must have in my archives."

"I can't let it get into the hands of the Army—it would be fatal for the men who are in the mountains. I can't betray them, and I'm sure you would feel the same way."

The Director of National Television puffed on his cigar in silence, studying his disciple through a haze of smoke, without a trace of sarcasm, thinking, remembering his own years of opposition to the dictatorship of the General, reliving his emotions from that time.

"You don't like to accept advice, but this time you'd better listen to me, Rolf," he said finally. "Hide that film, because the government knows it exists and will try to get it from you one way or another. Edit it, make your cuts, keep what you think is necessary—but I warn you, you're sitting on dynamite. Finally, someday soon we can air your documentary, and—who knows—maybe in ten years we can even show what now you think would change the course of history."

On Saturday, Rolf Carlé arrived at La Colonia with a locked suitcase. He handed it to his aunt and uncle, asking them not to say anything about it, and to hide it until he came for it. Without comment,

Burgel wrapped it in a plastic curtain and Rupert hid it beneath some boards in the carpentry shop.

The factory whistle blew at 7 a.m.; the door opened and two hundred women crowded in, filing by in a line past women supervisors who checked us from head to toe as a precaution against possible sabotage. Everything from soldiers' boots to generals' ribbons were manufactured there, all of it measured and weighed so that not a button, a buckle, a thread would fall into unauthorized hands. As the captain in charge of the factory often said, Those sons of bitches are capable of copying our uniforms and infiltrating our troops so they can hand the country over to the Communists, damn them. The enormous windowless rooms were lighted with fluorescent lights and air was forced in through a ventilation system in the ceiling. All along the walls, two meters above the rows of sewing machines, ran a narrow balcony patrolled by guards whose duty was to control the pace of the work so that no stutter, no shudder, no sneeze should slow production. The offices were on that level: small cubicles for officers, bookkeepers, and secretaries. A constant roar like a great waterfall obliged everyone to wear earplugs and to communicate with gestures. At noon, above the deafening noise, everyone listened for the whistle that called them to the lunchrooms where an unappetizing but filling meal was served, not unlike Army mess. For many of the women that was the only meal of the day, and some even put food aside to take home, despite the embarrassment of passing before the supervisors with paper-wrapped leftovers. Makeup was strictly forbidden, and hair had either to be short or covered by a kerchief, because once a woman's hair had caught in the spindle of a winding machine, and before the electricity was cut off her hair had been torn from her scalp. The young girls, nevertheless, worked hard to look attractive—colorful kerchiefs, short skirts, and a touch of lipstick—hoping to catch the eye of one of their bosses and better their fortune by moving up two meters to the balcony of the office workers, where both salary and treatment were more dignified. An uncorroborated story about an operator who had married an officer fed the imagination of the new workers, but the older women never lifted their eyes toward such fancies; they labored silently and quickly to add to their quota.

Colonel Tolomeo Rodríguez came regularly to inspect the factory. He was accompanied by a noticeable chill in the air and an increase in noise level. The effect of his rank and the power emanating from his person were so great that he gained respect without having to raise his voice or gesticulate—a look was sufficient. He examined every detail, leafing through the books, poking into the kitchen, quizzing the operators: Are you new? What did you eat today? It's too hot in here, turn up the ventilation. Your eyes are red, go to the office and get a pass. Nothing escaped him. Some subordinates hated him; everyone feared him. It was rumored that even the President was cautious when dealing with him, because he had the respect of the young officers and at any moment might yield to the temptation to rise up against the constitutional government.

I had always seen him from a distance; my office was at the end of a corridor and my work did not require his inspection, but even from afar his authority was evident. But then, one day in March, I met him. I was watching him through the glass that separated me from the corridor, when suddenly he turned and our eyes met. Usually when he spoke, everyone avoided looking directly at him, but for what seemed an eternity I could not even blink, hypnotized by his gaze. It seemed as if time stopped; then, finally, he was walking in my direction. I could not hear his footsteps above the noise; he seemed to be floating, followed at a short distance by his secretary and the captain. As the Colonel passed, he made a slight bow, and at this distance I could appreciate his size, his expressive hands, his thick hair, his large even teeth. He was attractive in the way a wild animal is attractive. That evening when I left the factory, a dark limousine was parked before the door; an orderly handed me a written note from Colonel Tolomeo Rodríguez asking me to have dinner with him.

"The Colonel is expecting an answer," the man said as he snapped to attention.

"Tell him I can't accept, I have another engagement."

As soon as I got home, I told Mimí, who ignored the fact that this man was Huberto Naranjo's enemy and appraised the situation from the point of view of the romances that nurtured her leisure hours. Her conclusion was that I had done the proper thing: It's always good to make a man beg, she repeated once again.

"You must be the first woman who ever rejected his invitation. I'll bet he calls tomorrow," she predicted.

But he did not call. I knew nothing more of him until the following Friday, when he made a surprise visit to the factory. When I heard he was in the building, I realized I had been waiting for him: glancing down the corridor, trying to hear his footsteps above the clatter of the machines, apprehensive about his appearing and at the same time hoping to see him with an impatience I had forgotten; I had not suffered that kind of torment since the beginning of my relationship with Huberto Naranjo. The Colonel, however, did not come near my office, and when the noon whistle blew I sighed with a mixture of relief and disappointment. In the days that followed, I thought of him only occasionally.

Nearly three weeks later, when I returned home from work I found Colonel Tolomeo Rodríguez having coffee with Mimí. He was sitting on one of the Oriental divans; he stood up, unsmiling, and offered his hand.

"I hope this visit does not come at an inconvenient time. I wanted to talk to you," he said.

"He wants to talk to you," Mimí parroted, pale as one of the Japanese prints on the wall.

"It has been some time since I've seen you, so I've taken the liberty of calling on you," he said, in the ceremonious tone he frequently affected.

"That's why he came," Mimí confirmed.

"Would you accept my invitation to have dinner?"

"He wants you to have dinner with him," Mimí translated once again. She was on the verge of collapse; she had recognized him the moment he walked in, and memories had flooded back. This was the man who had made the quarterly inspections of Santa María while she was imprisoned there. She was overwrought, even though she was certain the Colonel could not possibly connect the image of a wretched inmate of The Harem—half-dead from malaria, covered with sores, shaved head—with the astonishing woman now serving him coffee.

Why did I not refuse a second time? Not because of fear, as I rationalized then. I wanted to go with him. I showered, to rinse away the day's exhaustion, put on my black dress, brushed my hair, and returned to the living room, divided between curiosity and anger with myself for feeling I was betraying Huberto. The Colonel rather ostentatiously offered me his arm, but I swept by without taking it, to the distress of Mimí, who still had not recovered from her shock. I climbed into the limousine, hoping that the neighbors would not see the motorcycle escort and believe I had become the mistress of a general. The chauffeur drove us to one of the most exclusive restaurants in the city, a Versailles-style mansion where the chef greeted his most honored clients, and an ancient adorned in a Presidential sash and armed with a small silver cup tasted the wines himself. The Colonel seemed completely at ease, but I felt marooned amid the blue brocade chairs, the flamboyant candelabra, and the battalion of servants. I was handed a menu in French, but Rodríguez, perceiving my discomfort, ordered for me. I found myself facing a crab I did not know how to attack, but a waiter removed the meat from the shell and placed it on my plate. Regarding the array of curved and straight-bladed knives, assorted goblets, and finger bowls, I was grateful for Mimí's courses at the institute for beauty queens and for the coaching of our decorator friend. I was able to get by without making a fool of myself until I was served a mandarin orange sorbet between the entrée and the meat course. I stared at the small ball garnished with a mint leaf and asked why I was being served dessert before the second course. Rodríguez laughed, and that laughter erased the braid from his sleeves and several years from his face. Everything was easier after that. He no longer seemed a symbol of national power. I studied him in the glow of those resplendent candles and he asked why I was staring. I replied that he reminded me of a stuffed puma I knew.

"Tell me about your life, Colonel," I asked when dessert arrived.

I think my request surprised him, and he was instantly on guard, but then must have realized that I was not an enemy spy. I could almost read his thoughts: She's just a poor girl from the factory; I wonder what her connection is with that television actress—a gorgeous woman, certainly much prettier than this unfashionable girl; I was tempted to ask the other one out, but I've heard she's a fag—hard as it is to believe; at any rate, I can't run the risk of being seen with a pervert.

He eventually told me about his childhood on a hacienda in an arid province; high windblown plains where water and vegetation were particularly prized and where people were strong because life was so harsh. He was not a man of the tropics: his memories were of long horseback rides across desert land, of scorching noonday heat. His father, a local political boss, had sent him off to the Army when he was eighteen without asking his opinion. I want you to serve your country with honor, son. That's how it has to be. And he had done it without hesitation. Discipline comes first; the man who knows how to obey learns to command. He had studied engineering and political science; he had traveled; he read little; he liked music very much; he considered himself a frugal man, almost abstemious; he was married, the father of three daughters. Despite his reputation for severity, that night he exhibited a high good humor and, as we finished, thanked me for my company. He had enjoyed himself, he said; he thought I had an original mind—although he had not heard more than four sentences from me; he had dominated the conversation.

"I'm the one who's grateful, Colonel. I've never been here before—it's very elegant."

"It doesn't have to be the last time, Eva. Can we see each other next week?"

"Why?"

"Well, to get to know each other better . . ."

"Do you want to go to bed with me, Colonel?"

He dropped his fork, and for nearly a minute stared at his plate.

"That is a crude question and it deserves a crude answer," he replied finally. "Yes, that's what I want. Do you accept?"

"No, thank you very much. Sex without love makes me melancholy."

"I didn't say love is excluded."

"And your wife?"

"Let's be very clear on this point. My wife has nothing to do with this conversation and we will not mention her again. I'd rather talk about us. I'm not the one who should say it, but I can make you happy if you'll let me."

"Let's not beat about the bush, Colonel. You're a powerful man. You can do whatever you choose, and usually do—isn't that so?"

"You're mistaken. In my position I have certain responsibilities and duties. I carry them out on behalf of the nation. I am a soldier; I do not abuse my privileges, especially in personal matters. I intend to seduce you, not coerce you. I am sure I will succeed, because we're attracted to each other. I'll make you change your mind...and you may find yourself falling in love with me."

"I'm sorry, but I doubt that."

"Prepare your defenses, Eva, because I'm not going to give you a minute's peace until you accept me." He smiled.

"If that's your intention, let's not waste each other's time. I don't want to argue with you, because that could be dangerous for me. Let's go. We'll get this over with tonight, and then you'll leave me alone."

The Colonel leapt to his feet, his face fiery red. Two waiters rushed toward him, and people at neighboring tables turned to stare. He sat down stiffly, breathing rapidly, apparently composing his thoughts.

"I don't know what kind of woman you are," he said finally. His voice was icy. I could hear how angry he was. "Under normal circumstances, I would accept your challenge and we would immediately go somewhere private. But I've decided to go about this in a different way. I won't beg you. I am sure *you* will come to *me*, and if you are lucky my proposition will still stand. Call me when you want to see me," Rodríguez said curtly, handing me a card bearing the national coat of arms and beneath it his name printed in italic.

It was early when I got home. Mimí thought I was absolutely insane. The Colonel was a powerful man and could create all kinds of problems for us. Couldn't I have been more courteous? The next day, I resigned my job at the factory, collected my things, and left, hoping to escape from the man who represented everything that for so many years Huberto Naranjo had been risking his life to change.

"All's well that ends well," was Mimí's comment when she found that a spin of the wheel of fortune had set me on the road she considered I should always have been on. "Now you can write in earnest."

She was sitting at the dining-room table with her cards fanned out before her, where she could read that my destiny was to tell stories and everything else was wasted energy—something I myself had suspected the first time I read *A Thousand and One Nights*. Mimí maintained that each of us is born with a talent, and that happiness or misfortune depends on discovering what that talent is and whether there is a demand for it in the world, because there are remarkable skills that go unappreciated, like that of a friend of hers who could hold his breath underwater for three minutes, a gift that was of absolutely no use to him. She herself was happy, because she had found hers. She was starring in a telenovela as the evil Alejandra, the rival of Belinda, a blind girl who in the last episodes would recover her sight—predictably, in such dramas—and marry the hero. Her scripts were scattered about the house and I was helping her memorize her lines. I had to play all the other parts: (*Luis Alfredo presses his eyes to keep from crying, because men do not cry.*) Trust your feelings. . . . Let me pay for the operation on your eyes, my darling. (*Belinda trembles, she fears she will lose this man she loves.*) I want to believe you love me . . . but there is another woman in your life, Luis Alfredo. (*He looks into those beautiful, sightless eyes.*) Alejandra means nothing to me; she is only interested in the fortune of the Martínez de la Roca, but she won't get it. No one will ever separate us, my dearest Belinda. (*He kisses her, and she surrenders to that sublime embrace, suggesting to the audience that something may . . . or may not . . . happen. Camera pans to show Alejandra spying on them from the doorway, her face disfigured by jealousy. Cut to Studio B.*)

"You have to take these programs on faith. You have to believe in them, period," said Mimí, between two of Alejandra's speeches. "If you start analyzing them, you ruin them."

She argued that anyone can dream up dramas like Belinda's and Luis Alfredo's, but I better than anyone, since I had spent years listening to them in kitchens, believing they were true, and feeling betrayed when I learned that reality was not like the stories on the radio. Mimí outlined the undeniable advantages of working for television, where there was room for every absurdity and where every character, however extravagant, had a chance to win the hearts of an unsuspecting public—a privilege rarely accorded a book. That evening she came home carrying a dozen little cakes and a heavy, beautifully wrapped package. It was a typewriter. So you can get to work, she said. We spent part of the night sitting on the bed drinking wine, eating cookies, and discussing the ideal plot—a tangle of passions, divorces, bastards, ingénues and villains, wealthy and destitute, that would ensnare the viewers from the first word and keep them glued to the screen through two hundred emotional episodes. We were tipsy and covered with sugar by the time we went to bed, and I dreamed of blind girls and jealous men.

I awakened early. It was a soft and slightly rainy Wednesday, not very different from others in my life, but I treasure that Wednesday as a special day, one that belonged only to me. Ever since the schoolteacher Inés had taught me the alphabet, I had written almost every night, but I felt that today was different, something that could change my life. I poured a cup of black coffee and sat down at the typewriter. I took a clean white piece of paper—like a sheet freshly ironed for making love—and rolled it into the carriage. Then I felt something odd, like a pleasant tickling in my bones, a breeze blowing through the network of veins beneath my skin. I believed that that page had been waiting for me for more than twenty years, that I had lived only for that instant, and I hoped that from that moment my only task would be to capture the stories floating in the thin air, to make them mine. I wrote my name, and immediately the words began to flow, one thing linked to another and another. Characters stepped from the shadows where they had been hidden for years into the light of that Wednesday, each with a face, a voice, passions, and obsessions. I could see an order to the stories stored in my genetic memory since before my birth, and the many others I had been writing for years in my notebooks. I began to remember events that had happened long ago; I recalled the tales my mother told me when we were living among the Professor's idiots, cancer patients, and mummies; a snakebitten Indian appeared, and a tyrant with hands devoured by leprosy; I rescued an old maid who had been scalped as if by a spinning machine, a dignitary in a bishop's plush chair, an Arab with a generous heart, and the many other men and women whose lives were in my hands to dispose of at will. Little by little, the past was transformed into the present, and the future was also mine; the dead came alive with an illusion of eternity; those who had been separated were reunited, and all that had been lost in oblivion regained precise dimensions.

No one interrupted me, and I spent almost all day writing, so absorbed I forgot even to eat. At four that afternoon I saw a cup of chocolate before my eyes.

"Here, I brought you something warm."

I looked up at Mimí, tall and slim, wrapped in a blue kimono, and needed a few moments to recognize her; I had been deep in the jungle catching up with a little red-haired girl. I followed my own rhythm, ignoring the recommendations I had received: scripts are organized into two columns; each episode has twenty-five scenes; be careful, because scene changes are very expensive and the actors get confused if the speeches are too long; every key sentence must be repeated three times, and keep the plot simple; begin from the premise that your audience is composed of morons. A stack of pages grew on the table, spattered with notes, corrections, hieroglyphics, and coffee stains: but as soon as I had begun dusting off memories and weaving destinies, I saw that I did not know where I was going, or what the resolution would be—if there was one. I suspected that I would reach the end only at my own death, and was fascinated by the idea that I was another character in the story, and that I had the power to determine my fate, or invent a life for myself. The plot became more complicated, the characters more and more rebellious. I was working—if work is what that celebration can be called—many hours a day, from dawn till late at night. I forgot everything; I ate when Mimí fed me and went to sleep because she led me to bed. But even in dreams I was still deep in my new universe, hand in hand with my characters to keep them from escaping their faint outlines and returning to the nebula of stories that remained to be told.

After three weeks, Mimí thought it was time to reap some practical results from that delirium before I disappeared, swallowed up by my own words. She succeeded in getting an interview with the Director of National Television, to interest him in the story. She feared for my mental health if I continued to work without hope of seeing the product on the screen. When the day came, she dressed in white—according to her horoscope, the best color for that day—fastened a chain around her neck with a medallion of the Maharishi nesting deep in her cleavage, and dragged me off to the appointment. I felt peaceful and calm, as always when I was with her, secure in the aura of that mythological being.

Aravena received us in his office of plastic and glass, seated behind an imposing desk that could not disguise his gourmand's belly. I was disappointed when I saw that obese man with the cowlike eyes and the half-smoked cigar, so unlike the energetic man I had pictured when I read his articles. Inattentive, because the dullest part of his job was the unavoidable circus of theater people, Aravena acknowledged our presence, barely glancing toward us, his eyes focused on a window over-looking neighboring rooftops and the clouds of a gathering storm. He asked me how close I was to finishing the script; he glanced at the folder I handed him, picked it up in a dead-white paw, and murmured that he would read it when he had time. I reached out and took back my manu-script, but Mimí grabbed it from me and handed it to him once again, this time forcing him to look at her. She fluttered her eyelashes with deadly precision, moistened her bright red lips, and invited him to din-ner the following Saturday—only a few friends, an intimate gathering, she said in the irresistible purr she had cultivated to disguise the tenor voice she had been born with. Aravena was enmeshed in a visible fog, a lascivious aroma, a silken spiderweb. He sat mesmerized, folder in hand, totally nonplussed. I doubt whether he had ever received such a sexually loaded invitation. Cigar ash fell to the table, unnoticed.

"Did you have to ask him to our house?" I complained after we left.

"I'm going to get that script of yours accepted if it's the last thing I do in my life."

"You're not planning to seduce him . . ."

"How do you think things get done in this business?"

Saturday dawned. It was raining, and rain continued throughout the day and evening, while Mimí hurried around preparing an austere dinner based on brown rice, which had been considered elegant ever since the macrobioticians and vegetarians had instilled fear and trembling in hu-mankind with their dietary theories. Your fat man is going to die of hunger, I muttered, dicing carrots, but she was unmoved, primarily con-cerned with arranging flowers, lighting incense, selecting music, and plumping silk cushions—because it had also become fashionable to take off one's shoes and sit on the floor. She had invited eight guests, all theater people except Aravena, who brought the copper-haired man we always saw with his camera on the barricades of some remote revolution—what was his name? I shook his hand with the vague sen-sation of having met him before.

After dinner Aravena took me aside and confessed his fascination with Mimí. He had not been able to stop thinking about her; her absence was like a painful burn.

"She is the absolute female. We all have something of the andro-gyne about us, something male, something female, but she's stripped herself of any vestige of masculinity and built herself those splendid curves. She's totally *woman*, adorable," he said, wiping his forehead with his handkerchief.

I looked at my friend, so dear, so familiar, the features designed with pencils and lipsticks, the rounded hips and breasts, the sleek torso, innocent of maternity or pleasure, each line of her body won with un-yielding tenacity. Only I know the true nature of that fictional woman painfully created to satisfy the dreams of others, but never to live her own. I have seen her without makeup, exhausted and sad; I have been beside her through depression, illness, insomnia, and fatigue; I love with all my heart the fragile and ambiguous human being behind the feathers and glitter. I asked myself whether this man with the thick lips and swollen hands would know how to penetrate the surface and discover the companion, the mother, the sister, that Mimí truly is. From the other end of the room she was conscious of the stare of her new admirer. I had the impulse to stop her, to protect her, but I refrained.

"Come on, Eva. Tell our friend a story," said Mimí, dropping down beside Aravena.

"What would you like?"

"Something racy, don't you think?" she said suggestively.

I sat down with my legs folded like an Indian, closed my eyes, and let my mind wander through the dunes of a white desert, as I always do when I invent a story. Soon against those sands I saw a woman in a yellow taffeta petticoat, faint brushstrokes of the cold lands my mother had appropriated from Professor Jones's magazines, and the games La Señora had created for the General's revelries. I began my story. Mimí says I have a special voice for storytelling, a voice that, although mine, also seems to belong to someone else, as if it issued from the earth to rise through my body. I felt the room fading away, effaced by the new horizons I convoked. The guests grew still.

Times were hard in the south. Not in the south of this country, but the south of the world, where seasons are reversed and winter does not occur at Christmas-time as it does in civilized nations, but in the middle of the year, as in barbaric lands . . .

When I finished, Rolf Carlé was the only one who did not applaud.

Later he confessed to me that he was a long time returning from that austral pampa where I had left two lovers with a bag of gold coins, and when he did, he was determined to turn my story into a film before the ghosts of that pair of picaros absorbed his dreams. I wondered why Rolf Carlé seemed so familiar; it was more than having seen him on television. I looked into my past, trying to think where I might have met him, but I was sure I had not known him—or anyone like him. I wanted to touch him. I moved closer and ran my finger down the back of his hand.

"My mother had freckles, too . . ." Rolf Carlé did not move, but neither did he take my hand. "Someone told me you've been in the mountains with the guerrillas."

"I've been a lot of places."

"Tell me . . ."

We sat on the floor, and he answered almost all my questions. He talked about his career, how, observing the world through a lens, it had taken him around the globe. We had such a good time the rest of the evening that we did not notice as the others began to leave. He was the last to go, and he left only because Aravena hauled him away. At the door he told me he would be away for a few days filming uprisings in Prague, where the Czechs were confronting invading tanks with rocks and stones. I wanted to kiss him goodbye, but he shook my hand with a little nod of the head that I found rather solemn.

Four days later, when Aravena called me to sign a contract, it was still raining; pails were placed around his luxurious office to catch the leaks. As he explained without preliminaries, the script did not even remotely fit the usual patterns; in fact, the whole thing was a jumble of bizarre characters and unrealistic anecdotes; it lacked true romance; the protagonists were neither good-looking nor rich; it was almost impossible to follow the train of events; the audience would be totally lost. In sum, it was a mess and no one with an ounce of sense would run the risk of producing it, but he was going to do it because he could not resist the temptation to scandalize the country with such rubbish—and because Mimí had asked him to.

"Keep writing, Eva, I'm curious about how you're going to end such a mishmash," he said as he showed me to the door.

The floods began on the third day of the rains, and on the fifth day the government decreed a state of emergency. Since no agency took the precaution of cleaning the drainage ditches or storm sewers, catastrophes caused by bad weather were common, but this storm surpassed imagination. The rain dragged shacks from the hillsides, overflowed the river that runs through the city, flooded houses, carried away cars, trees, and half the sports stadium. Cameramen from National Television climbed into rubber boats and filmed victims on the roofs of houses waiting patiently to be rescued by military helicopters. Although stunned and hungry, many sang, because it would have been pointless to aggravate misfortune by complaining. The rain ceased at the end of a week, the result of the same empirical solution used years before to combat the drought. Again the Bishop paraded the statue of the Nazarene, and a huge crowd followed with their umbrellas, praying and making vows, mocked by weather-bureau employees who had communicated with colleagues in Miami and found that, according to weather balloons and cloud measurements, the drenching rain would continue for nine more days. The sky, however, cleared only three hours after the Nazarene was returned to his altar in the Cathedral, wet as a dishrag despite the canopy that had been intended to protect him. Dye from his wig ran in dark rivulets down his face; the devout fell to their knees, crying that the statue was sweating blood. This purported miracle added to the prestige of the Catholic Church and calmed some souls worried by the ideological inroads of Marxists and the arrival of the first groups of Mormons, ingenuous and energetic youths in short-sleeved shirts who went about knocking on doors and converting the unwary.

When the rain had stopped and an accounting was being taken of the losses in order to repair the damage and return to normal life, a coffin, modest but in perfect condition, was found floating near the plaza of the Father of the Nation. The heavy rain had washed it down from a hovel in the hills of the western part of the city along streets turned into rushing torrents and deposited it unharmed in the center of the city. When it was opened, an elderly woman was discovered, peacefully asleep. I saw her on the nine-o'clock news, called the station for further details, and grabbed Mimí and rushed to the shelter the Army had set up to house the flood victims. There we found large campaign tents crammed with families waiting for good weather. Many had lost even their identification papers, but there was no melancholy in those tents: the disaster offered a good excuse to rest and an opportunity to make new friends; tomorrow they would worry about how they were going to get along; it was useless to weep today over what the floods had carried off. There, too, we found Elvira in her nightgown, thin and irate, sitting on a bare mattress recounting to a circle of listeners how she had been saved from the flood in her strange ark. And that is how I got back my *abuela*. Even with the white hair and the map of wrinkles that had transformed her face, I had recognized her the moment I saw her on the screen, for her spirit had not been dulled during our long separation: she was the same woman who had accepted my stories in exchange for fried bananas and the right to play funeral in her coffin. I pushed people aside, threw my arms around my *abuela*, and hugged her with the urgency stored during the long years she had been lost to me. Elvira made no fuss at all over me; she kissed me as if we had seen each other only yesterday and the changes in my appearance were nothing but a trick of her tired eyes.

"Imagine, little bird, all that sleeping in the box so that when death came for me I'd be ready, and then what came for me was life. I'm never going to lie down in a coffin again, not even when it's time to take me to the cemetery. I want to be buried standing up, like a tree."

We took Elvira home. In the taxi, all through the ride, Elvira was studying Mimí. She had never seen anyone like her; the nearest thing she could think of was a life-size doll. Later she felt her all over with her wise old cook's hands and commented that she had skin whiter and smoother than an onion and breasts as firm as green grapefruit, and she smelled like an almond-and-spice torte from the Swiss pastry shop. When she put on her eyeglasses to see her better, she was convinced beyond any doubt that Mimí was not a creature of this world. She's an archangel, she concluded. Mimí liked Elvira from the first moment, because besides me and her *mamma*—whose love had never faltered—Mimí had no family of her own; all her relatives had turned their back when they saw Melesio in a woman's body. She needed an *abuela*, too. Elvira accepted our hospitality because the flood had carried off all her material belongings except the coffin, to which Mimí had no objections although it did not harmonize with the décor. But Elvira did not want it. The coffin had saved her life once, and she was not prepared to run that risk a second time.

Rolf Carlé called me when he returned from Prague a few days later. He came looking for me in a jeep that had seen far better days, and we set off in the direction of the coast. By midmorning we found a beach with translucent water and rosy sands, very different from the sea of crashing waves on which I had so often sailed in the dining room of the spinster and the bachelor. We splashed around in the water and lay in the sun until we were hungry; then we dressed and went in search of a place that sold fried fish. We spent the afternoon sitting looking at the sea, drinking white wine and telling each other our life stories. I told him about my childhood as a servant in other people's homes, about how Elvira had been saved from the waters, about Riad Halabí, and many other things, but from the strong habit of secrecy I did not mention Huberto Naranjo. Rolf Carlé, in turn, told me about being hungry during the war, about the flight of his brother Jochen, about his father being hanged in the woods, and about the prison camp.

"It's strange," he said. "This is the first time I've put those things into words."

"Why?"

"I don't know, they seemed secret. They're the darkest part of my past," he said, and then in silence stared toward the sea with a different expression in his gray eyes.

"What happened to Katharina?"

"She died a sad death, alone in a hospital."

"All right, she died, but not the way you say. Let's find a happy ending for her. It was Sunday, the first sunny day of the season. Katharina felt very good when she woke up, and the nurse put her in a canvas chair on the terrace, her legs wrapped in a blanket. Your sister sat looking at the birds beginning to build nests beneath the eaves, the budding tree branches. She was warm and safe, the way she was when she slept in your arms beneath the kitchen table—in fact, she was dreaming of you at that very moment. She had no real memory, but her instinct retained intact the warmth you gave her, and every time she felt happy, she whispered your name. She was doing just that—happily saying your name—when, without her knowing, her spirit drifted away.

Your mother arrived a little later to visit her, as she did every Sunday, and found her motionless, but smiling. She closed her eyes, kissed her forehead, and bought a bride's coffin, where she lay wrapped in the white mantle."

"And my mother, do you have something good for her, too?" asked Rolf Carlé in an unsteady voice.

"Yes. She returned home from the cemetery and found that the neighbors had put flowers in all the vases so she wouldn't feel alone. Monday was baking day and she took off her best dress, put on her apron, and began to mix dough. She felt happy, because all her children were happy now—Jochen had found a good woman and started a family somewhere, Rolf was making his life in America, and now Katharina, freed of the bonds of the flesh, could at last fly."

"Why do you think my mother has never agreed to come here to live?"

"I don't know . . . maybe she didn't want to leave her country."

"She's old and alone—she would be much better off in La Colonia with my aunt and uncle."

"Not everyone is destined to emigrate, Rolf. She has found peace, cultivating her garden and her memories."

ELEVEN

The damage caused by the floods was so massive that for a week other news stories were overshadowed, and if it had not been for Rolf Carlé the massacre in one of the Army Operations Centers would have passed almost unnoticed, drowned in the turbid waters of the deluge and the duplicity of those in power. A group of political prisoners had rebelled and, after overpowering their guards and seizing their weapons, had entrenched themselves in one area of the compound. The *comandante*, a dauntless man given to hasty decisions, did not request instructions; he simply gave the order to pulverize the rioters, and his words were taken literally. His men attacked the prisoners with weapons of war, killing an undetermined number; no wounded remained because the survivors were rounded up in a courtyard and summarily executed. Once the guards recovered from their bloody frenzy and counted the bodies, they realized that it would be difficult to explain their action to the public, and that the press would not easily be diverted with a claim that they were dealing with an unsubstantiated rumor. The detonations of the mortars had killed birds in their flight, and dead birds had rained down for several kilometers around—an oddity impossible to justify, since few were prepared to accept a new miracle from the Nazarene. There was also the problem of the pervasive stench that rose from the common graves and fouled the air. As a first measure, no reporter was allowed in, and an attempt was made to cloak the zone in a mantle of solitude and silence. The government had no alternative but to back the *comandante*'s actions, but the President was furious and fumed in the privacy of his Cabinet, We can't interfere with the forces of order, but incidents like these jeopardize our democracy. Then the government spokesman improvised the story that the subversives had quarreled among themselves and killed each other, and they repeated this fabrication so often that they ended up believing it themselves. Rolf Carlé, however, knew too much about the situation to accept the official version and, without waiting for Aravena to assign him, pushed on ahead of everyone else. He obtained part of the truth from his friends in the mountains, and the rest he verified with the same guards who had exterminated the prisoners: they needed only a couple of beers to talk, because by then they were haunted by bad consciences. Three days later, by the time the odor of the corpses was dissipating and the last rotting birds had been swept away, Rolf Carlé had irrefutable proof of what had happened, and was ready to challenge the censors. Aravena warned him not to have any illusions: not a word of this could appear on television. Rolf had his first argument with his mentor; he accused him of cowardice and collusion, but Aravena was not to be swayed. Then Rolf spoke with a couple of deputies from the opposition party and showed them his films and photographs, so they could see for themselves the methods the government was using to combat the guerrillas, as well as the inhuman conditions in which the detainees were being held. That material was then exhibited in the Parliament, where politicians denounced the slaughter and demanded that the tombs be opened and the guilty parties be brought to justice. As the President was assuring the country that he was ready to push the investigation to its ultimate consequences, even if it meant resigning his office, a crew of new recruits was blacktopping a hastily constructed playing field and planting a double row of trees to cover the graves; files disappeared through cracks in the judicial process; and the directors of all the media were summoned by the Minister of the Interior and warned of the consequences of defaming the armed forces. Rolf Carlé continued to insist with a stubbornness that finally triumphed over Aravena's prudence and the evasions of the deputies, who at least approved a tepid reprimand of the *comandante* and a decree ordering that political prisoners should be treated in accord with the Constitution: they had a right to public trials and to serve their sentences in jails, not in special centers to which no civilian authority had access. As a result, nine guerrillas held in Fort El Tucán were transferred to the penal colony on Santa María—a measure that meant the same brutal conditions for them, but permitted the government to quash the scandal, which sank into the swamp of collective indifference.

That same week Elvira announced she had seen a ghost in the patio, but no one paid any attention to her. Mimí was in love, and I only half listened, absorbed in the turbulent passions of my script. The typewriter clicked all day, leaving me without energy for routine matters.

"There's a soul in pain wandering around this house, little bird," Elvira insisted.

"Where?"

"It keeps looking over the back wall. It's the spirit of a man. We ought to take precautions, I say. Tomorrow early I'll go buy a liquid that will protect us against wandering spirits."

"Is it something you take?"

"No, child, where do you get such ideas? It's to wash down the house. It has to be painted on all the walls and floors—everywhere."

"That sounds like a lot of work. Can't you buy a spray?"

"Of course not, child! Those modern contraptions don't work with dead spirits."

"But I didn't see anything, *abuela*."

"Well, I did. It's dressed like a person, and black as San Martín de Porres, but it isn't human. When I see it I get goose bumps all over, little bird. It must be someone who's lost and looking for his way. Maybe it hasn't finished dying."

"Maybe not, *abuela*."

We were not being haunted by an errant ectoplasm, however, as we learned that same day when El Negro finally rang the doorbell. Elvira was so terrified when she saw him that she fell flat on the floor. He had been sent by Comandante Rogelio and had loitered about in the street, not daring to ask for me for fear of attracting attention.

"Do you remember me? We met when you went to live with La Señora. I was working in that bar on Calle República," he said. "The first time I saw you, you were just a kid."

I was uneasy. Naranjo had never used an intermediary, and these were not times to trust anyone—but I followed El Negro to a gas station on the outskirts of the city. Comandante Rogelio was waiting for me, hiding in a storeroom for tires. My eyes took several seconds to adjust to the darkness before I saw the man I had loved so deeply but now seemed such a stranger. It had been some weeks since we had seen each other, and I had not had a chance to tell him about the changes in my life. After we kissed, there among the gasoline drums and old crankcase oil, Huberto told me he needed a plan of the factory, and asked me to get it for him. The guerrillas intended to disguise several men as Army officers, walk into Santa María, rescue their comrades— and, in passing, deliver a mortal blow to the government and an unforgettable embarrassment to the Army. The fact that I was not working there any longer and had no access to the building was a major setback. Then I made the mistake of telling Huberto about my dinner with Colonel Tolomeo Rodríguez. I could tell he was furious because he began asking entirely reasonable questions but with a mocking smile that I knew well. We agreed to meet at the zoo the following Sunday.

That night, after admiring herself in the current episode of her telenovela in the company of Elvira, for whom seeing Mimí in two places at the same time was further proof of her celestial nature, Mimí came to my room to tell me good night, as she always did, and found me drawing lines on a sheet of paper. She wanted to know what I was doing.

"Don't *you* get mixed up in it!" she exclaimed, terrified when she heard the plan.

"I have to do it, Mimí. We can't continue to ignore what's going on in our own country."

"Yes, we can. We've done it up till now, and because we have, we're doing fine. Besides, no one in this country cares about those things;

your guerrillas don't have the slightest chance. Remember where we started, Eva! I was cursed by being born a woman in a man's body, I've been persecuted for being homosexual. I've been raped, tortured, put in prison, but look where I am now—all on my own effort. And you? All you've ever done is work, work, work. You were born a bastard with blood of every color in your veins, you never had a family, no one sent you to school or had you vaccinated or gave you vitamins. But we've come out on top. And you want to throw it all away?"

In a way it was true that we had made our peace with life. We had been so poor that at first we hadn't known the value of money, and it had poured through our fingers like sand, but now we were earning enough for a few luxuries. We felt rich. I had received an advance for my script that seemed outrageous to me, and it lay very heavy in my purse. Mimí felt she was living the best years of her life. She had found the perfect balance for her many-colored pills, and felt so comfortable in her body that she might have been born with it. Nothing remained of her former timidity, and she could even joke about things that once had been a source of embarrassment. Besides her role as Alejandra in the television series, she was rehearsing the part of the Caballero de Eón, an eighteenth-century transvestite secret agent who spent his life in woman's clothing serving the kings of France, and was discovered only when, at the age of eighty-two, his corpse was being readied for burial. Mimí had every qualification for the role, and our most famous playwright had written the play especially for her. She was even happier because she believed she had finally found the man her horoscope had predicted, the man who would be beside her in her mature years. Ever since she had met Aravena, her youthful dreams had been reborn. She had never had such a relationship: he asked nothing of her, he lavished gifts and flattery upon her, he took her to all the fashionable places for everyone to admire, and coddled her the way an art collector cares for his works of art. For the first time in my life, everything is going well. Please, Eva, Mimí pleaded, don't go looking for trouble. But I countered with the teachings I had heard so often from Huberto Naranjo, arguing that we lived on the fringes of society and were condemned for all time to struggle for every crumb, and even if we broke the chains that had bound us from the day of our conception, we would still be captive behind the walls of a greater prison; it was not a question of changing our personal situation, but that of society as a whole. Mimí heard my speech to the end, and when she spoke it was in her man's voice and with a decisiveness that contrasted strangely with her curls and the salmon-colored lace on the sleeves of her negligee.

"Everything you've said is unbelievably naïve. In the unlikely event that your Naranjo wins his revolution, I'm sure in a very short time he would be acting with the arrogance of every man who attains power."

"That isn't true. He's different. He's thinking of the people, not himself."

"That's how it is now, because it doesn't cost him anything. He's on the run, hiding in the jungle, but it would be a different story if he came to power. Look, Eva, men like Naranjo can't ever change. They may modify the rules, but they always operate on the same principle: authority, competitiveness, greed, repression—it's always the same."

"But if he can't change things, who can?"

"You and I, for example. What has to change in this world are attitudes. But we're a long way from that, and since you've made up your mind and I can't let you do this alone, I'll go with you to the zoo. What that imbecile needs isn't a plan of the uniform factory, but of Santa María."

The last time Comandante Rogelio had seen Mimí, her name had been Melesio; she had looked like a normal man and was teaching Italian in a language institute. Even though Mimí frequently appeared on television and in the pages of the most popular magazines, he did not recognize her. He lived in a different dimension, light-years away from such frivolity: crushing snakes in the jungle, hefting firearms. I had often spoken of my friend, but nothing had prepared him for the woman in the red dress near the monkey cages; her beauty stunned him, obliterating his prejudices. No, this wasn't a queer in drag, this was a truly Olympian female who would steal the breath of a fire-eating dragon.

It was impossible for Mimí to pass unnoticed, but we tried to blend into the crowd, strolling among throngs of children with parents in tow and tossing corn to the pigeons like any family on a Sunday outing. On Comandante Rogelio's first attempt to quote theory, however, Mimí pulled him up short with one of those barrages reserved for extreme situations. She told him very explicitly to stow his speeches, because she was not as innocent as I was; that she was agreeing to help him this one time in order to be rid of him as quickly as possible, and it was her fondest hope that he would catch a bullet and land in hell so she wouldn't be bothered with any more of his shit; but she was not going to put up with him trying to sell her his Cuban ideas—he could put them he knew where; she had enough problems without taking on someone's revolution. What was he thinking of? She didn't give a fart for Marxism or any of his crew of bearded rebels; all she wanted was to live in peace, and she hoped to God he understood that, because if not, she'd explain it a different way. Then she stretched out her legs on a concrete bench and took eye pencil in hand to draw him a map on the cover of her checkbook.

The nine guerrilla fighters who had been transferred from Fort El Tucán were assigned in Santa María to a cell block for incorrigible prisoners. They had been detained seven months earlier, but had emerged from all interrogations without having talked and with an unswerving determination to return to the mountains to continue the fight. The debate in Parliament had made them front-page news, and elevated them to the status of heroes in the eyes of the university students, who papered the city with their posters.

"Put a news blackout on all their activities," ordered the President, counting on the public's forgetfulness.

"Tell the *compañeros* we're coming to free them," ordered Comandante Rogelio, counting on his men's daring.

Only one person had ever escaped from Santa María, and that had been years earlier, when a French bandit had reached the sea by drifting downriver on an improvised raft kept afloat on swollen dog cadavers; no one had attempted it since. Debilitated by heat, poor food, illness, and unrelenting violence, ordinary inmates lacked the strength to drag themselves across the courtyard, much less fight their way through the jungle in the unlikely case of a breakout. Specially guarded prisoners had no chance at all of escaping, unless they could somehow open steel doors, overpower guards armed with machine guns, pass unseen through the entire compound, leap the wall, swim a swift, piranha-infested river, and make their way through the jungle—all this bare-handed and in the last stages of enervation. Comandante Rogelio was not unaware of those colossal obstacles; nevertheless, he swore unemotionally that he would rescue the prisoners, and none of his men doubted his word, least of all the nine inmates in the escape-proof cell block. Once he had mastered his initial anger at my mention of Colonel Tolomeo Rodríguez, Huberto conceived the idea of using me as a decoy to lure the Colonel into a trap.

"All right, as long as you don't hurt him," I said.

"We're talking about kidnapping him, not killing him. We'll treat him like a princess, so we can swap him for our *compañeros*. Why are you so concerned about the man?"

"No reason ... But I warn you, it won't be easy to catch him off guard—he's accompanied by bodyguards, and he carries a weapon himself. He's no fool."

"I don't suppose he takes his escort along when he's with a woman."

"Are you asking me to seduce him?"

"No! All I want you to do is arrange to meet him in a place we will name, and then distract him briefly. We'll arrive immediately. A clean operation, no shooting, no noise."

"I'll need to gain his confidence, and that won't be possible the first time I'm out with him. I'll need time."

"I think you like this Rodríguez. You'd think you *wanted* to go to bed with him." Huberto intended his comment as a joke, but his voice was strained.

I did not reply; I was thinking that seducing Rodríguez might be very interesting, even though I was not sure whether when the time came I would hand him over to his enemies or try to warn him instead. As Mimí had said, I was not ideologically prepared for that war. Unconsciously, I smiled, and I believe that secret smile changed Huberto's plans on the spot, because he decided to return to his first scheme. Mimí thought it was suicidal; she knew how closely the prison was guarded. The arrival of visitors was announced in advance by radio, and if the visitors were officers, as Naranjo intended disguising his men, the prison commander would meet them in person at the military airport. Not even the Pope could get into Santa María without a security check.

"Then we'll have to get weapons to the *compañeros* inside," said Comandante Rogelio.

"You must be out of your mind," Mimí laughed. "Even in my time that would have been difficult—they searched everyone, coming and going—but now it's impossible. They had metal detectors, and they'd discover the weapons even if you swallowed them."

"No matter. I'll get them out of there."

In the days following our meeting at the zoo, Naranjo met us in various places to work out the details, which, as they were added to the list, made the insanity of the project even more evident. Nothing could dissuade him. Victory is for the bold, he replied whenever we pointed out the dangers. I sketched the plan of the uniform factory, and Mimí drew details of the prison; we calculated the movements of the guards; we clocked their routines; we even studied the wind direction, light, and temperature at every hour of the day. In the course of the process Mimí became infected with Huberto's excitement, and lost sight of the final goal; she forgot they were trying to free prisoners and thought of it as a kind of parlor game. Fascinated, she drew maps, made lists, imagined strategies—totally overlooking the risks—believing in her heart that, like so many other things in the nation's history, nothing would go beyond the planning stages. The undertaking was so audacious that it deserved to succeed. Comandante Rogelio, along with six companions chosen from among the most experienced and courageous guerrillas, would camp with Indians near Santa María. The tribal chieftain—motivated to cooperate after the Army had swept through his village leaving a swath of burned huts, gutted animals, and raped girls—had agreed to take the men across the river and lead them through the jungle. They would communicate with the prisoners through two Indians who worked in the prison kitchen. The day of the attempt, the detainees would be ready to disarm their guards and slip into the prison yard, where Comandante Rogelio and his men would rescue them. The weakest part of the plan—as Mimí pointed out, although no experience was needed to reach that conclusion—was how the guerrillas were going to get out of their cells. When Comandante Rogelio set Tuesday of the following week as the latest possible date for the attempt, Mimí stared at him through long mink eyelashes, realizing for the first time that he was truly serious. A decision of such magnitude could not be left to chance, so she pulled out her cards, told him to cut the deck with his left hand, laid out the cards according to an order established in an ancient Egyptian civilization, and read the message from the supernatural forces while he observed with a sarcastic smile, muttering that he must be crazy to entrust the success of such a venture to this bizarre creature.

"It can't be Tuesday, it has to be Saturday," she determined when she turned over the Magus and his head was upside down.

"It will be when I say," the Comandante replied, leaving no doubt about his opinion of such madness.

"It says Saturday here, and you're in no position to defy the tarot cards."

"Tuesday."

"Saturday afternoons half the guards go on a spree in the whore-house in Agua Santa, and the other half watch baseball on television."

That was the argument that tilted the scales in favor of the stars. It was at precisely that moment, as they were arguing, that I remembered the Universal Matter. Comandante Rogelio and Mimí looked up from the cards and stared at me, perplexed. And that is how, without ever intending it, I ended up in the company of half a dozen guerrillas mixing *porcelana* in a native hut a short distance from the house of the Turk where I had spent the best years of my adolescence.

I rode into Agua Santa in a battered car with stolen license plates, driven by El Negro. The place hadn't changed much. The main street had grown a little: there were new houses, several shops, and an occasional television antenna. Absolutely unchanged were the sound of the crick-ets, the implacable noonday heat, and the nightmare of jungle that began at the edge of the highway. Tenacious and patient, the townspeople had endured its steamy breath, and the erosion of time, virtually isolated from the rest of the country by that merciless vegetation. In principle, we should not have stopped. Our destination was the Indian village that lay halfway to Santa María, but when I saw the tiled-roof houses, the streets gleaming from the most recent rain, the women sitting in rush chairs in shadowy doorways, memories swept over me with irresistible force and I begged El Negro to drive past The Pearl of the Orient so I could take one look, if only from a distance. So many things had dis-integrated during the years since I had left, so many people had died or gone away without a goodbye, that I expected to find an unrecognizable fossil, ravaged by time and tricks of memory. To my amazement, the shop appeared unscathed before my eyes, like a mirage. The front had been rebuilt, the sign newly painted; the shopwindow displayed agricultural tools, foodstuffs, aluminum pots and pans, and two brand-new mannequins with yellow wigs. There was such an air of renewal about it that I could not resist getting out of the car to take a peek inside. The interior had also been rejuvenated with a modern counter, but the grain sacks, bolts of cheap cloth, and jars of candies were as they had been.

Riad Halabí, dressed in a batiste guayabera, his mouth covered with a white handkerchief, was adding up his accounts beside the cash register. He was exactly as I remembered him, not a minute older—as sometimes the memory of our first love remains. I walked forward timidly, moved by the tenderness I had felt when I was seventeen and I sat on his lap to ask him for the gift of a night of love, and to offer him the virginity my *madrina* used to measure with a cord of seven knots.

"Good afternoon . . . Do you sell aspirin?" was all I could say.

Riad Halabí did not look up or lift his pencil from his account book, but gestured toward the far end of the counter.

"My wife will help you, *señorita*," he said with the lisp caused by his harelip. I turned, expecting to see the schoolteacher Inés converted into the Turk's wife, as I had so often imagined; instead, I saw a girl who was probably no more than fourteen, a short, plump little brunette with red lips and an obsequious expression. I bought the aspirin, musing that years ago when this man had rejected me because I was too young, his present wife must have been crawling around in diapers. I will never know what my fate would have been had I stayed with him, but of one thing I am sure: I would have been very happy in bed. I smiled at the red-lipped girl with a mixture of complicity and envy, and left without exchanging a word or a glance with Riad Halabí. I was happy for him, for how well he looked. From that moment I have thought of him as the father that in fact he was; the image fitted him much better than that of lover for one night. Outside, El Negro was grumbling with impatience; this stop had not been included in his orders.

"Let's get out of here. The Comandante said that no one should see us in this crummy town where everyone knows you," he complained.

"It isn't a crummy town. Do you know why it's called Agua Santa? Because it has a holy spring that washes away sins."

"The hell you say!"

"It's true—if you bathe in the waters, you will never again feel guilt."

"Please, Eva, get in the car and let's go."

"Not yet, there's something I have to do, but we'll have to wait till dark, when it's safer."

It was useless for El Negro to threaten to leave me stranded, because when I get an idea in my head I seldom change my mind. Besides, I was indispensable to the rescue. He not only had to wait, I also set him to work digging as soon as the sun went down.

I led him behind the houses to some rough ground covered with heavy undergrowth, and pointed to the spot.

"We're going to dig something up," I told him, and he obeyed because he had decided that unless the heat had melted my brains, this must be part of the plan.

He did not have to expend much energy; the clayey soil was wet and soft. A little more than half a meter down we found a plastic-wrapped package covered with mud. I wiped it off on my shirttail and, without opening it, stuck it in my purse.

"What's inside?" El Negro wanted to know.

"A dowry."

The Indians met us in a cleared ellipse, their fire the only source of light in the dense jungle darkness. A large triangular roof of branches and leaves served as a communal shelter, and numbers of hammocks were strung beneath it at different heights. The adults wore minimal clothing, a habit acquired through contact with nearby towns, but the children were naked, since parasites and a pale, unhealthy mold thrived in fabrics never free of the damp. Girls wore feathers and flowers above their ears; a woman was nursing a child at one breast and a puppy at the other. I studied those faces, searching for my own image in each of them, but I saw only the tranquil expression of those who have encountered and answered all questions. The chief stepped forward two paces and welcomed us with a slight bow. He held himself very straight; his eyes were large and wide-set, his lips fleshy, and his hair cut like a round helmet, clipped at the back of the neck to reveal the proud scars of many cudgeling tourneys. I recognized him immediately; he was the man who every Saturday led the tribe into Agua Santa to ask for charity; the man who one morning found me sitting beside the body of Zulema; the same man who sent news of the calamity to Riad Halabí and, when I was arrested, lingered outside police headquarters to stamp the ground as if a drum of warning. I wanted to know his name, but El Negro had explained beforehand that it would be discourteous to ask. For these Indians, he said, to name is to touch the heart; they consider it offensive to call a stranger by name or to be named by him, and it would be best to avoid questions that might be misinterpreted. The chief looked at me without a hint of expression, but I was sure he recognized me. He pointed to indicate the way, and led us to a windowless cabin smelling of scorched rags and containing two campstools, a hammock, and a kerosene lamp.

Our instructions were that we were to wait for the other members of the party, who would join us sometime before Friday night. I asked about Huberto Naranjo, because I was counting on our spending those days together, but no one had news of him. I lay in the hammock without removing my clothes, disturbed by the incessant hum of the jungle, the humidity, the mosquitoes and ants, my fear that snakes and poisonous spiders would crawl down the ropes, or might be nesting in the palm thatch and drop on me during the night. I could not get to sleep. I spent two hours examining my reasons for coming there—without reaching a conclusion; my feelings for Huberto did not seem sufficient pretext. Every day I felt more remote from the times when I had lived only for our furtive meetings, fluttering like a firefly around a guttering flame. I think I had agreed to be a part of that adventure in order to test myself, with the hope that by sharing in that unconventional war I could again be close to the man I had loved but asked nothing of. But now I was alone, huddled in a bedbug-infested hammock reeking of dog and smoke. I was not acting from any compelling political conviction, because even though I had accepted the principles of that utopian revolution, and was moved by the desperate courage of the small band of guerrilla fighters, I sensed they were already defeated. I could not escape the prickle of disaster that had haunted me for some time, a vague uneasiness that flared into certainty when I was near Huberto Naranjo. In spite of the revolutionary passion that still blazed in his eyes, I felt an air of calamity closing in about him. I had espoused his rhetoric to impress Mimí, but in fact I believed that the guerrilla movement would never triumph in this country. I did not like to think about what might finally happen to those men and their dreams. That night in the Indian hut, unable to sleep, I was disconsolate. As the temperature dropped I grew cold; I went outside to spend the night huddled beside the coals of the fire. Pale, barely visible light filtered through the leaves, and I was aware that, as always, I was calmed by the moon.

At dawn I heard the Indians, still numb in their hammocks, stirring beneath the communal roof, talking and laughing. A few women went to fetch water, followed by their children imitating bird cries and animal sounds. In the morning light I could see the village better: a handful of huts wasted by the breath of the jungle, stained to the color of clay, surrounded by a strip of cultivated earth with patches of yucca and maize and small bananas—the tribe's only wealth, despoiled for generations by the greed of the outside world. Those Indians, as poor as their ancestors at the beginnings of American history, had, even with the intrusion of colonizers, maintained their customs, language, and gods. Of the proud tribe of hunters they once were, there remained only a few sad indigents, but the long record of misery had not erased the memory of their lost paradise, nor their faith in the legends that promised they would regain it. They were a smiling people. They owned a few chickens, two pigs, three dugouts, some fishing spears, and the unproductive patches of land they had wrested from the jungle through extraordinary effort. They spent their days looking for food and firewood, weaving hammocks and baskets, carving arrows to sell to tourists by the roadside. Occasionally one of them hunted and, if he was lucky, returned with a bird or two, or a small jaguar that he shared with the tribe but did not taste himself, in order not to offend the spirit of his prey.

It was time to get rid of the car. El Negro and I drove to a place where the undergrowth was particularly heavy, and pushed the car into a bottomless barranca; we watched it plunge downward noiselessly, past chattering parrots and unimpressed monkeys, silenced by gigantic leaves and curling lianas, disappearing into a jungle that closed over its trail without a trace. The guerrillas arrived throughout the day, one by one —all on foot and by different routes—with the composure of men who have lived long in the outdoors. They were young, resolute, serene, and solitary; their jaws were firm, their eyes sharp, their skins roughened by weather, their bodies scarred. They had little to say to me; their movements were measured, avoiding any waste of energy. They had cached part of their weapons and would not recover them until the moment for the attack on Santa María. One of them, with an Indian guide, left to take up a position on the riverbank where he could observe the prison through binoculars; three others went off toward the airport to lay explosives, under the direction of El Negro; the remaining two set about organizing the retreat. Each carried out his task without fuss or comment, as if it were routine. At dusk I heard a jeep and ran to meet it, hoping that at last it was Huberto Naranjo. I had been thinking about him constantly, hoping that with luck, after a couple of days, the love that now seemed so cool might be rekindled. The last thing I expected was to see Rolf Carlé descending from the vehicle with knapsack and camera. We stared at each other in amazement; neither had anticipated finding the other in this place and under these circumstances.

"What are you doing here?" I asked.

"I've come to cover the story," he smiled.

"What story?"

"The story that's going to happen Saturday."

"Really. How did you know that?"

"Comandante Rogelio asked me to film what happens. The authorities will try to suppress the truth, and I came to see whether it can be told. And what are *you* here for?"

"To make dough."

Rolf Carlé hid the jeep and left with some of the guerrillas who, to avoid later identification, covered their faces when they saw the camera. Meanwhile I was responsible for the Universal Matter. In the darkness of the hut, on a piece of plastic unrolled on the hard dirt floor, I mixed the ingredients as I had learned from my Yugoslavian *patrona*. To shredded wet newspaper I added equal portions of flour and dental cement; I bound it with water, and kneaded it to obtain a firm paste more or less the color of wet ashes; then I rolled it out with a bottle—all under the observant eye of the tribal chief and some children chattering among themselves in their musical language, gesturing and making faces. I now had a thick, pliable dough, which I wrapped around stones chosen for their oval shape. My model was a dark metal Army hand grenade, three hundred grams in weight, ten meters killing range, twenty-five meters bursting radius. It looked like a small ripe guanábana. The false grenade was simple in comparison to the Indian elephant, the musketeers, the pharaonic-tomb bas-reliefs, and other works fabricated by my *patrona*. Even so, I needed several trial runs; it had been a long time since I had practiced, and anxiety made my wits slow and my hands clumsy. Once I obtained the exact proportions, it seemed clear that there would not be enough time to shape the grenades, let them harden, paint them, and wait for the varnish to dry. It occurred to me that I might dye the dough to save painting it after it dried, but when I mixed dough with paint it lost its malleability. I began to mutter curses, and impatiently scratched my mosquito bites till I drew blood.

The chief, who had followed every step of the process with obvious curiosity, left the hut and soon returned with a handful of leaves and a clay ladle. He squatted beside me and began methodically chewing the leaves. As he reduced them to a kind of cud that he spit into the receptable, his mouth and teeth became blackened. He pressed the wad in a rag, squeezed out a dark oily liquid—a vegetal blood—and handed the wad to me. I added the spittle to a portion of the dough. The experiment worked: when it dried, it was the color of the original grenade and had not altered the admirable versatility of Universal Matter.

The guerrillas returned at nightfall, and after sharing a few slices of cassava bread and grilled fish with the Indians, they lay down to sleep in the hut that had been assigned to them. The jungle turned heavy and black, like a temple; we lowered our voices, and even the Indians talked in whispers. Rolf Carlé returned shortly afterward and found me sitting before the still-burning fire hugging my legs, my face buried between my knees. He knelt beside me.

"What's the matter?"

"I'm afraid?"

"Of what?"

"Of the sounds, of this darkness, of evil spirits, of snakes and bugs, of the soldiers, of what we're going to do Saturday—that we'll all be killed . . ."

"I'm afraid, too, but I wouldn't miss this for anything."

I took his hand and held it firmly for a moment; his skin felt warm to the touch, and again I had the impression I had known him for thousands of years.

"What a pair of fools we are!" I tried to laugh.

"Tell me a story, to get our minds off things," Rolf Carlé requested.

"What about?"

"Tell me one you've never told anyone. Make it up for me."

"Well . . . *Once there was a woman whose lifework was telling stories. She traveled far and wide, offering her wares: stories of adventure, suspense, horror, lust, all at a fair price. One noon in August she was standing in the center of a plaza when she saw an imposing man walking toward her, slim and hard as a sword. He was weary; he had a weapon in his hand and was covered with the dust of faraway places, and when he stopped before her she noticed a strong odor of melancholy. She knew immediately that the man had been at war. Solitude and violence had driven steel splinters deep into his heart, and had robbed him of the ability to love himself. Are you the one who tells stories? the stranger asked. At your pleasure, she replied. The man took five gold coins from his pocket and placed them in her hand. Then sell me a past, because mine is filled with blood and lamentation, and I cannot use it in my way through life. I have been in so many battles that somewhere out there I forgot even my mother's name, he said. She could not refuse him, because she feared that there before her in the plaza the stranger would shrivel into a little pile of dust—which is what happens to those who are not blessed with good memories. She motioned for him to sit beside her, and when she could look into his eyes, she was once again overcome with pity, and was moved by a desire to take him in her arms. She began to speak. All that afternoon and all that night she spun her tale, inventing a worthy past for the warrior, putting into the task all her vast experience and the passion the stranger had evoked. She spoke for a very long time, because she wanted to offer him the novel of his life, and she had to invent it all—from his birth to the present day, his dreams, his desires, his secrets, the lives of his parents and his brothers and sisters, even the geography and history of his homeland. Finally it was dawn, and with the first light of day she could tell that the odor of melancholy had faded from the air. She sighed, closed her eyes, and when she felt her spirit as empty as that of a newborn child, she understood that in her desire to please him she had given him her own memory: she no longer knew what was hers or how much now belonged to him; their pasts had been woven into a single strand. She had delved deeply into her own story and now could not take back her words; but neither did she want to take them back, and she surrendered herself to the pleasure of blending with him into a single story. . . ."*

When I finished I stood up, brushed the dust and leaves from my clothes, and went to my hammock in the hut. Rolf Carlé stayed before the fire.

Comandante Rogelio arrived very early Friday morning, so stealthily that the dogs did not bark when he entered the village; but his men knew, because they slept with one eye open. I shook off the numbness of the last two nights and ran to hug him, but he stopped me with a gesture only I would notice. He was right, it was thoughtless to show signs of intimacy before men who had not loved in such a long time. The guerrillas welcomed him with crude jokes and backslapping, and it was obvious how much they counted on him, because from that moment the tension eased, as if his mere presence were a safeguard for them. He had brought a suitcase filled with uniforms, neatly ironed and folded, officers' stripes, caps, and regulation boots. I went and got the trial grenade and placed it in his hand.

"Good," he said approvingly. "Today we'll send the dough to the prison. It won't show up on the metal detector. Tonight the *compañeros* can make their weapons."

"Will they know how?" Rolf Carlé asked.

"Do you think we'd forget that little detail?" Comandante Rogelio laughed. "We've already sent the instructions, and by now they have the stones. All they have to do is cover them with the dough and give them a few hours to dry."

"The dough has to be kept wrapped in plastic so it doesn't dry out," I explained. "You score the surface with a spoon, and let it get hard. It darkens as it dries, and looks like metal. I hope they don't forget to put in the fake fuses before it sets."

"This is a country where anything can happen, even making weapons from bread dough. No one is going to believe this," sighed Rolf Carlé.

Two of the village Indians paddled a dugout to Santa Mariá to deliver food to the Indians in the prison kitchen. Among bunches of bananas, chunks of yucca, and two cheeses lay the mound of Universal

Matter, looking for all the world like unbaked bread. It drew no reaction from the guards, who were used to sending food packages through. Meanwhile the guerrillas reviewed the details of the plan one last time, then helped the tribe complete their preparations. Families were packing their miserable belongings, tying cord around the feet of their chickens, collecting provisions and utensils. Although it was not the first time they had been forced to a different area, they were disheartened; they had lived several years in that jungle clearing and it was a good place—near Agua Santa, the highway, and the river. The next day they would have to leave their primitive plots, because as soon as the soldiers found out about their role in the escape, the reprisals would be fierce. For lesser reasons the military had swept down like a cyclone on the hapless natives, wiping out entire tribes and erasing every trace of their passage on earth.

"These poor people . . . there are so few left!" I said.

"They have their place in the Revolution," Comandante Rogelio declared.

But the Indians were not interested in his revolution, or anything else that came from that hated race; they could not even repeat the long word he had used. They did not share the guerrilla's ideals; they did not believe their promises or understand their reasoning; and if they had agreed to help in a venture whose outcome they were not capable of measuring, it was because the military were their enemies and this gave them an opportunity to avenge some of the harm done to them over the years. The chief knew that even if the Indians had not been involved, the soldiers would hold them responsible because the village was so close to the prison. They would not be given a chance to explain; so if they were to suffer the consequences whatever they did, it might as well be in a good cause. They would cooperate with those silent, bearded men who at least had not stolen their food or mistreated their daughters, and then find a home somewhere else. Several weeks in advance they had decided where: ever deeper into the jungle, with the hope that the impenetrable vegetation would prevent the Army from following them, and would protect them for a while longer. That had been their lot for the last five hundred years: persecution and extermination.

Comandante Rogelio sent El Negro in the jeep to buy a pair of young goats. That night we sat with the Indians around the fire; we

roasted the animals in the coals and opened some bottles of rum that
had been reserved for the last meal. It was a good farewell in spite of
the restlessness in the air. We drank with moderation; the young guerrillas sang a song or two, and Rolf Carlé entertained everyone with
magic tricks and with photographs from a miraculous machine that in
only a minute spit out images of the dumbstruck Indians. Finally, two
men stood guard and the rest of us went to bed; we anticipated a very
heavy day.

In the only available hut, lighted by the kerosene lamp flickering in a corner,
the guerrillas lay on the floor and I in the hammock. I had imagined I
would spend those hours alone with Huberto; we had never spent an
entire night together. Nevertheless I was content with the arrangement;
the young men's company soothed me and I was able finally to control
my fears, relax, and doze. I dreamed I was making love in a swing. My
knees and thighs were bared in a flutter of lace and yellow taffeta petticoats. On the backward arc of the swing I was suspended in air, and I
saw the powerful sex of a man waiting below. The swing hung for an
instant at the height of the arc; I lifted my face to the sky, which had
turned purple, then plummeted downward to be impaled. My eyes opened
in fright; the room was filled with warm mist. I heard the roar of the
river in the distance, the crying of night birds and the sounds of animals
among the dense trees. The rough cords of the hammock irritated my
back through the fabric of my blouse and the mosquitoes were pure
torment, but I could not move to brush them away; I was dazed. I sank
back into a stupor, soaked in sweat, dreaming this time that I was adrift
on the ocean in a narrow boat, in the arms of a lover whose face was
covered with a mask of Universal Matter and who thrust deep inside
me with every swell of the waves, leaving me bruised, swollen, thirsty,
and happy: desperate kisses, omens, the wall of that hallucinatory jungle, a tooth-shaped gold nugget given as a gift of love, a knapsack of
grenades that exploded noiselessly and filled the air with glowing insects. I started in my sleep and awoke in the darkness of the hut, and
for a moment did not know where I was, or the meaning of those
spasms in my belly. I did not sense, as at other times, the ghost of Riad
Halabí caressing me from the far side of memory but, instead, the pres-

ence of Rolf Carlé sitting on the floor beside me, resting against his knapsack, one leg doubled, the other extended, arms folded across his chest, watching me. I could not see his features, but I saw the gleam of his eyes and teeth when he smiled.

"What are you doing?" I whispered.

"The same thing you are," he replied, also in a low voice, to keep from waking the others.

"I think I was dreaming . . ."

"So was I."

We slipped quietly from the hut and went to the small open space in the center of the village. We sat beside the dying coals of the fire, listening to the eternal murmur of the jungle, in the light of the faint moon rays penetrating the foliage. We did not speak; we did not touch; we did not try to sleep. Together, we waited for Saturday to dawn.

When it began to grow light, Rolf Carlé went to get water to boil coffee. I stood up and stretched; my body ached as if I had been beaten, but I felt at peace. It was then I noticed the reddish stain on my slacks. That hadn't happened for so many years that I had almost forgotten what it was. I smiled, content, because I knew that it meant I would never dream of Zulema again, and that my body had overcome its fear of love. While Rolf Carlé fanned the coals to start the fire, and set the coffeepot on a hook over the flames, I went to the cabin, pulled a clean blouse from my bag, tore it into rags to use as sanitary napkins, and went to the river. When I returned, my clothing was wet, and I was singing.

By six o'clock everyone was ready to begin that decisive day in our lives. We said goodbye to the Indians, and watched them leave in silence, carrying children, pigs, chickens, dogs, and bundles, fading into the foliage like a row of shadows. The only ones who stayed behind were those who were to help the guerrillas cross the river and guide them through the jungle. Rolf Carlé was one of the first to go, camera in hand and knapsack on his back. The others followed, each to his own task.

Huberto Naranjo kissed me goodbye on the lips, a chaste and sentimental kiss: Be careful. You, too. Go straight home and try not to attract attention, and don't worry, everything will work out fine. When will we see each other? I'll have to hide for a while—don't expect me.

Another kiss, and I put my arms around his neck and hugged him hard, rubbing my face against his beard, my eyes moist because I was saying goodbye to a passion shared for many years. I climbed into the jeep; El Negro was waiting with the motor running to drive me north to the distant town from which I would take a bus to the capital. Huberto Naranjo waved, and we both smiled. My best friend, don't let anything happen to you, I love you very much, I whispered. I was sure that he was echoing the same words, knowing it was good we could count on and always be near to help and protect each other; at peace because our relationship had taken a turn and finally slipped into the track where it should always have been. We were two best friends, affectionate and slightly incestuous brother and sister. Be very careful. You, too.

All day I was buffeted by the jolting of the bus, bumping along a treacherous road constructed for heavy trucks and eroded to its skeleton by rains that had washed out potholes big enough for boas to nest in. At a certain bend in the road the vegetation suddenly opened into a fan of impossible greens and the daylight turned stark white, illuminating the perfect illusion of the Palace of the Poor floating some fifteen centimeters above the rich humus of the jungle soil. The driver stopped the bus and all of us passengers pressed our hands to our breast, not daring to breathe during the brief seconds the sorcery lasted before gently fading away. The palace vanished, the jungle reappeared, the day recovered its normal transparency. The driver started the motor and, awed, we returned to our seats. No one spoke until we reached the capital many hours later; each was searching for the meaning of that revelation. I did not know how to interpret it, either, but it seemed almost natural since I had seen it years before from Riad Halabí's truck. That first time, I had been dozing and he had shaken me awake when the night sky turned bright from the lights of the palace; we had left the truck and run toward the vision but before we could reach it, it was enveloped by shadow. I could not stop thinking about what was to happen at five o'clock in Santa María. I felt a racking pain in my temples, and I cursed the morbidity that tortured me with visions of disaster. Let it go well, oh, let it go well; help them, I begged my mother, as I always did in moments of crisis, but once again her spirit was unpredictable: sometimes she appeared without warning, startling me, but at times like these, when I needed her urgently, she gave me no sign that she had heard. The landscape and the sweltering heat reminded me of when I was seventeen years old, of the day I had made this journey carrying a suitcase with new clothes, the address of a boardinghouse for young ladies, and the still-vibrant discovery of pleasure. I had wanted to take my fate into my own hands, and since then much has happened to me. It seemed as if I had lived many lives, that I had turned to smoke each night, and been reborn each morning. I tried to sleep, but the sense of impending disaster would not leave me in peace, and not even the mirage of the Palace of the Poor could rid me of the sulfurous taste in my mouth. Using the rather vague criteria in the Maharishi's manual, Mimí once had analyzed my premonitions, and had concluded that I should not trust them because they never predicted anything important, only trivial events, and when anything significant happened to me, it always came as a surprise. Mimí had demonstrated that my rudimentary divining powers were completely unreliable. But again I begged my mother to make everything all right.

I arrived home that Saturday night looking like the victim of some disaster, filthy from sweat and dust, in a taxi that drove me from the bus terminal to my door, passing through the park illuminated with coach lamps, past the Country Club with its rows of palm trees, the mansions of the millionaires and ambassadors, the new buildings of glass and steel. I was on a different planet, at an incalculable distance from the Indian village and young men with burning eyes ready to fight to the death with absurd grenades. When I saw the house ablaze with light, I had an instant of panic, imagining that the police had preceded me, but before I could turn back Mimí and Elvira threw open the door. I went inside like a sleepwalker and fell into a chair, wishing that everything that had happened was only an invention of my feverish brain and it wasn't true that at that very hour Huberto Naranjo, Rolf Carlé, and all the others might be dead. I looked around the living room as if I were seeing it for the first time; it seemed more welcoming than ever with its eclectic furniture, my improbable ancestors looking over me from their ornate frames, and the stuffed puma in a corner, its ferocity intact in spite of all the abuse and upheaval it had endured in its half-century of existence.

"I'm happy to be home!" I said from the bottom of my heart.

"How the devil did it turn out?" Mimí asked after examining me to be sure I was all right.

"I don't know. I left just as everything was about to start. The escape was planned for around five, before the prisoners were locked in their cells. There was supposed to be a riot in the yard about that time to distract the guards' attention."

"Then it should have been on the radio or television by now, but there hasn't been a word about it."

"That's *good* news. If they'd been killed we'd have heard, but if they escaped, the government will keep it quiet until they can concoct their version of what happened."

"These last few days have been terrible, Eva. I haven't been able to work. I've been sick with fear. I imagined you captured, dead, poisoned by snakebite, devoured by piranhas. Damn Huberto Naranjo! Mimí exclaimed. I don't know why we ever got mixed up in this crazy mess."

"Oh, little bird. You look like a sparrow hawk. I'm of the old ways, I don't like all these goings-on. What is a girl doing mixed up in a man's affairs, I'd like to know? I didn't boil lemons and make you drink them for this," Elvira sighed, as she scurried around serving coffee, preparing a hot bath, and laying out clean clothes. "A good soak in a hot tub full of linden leaves is good for getting over a fright."

"I'd better shower instead, *abuela*."

The news that I have begun to menstruate after so many years was welcomed by Mimí, but Elvira saw no cause for celebration; for her it was nothing but a dirty nuisance, and she thanked her lucky stars she was too old for all that business. She'd always wondered why humans didn't just lay eggs, like chickens. I searched through my bag and pulled out the package I had dug up in Agua Santa; I placed it on Mimí's lap.

"What's this?"

"Your dowry. I want to sell what's inside so you can have your operation in Los Angeles and then get married if you want to."

Mimí ripped off the dirt-stained wrapping and exposed a box damaged by mildew and termites. When she prized open the lid, Zulema's jewels fell into her lap, as brilliant as if they had just been cleaned, the gold gleaming yellower than ever: emeralds, topazes, garnets, pearls, amethysts, all glowing with new light. The pieces I had thought so wretched when I aired them in the sunlight of Riad Halabí's patio now glittered like the treasure of a caliph in the hands of the world's most beautiful woman.

"Where did you steal those?" Elvira whispered, frightened. "Didn't I teach you to do right, little bird?"

"I didn't steal them, *abuela*. Out in the jungle there is a city of pure gold. The cobblestones of the streets are gold, the roof tiles are all of gold, the carts in the marketplace are gold, and all the benches in the plaza—even people's teeth are gold! And there children play with colored stones like these."

"I'm not going to sell them, Eva, I'm going to wear them. That operation is barbaric! First they cut off everything and then they take a piece of your intestine and construct a vagina."

"And Aravena?"

"He likes me the way I am."

Elvira and I breathed a dual sigh of relief. I had always hated the idea of that operation, the result seemed nothing more than a mockery of nature—and to Elvira, the idea of mutilating her archangel was a sacrilege.

Very early Sunday morning, when we were all still asleep, the doorbell rang. Elvira got up, grumbling, and opened the door to an unshaven man with a knapsack over one arm, a black machine on his shoulder, and teeth gleaming in a face blackened from dirt, sun, and fatigue. She did not recognize Rolf Carlé. Mimí and I, in our nightgowns, were not far behind. We did not even have to ask: Carlé's smile was eloquent. He had come to take me away until things had calmed down; he was sure the escape would unleash a maelstrom of unpredictable consequences. He was afraid someone in Agua Santa might have seen me and identified me as the girl who years before had worked in The Pearl of the Orient.

"I told you we should have kept our hands clean of this business!" Mimí wailed, unrecognizable without her makeup.

I dressed and packed a small suitcase. Aravena's car was waiting outside; he had lent it to Rolf when he went to his house at dawn to deliver several rolls of film, along with the most astounding news of recent years. El Negro had driven the car to our house and then taken Rolf's jeep, his mission to dispose of it so no one could follow its

owner's trail. The Director of National Television was not used to getting up early, and when Rolf told him why he was there, he thought he
must be dreaming. To clear the cobwebs from his head, Aravena had
drunk half a glass of whisky and lighted his first cigar of the day; then
he sat down to ponder what to do with what had been placed in his
hands. Carlé, however, did not have time to wait, and asked for the
keys to his car: his job was not finished. Aravena handed him the keys
with Mimí's words: Keep your hands clean, son. I'm already in it up to
my neck, Rolf had replied.

"Do you know how to drive, Eva?"

"I took a course, but I haven't had much practice."

"I can't keep my eyes open. There's no traffic at this hour; drive
slowly and take the highway to Los Altos, toward the mountains."

Rather nervous, I got behind the wheel of that red leather-uphol-
stered yacht, turned the key with unsteady fingers, started the motor,
and lurched away from the curb. In a few minutes my friend was asleep,
and did not wake until I shook him two hours later to ask which road
to take at an intersection. And that is how we arrived at La Colonia on
Sunday.

Burgel and Rupert welcomed us with their characteristic noisy and unrestrained affection and immediately prepared a bath for their nephew,
who, in spite of his nap in the car, wore the ravaged expression of an
earthquake survivor. Rolf Carlé was reviving in a nirvana of warm water
when his two cousins arrived, breathless, overcome with curiosity to see
the first woman he had ever brought there. The three of us met in the
kitchen, and for a good half-minute stood studying, measuring, and siz-
ing one another up, at first with natural suspicion and then with good
will: on the one side, two opulent, blonde, apple-cheeked hausfraus in
the embroidered felt skirts, starched blouses, and lace aprons they wore
to impress the tourists; on the other, myself, considerably less engaging.
The cousins were just as I had pictured them from Rolf's description,
although ten years older; I was enchanted to think that in his eyes they
lived in an eternal adolescence. They must have understood at a glance
that they were in the presence of a real rival, and shocked that I was so
different from them—no doubt they would have been flattered if Rolf

had chosen a replica of themselves—but since both were good-natured, they conquered their jealousy and welcomed me like a sister. They ran off to look for their children, then introduced me to their husbands— hulking, genial, and smelling of scented candles. Then they went to help their mother prepare a meal. A little later, sitting at the table surrounded by that wholesome tribe, with a German shepherd pup at my feet and the taste of ham hock and mashed sweet potatoes in my mouth, I felt so remote from Santa María, Huberto Naranjo, and the Universal Matter grenades that when someone turned on the television to watch the news and we saw a military officer recounting details of the escape of nine guerrilla fighters, I had to make an effort to comprehend what he was saying.

Sweating, obviously apprehensive, the prison warden stated that a group of terrorists in helicopters had attacked the facility, armed with bazookas and machine guns, while inside the compound prisoners had incapacitated their guards with grenades. With a pointer he illustrated the layout of the building and described the movements of those impli- cated in the breakout, from the instant they fled their cells until they disappeared into the jungle. He had no explanation of how the weapons might have come into their hands, somehow getting past the metal de- tectors; it had happened as if by magic; the grenades simply bloomed in their hands. Saturday, at five in the afternoon, as the detainees were being returned to their cells from the prison latrines, they suddenly brandished these explosives before the guards and threatened to blow up the entire compound if the guards did not surrender. According to the warden—pale from lack of sleep and with a two-day growth of beard—the guards on duty in that sector had resisted courageously, but finally had no alternative but to hand over their weapons. These ser- vants of the nation—at present confined in the Military Hospital under orders not to receive visitors, much less reporters—had suffered minor wounds and had been locked in cells to prevent their sounding the alarm. While this was happening, the detainees' accomplices had provoked a riot among the prisoners in the yard as squadrons of subversives on the outside cut the electric power lines, blew up the landing strip five kilo- meters from the prison, blocked the highway to motor vehicles, and stole the patrol launches. They threw mountaineering lines and grapples over the walls, then dropped the rope ladders by which the detainees made their escape, concluded the warden, trembling pointer in hand. He was replaced by an announcer with a pompous voice who affirmed that the escape was obviously the work of international Communists; the peace of the continent lay in the balance; the authorities would not rest until the guilty were apprehended and their accomplices revealed. The newscast ended with a brief announcement: General Tolomeo Rodríguez had been named Commander in Chief of the armed forces.

Between swallows of beer, Uncle Rupert commented that all those guerrillas should be shipped off to Siberia to see how they liked it there; you never heard of anyone scaling the Berlin Wall to the Communist side, it was always to escape from the Reds. And look what they had made out of Cuba! They don't even have toilet paper there. And don't give me that crap about health and education and sports, he grumbled, that's no good at all when a man needs to wipe his ass. A wink from Rolf Carlé warned me it would be best to refrain from comment. Burgel switched channels to watch the nightly episode of the telenovela, having lived in suspense since the previous night when the evil Alejandra stood spying from behind a half-open door, watching Belinda and Luis Alfredo, who were wrapped in a passionate embrace. That's how I like it, now they're showing the kisses up close. They used to cheat. The lovers looked at each other, took each other's hands, and just as they were getting to the good part, they showed us a picture of the moon. I wonder how many moons we had to put up with when we were dying to see what followed. Look at that! Belinda is moving her eyes. I don't think she's blind at all. . . . I was tempted to tell her the convolutions of the story I had rehearsed so many times with Mimí, but I did not; it would have destroyed her illusions. The two cousins and their husbands were hanging on every word, and their children were asleep in big armchairs; dusk was falling, gentle and cool. Rolf took my arm and led me outside.

We walked through the twisting streets of that unbelievable town clinging to a tropical mountainside, a relic from another century, with its spotless houses, lush gardens, shopwindows filled with cuckoo clocks, and its minuscule cemetery with graves in perfectly symmetrical rows —everything gleaming and absurd. We paused at the curve of the highest street to observe the dome of the sky and the lights of La Colonia stretching down the slopes of the mountain like an enormous tapestry.

When the sidewalk ended and there was no sound from our footsteps, I had the feeling I was in a world so new that sound had not yet been created. For the first time, I was hearing real silence. Until that moment there had always been noise in my life: often barely perceptible, like the whispers of Zulema's and Kamal's ghosts or the murmur of the jungle at dawn; other times thunderous, like the radios in the kitchens of my childhood. I was as elated as when I was making love, or spinning my stories, and I wanted to capture that mute space and guard it forever as a treasure. I inhaled the smell of the pines and surrendered myself to this new delight. When Rolf Carlé spoke, the spell evaporated, and I was left with the same frustration I had felt as a child when a handful of snow turned to water in my hands. But he was telling me what had happened at Santa María, some of which he had filmed, and the rest learned from El Negro.

Saturday afternoon the warden and half the guards were at the brothel in Agua Santa, just as Mimí had said they would be, so drunk that when they heard the explosions at the airport they thought it was New Year's and did not even put on their pants. While Rolf Carlé was approaching the island in a dugout, his camera equipment concealed under a layer of palm leaves, Comandante Rogelio and his men in their stolen uniforms were nearing the main gate from the river in a launch commandeered from guards at the dock, sirens blaring like the finale of a circus act. In the absence of their superiors, no one had stopped the party of men, because they looked like high-ranking officers. At that moment the only meal of the day was being distributed to the guerrillas in their cells, through a hole in the metal doors. One of the prisoners began to complain of terrible stomach pains—I'm dying, help, I've been poisoned—and from their cells his *compañeros* immediately joined in the uproar: Murderers! Murderers! They're killing us! Two guards went in to calm the stricken man, and found him waiting with a grenade in each hand and such fierce determination in his eyes that they did not dare breathe. Comandante Rogelio had freed his *compañeros* and their accomplices in the kitchen without firing a single shot, without violence and without haste, and in the same commandeered launch transported them to the opposite bank, where they plunged into the jungle, led by the Indians. Rolf had filmed everything with a telephoto lens and then drifted downriver to where El Negro was waiting. Before the military had time to organize a roadblock or begin the manhunt, the two men were roaring at top speed toward the capital.

"I'm happy they succeeded, but I don't know what good the film is going to do them if everything's censored."

"We'll run it," he said.

"You know what kind of democracy this is, Rolf. They use the excuse they're fighting Communism, but there's really no more freedom than we had in the General's time."

"If they censor this news, the way they did with the slaughter in the Operations Center, we're going to tell the real story in the next telenovela."

"What do you mean?"

"Your drama is scheduled to air as soon as that pap about the blind girl and the millionaire is over. You have to write the guerrilla struggle and the attack on Santa María into your script. I have a suitcase full of film on the guerrillas. There's a lot of it you can use."

"You'll never get away with it . . . "

"An election is coming up in three weeks. The next President will want to give the impression of liberalism and will go easy on censorship. Anyway, we can always claim that it's only fiction, and since the telenovela is much more popular than the newscast, the whole country will know what happened at Santa María."

"What about me? The police will ask how I knew about it."

"They won't lay a finger on you—that would be the same as admitting that what you've written is true," Rolf Carlé replied. "And, speaking of stories," he said, "I've been thinking a lot about your story of the girl who sold a past to a weary warrior . . . "

"Are you still mulling that over? I can see you're a man of slow reactions."

The Presidential elections took place in orderly fashion and with good feeling, as if the exercise of democratic rights was of long standing and not the fairly recent miracle it was. The opposition candidate won, as Aravena, whose political acumen had sharpened rather than diminished with age, had predicted. Shortly afterward, Alejandra died in an automobile accident and Belinda recovered her sight and was married—

enveloped in clouds of white tulle and crowned with rhinestones and wax orange blossoms—to her suitor Martínez de la Roca. The country breathed a deep sigh of relief; it had been a severe test of patience to endure the misfortunes of those three day after day for nearly a year. The National Television, however, gave their patient viewers no respite, but immediately premiered my drama, which in a fit of sentimentality I had called *Bolero*, as homage to the songs that had nurtured my girlhood hours and served as a basis for so many of my stories. The public was thrown off balance in the first episode, and never recovered from their daze during the episodes that followed. I doubt that anyone understood that eccentric story, habituated as they were to jealousy, scorn, ambition, or at least virginity, but none of these appeared on their screens; and they went off to bed every night with their heads spinning from clashes of snakebitten Indians, embalmers in wheelchairs, teachers hanged by their students, Ministers of State defecating in bishop's plush chairs, and other atrocities that would not bear logical analysis and that defied all laws of the commercial television romance. In spite of the confusion it produced, *Bolero* caught on, and within a short time some husbands were coming home from work in time to watch the day's episode. The government warned *señor* Aravena, entrenched in his post by reason of prestige—and the guile befitting an old fox—that it was his duty to uphold standards of morality, good conduct, and patriotism. As a result, I had to omit several of La Señora's bawdy activities, and to muddy the origins of the Revolt of the Whores, but everything else survived nearly intact. Mimí had an important role, playing herself so successfully that she became the most popular actress in the company. The uncertainty about her sex added to her fame; anyone seeing her found it difficult to believe that she had once been a man, or, even more, that she was still masculine in some details of her anatomy. There were those who attributed her triumph to her love affair with the National Television's director, but as neither of them made the slightest effort to deny the rumor, the gossip died a natural death.

I was writing a new episode each day, totally immersed in the world I was creating with the all-encompassing power of words, transformed into a multifaceted being, reproduced to infinity, seeing my own reflection in multiple mirrors, living countless lives, speaking with many voices. The characters became so real that they invaded the house, all together, without respect for the chronology of the story, the living with the dead and each in every phase of his or her life, so that while Consuelo-the-child was prying open the beaks of chickens, a naked Consuelo-the-woman was letting down her hair to console a dying man; Huberto Naranjo wandered about the living room in short pants, conning the gullible with tailless fish, then suddenly materialized on the second floor with the mud of war on his *comandante*'s boots; my *madrina* went sashaying through the house, swinging her hips as she had in her best years, and met herself, toothless and with a seam across her throat, praying on the terrace before a hair from the Pope's head. Their presence in the house upset Elvira's routine; she spent much of her time arguing with them and cleaning up the chaos of hurricane they left in passing. Oh, little bird, get these lunatics out of my kitchen, I'm weary of chasing after them with my broom, she complained; but when she saw them at night, fulfilling their roles on the television screen, she would sigh with pride. In the end, she considered them all members of her family.

Twelve days before we began to shoot the episodes involving the guerrillas, I received a communication from the Ministry of Defense. I had no idea why I was being summoned to the office rather than picked up by agents of the Political Police in one of their unmistakable black automobiles, but I said nothing to Mimí or my *abuela*, not wanting to frighten them. Nor could I warn Rolf, who was in Paris filming the first negotiations on the Vietnam peace. I had been expecting this bad news ever since months before I had shaped the grenades of Universal Matter, and I was actually relieved to confront it once and for all and be rid of the vague uneasiness that kept prickling my skin like a rash. I put the cover on my typewriter, straightened my papers, and dressed, about as happy as someone trying on her shroud. I twisted my hair into a bun at my neck and left the house, waving a hand in farewell to the spirits I left behind. I reached the Ministry, went up the double staircase of marble, walked through the bronze doors protected by guards in plumed caps, and showed my documents to a doorkeeper. A soldier led me down a carpeted hallway and through a door embossed with the national seal;

I found myself in a room adorned with rich drapery and crystal chandeliers. In a stained-glass window Christopher Columbus was immortalized with one foot on the coast of America and the other still in his dory. Then, behind a mahogany desk, I saw General Tolomeo Rodríguez. His commanding figure was outlined against the exotic flora of the New World and the boot of the conquistador. I recognized him immediately by the sudden vertigo that stopped me short, even before I could distinguish his feline eyes, expressive hands, and perfect teeth. He rose, greeted me with his slightly ostentatious courtesy, and offered me a seat in one of the armchairs. He took a chair beside me and asked his secretary to bring coffee.

"You remember me, Eva?"

How could I have forgotten him? It had not been that long since our only evening together, and it was because of his attentions that I had quit my job at the factory and begun to earn my living by writing stories. We spent a few moments exchanging banalities—I, sitting on the edge of my seat, holding my cup in a trembling hand, and he, relaxed, observing me with an unfathomable expression. Once we had exhausted the formulas of politeness, we sat silent for a moment that I found unbearable.

"Why did you call me here, General?" I blurted out finally, unable to stop myself.

"To offer you a deal," he said, then proceeded to inform me, always in the same doctrinaire tone, that he had an almost complete file of my life, dating from the press clippings at the time of Zulema's death to proof of my recent relationship with Rolf Carlé, the polemical television newsman whom the Security Force also had under scrutiny. No, he was not threatening me—on the contrary, he was my friend, or, to put it more exactly, my ardent admirer. He had read the entire script of *Bolero*, in which, among many other events, he had found amazing details about the guerrilla war as well as that unfortunate escape of detainees from Santa María.

"You owe me an explanation, Eva."

I had to fight to keep from pulling up my knees in the leather armchair and burying my face in my arms, but I controlled myself, staring at the design in the carpet with exaggerated attention, unable to find in the vast archives of my fantasy anything sensible I could say. General Tolomeo Rodríguez's hand rested ever so briefly on my shoulder: I had nothing to fear, he had already told me that; furthermore, he had no intention of interfering with my work; I could continue my drama; he did not even object to that colonel in Episode 108, the one who resembled him so closely; he had laughed when he read that section—the character wasn't at all bad, he was rather decent—yes, decent. But I must be careful when it came to the sacred honor of the armed forces; that was not something I could toy with. He had only one observation, as he had told the Director of National Television in a recent conference: the nonsense about the weapons made with a kind of play dough would have to be modified and any mention of the brothel in Agua Santa would have to be deleted. It not only made the prison guards and the officers look ridiculous, it was totally unrealistic. He was doing me a favor by ordering those changes; the series would undoubtedly be improved if I tossed in a few dead and wounded on both sides; the public would like it and it would avoid the touch of buffoonery that was so inappropriate in matters of such gravity.

"What you propose would be more dramatic, General, but the fact is that the guerrillas escaped without violence."

"I see that you are better informed than I am. Let's not get into discussions of military secrets, Eva. I hope you will not force me to take certain measures—just follow my suggestion. Let me say, in passing, that I admire your work. How do you do it? I mean, how does one write?"

"I just do what I can. Reality is a jumble we can't always measure or decipher, because everything is happening at the same time. While you and I are speaking here, behind your back Christopher Columbus is inventing America, and the same Indians that welcome him in the stained-glass window are still naked in a jungle a few hours from this office, and will be there a hundred years from now. I try to open a path through that maze, to put a little order in that chaos, to make life more bearable. When I write, I describe life as I would like it to be."

"Where do you get your ideas?"

"From things that are happening and from things that happened before I was born—from newspapers, from what people tell me."

"And from Rolf Carlé's films, I imagine?"

"You didn't call me here to talk about *Bolero*, General. Tell me what you have on your mind."

"You're right. I have already discussed the series with *señor* Aravena. I called you here because the guerrilla forces have been defeated. The President plans to end this struggle that has been so harmful for our democracy and so costly for the nation. Soon he will be announcing a plan for pacification, and will offer amnesty to those guerrillas who are willing to lay down their arms and who are prepared to obey our laws and become a part of our society. I can tell you something more. The President plans to legalize the Communist Party. I don't agree with this measure, I must admit, but it is not my place to dispute the actions of the Executive. So that's it. I warn you that the armed forces will never allow outside interests to sow pernicious ideas in the minds of the people. We shall defend with our lives the ideals of the Founders of the Nation. In sum, we are making a unique offer to the guerrillas, Eva. Your friends will be able to return to everyday life," he concluded.

"My friends?"

"I am referring to Comandante Rogelio. I believe that the majority of his men will accept the amnesty if he does, and that's why I wanted to explain to you that this is an honorable way out, his only opportunity—I shall not offer him a second chance. I need someone who has his confidence to arrange a meeting, and you can be that person."

For the first time in the interview, I looked directly into his eyes, convinced that General Tolomeo Rodríguez had taken leave of his senses if he thought I would lead my own brother into a trap. My God, the turns of fate . . . Not so very long ago Huberto Naranjo asked me to do the same thing to you, I thought.

"I see that you don't trust me," he murmured, never taking his eyes from mine.

"I can't imagine what you mean."

"Please, Eva. At the very least, I deserve not to be underestimated. I know about your friendship with Comandante Rogelio."

"Then don't ask me to do this."

"I'm asking you because it's a fair arrangement. You can save their lives, and save me time—but I understand your hesitation. Thursday the President will announce these measures to the nation. I hope then you will believe me and be prepared to cooperate for the best interests of everyone concerned—especially the terrorists, whose only alternatives will be pacification or death."

"They are guerrillas, General, not terrorists."

"Call them what you will, that doesn't change the fact that they are operating outside the laws of the nation, and I have the means to destroy them. Instead, I am throwing them a life preserver."

I agreed to think about it, reasoning that the delay would give me time to think. For an instant I remembered Mimí exploring the position of the planets in the firmament and decoding the secrets of the cards to tell Huberto Naranjo's fortune: I've always said it—that one was born to be a bandit or a tycoon. I could not help smiling, because maybe astrology and the cards were wrong once again. Suddenly before my eyes flashed a fleeting glimpse of Comandante Rogelio in the Congress of the Republic, fighting from his velvet-upholstered chair the battles he now was fighting with a rifle in the mountains. General Tolomeo Rodríguez accompanied me to the door and, as he said goodbye, held my hand in his.

"I was mistaken about you, Eva. For months I have impatiently awaited your call. But I have my pride, and I always keep my word. I said I would not force you and I haven't done so, although I regret it now."

"Are you referring to Rolf Carlé?"

"I imagine that is a passing relationship?"

"I hope it will be forever."

"Nothing is forever, my dear, except death."

"I also try to live my life as I would like it . . . like a novel."

"Then there's no hope for me?"

"I'm afraid not. But I thank you for your gallantry, General Rodríguez."

And, standing on tiptoe to reach his martial height, I kissed him lightly on the cheek.

A FINAL WORD

Just as I had diagnosed, in certain matters Rolf Carlé is very slow to react. That man who is so quick when it comes to capturing an image on film is rather awkward when faced with his own emotions. In his thirty-some years of existence, he had learned to live with solitude, and he had persisted in protecting those habits despite his Aunt Burgel's sermons on the virtues of domestic life. Perhaps that was why he was so slow to perceive that something had changed when I had sat on a silk cushion at his feet and he had listened to me tell a story.

After the breakout from Santa María, Rolf placed me in his aunt and uncle's care at La Colonia and returned that same night to the capital; he could not be absent during the pandemonium that swept the country when the guerrilla radio broadcast the voices of the escapees flaunting their revolutionary slogans and ridiculing the authorities. He spent the following four days—exhausted, hungry, short of sleep—interviewing everyone related to the events, from the madam of the brothel in Agua Santa and the demoted prison warden to Comandante Rogelio himself, who appeared for twenty seconds on the television screens, with a star on his black beret and a kerchief covering the lower half of his face, before the transmission was interrupted—it was said—because of technical difficulties. On Thursday Aravena was summoned to the Presidential Palace, where he received the explicit recommendation that he control his team of reporters if he wanted to retain his post. Isn't that Carlé fellow a foreigner? No, Excellency, he's a citizen—check his papers. Aha! Well, at any rate, warn him not to poke into matters of national security or he might regret it. The Director called his protégé to the office and closeted himself with him for five minutes; the result was that Rolf returned to La Colonia that same day under unequivocal orders to stay out of the limelight until the complaints about him died down.

He walked into the large frame house, still empty of weekend tourists, shouting hello, as he always did, but without pausing to allow his aunt the opportunity to feed him the first bite of pastry or the dogs to lick him from head to foot. He walked straight through, looking for me, because for several weeks a ghost in yellow petticoats had been haunting his dreams, teasing him, eluding him, inflaming him, lifting him to glory moments before dawn when at last after hours of impassioned pursuit he had managed to embrace her, plunging him into frustration when he awakened alone, sweating and calling her. The time had come to put a name to that ridiculous vexation. He found me sitting beneath a eucalyptus tree, seemingly absorbed in writing my script, but in fact watching him out of the corner of my eye. I shifted position so that the breeze fluttered the fabric of my dress and the late afternoon sun gave me an aspect of tranquility—utterly unlike the voracious female who tormented him every night in his dreams. I could feel him observing me from a distance. I suppose that finally he decided there had been enough time wasted and it was the moment to demonstrate his thoughts in clearer terms, always within the bounds of his usual courtliness. He strode forward, and kissed me exactly as it happens in romantic novels, exactly as I had been wanting him to do for a century, and exactly as I had been describing moments before in a scene between the protagonists of my *Bolero*. Once we were close, I was able unobtrusively to drink in the smell of the man, recognizing, at long last, the scent of the other half of my being. I understood then why from the first I thought I had known him before. Quite simply, it all came down to the elemental fact that I had found my mate, after so many weary years searching for him. It seemed that he felt the same, and may have reached the identical conclusion, although—always bearing in mind his rational temperament—perhaps with some small reservations. We stood caressing and whispering those words that only new lovers, to whom all the familiar words sound freshly coined, dare speak.

As we kissed beneath the eucalyptus tree, the sun had set; dusk had fallen and the temperature suddenly dropped, as it always does at nightfall in those mountains. We then levitated and went inside to tell the good news of our just-declared love. Rupert went first to inform his daughters and then to the cellar to look for bottles of the best wine while Burgel, moved to the point of bursting into song in her mother tongue, began to chop and season the ingredients of her aphrodisiac stew; in the patio the dogs, who had been the first to scent the emanations of our happiness, created an unbelievable ruckus. The table was laid for a stupendous feast, with the best china, while the candlemakers, all qualms allayed, drank to the happiness of their former rival, and the two cousins, whispering and giggling, went to plump up the feather bed and place fresh flowers in the best guest room—the same room where years before the three of them had performed their first experiments in voluptuousness. When the family feast was over, Rolf and I retired to the large room they had prepared for us. Hawthorn logs were blazing in the fireplace and the high bed was covered by the lightest eiderdown in the world and enveloped in mosquito netting as white as a bridal veil. That night, and many following nights, we made love with such ardor that all the wood in the house glowed like polished gold.

Later, for a judicious period of time, we loved each other more modestly until that love wore thin and nothing was left but shreds.

Or maybe that isn't how it happened. Perhaps we had the good fortune to stumble into an exceptional love, a love I did not have to invent, only clothe in all its glory so it could endure in memory—in keeping with the principle that we can construct reality in the image of our desires. I exaggerated slightly, describing, for example, our honeymoon as prodigious: I said that it changed the soul of that comic-opera town and the very order of nature; that every lane echoed with sighs, that doves nested in the cuckoo clocks, that the almond trees in the cemetery flowered for a night, and that Uncle Rupert's bitches came in heat before season. I wrote that during those enchanted weeks time expanded, curled back on itself, turned inside out like a magician's handkerchief, and that Rolf Carlé—his solemnity shattered to bits and his vanity somewhere in the clouds—was able to exorcise his nightmares and again sing the songs of his boyhood, and that I at last danced the belly dance I had learned in the kitchen of Riad Halabí, and amid laughter and sips of wine told many stories, including some with a happy ending.

A NOTE ON THE TYPE

*This book was set in Fournier, a type face named for Pierre Simon
Fournier, a celebrated type designer in eighteenth-century France.
Fournier's type is considered transitional in that it drew its inspiration
from the old style yet was ingeniously innovational, providing for an
elegant yet legible appearance. For some time after his death in 1768,
Fournier was remembered primarily as the author of a famous manual
of typography and as a pioneer of the point system. However, in 1925,
his reputation was enhanced when The Monotype Corporation of
London revived Fournier's roman and italic.*

*Composed by Crane Typesetting Service, Inc.,
West Barnstable, Massachusetts*

Printed and bound by R. R. Donnelley & Sons, Harrisonburg, Virginia

DESIGNED BY MARYSARAH QUINN